Homer *Realized*

A NOVEL

For Margaret – my talented friend –
Enjoy –
Martha Battle

Martha Battle

2005

To order additional copies, please contact us.
BookSurge, LLC
www.booksurge.com
1-866-308-6235
orders@booksurge.com

Dedicated to my husband Guy and our children Guy, Kemp, Anne, and Maggie who have shared these times, Jane, Ruth, Steve, and Todd, and our grandchildren.

☆☆☆

Cover: Watercolor by Martha Battle based on a photograph of a bust in the Museum at Naples reproduced in History of Greece and the Greek People from the Earliest Times to the Roman Conquest by Victor Duruy, translated and edited by M.M.Ripley. Boston: Estes and Lauriat, 1895. Vol. 1, opposite page 1. No one knows how Homer looked.

Homer *Realized*

CONTENTS

Chapter 1 Places in the Mind I

Chapter 2 Songs of a Lydian Summer 19

Chapter 3 Mousike and the Oracle 39

Chapter 4 Love and Death 57

Chapter 5 The Margites 69

Chapter 6 The Sibyl 79

Chapter 7 Shipwreck 95

Chapter 8 Initiation 107

Chapter 9 Making the Iliad 115

Chapter 10 Singing the Iliad 129

Chapter 11 The Scarf 139

Chapter 12 Zoe 149

Chapter 13 In the Court of the Archon 161

Chapter 14 Sons or Fathers 175

Chapter 15 "Homer" 191

Chapter 16 Odysseus Found 203

Chapter 17 The Long Way Home 227

Chapter 18 Earthquake 239

Chapter 19 "The Blind Singer of Rocky Chios" 247

Chapter 20 Making the Odyssey 255

Chapter 21 Homer Speaks 265

Chapter 22 Death of Homer 279

Chapter 23 The Paulus Letter 291

Chapter 24 Nonnos 299

Afterword 313

This map depicts only sites in text.

Samothrace

Imbros

Lemnos

Troy

Tenedos

Lesbos — Mytilene

Phoinikous

Kyme

Phokaia

Sardis

Valissos
Chios Town
Emporio
Chios

Smyrna

Teos

Kolophon

Klaros

Erythrai

Samos

Mycale

Miletos

Delos

Ios

Rhodes

To Cyprus

Map 1

PREFACE: THE VOICE OF LETHA GOODING

It started with a marginal note, a casual allusion by an unknown scholiast in the text of a Florentine manuscript, and it grew into my obsession. Through years of family and career it was there, bumping into consciousness more and more, like a palpable thing, like a mysterious bottle washing ashore with clues to a buried treasure. Let me find a simile for this experience, one from our own century, as Homer's were from his.

It has been like a Mandelbrot set. I look at that incomprehensible figure and know I have been there. Amid its rich chaos come pattern and infinite dimension. Laughter, awe, suspense, surprise, and at the root of it recognition but never predictability. I live between system and apparent randomness, between knowing and unknowing, on the fractal edge. Like Faust reclaiming land from the sea. Like Orpheus turning to look too soon.

Well. If you are going to enter the mystery with me, I had better let you read the sentence that was in the bottle. It will not amaze you —at first.

He (Apollonius) is referring to the initiatory rites performed at Samothrace. If a person is initiated into these, he is saved from storms at sea. So Odysseus is said to have used the veil (of Leucothea) in place of a fillet, since he had been initiated at Samothrace—for the initiates bind purple fillets (scarves) about their abdomens. (Scholia Laurentiana to Apollonius Rhodius <u>Argonautica</u> I.917-18 in Lehmann, <u>Samothrace: A Guide</u>. Vol. I p. 107)

You see here the seed of an absorbing discovery: that Homer is the most remarkable Trickster of all time, greater even than Odysseus. Worthy of Hermes, whose spirit guides him. For we will find embedded in the Odyssey two references to Samothrace, deftly concealed but unmistakably there. They stand like secret parentheses around Odysseus' telling of the Fantastic Voyages, like hands cupped around a treasure newly lifted from the sea.

But why? And why are they concealed?

It began to haunt me.

By the way, I am Letha Gooding. At least, that will be my name. During my leave here in Cyprus, where I am studying the "Paulus" letter to the last Greek epic poet Nonnos, I have finally finished this life of Homer, the first and greatest Greek epic composer, the man the Greeks simply call The Poet. It has stretched my leave to four years, but I will soon be going home again.

The sentence from the scholiast grew, here for you to enjoy. I must ease our way from time to time through strange waters, acting as a scholiast myself when it seems useful, a kind of interlocutory. I like connections like that—scholiast/boundary-crosser.

Well. To explain a few conventions: the time vocabulary has been modernized (and placed in parentheses) and familiar spellings kept familiar. As a general principle, all private events are suppositional, and public affairs, place descriptions, chronicles are documentable. Where critics do not agree on the date of a public event, I choose one well within the parameters of historical debate.

Of the vast commentary on Homer's work, some is recognizable in this imagined life, as are a number of epic conventions. I make use of lives written about Homer in classical times, though they are contradictory and unreliable; no testimony, no letters, no images, no proven facts remain. But the epics themselves loom before us, and knowledge of the times grows rapidly. A kind of narrative criticism is the result—a plausible recreation of a life from which the greatest works of western literature emerged—a new kind of "mystery."

It is a story we must try to tell. We will linger at first in Smyrna, savoring what the memory of home would have evoked in the poet. It is a boyhood seen from a distance. Let yourself in gently and be patient at first as we set the scene. Honor the images there, mirrored in his own words.

So let us begin. It is the morning of our world, as Thoreau has said. The making of great-hearted Homer lies before us. Pour a libation to Hermes, the boundary-crosser, breathe deeply, loosen your spirit and let's be on our way.

PART ONE

Axieros, First Goddess, of the Earth,/ Matter of mind, not circumstance alone,/ Substance from which the mortal clay is shaped/ Before the Muse can claim him as her own.

CHAPTER I

Places in the Mind

750 B.C.E. Smyrna

Maion the Lydian found him, a child of about two years, the sole survivor of an Enkomian ship which foundered in a wild storm off the western coast of Cyprus.

"I was easing my way through the misty morning sea, just off Paleokastro, when I heard a voice and came upon the wreckage," Maion told his family. "There was a mast in a tangle of sail and this boy, tied to the step-box with a length of purple wool. I searched round for the others, but the broad sea had taken them. Shoremen told me it had been an outbound pirate vessel, common in those waters, one often trading in slaves and copper. So of course I brought him home with me."

He held out the strip of cloth for them all to examine, as if it would give them clues. It seemed to be a sash or loin cloth, and they would store it away for safekeeping, hoping it would be useful some day. His wife Charite and her family were more interested in the child, gazing at the foundling with wonder and admiration. He was beautiful indeed.

Some in Smyrna found Maion's story remarkable and—since the stories people love to tell are always about the latest news—some said the boy was Maion's child by a woman of Chios, others by a woman of Ios. Because of his blue-green eyes others said he was the child of the river-god Meles and a water-nymph. Because of his sun-lit hair, some said he was the child of Cyprus' golden Aphrodite. Later, when his songs enchanted all the world, they said he must have been born of Poseidon and the Muse.

Smyrna was an Ionian settlement then, and Maion's wife Charite was a member of one of the leading families of Ionian Greeks. It had been a useful practice for Greek colonizers to marry their daughters to the landed natives, in this case Lydians; many advantages developed and, as generations passed, much could be peaceably acquired. While her Ionian kinswomen had wept with sympathy, fair-cheeked Charite had been married to Maion, this Lydian who had high honor among both Lydians and Greeks and sleek fat trading ships in the Hermaian gulf. The gods had not given them children, so Charite took the boy in and loved him as her own.

"He surely has a name already," Maion pointed out, and they prompted him, with no result. Then Maion said, "You choose a name, Charite. He is a gift to you."

"Yes," she said. "A gift. Telos. And you found him at just the right time."

"Kairos." Maion added. "The right time and place."

"Yes." They agreed. He was Teleokairos from that moment on.

Indeed, the few words the child knew proved him to be Ionian. He named weapons, and when he heard the word "phorminx," he sang a note clear as a swallow. Because he was found in the summer that Melia was destroyed, Charite thought to her dying day that he had been a prince of that doomed city. Her father Leonidas, an important man in Smyrna, accepted the boy into the family and exerted every influence to see that he was brought up Ionian.

It was by no means automatic that any child be accepted, even by his natural parents, and, until the ritual of the amphidromia, he had no existence. This was a simple ritual of purification by water and fire: A runner would race around the family hearth with the baby, freeing him of bad influences from the birth. While Teleo had probably already been through the ritual, his new parents did it again anyway, naming him anew and giving him the presents of squid.

There were other recognitions, too. At the Apoteria in October his name was presented to the extended family, the gens, along with those of newborn males, the new names of the women who had married, and the names of the boys who had been accepted into manhood. This was the time when full legitimacy was acknowledged and social acceptance given or refused. Later, at the Panionian festival at Mycale, new crops of sons of all the Ionian cities were introduced to the gennetai. One of the mnemonoi, official rememberers for the city, had spoken for Smyrna, and Teleokairos Maionides was enrolled rather matter-of-factly. It was only later, when his fame was great, that people claimed Poseidon shook the earth at Mycale when his name was enrolled. Perhaps he did. The earth shook frequently there—-and everywhere else in Ionia. Poseidon Earthshaker was a potent deity.

✵✵✵

Teleokairos Maionides spent his seedtime in sunny Smyrna, in the fertile valley of the Hermos that Herodotus would call the loveliest climate on earth. It lies halfway down the coast of Asia Minor behind the island of Chios and Mimas peninsula. Gusty Mimas and its mountain chain form the western and southern sides of the Hermaian gulf, and the Hermos river delta dominates the eastern side of the gulf whose great northern entrance ten miles wide looks north to Lesbos and the Troad. Smyrna was tucked safely at the eastern toe of the gulf, forty miles from the stormy Aegean and strategically astride the river valley. Greek settlements were only along the coast, except for Greek-speaking Sardis; but Sardis was not Ionian, because the ruling house of the Heraclidae there had come centuries earlier and had become very easternized. Away from the coast, then, as far as the high plains ten days inland, the country was called Lydia, and within it lay the province of Maionia, the ancestral home which gave its name to Teleo's new father.

The Greek coastal cities, founded during the Great Migration nearly six generations before, were divided into three dialect, or tribal, areas: the Aiolians held the north as far south as the Hermaian gulf, the Ionians the middle as far south as Miletos, and the Dorians south to the Levant.

One of the very first stories Teleo would certainly have learned was the tale of the taking of Smyrna from the Aiolian Greeks in his grandfather's time. It was a tale of conquest through trickery. Leonidas and his friends were from Ionian Kolophon, a powerful city fifteen miles to the south. Exiled as the result of a violent political conflict (in 760) they fled to Smyrna for sanctuary, and were taken in by the Aiolian population. Now, it was the tradition that during the festival of Dionysos all of the Aiolian men would go to the sacred ground in the swamp south of the city to celebrate the tasting of their renowned Pramneian wine—to sample the new and open up the old year's supply—while the women stayed in the city to welcome the celebrants in joyful union with the dying and resurrected god. But this year when the Aiolian men were at the swamp, the Kolophonian refugees rose up and closed the gates, taking the city as well as all the waiting women.

So the Aiolians sent for their allies who helped them negotiate a settlement. All moveable goods were sent out to the dispossessed men who were welcomed into citizenship in the Aiolian towns to the north. Some of the women were held to prevent reprisals, and Smyrna became Ionian. Though some of the victors sent for their families in Kolophon, many took Aiolian wives, and by the time Teleo was learning songs of the capture, it was a part of the village's heroic history. Leonidas loved it.

So clearly it meant a great deal to his family that Teleo be Ionian. They saw to it that he was brought to feasts and festivals and heard the songs of the heroes, in Ionian. He was corrected if he slipped into Aiolian or sang a Lydian song of the shipwrights. Then his Lydian father would flush with anger and refuse to speak for awhile. Then Teleo could feel a knife touch his heart, leaving an ache there. But they all loved each other well and thrived as the time passed.

Indeed, it would have been strange not to be happy in Smyrna. It was a walled village of dozens of houses on a low hill surrounded on three sides by water, because here the short river Meles ran into the sparkling gulf. The small acropolis, the high defensive outpost, was 1200 feet up the hillside to the north, part of Mt. Sipylos. There was no sweeter prospect—gulf and sea and islands to the west and fruitful plain to the east, all ringed with forested mountains. Below the acropolis freshets tumbled down the hills, carving caves and shaded pools sacred to the gods. One cave by the Meles would become a fabled place where the bard-to-become-Homer would practice his hexameters. Myrtles abounded everywhere, for which some said the city had been named.

Smyrna was blest with winds and fragrant breezes. Zephyros, the cool northwester, would rise in the heat of the day and blow, sometimes very strongly, all through the long summer afternoons, settling only at sundown. Then land breezes came, and the nights were filled with green stars. Rain fell seasonally, from November to March, and winter touched them, though snow seldom fell except in the high mountains. Spring and fall were wonderful—temperate, sunny, with a clarity of air and light that dazzled his brain. Even the intense summers were dry and breezy, and the pace of life was good.

Who built the high, thick walls of Smyrna was a mystery to the recent settlers who understood the excellence of an ancient locale. In fact, only Emporio on Chios and the doomed Melia had also been completely wall-girt. The wall was made of huge ashlar blocks, each over three feet long, beautifully finished and positioned, like those of the Hatti cities, or Mycenae, or Troy. Other remnants of past glories with unknown histories were all over the neighboring countryside, but no one could imagine a time when Smyrna had ever been important enough to merit such a magnificent enclosure. The walls, however, were the end of it; inside them, the houses of Smyrna were simply made.

They were not laid out, as they would be later, in a grid, with courts and public places. They were cottages, haphazardly situated, oval in shape and made of mud brick, the oldest kind of Greek house. When Mycenaean civilization in mainland Greece collapsed (twelfth century B. C.E.) after thriving for five hundred years, the survivors had abandoned the ruined cities and scattered into safer backward areas of the mainland to live, where such houses as these had always been in steady use. Thus, when the Ionians and Aiolians migrated to this coast, they brought the modest and familiar style with them. Here in Smyrna life was still a struggle, and there were no palaces yet. Its sister cities considered it prosperous and important but still a country town.

Teleokairos Maionides grew up in one of the larger houses, long and oval, with the walled courtyard taking one end of the oval and the rounded end of the house the other. The entrance to the house from the courtyard was squared;, only the large doors and the roof vents provided natural light, for there were no windows. The walls had a dressed stone base, and two poles held up the thatched roof. Some said the shape could not be changed, for it was an omphalos, the navel of the earth and center of life. Others said it was a beehive, where magical transformations could take place, or a cave, or the world egg, in which life was nourished. Even while it was becoming impractical, as the city population grew, no one would change it.

The walls and houses gleamed. White lead, found in its pure state near Smyrna and mixed with vinegar, made an excellent paint. Lovely green malachite, also nearby, was a favorite pigment, and was sometimes carved into graceful utensils. The murex snail lived in the warm waters of the gulf and all around Mimas peninsula; it was the source of a dye called Tyrian purple because it was made famous by the Phoenicians. There was, in fact, a small and friendly Phoenician settlement on the far side of Mimas, facing Chios. A great salt flat lay at the mouth of the gulf. The finest clay in the world was nearby, and over the pass inland, at Sardis, the Pactolas river ran with gold.

The valley about the city was farmed by various gens, and by Greek tradition ownership would pass from one first son to the next. Those not owners worked for the others, as did Lydians—and of course a few slaves—and almost everyone left the village in the morning to go to the fields and orchards or to tend the flocks in the hills.

Fragile Charite did not work often in the fields but in her house, a lovely place. A sacred hearth was in the center and benches edged the wall, for sleeping and for storage underneath. The floors were hard and level, swept and sprinkled down every day and dusted with herbs—lavender, rue, and juniper—to keep insects away. A rich growth of catnip flourished outside the walls to assure that no rats would come in, and she made small ropes of artemesia twigs to drive away mosquitoes.

She grew marigolds in the courtyard, for seasoning and headaches and to rub into bee stings. She gathered thyme nearby too, burning it in the hearthfire to clear the air, feeding it to the sheep to give them a delicate flavor. Periwinkle spread by the doorway, the leaves handy for crushing to treat nosebleeds and the small wounds of boyhood. She kept a vial of lavender vinegar next to the small footbath by the hearth, pouring a few drops into the steaming water to ease the fatigue of travelers and weary little boys. That pungent aroma would always flood Teleo's mind with memories of mountains, of stony paths and the pebbles of the river, of dusty walking sticks, the shade of orchards, the narrow shingled beach. And of gentle Charite.

The men always roasted the sacrifice on spits in the courtyard, in the open air where the women also cooked. A circular granary with a thatched roof, dug very deeply and lined with stones, stood near the city wall; Teleo clambered down the ladder to the bottom many a time on errands for his mother. Nearby was the public oven for baking.

The doors to their home faced to the east, to catch the land breezes at night and avoid the cold winter northwesterly. Life was lived out of doors for the most part, but Teleo always remembered how the tall roof of the house would cast cool shadows across the yard and how the courtyard wall would turn from bright white at noonday into orange and rose and lavender at sundown. He and the other children, after a busy day, would go to the new fountain house, which had been built in corbelled masonry by the Ionians when he was just a little boy. There they would wash in the spring, rub themselves vigorously, race a thin layer of oil over their bodies, and comb and inspect their hair with practiced fingers. Then they would run home to eat and, on feasting days, after eating, creep in to listen to the bard sing until they fell asleep.

Teleokairos Maionides was enthralled by the singers of songs—singers of the old tales of Troy, of Jason, of Thebes and the sacking of cities. They were working men of Smyrna blessed with skill in remembering, the mnemonoi, who kept in their minds the lives of the villagers, their births and their deaths, along with the songs of fathers and kings. Men of Ionian Smyrna, of course. The bards of Aiolian days had left long ago with the revelers, singing their songs to the wine god in the swamp when the city was taken.

As Teleo blossomed into active youth, a conviction took root in his heart that bards had sung for him somewhere in his mysterious infancy. In a certain slant of evening light, at a certain late hour suddenly awakened from sleep, he would hear the twang of a phorminx string and his body would vibrate with it. His body knew why but, no matter how still he lay, no matter how patiently he listened, what his knees and the back of his neck knew would not open to his mind. Something in him watched the sweet singers. And they knew so many tales! As richly as acacia leaves overlay each other in the bud, so that a single thumbnail can cover leaves numbering the days of the lunar year, so richly were the tales of the Greeks enfolded in the hearts of the bards.

Well-told stories may often be more real in childhood than daily life, perhaps because they take image from youthful imagination with the full sanction and impress of adult authority. Implicit in the telling of them is a sense of their human value. There is, after all, a great difference between walking over a mountain, then learning the story of its creation and walking over it again. Between drinking the Pramneian wine and hearing stories of its power. Could a beaker of that fabled vintage ever be only itself again, however glorious that self might be, after Homer had sung of it in Circe's hands?

As he grew an instinct grew in him which knew that words make the human world. He accepted the bard's voice as more than human, his song carrying the wealth of all that had gone before him, his memory a gift of the god. When the bard failed, it was a human failure; his Muse had abandoned him. But when he sang well! Ah, then divinity sang through him. He colored the world. He brought the powers of life into the hearts of mortals. He made them glad to be alive and see the light of the sun. The boy listened to voices rumbling in the chests of men, as natural as birdsong and water over the river rapids, a music of regularity and variation that spoke to his soul even then.

And there was one bard above all others that Teleo remembered from his childhood, Laocoon, whose voice would resonate in him all through the deep nights of his life. Laocoon was a bard of extraordinary talent, a wanderer from nowhere who came to Smyrna only once, when the boy was eight. So extraordinary was he that people said there was a light around his body when he sang. The air was rare and pure, and his voice would move to the ear in such a way that each listener felt as if the gods spoke to his heart alone. So remarkable was he that people feared his eye, the penetration of his look, his very blue gaze that reached the soul. He was a disturbing man who could not stay long in any place. With disturbing ways as well, for he brought the alphabet to Smyrna.

Teleokairos Maionides always remembered him for the simple song he would sing to the children about Hermes and his new alphabet. Often Laocoon wrote the symbols in the sand of their courtyards as he sang. But trouble followed Laocoon. The priests of the Great Goddess Artemis/Kybele were outraged by his actions, and it was not long before this magical man had been driven from town, for he had breached the laws of hospitality and taught blasphemy to children. He had written among his letters the sacred and secret vowels, separate. Teleo did not understand why this was wrong, but he knew it was forbidden to defy the gods, and he was hurt and made ashamed of his love for his new idol. For he had loved him as he sang.

Thus it was shattering to hear the news from Mycale the following spring. Laocoon had gone to the Panionian festival, and there he had been murdered most horribly. He had been found below the Temenos by the sea, brutally beaten and tortured, his right hand hacked off and his tongue cut out. Those offending parts were never found.

People spoke of the event in hushed tones, for it seemed to be a ritual act. Some said his eyes had been burned out and that a god had done it. Others said a Phoenician vessel had put into Samos across the channel and had abruptly left again. The Phoenicians were known to consider certain symbols sacrosanct, and thoughtful men believed that Laocoon's blaspheming members had been taken as prizes to be placed on the altar of their strange gods. Such things still happened in the world.

There were influential men even among the Greeks who saw the new writing as a violation to be avenged. The stones upon which Laocoon had been carving his letters, to leave as an offering to Poseidon Heliconian, had been cruelly smashed and scattered so that no one could reassemble them.

And no one dared. In Smyrna when the news arrived there was shock but no surprise. Many mourned for the singer and the loss of his miraculous voice. But he had been too bold. The priests of the Great Goddess let it be known that the gods had punished Laocoon for giving to mortals the letters of power, and they instructed parents to see that their children did not write what Laocoon had taught them. Each young mind felt terror at the thoughts of mutilation and disgrace, though the prohibition fixed the letters indelibly in many of their minds.

Teleo had not really thought about the 24 alphabet symbols. He had been entranced by the voice of the man, by the sheer energy and music of his words, by some freshness in his song. In fact, by the time he began to think deeply about him, Laocoon was long since dead. Nobody knew his birthplace or lineage, for he had chosen the name Laocoon, meaning very perceptive, after becoming a bard, according to the custom of the Aegean islands and the Greek mainland. He was simply a child of the Muse. But as one who had offended the gods, his body had been cast into the sea.

**

Teleo's was a productive childhood, full of hard work. He toiled in the fields and did house duties for his mother, even after he was seven and old enough to spend his time with men, and with his father's ships.

The women and children grew flax, a three-month crop they tended together. After a lazy start, the plants would grow an inch a day for forty days and then would stop to blossom. A month later, when the leaves had fallen, the women and children would pull them up for soaking before they became too woody. They would haul piles of stalks to the running streams in the valley and weight them down with stones. Or the stalks would be left in the fields if the dews were heavy, to soak and separate, a process of a week or so. After that they would gather them, strip off the woody part, boil and bleach the linen fibers, and dry and comb them for weaving.

It was hard work: linen fibers were strong, even when they were wet. An ancient woman, captured out of Egypt long ago, told Teleo one day as they worked that in her country she had mixed lavender oil and asphalt and soaked fine linen in it to wrap around the bodies of kings. The cloth was so strong it would last a thousand years, she said, and Teleo was amazed at the thought. He looked at the shreds in his work-weary hands with a new respect. This must be the stuff of the imperishable robes of the gods, woven in delicate thinness and softened in scented oils.

Everyone, of course, learned to work in wood, and it was plenteous along the rivers and in the mountains. Maion and Tel, when he was five, together had made small tables of poplar—a soft and lovely wood with rivers of green-grey and golden tan—smoothing and polishing them with sand and many coats of fragrant lemon oil his father had brought from Al-Mina. They made door frames of cypress. The coffer for clothes was of cedar, a fine protector of woven stuffs. Charite would joke that she wanted to be buried in such a box, where the worm could not fasten on her and her body would be immortal as the linens she made for her family. By the time he was crafting his own instruments for singing, working in fine wood was second nature to Teleo, his phorminx an extension of his own strong fingers.

So his was a happy boyhood. But there was a turmoil near his heart; it seemed always to have been there. It made a wildness in him that he sometimes could not check, no matter what the cost, a need to seek his own limits, an appetite for something that lay on the edge of endurance. How long could he stay underwater? How many figs could he eat? How long could he go without eating, work without stopping, go without speaking, run before dropping? His grandfather Leonidas was proud when he saw this.

"Tel is a competitor. He will win many prizes at funeral games, maybe even in Olympia." And he would grunt with satisfaction and slap the boy heartily on the shoulder. Gentle Charite saw in her son things alien to her own fragile nature, but she sensed that his rashness lay deeper than that. She envied the boy his energy and silently sought it within herself. She worried at his risk-taking.

"Let the boy alone," Maion would say. "He has to look out for himself in this world if he is to be a trader and visit the cities of men." But none of them understood that he just had to see what a mortal could do, what was possible for him. He began to memorize, to see how much he could remember, and it astonished him. He decided to see how many stories he could learn.

INTERLOCUTORY

The Voice of Letha Gooding

I am taken by the memory of lines from Walt Whitman, which surprises me because I never cared for him. He thought he was God, and I read him at a time when that offended me. But I read him today with more understanding: "There was a child went forth every day,/ And the first object he look'd upon, that object he became/...that object became part of him for that day or a certain part of the day,/ Or for many years or stretching cycles of years." ("There Was a Child Went Forth") The poem moves from the simplest Spring images of animal and plant birth into the family and the town, gradually growing, as the length of the verses and stanzas do, until the eyes see whole sweeps of space, vistas of sky and sea.

And when the child Homer went forth at Smyrna, what did he see?

***

A high and legendary blue mountain was in his line of vision when he rose to see the sun every morning, its cool sides veiled in milky mist. It was part of the mass called Sipylos that lay between the village and the delta of the Hermos. Sipylos, ten miles wide and thirty miles long, was actually two distinct mountain masses, this portion lying farthest east and rising to almost 5000 feet above the gulf. Its northern side, ragged and precipitous, faced toward the Hermos, and even on the south its cliffs of blue slate and grey-blue limestone awed the boy standing in the village. It had once been called Thunder Mountain, but the story went that Sipylos, son of Agenor and Dioxippe, had hanged himself there in grief at accidentally murdering his mother, and so it had been named for him. Through the ages Poseidon Earthshaker had cast parts of it into the valley, and the rubble from its harsh peaks had gradually become low green hills, full of flowering trees and dark cypress.

The rest of the mass was directly behind Smyrna and on the gulf immediately north of the village, the acropolis being atop one of its foothills. This was a disheveled and warm-looking mountain but full of mystery. Its lower slopes were largely volcanic white tuff glistening with feldspar; higher up among the forests it was a tumble of yellow-brown and brown-grey rock mixed with red granite and layers of sandstone. It was the peak that held Teleo's mind most often because there were two lakes on it.The one on the south side toward Smyrna was 2000 feet above the village,and he thought it was remarkable that such a thing could be. But the lake on the northern watershed, Lake Saloe, at almost 2700 feet, was profoundly deep and full of mystery.

Some said that at its bottom lay the lost city of Tantalis. He knew well the tomb of Tantalos that was near Smyrna in the eastern foothills. He could never hear the story of that king without feeling thrills up his spine or lingering over thoughts of that high doomed city.

Tantalos was king of the region in early Mycenaean times and his power was so great that he dined with the gods, for Zeus was his friend. Even the local Lydians said that the Kouretes, the famous guardians of Zeus, danced on Sipylos, and men and gods had lived together there. Then in his pride Tantalos forgot the gods, stealing their nectar and ambrosia to share with his mortal friends. Entertaining the gods one day and running out of food, he killed his son Pelops, cutting him up in the stew and serving him to the gods; only Demeter ate. The gods, in horror at his act, restored Pelops to life and made a new left shoulder of ivory to take the place of what Demeter had eaten. To punish Tantalos the gods sent a savage earthquake, casting his beautiful city of Tantalis into a chasm, where water covered it. After other deceptions Tantalos died, and in his Odyssey Teleo would picture the old man in the underworld:

> And I saw Tantalos in endless pain, standing up to his chin in water not able to slake his thirst. Time and again he stooped to drink but time and again the water drained away into black earth, miraculously gone. Tall trees heavy with fruit hung over him—pears and pomegranates, bright apples, figs, and rich ripe olives—but when the old man reached for them, the gusty wind snatched them away into the blustery sky. (Odyssey Book II)

Because of the presumption of Tantalos, now only the water nymphs knew the whereabouts of the city somewhere on the peak of Sipylos.

Tantalos was only the first of his line to run afoul of the gods. Pelops, his twice-born son, went to the Troad where he was driven out by Ilios, and then migrated to Greece where his fame became so great that an entire peninsula now has his name—the Peloponnesos. But he wronged Myrtilus, the charioteer who won him his wife, and the curse was renewed. The terrible acts of his sons Atreus and Thyestes followed. The house of Atreus was especially cursed, for his sons were Agamemnon and Menelaos, who led the Greeks to Troy and that war which helped to bring down all the cities of men and drive them over the seas to find new homes. The Smyrnans had good reason to tell the tales of Tantalos, for in a curious way the children of Pelops had brought them here, to the land of Tantalos who started it all. They told these stories often.

Teleo would beg to be taken to the lake and would stare in wonder into its depths where a ruined city lay, right here in the mountain above his home, the first touched by the Tantalids, as were Troy and Mycenae and Pylos and all the mainland and Peloponnesos, wonderful cities, gone because of mortal presumption toward the gods.

Gods were everywhere and he felt their power. They had to be recognized, their being acknowledged by prayers and gifts, or they would not hear when he called for them. Sometimes in the village he needed to be reminded that they were there, but the joy and fear he felt outside the city walls—in valley, bay, or mountain—were palpable. He loved the countryside. After he turned seven and was old enough to work away from the women, he could sometimes range freely with the other boys and young men hunting out into the fields and hills, and that was a whole new world.

Trout abounded in the tumbling rivers. Orchards and shepherd's stores were their provisions, and many a lonely herder smiled to see them coming up the hillside at sundown bringing laughter and stories and word from the village below. And Teleo began to recite tales for them by the campfire, the shadow of his slight figure stretching past the circle of light into the darkness.

***

A literate society cannot grasp the sense of loss an oral culture can feel when its stories are forgotten and the places remain. The country around Smyrna was rich with the evidence of past habitation. Ancient lookouts, watching places that were there long before the Greeks came, abounded, and the boys of Smyrna knew them well.

The favorite for the older boys was east of the city, about two and a half miles past the old necropolis on the east slope below the acropolis. The lookout was elaborate and very old, on top of a 400-foot hill above the plain, its crest leveled out into a five-sided platform 115 yards in diameter, big enough for a whole army, Teleo thought. It had wonderful towers, seven of them, solid and angled so that every direction could be covered, but no one knew who built them. It was a favorite place to play and practice soldiery, and the boys could tell when trouble brewed because then it would be manned. To the boys of Smyrna it was Troy and Thebes, Orchomenos and golden Mycenae. Many a battle was acted out here and many a brave hero fell, never to return home to his tall house and grieving parents.

Another lookout farther away was past the saddle of hill that ran between the mountain masses north and south of the city and which separated the fertile plain of Smyrna from inland territory. On the far side of the saddle and north of Black Pass were the remains of an old defensive fortress with cyclopean walls larger than the wall at Smyrna, and below it in the cliff were tombs hewn out of the living rock. The older boys would go there, still with a certain awe that goes with entering the works unknown men have abandoned. Travelers in the country would rest there at night, trusting the defensive sense of men long dead.

Even more sobering was a high place their parents did not want them to go. It lay east of the pass about three miles, and southsoutheast of the old fortress. At nine, Teleo approached it with dread and daring. He scrambled up the steep limestone cliff which rose abruptly from the plain to 1000 feet. On its top and upper slopes there were man-made ledges and hollows, and several tombs of strange design, all laboriously fashioned. The tomb treasures and human remains had long since been plundered, by animal or human.

It was strange to live in a country with such a long experience of habitation behind it, one that reached far back before the Trojan war. Something had changed and these people were gone, not even remembered. No one sang their songs or honored their names. And while their living place seemed crude, not at all modern as Smyrna was, he marveled at the patience and intention he saw in their works of stone. How long it must have taken, he thought, the wind whipping about him, twisting the pine trees. It came to him that their gods had died with them, and he wondered which had first abandoned the other.

But there were two places so numinous that Homer could call them up even in his blind old age: the Niobe and Black Pass.

The Niobe was a monumental carving on the old Hittite road to the harbor at Kyme on the north side of blue Sipylos. It was six or seven hundred years old at least, carved about 300 feet up on a sheer cliff overlooking the road, with a bottomless pool far below it. From a deep recess, facing due north, the huge figure of a seated woman looked out on passing humanity. The figure itself was thirty feet high and carved so as to be almost free of the mountain. She seemed to be leaning forward, as if to look down at him, her hands on her breast in an attitude of divinity. Her face and cheeks were damp with the waters of the mountain, which seeped down her breast and along the rock to the pool below. She wore a tall conical headdress, and her feet rested on a royal stool. Teleo had first seen writing there, for symbols were carved in the wall to her right, near her head, but no one could read them.

In Smyrna she was said to be Niobe, the daughter of old King Tantalos and sister of Pelops. She was married to the king of Thebes, Amphion, and bore him six sons and six daughters. But they came to grief, for—as his Iliad would say—Niobe compared herself to Leto who had only two children, Apollo and Artemis. Apollo shot the boys and Artemis the girls. Now on Sipylos Niobe broods, weeping over her troubles with the gods.

To Teleo from the very first this carving was a mother weeping for her lost child, and his heart would break with longing as he mourned for his own lost mother. It was here that he first seemed to hold within himself a shadowy memory of a warm lap and arms around him, before the hearth-fire. A dog was licking his toes, and there was singing. He felt it on his body rather than in his mind and wondered if it was just a wish or a half-remembered reality. It was too precious to voice. Here was an image from his life, mother and child, both infinitely lost. And yet it was a comfort to him.

But there was a darker tale about his Niobe. The old people of Magnesia-near-Sipylos said that it represented an Amazon goddess, carved when the Amazones fought along with the Hittites for control of the central coast of Anatolia. They had been warrior priestesses of a savage cult who worshipped the great mountain mother goddess, women said to have fought against the Greeks at Troy.

This was Amazon country, and the Greeks told frightening stories about them around the fires at night. Instead of giants and floods the children felt around their shoulders, in the shadows flickering on the walls, the great misshapen tribes of warrior women who had slashed off one breast so as to aim their arrows well, priestesses of Kybele, who, with unnatural savagery, rode through their dreams. Some of the stories said that the oldest cities—Smyrna, Ephesos, Pitane, Gryneia, Myrina, and Kyme—had been founded by Amazon queens. Never, said the children of Smyrna. Magnesia-near-Sipylos unabashedly claimed to have been founded by the Amazones, but Smyrnan children shuddered at the thought. There had been no women warriors since the Trojan war, and, anyway, war was man's affair.

Black Pass—or Warriors' Pass—reminded Smyrna that the Hittites had been there long ago. Travelers could not miss that famous landmark, for it stood where the road went south to Ephesos, west to Smyrna, north to Magnesia-near-Sipylos, and inland east to Sardis.

The pass was narrow and full of trees, with a stream running through it and flanked by Mount Olympos and Mount Draco, 5000- and 4500- foot peaks. Two warriors guarded Black Pass and no one—certainly no boy from Smyrna—came there without pausing in awe before them. Carved in the dark rock, 70 feet above the road on each side, were two larger-than-life Hittite warriors, one looking east and one west. Advancing figures in profile, except for the shoulders which faced the viewer, they were armed with bow and spear. Each wore a short tunic and vest, cone-shaped helmet and Hittite boots with slightly curled toes. There were symbols across their chests which tradition claimed to say, "I got this country with my own shoulders." They still stood there, in their neat and squared shadow boxes, guarding the road, for or against whom important now only to the traveler of the moment.

***

Teleo and his friends knew other old sites in the neighborhood, but most of them were still in regular use. Two older acropoli, one inland on the southern coast of the gulf and one northwest of the city's acropolis, both at about 1500 feet, served as excellent watch and signaling stations, as did Mount Pagos, a little closer on the gulf. Then there was the aforementioned lookout between Smyrna plain and the plains of Lydia inland; its wide view in both directions made its control essential. And last were the acropolis and its lower sentry post, an ancient sacrificial platform which commanded a strategic view of city and gulf. Teleo was to spend time on all of them as guard and soldier during his long life.

And of course the tomb of Tantalos was here, on the acropolis hill to the east of the village, the marvel of the countryside to such a boy. It was a bee-hive Mycenaean tomb, just like those at Mycenae and Pylos and all the heroic cities he would see in his long lifetime. But for him this was the first and most impressive. It was circular and large, almost 100 feet in diameter. Its base was shaped like a drum about eight feet tall, and the bee-hive cone sat on top of it. Within the drum was a closed chamber shaped like a rectangle, 11 by 7 feet, the burial room. The roof of the tholos tomb was vaulted, each block of the cone lying closer to the center than the one below until a single roof-stone completed the ceiling 90 feet above the floor. The inside surface was finished smoothly, but its decoration and the tomb's treasure had long since been stripped away—as well as the bones of the Tantalids. To Teleo it was a great thing, like the city walls, made by people who must have lived with the gods.

Signs everywhere near this ancient burial ground signaled existence of a city older and larger than his wonderful Smyrna. Some of the locals argued that Smyrna was really the old city of Tantalis; nobody would build a city as high as the lake was, they maintained. But others would argue that if they lived with the gods the lake was not too high a place for their city. In fact, the gods loved to live on mountains, and Ionia, like other places, had its own Mount Olympos. He imagined the gods flying back and forth across the valley from one peak to another. What a time that must have been, he thought.

Teleokairos Maionides noticed early that the gods seldom spoke to assemblies. In. the epic lays they came to men in their dreams and to women when they were alone in their beds, or in the fragrant meadows, or beside the rushing streams, in the sunshine, and lay upon them and begat heroes. It was only in battle that the gods flamed in glory before crowds of men, and even then they often hid themselves from common view. So from the earliest songs, he knew that if the gods were to speak in his life, he would have to make room for them.

Sometimes he thought that was the most important thing he ever learned.

He mentioned it to his grandfather once, when they were watching circling dancers at a wedding festival. The old man burst out laughing and lay his great hand on the nape of Teleo's neck, where he still wore a single lock of fair hair symbolizing boyhood.

"And the gods will find you if you seek solitude? You should probably hope they do not, for the gods do not enter the lives of mortals without an attendant curse. No, Tel. The gods help those who sacrifice to them, who honor their feast days, who follow their prohibitions, who give gifts to them before men. Go, dance in the festival. Thus do you honor the god." And Leonidas pushed him into the circling group, smiling expansively, and took his own place with the elders.

And always there was that wildness in him, a need to feel the edge of things. The Greeks called it akrasia. He swam often in the warm salt water of the gulf, diving for sponges in spite of the danger from sharks. If he were to be a sailor, he had to be used to the sea. If he were to find his family, his people, some day.

The war galley fighters would practice there, and boys were allowed to come along to learn the ropes. One hot afternoon as the city's two galleys practiced boarding maneuvers, he was on the ikria at the stern when a fighter fell into the water amidships. Laden with leather body armor, the man surfaced laboriously and began to swim back to the stern plank. Tel's quick eye sighted a fin, behind the boat and gliding slowly toward the splashing swimmer. Without thought he grabbed the long punting pole at his side and, as the shark passed below him, he struck the tough hide sharply, not six inches below the surface, pushing down with all his might. The fish veered away as the man pulled onto the boarding plank, safe by seconds. Tel was the talk of the town that evening and went to the feast with the sea warriors, seated in honor among them as the bard sang songs of Poseidon.

He knew he was not a hero, but he loved the feasts of men.

✵✵✵

Maionides could not see the Baths of Agamemnon from Smyrna, but he knew exactly where they lay along the gulf's south shore. For he grew up knowing that Agamemnon, the Great King of the Greeks, had been here. And the song went something like this.

During the long Trojan war, as everyone knows, the Achaean Greeks sacked other cities in the Troad and along the coast. Once Agamemnon himself had fought the Mysians near the Kaikos river 50 miles north of the Hermaian gulf. Telephos, a son of Herakles, had led the Mysians, and the battle was a memorable one. The victorious Greeks, however, saw that they could not linger on the shore while enemy reinforcements arrived from the countryside. So they stripped the bodies of the Mysians of their armor, according to their custom, and departed. Sailing out of the Elaitic gulf they turned south into Lydian waters and stopped at Erythrai, opposite Chios, to consult the legendary sibyl Herophile. She advised the tired and wounded men: "From the far side of my mountain you can look out over the safest and most hospitable of lands. At the far end of the gulf lies a town later to become Smyrna of the fair prospect. Between my mountain and that town, on the southern shore, are warm springs where you and your men can rest and heal your wounds. No enemy will seek you there, no storm will sink your ships. Hang up the captured Mysian helmets here, and I prophesy that in time to come you will become the most famous leader of warriors the world has ever known. And this fame will come out of Smyrna."

Agamemnon rejoiced in his heart to have the promise of such fame, and to rest and heal his men. So his ships set sail north again, rounded Old Black Nose, the headland of Mimas peninsula, and sailed into the gulf of the Hermos. Here at the hot springs they rested and feasted and hung the Mysian helmets as offerings to the sibyl. Then they sailed back to Troy. No one in Smyrna could know yet that the prophecy was being fulfilled in their lifetime.

✵✵✵

So this was where Teleo lived, in a sunny modern town steeped in stories of its past, not daunted by the ancient wreckage around it, and just at the edge of a breaking wave which would sweep them all into a new time. That was because of the ships. But ships are not born; men make them to sail over the broad back of the sea. And what makes them want to do that?

A boy who had stood on the acropolis and watched the black ships come down the gulf and beach beneath the city wall could answer. With the prevailing northerly winds bellying out the square sails, they would fly down the gulf like great sea birds, then turning east, they would furl the sails and the smooth rowers would take over, their oars glinting as they caught the sun to the tune of the pipes. It was miraculous to see.

There were two kinds of ships to watch for, very different in appearance, though their sails, the single square, were always the same. When the boat hulls were long and narrow, he would give the alarm, for that could only be war galleys manned for a fight. The merchantmen had wide beams and rounded sterns; usually the bows were rounded, too, though some were convex and had sharp projections at the waterline. But the city was not necessarily safe if it were a phortus, a merchant-man, for many of those were pirates. Or more correctly, most would become pirates if presented with the opportunity.

Maion was a naukleros, a ship owner who carried goods of his own as well as those of an emperos, a trader with foreign cities who sent his goods with ship owners. The settlers on Chios at Emporio were coastal traders marketing their famous wines and pottery through various carriers, Maion being one of them. Smyrna's wine was famous, too, the Pramneian wine which Maion took such pride and profit from and from whose miraculous vines two crops were harvested every year.

Frequent rapids made the Hermos unnavigable for any distance, so Teleo grew up with ships made for ocean and gulf. He was taught early that operating a war galley and sailing a merchantman were two totally separate skills, each looked down upon by those who practiced the other.

"My ships are built for sailing," Maion would say. "There are oars—20, in fact—to use when I must, but I carry goods, not an army, and the fewer crew and oars, the more space. I do not hug the coast running up the beach every night as warships do for food and rest. I strike out into the wine-dark sea, crossing where there is no land in sight, sometimes for days at a time. I am a sailor."

The warriors would agree, saying boastfully, "Warships never fight under sail. They are oared ships; we maneuver with our many oars, and attack with our powerful bow rams. Just as the epics say that the soldier rode to battle in his chariot and fought on foot, the sea warrior goes to battle by sail power and fights with oar and ram." So Tel learned early that his training as a builder and sailor of merchantmen was distinct from his training as a fighter, though the realities of each included the other.

Much trafficking passed between the cities of Ionia when Teleokairos was growing up, and commerce increased with the Lydians inland. Times were prosperous, the populations large enough to allow for specializations that made life more civilized. There was a modest amount of ship build-ing at Smyrna and, while the land was strictly parceled out and controlled by Greek citizens, the crafts of city and ocean were available to Lydians and other non-Greek craftsmen for a livelihood. In fact, the younger sons of the Greek aristos, who would not inherit the land, were turning to the sea. Even in the off season building and fitting kept many men busy.

The two sailing seasons were short: the spring and the time from mid-summer day until autumn. To sail was an audacious act, moving over the trackless waters pushed by the wind. The square sail was sturdy but it could not sail into the the wind, for tacking was unknown. There were frequent calms in the summer Aegean and unpredictable sudden shifts of weather. A trip south was fast, five knots an hour, even making 130 knots in a day and night, for the northerlies were strong;

but coming back was a different matter. A week's sail south could mean a month's return, with most of it spent waiting for favorable winds or rowing short distances between the villages.

By the time he was twelve Teleo had seen Ionian Miletos and Dorian Rhodes and had traded in Phokaia and Kyme, Aiolian towns immediately to the north of the Hermos. He spent a great deal of his time learning about the building and care of the vessel itself. He listened to the traders, too, but trading was second nature to everyone. Systems of coinage did not begin until a few decades later.

***

Ever since Athena had build the Argo, she had overseen the building of ships, and men had given them names and emblems. While Poseidon was the god of the sea, it was Athena who showed mortals how to sail across it and not be lost. There was a sense in which the two gods competed and myths told of their rivalry, the thundering natural force pitted against the skill of the city goddess' ship guided by the cunning mind of the mortal sailor.

Teleo could remember vividly every ship built in Smyrna, many of which he had a part in making. The phortes, merchants, were always made primarily of pine from the ample forests of Sipylon, with a false keel of oak or beech to minimize damage in hauling ashore. Mules would haul the timber down the mountain and building would begin before the wood was seasoned. It took time and a good eye to use wood properly.

He knew ship building from the very beginning. The shell of the craft was formed first, and then the frame to stiffen it was added. When the keel had been laid—an almost flat bottom—the stern post and stempost were scarfed to the keel with secure, overlapping joints. Then the slow work of planking would begin with the garboard strake, the plank next to the keel, rabbeted securely into the keel.

He connected every plank to the next with skillful and frequent mortise-and-tenon joints. The planks varied in width with the lumber available, but the patient joining, never more than eight inches from one to the next, went on until the shell was up to the gunwales. The tenons were deep, sometimes half the depth of the plank. He learned to cut the mortises in the upper edge of the attached plank, varying the position so that some were nearer the outer edge and some the inner. Then he would fill the mortise holes with charcoal and clamp the next board temporarily in place, thus marking where to cut. After matching tenons had been cut, he would grease both mortise and tenon heavily, for they had to fit tightly so as not to shrink and rattle but not to be so tight as to split the wood. Then, calling the strongest men, they would position the two boards together and hammer them home.

The inner skeleton was just as carefully done, the frame and shell connected every ten inches at the least. He used oaken treenails that he had made, cylinders of hard wood, and then the shipwright would drive bronze spikes through shell and frame and nail at an angle, spikes so long that the end would protrude and then be clenched. A strengthening keelson, notched over the frame, was laid inside for walking, and the mast stepping was put in.

If caulking were needed—it usually wasn't on a well-made ship- Teleo would patiently pack each crevice with flax debris called tow. He hated this step because it meant the fit was poor. But he loved the excitement of the sealing of the hull with pitch. While the pitch was melting in great cauldrons by the ship, every available man was swarming over the hull with brushes, soaking and filling every crack with the molten pitch. The fine black hull would begin to look seaworthy.

And then the decorating of the colored prow would begin. The owner would trace the great oculis on the prow, as well as the unique design to be painted in bright colors around it. The eye was often not a human eye but a wheel with spokes, much like a sun symbol or a chariot wheel, after the fashion of earlier times. Wax would be melted and mineral dyes added to each pot. When these were of painting consistency, the workers would fill the outlines with brushes full of bright color—purple, white, green, blue, yellow, and vermillion.

Red was the most popular and most visible from a distance, the coloring of the bow enabling others to see the direction of headway at a glance. The mast and yard and gunwales often were brightly painted too, but the rest of the hull was usually pitch black. The Phoenicians and some pirate vessels would paint the entire ship in mottled sea and sky tones in order to escape detection, something considered ignoble by the Smyrnans but nevertheless practiced on occasion.

The ships of each city and owner carried an identifying symbol painted or carved on each side of the stempost at the front of the ship. Maionides heard the stories of ancient stempost symbols: Achilles' ships were marked with golden nereids, Athens' with Athena in a golden chariot, and the Boeotians' with Kadmos and the golden snake. Wise Nestor's had been the river god Alpheus with the feet of a bull. Maion had chosen the meeting of Poseidon and the river god Hermos, represented by the silhouette of two horses' heads, manes flying, running into the wind. Tel loved the stempost figure with all his heart, always polishing it first of all, before any other duty called. The eye of Poseidon was rock crystal, and it seemed to watch him as he worked.

When the Pleiades set, the season was over, and he helped to bring in all the merchant ships that had made it back to port for winter beaching. They had to be scrubbed and drained, all plugs pulled so the winter rains could not collect and rot the bilges. Ballast had to be removed and the hard work of shoring up the ships with hermata, stones packed together around each ship, would begin. The packing had to be full and tight, around the length of the hull of each vessel, to protect it from weather, keep it dry, and make relaunching easier in the spring. All the wooden gear—oars, mast and yard—and all the hanging gear—the sail and ropes—were cleaned and taken home or stowed in the dockyard shed inside the watergate wall.

Smyrna kept two war galleys, maintained by the city and manned by the men of the aristoi. While every boy learned early how to fight with sword and spear, every family had a responsibility to arm a certain number of their men to fight on land and to work the war galleys in combat at sea. Members of the genos who did not fight were responsible for the making of armor and weapons and for maintenance of the galleys. Oarsmen trained hard for the intricate maneuvering of a war galley, sensing the glamour in such warfare. The galley was slim and black, with oars for fifty men, open decked with small platforms at either end and capable of carrying officers and extra fighters. As in Mycenaean times, the warriors were also the oarsmen. The discipline in a good galley was severe, and the speed and maneuverability astonishing.

Its most glamorous and menacing feature was the ram on the bow, a deadly and ancient weapon. Such rams were not extensions of the hull, but were installed so as to break away, if necessary, without undue damage to the keel. The rams were made of heavy bronze, fashioned with monstrous faces molded or painted on them, which gave life to the ship and spirit to the fighters.

That a warship would require a singer never seemed strange to Teleo Maionides, brought up where songs of war were sung at every feasting. The use was very practical on board ship, of course.

Oarsmen had to keep in rhythm, and to provide the strokes each ship would have a bosun, auletes, who would play the aulos pipe, standing by the mast amidships, giving a measure for sweep and pause during the hours of pulling. Most of the men would know the songs and strokes, but some were fine singers as well, and a ship was fortunate if, during a long passage, the bosun could sing as well as blow the pipe. The same thing was true on a merchantman, of course, and the bards could pay for their passage with songs. Even the Argo had Orpheus, and the dolphins were said to frolic by the dark prows of warships in order to hear the clear pipers.

There was drama in the departure of a vessel, and days when Teleo would be going along. The village folk came down to wish them fair journey. The sailors carried all the stuff down to the ship. Then they climbed aboard by the threnus—a projecting beam on the hull near the helmsman's seat—or by the boarding ladders at the stern. The captain, or archos, and passengers went aboard and sat at the stern in the ikria. The crew cast off the peismata, the mooring ropes, and poled out with the kontos away from the beach three lengths. As Telemachos and his crew in the Odyssey,

They hoisted the pinewood mast into its box amidships, made it fast, and hauled up the sail. A freshening wind caught the canvas full on and the deep blue waves hissed by the prow as the black ship got underway. When all was secure, they set out brimming bowls of wine, pouring libations to the deathless gods, and first to Athena with her flashing eyes, the daughter of Zeus. (Odyssey Book 2)

For Athena had made their bright-cheeked ships and shown them the paths of the sea.

INTERLOCUTORY

The Voice of Letha Gooding

Notice the boy has not spoken to you yet. Childhood memories are deep; just let them settle in. I wish I had time to stop here and tell you about Cadoux's <u>Ancient Smyrna</u>. His is truly a Homeric story. Tell me this: How free are you of the climate of opinion of your century? What do you think of an illiterate man who lived in a house with dirt floors and had one cloak for forty years? Can you see him creating a song light years ahead of you in psychological penetration and delicacy of expression? Can you believe in the full humanity of the villagers who understood his mastery as they licked their greasy fingers and made love in the family room? In Homer's time the individual was more intelligent than his environment, and nowadays the environment is more intelligent than the individual. What to make of that is beyond me. Today we worship Hephaistos, or we had better, as his technological net tightens around us.

There was more to the boy's world than Smyrna and the coast. In fact, Aristotle reports a tradition that Homer could have been Lydian. One of his traditional names, Melesigenes means "of the tribe of Meles", whether Lydian king or river is a mystery. Maionides is the traditional name of Homer or his father, Maionia denoting a region of Lydia. So we have to consider some non-Greek influence from Lydia or Phrygia, more than might be ordinary in the life of a Greek village boy, a double heritage for a great-hearted singer whose epics differ so radically from the norm in the compassionate characterization of both Greek and ancient antagonists.

Lydia was just beginning to feel the stirrings that in the next centuries would make it a paragon of wealth and worldliness. Sardis had its own double heritage and its own kind of sacred violence. What would have been the effect of it on a boy addicted to tales? And when did the Muse choose him for her own?

.

CHAPTER 2

Songs of a Lydian Summer

742 B.C.E. Sardis

During the spring that Teleo was ten, word came from Sardis that Maion's brother Ardys was gravely ill. After a hurried visit, Maion left his son there to spend the summer and tend his uncle.

The two brothers had had ships together but fate had set her hand against Ardys when his ship had sunk off Crete. Years passed, and then Ardys had come back again laden with treasure, but desperately ill with malaria. He had slowly rallied and then gone inland to their ancestral home in Sardis to join his wife and three small children. Since his return he had fathered a daughter. Now spring flooding had made part of the plain into swampland, and he had had a recurrence of malaria, the scourge of the Aegean coast which was again threatening his life.

"It is past time you knew my brother," Maion had said. "You know, Tel, there are other people in the world than Smyrnans, and other sounds than Ionian." It was the closest to a rebuke that Maion had ever spoken, and Tel thought for the first time about what living among Greeks had cost his father. But he realized too that he did not really value any other people, so thoroughly Ionian had he become.

He hated being in Sardis, bored with caring for a sick old man, missing the sailing season, hot and miserable away from the sea breezes, oppressed by the sounds of Lydian and Sardian Greek. At the same time he felt the optimism of the young and congratulated himself that he was destined for a better life than this one. So, with the condescension of the confident, most of the time he behaved himself and did his duty.

Teleo felt comfortable only with the animals, for an animal is the same everywhere. The horses especially drew him, glossy and spirited creatures; the Lydians had been famous horsemen even in Trojan times. He would gaze at the animal's fine head, musing at how one great eye contemplated his small being, and feel a god-like presence, the existence of a force which did not need to explain—or think that he could fathom—its own essence. There was a wildness under the liquid glance and a warmth, too, set in the huge skull, that gave him both an odd sense of his own validity and a knowledge of his fragility. He tried on the glance to see if he could know the power that lay behind it, if his was the same wildness. He could understand why any god would be happy to take on such a form, as Poseidon had.

But he had little time to be outside. His uncle Ardys was sallow, still shivering after many days of sickness. He seemed very old, too old to be strong Maion's brother. A passive patient at first, he finally began to rally enough to tell his nephew what to do to make him comfortable. He laughed quietly once when Tel commiserated with him over his illness.

"Never curse disease, my son. The gods send it for many reasons. Because of this fever I got away from the pirates who kept me so long from my home. They took all I had and left me to die. Some day—when I am able—I'll tell you that story."

He managed a trembling smile, and for the first time light came back into his eyes. They were dark eyes, much deeper-browed than his brother's, and they had frightened the boy. As Ardys had lain in the dim room he could see them catch the light, but they had been haunted and far, far away, living dreams of other times. Now they knew him and the room again. One morning they watched the boy sweeping, and his uncle turned toward him and spoke with a sober air.

"Tell me what you remember from your young days, Tel. Before you came to Smyrna with my brother. Is there anything?"

"Yes." Tel did not remember when anyone had asked him such a question. But it was natural for this old man. He looked at the floor to gather his mind together.

"Sometimes I can feel the swell of the sea, a gentle rocking. I think I am remembering my mother's breast—I think of the two together. I can hear voices and see shadows like huge trees standing on a polished floor and feel myself lifted. And dogs. There was a dog." He shrugged and turned back to his work.

"Tell me about your rescue again."

"I can only say what my father tells me; I don't remember for myself. He found me bound to floating debris in a tangle of mast and sails. I was tied to the step-box with a long cloth."

"What kind of cloth do you mean? Was it ship's gear or clothing?"

"I do know about that. My father has saved it all these years. It is deep purple wool. I plan to keep it always."

"Your father has told me something of this." He paused a long moment. "Tel, it is time I told you what I think about that cloth. I did tell your father but he may have let it fly out of his head. And my time seems now to be borrowed from the gods. I want you to know this."

Teleo felt a thrill pass through him. "Tell me," he said tightly.

Ardys smiled, pale and tired. "It is not much; don't fear it. Come, sit beside me. Let me hold your hand.

"Tel , I have traveled far in the world and heard the tales of men. Some are false, just as some dreams are false. But there are true stories that seem false because they are outside of our experience.

"A sailor told me this once. I had survived a savage storm off Mykonos and was resting in the harbor there, thankful to be alive, sitting on the stone quay drinking to the gods who rule the broad heavens. In the crowd that gathered about—a man always has friends when he's happy and spends—was a Thracian seaman. He was a boaster and we ended the night with blows. But among his outrageous boasts was one I especially remembered, that there were sailors who knew they could not drown, even in a storm like that one, because they wore a scarf given to them by the gods." He paused.

"We laughed hugely then and toasted his ingenuity. But as I have moved about the world I have caught sight of a few men who have such cloths. Hardy, rough men who will talk about much in the world but will not talk about this garment. They wear it wound about the abdomen. They only say that it was a gift of the great gods of Samothrace."

Teleo stared at him. Suddenly he needed to see the wrap again, but it was in the coffer at Smyrna. His head echoed and the light seemed to flicker.

"Where is that?"

"In the northern Aegean, north of Lemnos. An island." Ardys was talking more rapidly. "I do not know that this is such a sash. I have not seen it, nor do I know whether I would recognize it if I did."

He looked deep into the boy's eyes. "I do know that for your father you were indeed a gift of the gods. At just the right time."

"Do you think someone gave up his own life to save me?" He looked away. "I have always thought it was my parents." He turned back again. "Could my father have been a sailor? A sailor on a pirate ship? With a sash from the gods?"

Ardys felt his anxiety. "Tel, listen to me. Have you ever thought how strong each living person is? Just think of it. All the seeds of men. All the possibilities. Of all the seed your own father spilled, you grew instead of all the others that never had a chance for life. Remember that life is a gift you deserve because you earned it. You have brought creation into reality by living it yourself. Forced nature to give before your own spirit. You have asserted yourself and taken the great risk of being born. Right place, right time. You are well named. You survived the great trauma of breathing—of accepting life—long before you were found at sea. Everyone is a miracle, a hero in the deepest sense."

He lay back, exhausted by his intensity, then shifted his bones. " It may be I am misleading you about the scarf but I had to tell you while the breath is in me." He added lightly, " Life is so uncertain! If you should choose to go piping over the purple sea in search of fortune you may find some track of your people and this may be important. Only the gods can say. Now. Enough of that."

"Thank you, uncle. I will not forget. Surely you will live long and perhaps go roaming again. With me." He smoothed the rumpled pillows and gave his uncle a cup of cool water sweetened with honey and a little salt.

Ardys smiled at his attention and seemed to relax. "I hope you're right, Mr. Asclepios. But most voyagers pay a heavy price. Now let me sleep a while."

Teleo lingered at the door, then turned. "Do you think if I wore the sash that it would always save my life at sea?"

Ardys answered from a distance. "No. The gods probably did not give it to you." He laughed. "You would have remembered that."

Perhaps it was then that a new kind of consciousness began for Teleokairos. He had always known he was considered a gift of the sea god by his foster parents, and he had accepted that, aware of the pleasure he brought them, and confident that he could repay them in time to come.

Now he began to think more of a different matter. Life was a gift, yes, but he was less sure from whom it had come. Had he lived at sea at the expense of someone else? Of a parent or even of a stranger? Had giving the sash to him been an act of sacrifice? Was his life charmed or cursed because of it? He would observe that, when others are given their lives again, after thinking that they are lost, they seem to be born all over again, to become two people, one able to look back at the other and feel blessed, as if from a distance. Now he did this. He began to feel responsible to the giver of the sash. Perhaps it was not just a piece of someone's clothing. But how could he ever repay someone for such a gesture? For such a stranger's gift? He knew a helpless obligation, a kind of guilt.

***

One day when Ardys had recovered enough to sit in the shade of the courtyard, Tel sang a tale to him about the sack of Troy. Ardys listened with pleasure, and then he began to speak of those times from a Lydian point of view. The Lydians of Maionia had rallied behind Priam, the Trojan king, as had all of the other Hittite protectorates, against the invaders from across the Aegean. "Bring me the copper box from the bottom of the hearthside chest," Ardys said. "I want to show you something."

This done, Ardys fumbled with the intricate lock, his mind already inside the container. Finally he succeeded in opening it, revealing, on the soft cloth within, a cheekpiece, the kind that adorns the head of a war horse. It was of ivory stained with Tyrian dye, and intricately carved. Silken tassels lay beside it, long since fallen away and too fragile to lift. He spoke quietly.

"This is ivory, Tel. The ivory routes are finally opening up again. But this is very old. Worn in the battle against the 'long heads'—the Greeks—at Troy."

He looked up at Tel, smiling to reassure him. "We were a wealthy people, and fierce fighters. The equals of the Trojans themselves in the training of horses, and no one matched our skill in the use of war chariots. Two of our great princes died in the battle against the Greeks on the windy plain below many-towered Troy. Here. Hold it in your hand. Careful now."

And the precious ivory piece lay there, in Homer's hands, hands that would pluck the phorminx while he would remember it long afterwards in the Iliad.

It was strange to hear the story of Troy from the Trojan allies, enemies of the Greek heroes. From his father's people.

Ardys sensed his reserve.

"The fighters of Mycenaean Greece are legendary among the Lydians," Ardys continued. "Long before Troy they were on our coasts and in the islands of the Aegean. In the generation before the sack of Troy the Achaean King Atarissi was one of the most celebrated and feared men of his age."

Tel looked doubtful. "I never heard of him."

"You would have called him Atreus, perhaps."

Tel swallowed. "Father of Agamemnon and Menelaos. Yes." The names sounded unfamiliar here, as if he hestitated to share them with unsympathetic ears. He felt homesick.

Ardys continued. "Atarissi conquered the island of Rhodes. Miletos was already Greek. In league with coastal cities, he attacked the great Hittite kingdom itself. But his greatest conquest was in Cyprus." Tel was uncomfortable, hearing the tale of Greek conquest from the mind of someone whose peoples had fought against them. He thought of how Maion must have felt when Ionians referred to his people as barbarians.

"Tell me about Cyprus."

Cyprus was like magic to the boy, the first place he had probably known. He knew Ardys loved it, just as Maion had. "Cyprus is a lovely place. The first Greeks to colonize landed—guess where? On the very headland off which you were found. That's right. At Maa-Palaeokastro there is a spectacular promontory with such fine natural defenses from both land and sea that the Greeks made a beachhead there in Mycenaean times. Perhaps even that Atreus of yours. I have sailed by there several times, and it seems impregnable.

"Well, the Achaeans quickly assumed control of the area and moved to lusher fields. By the collapse of Mycenae, all of Cyprus was speaking Greek. Many refugees from Pylos and Mycenae went naturally to Rhodes and Cyprus. They destroyed the native cities at Kition and Enkomi and rebuilt them as Greek towns. Cyprus has been Greek for five hundred years.

Ardys shifted tone suddenly, looking at him intently. "You didn't come from that headland, if that's what you're thinking. It has been long abandoned."

How strangely and how easily precious information drops into one's mind, Ardys reflected when he saw how important his remark had been. Tel held it like a treasure in a treasure-box all day, mentioning it over and over.

They talked often about Troy for the boy knew many tales of that siege, and he sang them proudly for Ardys. Troy had been destroyed many times, Ardys told him quietly, for it was very ancient. It was as old as Egypt, he asserted. The Hittites themselves had taken it 1000 years before the Greeks came. Which did not diminish their achievement, he added, for Troy was the most magnificent citadel of the coast then.

Teleo observed one day that the term "Trojan War" was a misnomer. "Call it the sack of Ilion, not the Trojan war. It was really only one event in a long movement of people, wasn't it? And why is the sack of Ilion so important? Many other cities were sacked, too."

"It is famous. That is why it is important."

"You mean—famous because it was important."

"No. I meant what I said. In Mycenaean cities—in many cities of men—the bards sang. The bards made Ilion important."

***

What Teleo really wanted to know about was his uncle's travels, but Ardys always changed the subject or suddenly initiated some activity. Sensing something that was more than reluctance, he found himself wondering why this wonderful uncle, this fabulous teller of tales of the world, would not tell his own adventures.

"It is not a hero's tale, my boy ," Ardys said in reply to his urging one day as they sat eating a lunch they had brought with them onto the acropolis hill. The climb had been arduous for his uncle, his first strenuous effort since his illness, and they shared a sense of triumph as they sat looking out over the broad plain below them, like gods or kings in a happy world .

"Has Maion told you about our great ancestor Piyamaradush?"

Ardys was evasive again, but Teleo did not notice. He was anxious to hear a family tale retold. "Yes, but tell me your story. He never said much. Just that Piyamaradush was a great Lydian honored by the Greek cities. That as his descendent the Greeks honored your family."

"Now he was a hero ! " Ardys' eyes sparkled. "He lived here in the valley not long after the Trojan War. He had been a powerful prince under the protectorate of the Hittites. But in a brutal violation of the traditional hospitality due tributary lords, the Hittite king ravaged his estates, killed his sons, and carried the women into slavery while Piyamaradush was fighting in the east.

"Our Lydian ancestor swore vengeance and, taking the remnants of his tribe with him, waged guerrilla warfare throughout the southern territories, from Assyria to Cyprus and all along the coasts of the Aegean.

"Piyamaradush was a swashbuckling figure, the terror of the coast. The Mycenaean Greek cities gave him sanctuary, and the ruler of Miletos fitted him with gear and supplies to sail the coast as far north as the Hellespont! This he did to the great discomfort of the toppling Hittite regime.

"The story goes that the Hittite king Hattushish left his capital city Bogazkoy, far inland, and traveled all the way to Miletos to try to persuade the Greeks to betray the Lydian prince to him, or at least to refuse him sanctuary.

"On the way he fought against our guerrilla forces, capturing 7000 in one battle! But when he woke the next morning, they had all been rescued and had melted away into the mountains!

"When after a month's march Hattushish came to Miletos, the king was out of town and the pirate nowhere to be seen. Enraged, he wrote to the Achaean king at Mycenae to protest such insulting treatment of a Great King.

"To breach the aristocratic code of hospitality was a grave offense, replied the Mycenaean, but it had been the breach of the same code in his treatment of Piyamaradush that had caused the trouble to begin with."

"Why isn't there a song about him?"

Ardys laughed. "There should be. There should be. Our ancestor, the great Lydian corsair Piyamaradush, became a Greek hero, and his name is still honored among the Panionians, even though Miletos has been burned and resettled in the twenty generations since. That is why Maion and I are honored in the Greek cities." He added, "And why I want always to live here, in the land of my people. No matter who holds the high city, it is my home. Just look at it, Tel. Have you ever seen anything more beautiful?"

He had—at Smyrna—but kept a tactful silence in the face of such emotion.

Sardis sprawled before them, along the three miles to the junction of the Hermos and Pactolas rivers in the northwest. Its spectacular acropolis where they sat had been the site of an ancient town called Hyde. In fact, the high citadel was still sometimes called by that name. It was now impregnable, since the great King Meles had built an impressive wall around its summit generations ago. It held the palace of the ruling house, the Heraclidae, still a fairly simple structure, for the great gold rush was just beginning. Here the Greek-speaking Mycenaean aristoi had ruled for almost 500 years, and much tradition still was Greek. But the people of the city and countryside were Lydian, and they lived their lives on the fertile and well-watered Sardian plain below them.

Ardys did not have much respect for the present generation of Heraclidae, saying that they had exchanged their own strengths for the weaknesses of Lydia, and no one respects a poor trader. Greek influence now came primarily through trade with Ephesos and Smyrna, and lately with the city of Corinth across the Aegean. Ardys saw trouble coming from Phrygian inroads from the north, and he wished the Lydian towns and villages held the high citadel at Hyde. "Waves of people have washed over this lovely land. Soon it will be the Phrygians. The Cimmerians are behind them, pushing south. And northeast, behind them, are the savages, the Scythians." Ardys felt the inevitability of conquest. There was some time still, he thought, before they would come to Sardis.

His nephew stared at the distant horizon, trying to imagine horsemen sweeping toward them from the north, soldiers burning and killing on the plain below, warriors storming the steep path they had climbed. He tried to imagine himself fighting and dying, or a bard, sitting where he was, watching a city fall. He shivered and looked at Ardys, who was smiling at the serene countryside.

***

Teleokairos Maionides encountered new gods In Sardis, something he would have expected, for each place had new and distinct ones. But there was an element in Sardian worship that was deeply new to him, for Sardis was still emerging from matriarchal patterns of religion, patterns that had ruled the world for many ages. The ancient Great Mother held sway among many Lydians, who called her Kybele or Kuvava. The Greek Artemis had taken on a prominence there in the city of the plain, her worship fused with the feast days of Kybele, absorbing some of her great power in Sardian minds. Ardys worshipped such an Artemis, and took his nephew with him to sacrifice and festival.

But it was the Sardian Heracles that Tel asked his uncle about, because Heracles was the ancestor of the ruling Greek house, the Heraclidae or Children of Heracles, and seemed to be both divine and human. Ardys laughed at his confusion and threw his arm over Tel's shoulder as they walked along the Pactolas to exercise.

"If you can understand these gods, my boy, you are better than most mortals. But I can tell you the story of how Heracles carne to Sardis, and that will help." He sat down on a flat rock in the shade by the rushing stream and began. The boy dangled his feet in the sacred water, full of gold dust from the mountain above, innocent of the role this stream would play in his life, and of the importance of the myth, to haunt him until his dying hour.

"Long ago the rulers of Sardis were Lydian, Queen Omphale and King Tmolus. But Tmolus became enamored of a priestess of Artemis whom he ravished in the sacred temple. The girl hanged herself in despair, and Artemis slew Tmolus, casting him down upon spikes, from her mountain. From that time it became Mt. Tmolus, in memory of the slain king." Here Ardys broke and seemed to pale. "He was clearly a sacrifice you see."

Tel thought the death was brutal, but it did not move him as it clearly did his uncle. After a pause, his uncle began to speak again, more surely.

"It was after this that Omphale the Queen, ruling alone, bought a strong young slave to take as a lover. He proved to be Heracles the Greek hero, who had been sentenced to a year of slavery by the Delphic oracle because of murders he had done in a fit of madness. While Heracles served the great passion of Omphale—for the navel, or omphale, is considered to be the seat of the passions—he managed to rid the country round about of various perils, almost as great as passions"—Ardys could smile again—"and the lions, who were his companions, became the sacred animals of the city.

"Heracles even adopted the dress of the queen's court, adorning himself with jewels and luxurious silks. Omphale bore Heracles three sons. They were the first Heraclidae, whose descendants have ruled Sardis ever since, in unbroken patriarchal succession, father to son. That, Teleo, is what you will hear from the Greeks of the story of Sardis.

"The truth is that the struggle between patriarchy and the old Lydian matriarchal descent is still going on here, as it must have done once in the Greek world, the ancient line of familial authority having formerly gone through the mother's line and vested in the uncle, her brother, rather than in the father. Tmolus represents the old order—the brother/husband in the myth—and Heracles stands for the new power of the patriarchy. Do you see? Somewhere in the marriage Heracles moved from slave to master, for authority shows forth in the family name. The Heracles family."

"Was Heracles really here?" Tel asked. "Was he a mortal then or a god?"

Ardys sighed. "He may have been. Who knows? I think he stands for the blood of the Greek line who conquered Sardis (in 1185 B.C) part of those displaced Mycenaeans after the Trojan destruction, when civilization was disintegrating everywhere. They came here, whoever they were. They are still here, though after 450 years, they are more Lydian than Sardis is Greek.

"Heracles, you see," Ardys said, "is really an interesting hero. You sing of Achilles, a half-god who became a mortal. But Heracles is a half-mortal who succeeds in becoming a god. He may still be plagued by Hera—what the Greeks will allow of the old earth goddess' power—but he finally triumphs. He is the first ingenious technocrat you Greeks have, always solving unsolvable problems in nature by his inventiveness, his strength, and his prodigious will. He uses animals to conquer animals or to turn away their raw power from the cities of men. Now let me qualify what I say—the first technocrat not to be punished, as Prometheus was. Prometheus was the first, bringing fire. And fire is the beginning of technology; the rest is inevitable. But innovators are always punished."

Ardys looked closely at Teleo and, after seeming to make a decision of some kind, he went on.

"You are old enough," he said urgently, "to know that myths are more than just tales. They carry meanings that are too numinous to express in other ways.

"For example. Here in Sardis Heracles and Dionysos are both important—both sons of Zeus, persecuted by Hera during their lifetimes, both sacrificed and deified—fundamentally alike as rebel sons of the Great Mother, for Hera is the pale remnant of the goddess. Successful rebel sons. They are different only in their spheres of power, but that difference is a telling one.

"Heracles is that child who usurped the goddess' power over the animal kingdom, that attribute which removed the divinity implicit in animals from the province of the Goddess of the Wild Beasts into the province of the Strong Man, the male offspring named Heracles, 'glory of Hera.' Dionysos/Baki usurped power—from the goddess—over vegetation, in a similar shift. The perilous shift of power from the Great Goddess and her servant-lover or son toward the son-lover who subdues the power of the Great Goddess and eventually reduces her to a jealous wife of the sky-god—that perilous shift is still in progress here in Sardis—and it is perilous indeed. That shift is farther advanced in the animal world, the realm of Heracles, than in the plant world of Dionysos. For here at Sardis the Children of Heracles sit on the throne while Bakis, or Dionysos, is still the son of the Great Goddess Kybele."

Ardys looked with affection at his nephew, wondering how much of what he was saying he would understand. Ardys knew that power, political and religious, went hand in hand, and his beloved Sardis was doomed to suffering. There was the growing threat of Phrygia in the north. And the deep-rooted worship of Artemis/Kuvava that still demanded its sacrifices, cast from the mountain or hanged. Trade flourished and Greek was spoken in the citadel, but the heart of Sardis still belonged to the Mountain Mother: when rash young Lydians resented the Greekness in Sardis, the older men of Lydia would tell them to bide their time, because Sardis at heart was Lydian again. To drive out the ruling Greek house now would invite attack from the coastal cities. Extremists on either side were dealt with quietly while Sardis rulers spoke Greek and thought Lydian.

Ardys did not explain all that to Teleo.

***

As his uncle's health had returned, Teleo and Ardys knew a friendship few experience. They balanced in the delight of the moment, Ardys thriving on the quick wit and natural spirits of youth and Teleo enthralled with the inexhaustible tales and judgments of an experienced man. His uncle would sing with a gusto that made up for talent, and the boy would echo him. Ardys could draw out of him patterns of words that he didn't know he knew, both in Greek and in Lydian. They began to play word contests which became so vigorous and competitive that the family would stand in the doorway to listen, grinning. Both of them would roll with laughter at some absurdity or cackle with pleasure at defeating the other. What joy they had found in words—Lydian words, barbarisms in Smyrna! And he began to revel in the sounds of language.

Along with song and feast, the Lydians loved games. As Ardys recovered they played dice, and knuckle-bones. Intricate ball games and dances occupied everyone's feast days, and Tel was infected with the Lydian spirit released in the interaction of mind and body that all these activities wakened. There was celebration and sensuality there, and total absorption. He could get lost in them.

Ardys would shake his head. "Don't love games too much. Lydians do, but they understand them. Because they invented them! Did you know that?"

His attention was caught. "Tell me the story—why did they do it? Like funeral games at home?"

"Oh no," Ardys countered. "Nothing like that.

"Once long ago there was a terrible famine, severe and very prolonged. The people were suffering, so Lydia's leaders decided to invent games to play that would distract everyone from their hunger. Absorb all their attention. King Atys decreed a plan whereby on one day they would all play games and refrain from eating, and on the next day they would eat and work. It was then that the people rallied, their imaginations engaged. Lydians invented ball games, and dice, and knuckle-bones, and many delightful pursuits. They lived that way for a generation, before the drought passed."

Tel laughed uproariously at the prospect of such a life, but Ardys shook his head and repeated. "Don't love games too much. Remember what the Lydians did. Play games, but never two days in a row, for they can make a person forget he has a home and family."

He sobered. "Not likely for me. I will never forget that."

Stories and games, song and sleep. Tales of Lydia and tales of Greeks. Teleo sang all he knew for his uncle, and Ardys was never weary of hearing him. "How you can sing, " Ardys would say. "You can make me feel like a Greek!"

"Tonight I have a treat for you," Ardys told him one day. "A bard will sing at our feast tonight, one of my favorite tales. Just for you."

Teleo was pleased, and impatient until evening. The singer Asie sat with him at the feast, hanging his phorminx by its strap on the column beside him.

Tel beheld it with full admiration. It was a beautiful instrument, small and heavy with a bulging sound box and strong hollow arms. This one had inlays of ivory and gold and elaborate embossed designs all along the arms and body, even on the crossbar. The strings, which ran from the tail piece over a bridge to the crossbar between the arms, were made of linon instead of sheep gut, and he wondered how it would sound. Asie tuned the four strings, tightening them around the "bulges" made of oxhide which wrapped the crossbar—the oxhide kept them oiled so they would stretch without breaking. The beauty of this phorminx surpassed anything he had ever seen.

The old bard Asie smiled at the boy's whole-hearted fascination. "Play it, my friend. It's the oldest phorminx I know of. Belonged to my great-grandfather who said it was made in Assyria long before his time."

"Maybe later. I want to hear you sing." He was uncharacteristically shy, overwhelmed with the power of the instrument. It seemed to have a personality, as if its Muse lived within it. All through the feast he sat next to it, aware of its presence without looking, as if it were a silent companion waiting for a time to speak.

And that night when it did, he heard a famous Lydian epic, an elaborate and beautiful poem of suffering and loss and eventual victory. It was set in the time of Atys, the time of the invention of games, but it was a different story, one that would touch his own life.

The poem said that finally came terrible famine. The sun rolled daily close to the earth in its brass chariot. The nymphs of the waters fled and the birds all flew away. Finally good king Atys called all the people together and said half of them would have to leave so the other half could survive until better times. Tyrsenos, the king's son, would lead the emigrants. Everyone wept, for no one wanted to leave, so they drew lots. With heavy hearts they bid each other farewell and half of them left the fields of home.

Teleokairos sat entranced, captured by the bard and his phorminx, aching for the beauty of the language and for the lost homeland and for the parting of fathers and sons.

After a rest the bard continued: They traveled down the parched valley to Smyrna where they built their black ships and launched them on to the broad back of the sea. They traveled far and long—past Rhodes and Naxos, to Crete and beyond, north and west past the land of Odysseus. After great tribulation they settled in a lovely land near the Umbrians and still live there and flourish, calling themselves the Tyrsenians. Some call them the Etruscans, who still celebrate their ancient homeland in Lydia, and welcome all Lydians to Tuscany.

That song was especially well regarded, and, as Ardys had pointed out, it would live because it was well told. The Lydians were fine musicians and had a scale of music especially pleasing to the ear. Teleokairos began to sing other Lydian songs and love them.

✻✻✻

The mornings were cold now, and the fires felt good. Maionia was fine hunting country, and one expedition into the countryside was a lion hunt. The Heraclidai had adopted the lion as the symbol of Sardis, as a tribute to Heracles, and it was much admired as a trophy. Three magnificent animals were taken in the five-day hunt. The most important part of the episode for Tel was a gift of two lion cubs orphaned when their mother was killed. He kept one for himself and gave the other to his cousin, the youngest of Ardys' children who was just turning six, the child of his return. Ardys had named her Amygdale after the flowering almond tree. He had been saved from death in Egypt by a balm made from its bark and since that time had loved the tree with its delicate pink cloud of blossoms. It was a gift of the gods, he said, as was his beautiful dark-eyed daughter. Amygdale was delighted with Tel's gift, and they marched their cubs around the wall of the house in imitation of a story that Ardys had the bard sing for them. The story went that Meles the king and builder of the acropolis wall had carried a lion cub (which one of his concubines had birthed!) around the walls of Sardis because an oracle had said that Sardis would then be impregnable. The idea delighted them, and so they gave the house that same protection, careful to go completely around and not leave a fatal gap, as Meles had done.

Teleo was to remember that day. He was to take his own cub back to Smyrna where, after considerable troubles, he was persuaded to give it as a sacrifice to Artemis. He did it with resentment, with dark places in his heart, weeping over the lion's skin, dreaming many times of that mother lion trying to protect her cubs, thinking of her anxious heart.

Here in Maionia hearing of the other peoples of the earth, close to animal life that did not recognize citizenship or blood, Teleo saw at last the beauty of his foster father's people. And here he was called Melesigenes, one of the people of Meles, though he did not look like kin. Lydians were black-haired, with heavy-lidded almond-shaped eyes, prominent noses and flat cheeks. Men wore their hair long, in rows of corkscrew curls, and their heavy beards were fashionably styled. The women's triangular faces, their foreheads smooth over a domed skull, were framed with dramatic and exquisite wide earrings. They wore rings on their elegant long-fingered hands, and clasps on their clinging tubular dresses. There was an air of luxury about them, as if they loved the style more than the matter. His uncle's favorite ring, for example, was made in Cyprus, a finger ring which he loved more for its elaborate crafting than for its materials. Thin sheets of gold had been arranged on the bezel to make a pattern of intricate ridges. Then white enamel was laid over it all and polished to a level so that both enamel and metal were visible together. He wore it always.

Now Ardys was active again, busy assessing and managing, a man who confined much of his conversation with others to a functional level. He was even-tempered and temperate, quiet, ever-observant, sometimes deeply sad. But the habit of easy dialog they had developed still continued between them. Teleo realized that most of what his uncle had recounted to him he had wanted him to remember well. And he had done so, almost verbatim, so close was their sense of each other. In fact, Ardys had often commented on his remarkable memory.

"If you ever give up ships, my boy," he said, "you could make a living as a bard. There can never be too many bards, for when one dies or is slain, his unique memory is gone and many people die with him."

Tel had always been quick and accurate and he loved the songs and the songmen, but he would be a trader. He could not disappoint the seaman who had saved his life. And he loved the sleek black ships with a passion.

✵✵✵

Then something important happened in the house in Maionia. Two traveling bards arrived, Phrygians on their way home from Egypt. As the cold began, the feasting season did too—the forty nights of song—and every night they all gathered—slave and shepherd, noble and child—in the Lydian homes to hear the bards. The Phrygians had brought with them a new instrument that no one had ever seen before and that created a sensation in the household. It was a tortoise shell lyra, supposedly invented by the Thracians, a design that would sweep into common use toward the end of Homer's life, perhaps because it was so light and simply made, so elegant that everyone who saw it was enthralled by it. The body was literally the shell of a tortoise, a beautiful shape and material in itself. A piece of skin served as the top of the soundbox, and the arms that held the crossbar and strings in positon were the horns of an animal, gracefully curving in a balanced symmetry. The strings, attached to the underside of the shell and held away from the soundboard by a bridge, were the same as for the phorminx, but the player slanted the lyra away from his body and played seated or reclining.

Simply the sight of this lyrical instrument delighted the household, and for his first performance, the Phrygian sang the song of its inventor. It became one of the Homeric Hymns, and the Greeks as you recall tell it like this: Hermes invented the tortoise-shell lyra on the day he was born in his mother's cave on Mount Kyllene in Arcadia. A child of Zeus and the mountain mother Maia, he was a precocious baby, leaving his cradle to explore that very morning. Before noon he had killed the tortoise and made the lyra; then he stole fifty cows of Apollo, leading them backwards so their hoof marks would not reveal his hiding place. When he was discovered, the clever baby gave the lyra to Apollo who was so delighted that he gave his herd to Hermes, so greatly did he value this lovely music maker.

It was not a concert instrument, lacking the resonance of the phorminx, but its grace and novelty brought it into use that fall in the home of Ardys near the Pactolas in Maionia. For epic song the Phrygians picked up the phorminx again.

It was here, in his eleventh year, that Teleo first heard the ancient epic of Gilgamesh, a favorite tale throughout all of Anatolia and Assyria, one whose ghost would echo behind his great poem the Iliad. Gilgamesh was 2/3 god and 1/3 man, a king of Uruk in Babylon in the third millennium. He was the fifth king after the great flood, his mother the goddess Ninsun and his father Lugulbanda who journeyed to the underworld. The song told the story of his great friendship with Enkidu of the Forest and that man's death, of Gilgamesh's search for immortality and his final return to Uruk without it, of his acceptance of his fate and his writing down of the whole story for other men to know. It, as the Iliad later, was the story of a god's spirit in a mortal body.

Never had a performance had such an impact on Melesigenes as the story of Gilgamesh. It had been polished for a thousand years, a masterpiece. He sought out the singer, the Phrygian named Phryxis, the next morning. "What do you mean, he wrote down the story when he returned to Uruk?"

The bard was polishing his tortoise-shell lyre and looked up. "Just what I said. He wrote it down."

Silence.

"Why?"

"Well, I learned this story in the north, where it was written down on tablets during the time of the Hittites. So why wouldn't Gilgamesh write it down? I have just repeated what I learned from others, who read it long ago from the old Hatti tablets."

"But why did Gilgamesh write down the story? Why did he not sing it?"

The Phrygian smiled. "Maybe a king has other things to do than to sing to his people. Besides, there are many countries where writing is in use. But only a few people can read, and fewer can write. They are called scribes, and it takes many years for them to master the thousands of marks that give meaning to the tablet. It is a sign of special talent and education when a prince can read and write.

"Gilgamesh is a special king because he wrote down the secrets he learned so that everyone could know the truth of his adventure. But I sing the song for other reasons. Every man must learn to die. If my song can help him, I will sing it."

Teleo was persistent, disturbed. He was thinking of Laocoon's fate. "But it is so much easier just to sing. I do not see why anyone should write down a story when the bard can sing it whenever he likes. Writing is for temples. Forbidden to bards."

The singer hardly looked up from his task. "Well, if someone could not remember the song, or had never heard it—he could look at the symbols and sing them. And he would not have to remember."

"Then why learn to compose?" He was confused. "He would not have to remember the rules of composing poetry. He would just repeat without composing."

"Yes," said the Phrygian.

"Then anyone who can read can be a bard? Can sing in any fashion?"

Is that what Laocoon had wanted?

The Phrygian stopped and looked up with curious eyes. "If he learns to read and compose—I suppose so. But it is far more difficult to learn all the symbols than to learn the rules of epic composition. No one in his right mind would try to do both." They laughed together. Perhaps Laocoon had been mad.

"But the new alphabet is easy"—he stopped. The Phrygian would not know about that.

"Well, I think I would learn to compose, and learn the song by listening. My memory is fine, thank you." And to prove it he sang of the taming of Enkidu and his fight with Gilgamesh.

The bard was pleased and went to tell Ardys. "The boy is phenomenal. He heard the song once. Once! And his singing was beautiful. You should train him as a bard."

"Ah, he is remarkable, that one. He has the gift. Teach him all you can. Your rewards from me will be handsome."

And so Phryxis was willing to talk to Teleokairos about singers and scribes. In Egypt, he said, scribes have been honored above most men. They write down stories that do not even have metric patterns, in a form of prose. Eloquence, the gift of appropriate language, is admired above all else in Egypt.

"But let me give you a tale from Egypt that was old when Gilgamesh was born. It is my favorite, and I have turned it into song. I will sing it tonight for the company."

Later men were to see the Egyptian "Tale of the Shipwrecked Sailor" as an ancestor of the Odyssey. It was a clever story, a triple tale-within-a-tale, with a fabulous myth at the center. The worthy attendant would strive to save his master by telling a tale which enclosed a tale intended to be his salvation.

Ah, Teleo reflected. To tell what man has tasted when calamity is over. The island of the soul. His eyes shone with wonder. A man's speech can save him. If you are brave and control your heart you can see home. It is better than anything else. He would remember.

There was a silence in the great hall and he turned to his uncle to find him weeping, his head concealed in his cloak. Only then did he realize how thoughtless he had been not to warn the singer away from such a subject. "Ah, my uncle, it is my fault you are weeping, remembering your own tribulation on the seas. How stupid I have been not to warn Phryxis away from such a subject."

Ardys cleared his face and spoke. "That tale is an old one to a man who has been shipwrecked and has lost a good crew, as I have. There are islands in the sea that hold miraculous things, and I have seen some of them. And it is true that a man's tongue can save him. It can ruin him, too. The gods attend the man whose eloquence can match the situation. It is better than gold and strength to know the dangers of language. I have lacked the eloquence to tell a good story, though I love that more than anything. Except my home and kinsmen."

Teleo spoke up boldly to his uncle now. "You have told me many wonderful tales during my visit, and I have loved them all. But you have never told me your own adventures while you were away. It cannot be that everyone has heard them. What is the reason?"

Ardys replied, "I know that the snake god says, as he begins his tale, that nothing is more entertaining than troubles past. But I have never been able to tell of the things that happened to me. Why will become apparent all too soon.

"What happened to me is simply told: I was saved from drowning by a dolphin, perhaps a god, which carried me on his back to nearby Crete. When I told the villagers there, they took me for a liar and enslaved me, finally selling me into Egypt. There I lived among the ship builders until a Phoenician war galley freed me, and I became a mercenary for them.

"I was taken hostage by the Persians during a raid near Cyprus and escaped to the Greek trading post at Al-Mina. Then I hired on a Greek ship out of Miletos and, when we were rounding Cos we were taken by Taphian pirates. They stowed their booty in their secret landfall on a swampy stretch of island north of there, celebrating and waiting for good weather. It was there that I contracted malaria; when we sailed for Corinth to sell the ship they put me ashore on a barren island to die. I wept and prayed to Artemis, promising her the greatest treasure. And she heard me."

He had spoken flatly and now paused a very long time, overcome by some deep emotion. "A merchant ship from Thasos saw my fires. They treated me with herbs they know, and I was grateful. I told them where the pirates' treasure lay , and together we looted their hoard, taking with us all that we could carry and loading the tender to the gunwales. Then they brought me back to Smyrna where I was welcomed and nursed back to health by my dear brother Maion. That would make a good tale for someone else to sing, anyone but the man who endured it." He looked earnestly at Teleo.

"As time passed I found that these things which I have just told you were not the important things at all. Not the real things I had tasted. For me the most memorable things—what I want you to know—are the ways the world seems to the minds of men." Tel persisted. "I wondered"—but Ardys interrupted him. "—because I want you to know the patterns in life, the marvelous systems and thoughts of men. You do not need to have a chronicle of disasters. We see enough pain and calamity every day. And death will come soon enough.

"Look to the beauty men have brought, to the return of civilized, settled commerce between peoples. Anyone can be a sacker of cities, a pirate, a murderer. How many men can make an iron hammer? Survive a drought? Heal a sickness? Invent games and songs? Carve an ivory cheekpiece for my horse? Who are the carpenters? The singers of tales? The fathers of sons?"

And he sang—very haltingly-words that Homer would put into the mouth of Odysseus when he has survived years of disastrous wandering:

"What a pleasure to listen to such a divinely inspired bard. There is nothing better in life than this—a peaceful kingdom, a palace full of festive guests listening to music, and tables laden with breads and meats, with the steward topping their wine cups. I do believe that this is the best man can know" (Odyssey Book 9)

Ardys added, "And remember what Siduri told Gilgamesh—family, home, goods, loving children—" and he trembled. "That is the happy lot of mortal men."

Later they talked about writing. "Tell me what you know of this, uncle. The Phrygian told me of the scribes of Egypt. I wonder at Gilgamesh writing down his own story."

"Writing is in many places now. It faded in Greece when Mycenae fell because the things writing was used for disappeared—the records of court life, the scribes. Now we are sailing again and in contact with societies that have been writing for a thousand years. I hear the new Greek alphabet is different, though, and much easier to learn. It is probably already in Smyrna. I saw it at Al-Mina where many say it began. It is coming. I will show you what I know."

But that was not to be. A messenger came from Smyrna calling Teleo home. His mother was dying and wanted to see him once more. He and a servant left hastily, but by the time he reached Smyrna, Charite was dead. And everything changed.

***

Grandfather Leonidas prevailed upon Maion to marry Sophie, Charite's younger sister, a common recourse in those days to solve two family problems at once. When she proved fruitful, bearing two boys in two years, it became evident that all of the family except Maion regretted having Teleokairos recognized before the Apoteria, for as oldest he stood to inherit all of Maion's property. Sophie and Leonidas began to put pressure on Maion to announce that his oldest natural son would be his heir.

While Maion loved his foster son with all his heart, his young wife, only nine years older than Teleo, did not. Maion was gone a great deal and life was not pleasant at home.

After the second son was born, Maion took Teleo on his next trip to Cyprus and they talked long about the situation. Maion may even have intended to look for clues of Teleo's parentage there, for he raised the subject more than once. Finally, on the eve of their return, it was agreed that Sophie's first-born would receive the Ionian lands. The other natural son would be given the ships, except for one vessel, which would go to Teleo. He would have to be content with that, for Maion had to recognize his wife's children and his own blood.

Teleo understood. He did not really care about the land, and the decisions came as no surprise. But the recognition of belonging had been painfully important to him. By the time this happened it had been very long since he had been happy in Smyrna, where feelings toward him had changed so much. He looked away to sea most of the way home, staring at Maa Paleokastro with an intensity that commanded it to give up its secrets. But only sea birds wheeled above it and no gods came to help him. A long line of sea-skimmers, great birds of the sea, passed by, not an elbow's length above the surface of a great wave, smooth and sure, intent on their own survival. They did not so much as acknowledge him. He felt lost again, whoever he was, and tried to comfort his father who could not forgive himself.

By this time—fourteen—skill with language was his most obvious talent. His short lays and hymns as well as the bawdy lyrics with which he regaled his father's shipmen and the festival crowds of Smyrna were exceptionally good. He was handsome and reckless, and life went on for a while.

He worked in the fields and lay with the women young boys can find, especially during festival in the furrowed fields at spring planting, and in the ripened fields under the harvest moon. He

33

often would sit on the promontory of the acropolis, looking out to sea. He sang and danced in the firelight until the embers were grey with ash and the darkness took him. He wept when children drowned, unwary, in ponds and rivers, and wondered at the scarf hidden away in Charite's storage chest, along with her imperishable linens. At the feasts he heard and sang only the tales of war and betrayal.

At last his father confronted him: he could go to Ardys in Lydia, or to Kolophon to Theophilos the bard, in order to make his way as a bard in an Ionian world. He suffered and chose Kolophon. Maion's struggle was great, and they both were bitter that he had to choose, though all of Smyrna applauded his decision.

He had been in Kolophon less than a year when word came that Maion was overdue on a trip to Ios. Ardys later told Teleo that he knew his brother was lost or he would have got word of him, for they had arranged a signal between them. None ever came. But sometimes in the dead of night he would dream that Ardys had gone to find him and both of them would return, triumphant, just when he needed them most.

In later years, in his travels, when he was weary, he imagined he might look up and there Maion would be, listening to him sing. But it never happened, and then it was too late. There had been no scarf of Samothrace for Maion Melesigenes.

INTERLOCUTORY

The Voice of Letha Gooding

I first read the Iliad when I was thirteen; I can still see the library wall where I looked up from the page, my head full of clamor and death. Each individual death, and the gods looking on. Terrible honesty was there, clarity of light, sun and fire. The roll of chariots, the sound of horses and bronze and leather, of desperate struggle. No suffering. I was too naive to expect it on the the field or see it in Achilles. Nothing in between the reality of life or death except hideous surprise as darkness came over men's eyes.

I felt I had happened on the truth of things, quite by accident. It wasn't that I saw the battle before me on the wall. What happened was that I looked up and really saw the wall.

It was an event in my life.

I couldn't understand why Homer hadn't finished the story. He had left out Achilles' death! Part of the work was missing, but the library had no second volume. I started the Odyssey full of questions it didn't answer. When I got to the fairy tales I quit in disappointment and read the rest of the plot from a classical handbook I found. I couldn't believe that Achilles died at the hands of Paris.

I had read Lang Leaf and Myers' prose translation. To what degree that diminishes Homer from his live performance for his peers I can never know. The last live performance I have even heard of was a continuous read-in in the sixties at a university student center, with readers spelling each other through twenty-four hours. At Stanford perhaps. Now years later I hear Homer has been dropped from humanities courses there! Bleak. Really bleak. Some committee chaired by a literalist wanting to be "contemporary." Someone who'd call "Jesus wept" a simple sentence.

Well. Can you imagine a mind with no symbolic furniture for mousike—no alphabet and no musical notation? Then do it. The whole reality of Homer's composition lay in trusting body memory and the Muse. That must have meant constant rehearsal. Music was an accompaniment for metrical language, and metrical language was a kind of plainsong with a melody of its own made by the vowels. To the everyday ear of Homer's time spoken language was indeed a kind of music, a beloved human art, not an indifferent thing. There would never be a people who cared more for or heard more fully the sound of passion and thought, and finally of passionate Reason, in the words themselves.

The web of poetic formulae and traditional tale—to what degree was it for Homer a supporting net and to what degree a fetter? While the particulars are unique to Homeric problems, the issue of plot is the same with all great writers. Chaucer, Shakespeare, the tragedians of classical times always tell the thrice-told tales. These people all begin within traditions of composition, as Homer does, subject to the reactions, festive or economic, of an audience, as Homer was.

So what kind of performance was it? You need to know what Homer knew of music and what his basic utterance—the hexameter line-—was. I'll be concise. Homer played the phorminx, as his bards did—Demodocus and Phemius, and even Achilles in his tent.

You know already how the phorminx looked. Homer would have held it on his left, above the waist and slanting away at the top a little, and would have stood to be heard, a strap helping distribute the weight. He would have trimmed his beard out of the way. His left hand would have plucked or damped the strings, damping meaning to stop the vibes. His right hand plucked and occasionally strummed. Some say the left hand, with a bone or metal thimble on the fingers, could have stopped the strings into infinite numbers of notes and created harmonic effects. I like that idea immensely. Others say such tools were not yet in use there. It would be a few decades before Terpander would live, the man credited with inventing the octave on a seven-stringed kithara. All I can say is that Homer's phorminx had these capacities; still, if he thought of his phorminx as a simple background instrument, he may indeed not have used its full capability. I honor the caution of scholars as they keep looking for evidence. What we need to find now is an eighth century vase painting showing a plectrum in the bard's hand. That would settle the matter.

Homer had melody alone, one note played at a time. He could have played one note for each syllable of language, though I doubt that. More likely he accented each foot- -six to the line. No, six to the utterance, because he had no sense of a line, did he? For all I know there was a formula of phorminx music which told the listener what the content of the passage would be, whether battle, assembly or funeral game. I've never run across a discussion of that. The basic musical figure of Homer was the tetrachord (4-note), notes separated by four spaces. There were double tetrachords, which were disjunct—that is, separate units—or conjunct—sharing a fixed note. Each tetrachordal frame had two "moveable" notes in three genera: the enharmonic said to be earliest, the chromatic, and the diatonic. The diatonic was made of five whole tones and two semi- tones, one semi- tone in each tetrachord of a double tetrachord. The chromatic genus had a minor third and two semi-tones in each tetrachord, and the enharmonic was a major third and two micro-tones of a quarter of a tone, or less, each. A double tetrechord could be made up of different genera. From this basic skeleton the melody would take its form, using division into many unequal intervals—semi-tones, quarter-tones, and even less.

If you're into music, you liked that paragraph. If you aren't, maybe you did anyway. You probably know about the modes: Dorian, Phrygian, and Lydian. Dorian, most admired for its virile and courageous sounds, was the basic mode for epic. It was a double conjunct tetrachord. The Phrygian mode was considered lively and ecstatic. Lydian, which our bard would have known early, was considered amorous and sentimental, romantic and relaxing. These modes were nomoi- -the law. How extensively they were used at the time of Homer is anybody's guess. Given Homer's ambiguous double heritage and his high intelligence, we should assume he knew at least two. The other modes you find in the texts are from a later time. These three, however incomplete conceptually, provided a complex effect with such numerous intervals, both clear and subtle, that invited the ear to a sharp attention.

Well. That leaves the hexameter line to learn about. I've saved the best til last because this boring little paragraph is going to bloom into magnificence about six chapters from now. Briefly, this is what you need to know:

The epic line (?) was the oldest of all Greek metric forms: six units of dactyls—dactylic hexameter. The sixth unit, or foot, had to be a spondee (two long syllables of the same duration as a dactyl foot); the last syllable was anceps, that is, the bard could substitute a short syllable and a pause. A spondee could also be substituted in any foot except the fifth. While all of this sounds restrictive, there was a freedom in the form of pauses, or caesuras, which broke the utterance into unequal parts, usually somewhere in the third foot, occasionally in the fourth. Thus variety occurred, and the bard could breathe. Smaller pauses, necessary for sense, were allowable too. They were most effective in the second foot when the caesura was in the fourth or after the fourth when the caesura was in the third. The Iliad and the Odyssey, and even this manuscript, are built on this design. So the variety, coupled with the vocal range and length of vowel sounds, made infinite possibilities for the bard. Dropping in formulaic music and formulaic language, the bard would sing his wonderful tales.

Of course I invented Phanes, but I tend to agree with Wade-Gery that the invention of the Greek alphabet was for poetry's sake. You will recognize the songs of Thaddeus and Teleo as two of the Homeric Hymns.

That was Homer's heritage. I know you can read a novel about an architect which contains precious little about architecture. But you have experienced architecture, haven't you? How can you get a kick out of what this incredible man did unless you know something of his art? The art of every bard, for there were generations of these people, and numberless souls who thirsted after their stories.. As to the specifics of formulaic composition—what did the bard know and when did he know he knew it- -I must leave that fascinating subject to others whom I continue to read with the profoundest awe.

CHAPTER 3

Mousike and the Oracle

735 B.C.E. Kolophon

Theophilos would say: "I love to feel the language on my tongue, to shape the words and send them singing on my breath out into the wide world. Some will reach the ears of men and some will reach their hearts. Others will strike their loins and engender passion. Some will make men bodiless—floating like ice crystals in the light of a winter morning, clearing their spirits. Or free men from the bondage of old pains, as sharp against the blue floor of a fountain lie magnified skeletons of leaves, their instincts spent."

The practical Theophilos would say:

"Remember, syllables and musical notes share common elements. They are loud or soft, fast or slow. They are high or low in turn, and especially in Greek, which is a tone language. And they vary in texture and color. Right now most of you sing far too rapidly. Young people are always in a hurry. Do not hurry! Practice at half or three-quarters the speed of conversation, which is 300 syllables a minute. It is a good way to learn, to gain confidence, to hear yourself, to acquire a control of your rhythmic body."

Then he would sing for awhile, to illustrate his meaning. He was strong and heavy at sixty, and his voice was golden, rich as honey.

Theophilos would say:

"Our audience believes that high-minded men speak steadily in a deep voice, neither eager nor halting. And when your noble characters speak, you must reveal their nature in your style. Choose your language skillfully, know how rhythm and pacing is affecting your listeners and how it helps them understand your song. There is no more complicated art, no higher calling than to be a child of the Muse."

Teleo and the other boys lived with Theophilos at his fine house in Kolophon, learning mousike—poetry and music—in the best bardic tradition of Ionia. The elegant city fifteen miles south of Smyrna near the coast was one of the original twelve of the Panionian league and was distinguished for its cultural atmosphere and broad control of the lands around it. The famous oracle of Klaros five miles away belonged to the city, and in these prosperous days it brought a stream of visitors from foreign parts. Manto, the daughter of the prophet Teiresias, had moved to Kolophon, as the Delphic oracle had instructed, when she had married Rhacius. Teiresias was said to have died here.

The city was cosmopolitan and bards were in demand. Even though much bardic training ran in families, the best young talents of Ionia wanted to practice under Theophilos for a time, and he would do what he could to improve their singing while they were learning the canon that they did not already know. For there were many songs and stories to be remembered and passed along. Boys came and went according to the demands of life, and everyone performed for everyone else. Teleo already knew most of the old tales, but he had never really thought seriously about composition and performance. He learned most from what Theophilos would say.

Theophilos would say: "Bards have secrets, things they know about language. But nowadays the greatest secret has become common knowledge. Everyone knows about vowels."

Teleo thought with a pang of Laocoon.

"Vowels are the music of language. They are separate sounds and letters in the new alphabet. They cover about a fifth in range—do to sol. Sing them. Listen to each other. The Egyptians train their singers with the Chant of the Seven vowels. It is music. Pure music." Egypt was four days sail south of Samos, and Theophilos was very much aware of musical debts to the Egyptians.

Teleokairos sang, listening to himself, sounding out the mysterious vowels, hearing them in the words he knew so well. The alphas and omegas open and clear like trumpets, the thin upsilon and iota, the cerebral eta; and he heard too the liquid consonants as separate mu and nu and ever lovely lambda and rho, the cacaphony of kappa and the hissing of sigma, so dominant when repeated, and obvious to the ear. Audiences did not like too many sigmas. Spoken language and music, in fact, were not really distinct entities to the Greek ear.

Ideal delivery for a bard was steady, clear, in a slightly raised voice sliding between vowel sounds. Theophilos again:

"The narrative is long, and this delivery is the best for articulation, endurance, and modulation. Your audience dislikes too much broken or throaty sound. Use that only for emphasis. Remember, while your audience cannot sing especially well themselves, they are expert listeners. The sound of Greek is one of their greatest pleasures."

Theophilos thought the tone and timber of a syllable should be at once strong and delicate, precise of tone but with hovering overtones, and light enough to carry over the audience. Sound variation in a line was infinite, though the tones were tied inexorably to meaning. Syllables should be measured, and most of all appropriate. "Euphonia means well-voiced. Eustomia means well-mouthed. It is not a simple matter. There is pleasure in hearing harsh sounds when they are suitable or are parts of a skillful combination. There is pleasure in seeing some distortion of the face when it enhances meaning. The cicada sometimes sings as beautifully as does the nightingale."

Theophilos raged at them:

"Do not run together important words. No elision! And hiatus can be effective, noble, especially with long-vowel repetition. So be intelligent! Be careful. The mind remembers unusual effects over an evening, and they must be rare."

Theophilos looked at them soberly, wondering how much his students understood of what they did so well. " Anyone can learn to echo someone else's rousing hero's tale. But do you think about how the words work? Do you memorize the useful phrases and fit them in rhythmically as you go? Can you make puns on the run by distorting pitch accent? Are games of sound and meaning buried in your song? That is how you entertain the quick-witted who have heard a story many times.

"We have a language here that is capable of saying anything. Eloquence is the finest gift the Muse can give to a pure heart."

And so it went.

Teleo had loved the stories first, and then the language. Here in Kolophon, while they talked thoroughly about the tales and their variations, the emphasis was upon the craft of composition. They looked at what it was they did and tried to keep on doing it, better and more constantly.

A good bard at that time only seldom memorized verbatim. Although the basic line form was strict, he would tell and retell tales using his own words whenever the impulse struck him, cutting down passages that bored his listeners, adding similes and myths on the spot, always responding to his audiences. All of the boys in Theophilos' school were skilled in the use of the hexameter line, the unit of epic song, and a song was as long or as short as the singer wanted to make it.

Theophilos would remind them:

"Remember you are entertainers. While priests and teachers live for the future, you live for the present audience. If you want to be asked again to sing you must give something to everyone: the pleasure of repeated sound, the anticipation of repeated passages, the shock of the unexpected, the horror and fascination of the grotesque and fantastic. The fulfilling of all possibilities. You must give them what they expect and always something more.

"I love to tell a story so that it leads to surprise and delight that echoes in the head for days, that leads men to ask for the tale again, brings the heart pleasurably into the mind where it warms the clear image and gives it golden life."

Theophilos had been astonished when this boy had arrived for training. He had never encountered such a keen memory or clear true tone. But it was the boy's abundance of talent—a copious fire—that was unique. Whenever he sang Theophilos would feel an excitement in the air, as he did before the earth would quake or a summer storm approached from the sea. The promise of great power. He knew the Muse was his companion and wondered at his own role in this life.

Most of the time, since Teleo was very good at what he did, he was happy. But when he was lonely he would despair. His would be a precarious profession. While the bard is deeply respected, what is the meaning of a life spent in telling tales for the pleasure of the feast? Isn't it better, more noble, to act? To grow wheat or make pottery? To trade or to fight? The song is gone into the air and lives only in the quality of memory, often memory in minds weary or distracted or sodden. Does one become the slave of others when he seeks their approval with his song? Was singing much sweeter to him when he thought of himself as a merchant sailor singing for his ship and his friends? Singing for himself and the Muse?

Theophilos would tell them all:

"Do not confuse your own pleasure with the pleasure of the audience. Yes, you must please or you will not have an audience. But your own pleasure lies in knowing how, and in composing well, in finding the sounds and words that create life in the imagination, in opening yourself to the Muse. People will tell you that the stories are what make your profession important. And that is true. But it is truer that you choose to be a bard because of a language that you love. Because of the many effective ways of telling a story. And that comes with attention and practice."

They attended and practiced endlessly, with inventive games, with finish-the-line riddling, and memory contests. As soon as they were good enough, they were sent to houses in Kolophon to sing for their supper and to get used to audiences of strangers, for most had performed only in familiar surroundings amid general familial approval. They sang in the streets on festival days, to the great delight of the populace, and Teleo was surprised to find how much he enjoyed the turbulent marketplace audiences. Then life began to seem a perpetual festival celebrated with words.

***

Though the boys at Kolophon enjoyed exuberant life, they were not like schoolboys of later literate societies. For theirs was an oral culture where the mature use of language came as early as seven years, where small quick hands could cast and decorate a pot better than a grown-up could; speech and manual manipulation, the marks of human culture, were theirs in full measure. After puberty only strength and a little height separated youth from the full duties of manhood. By the time Teleo, at fourteen, came to Kolophon, he thought of himself as a man, a youth, as did everyone else; there was no such thing as adolescence. His apprenticeship, then, was no trivial pastime. And he would find that apprenticeship at this numinous juncture in time would differ from all that had gone before because of the new alphabet.

Actually, he and his compatriots were a rowdy bunch, clever but less clever than they thought. They always had supplies of food—thin cakes full of sesame and cheese, leeks and radishes, bread and ham, liver paste and parsley, honey-cakes, tomatoes, figs—and wine scrounged from the kitchens. And, being skilled with words, they sang and fumbled their way into many a servant girl's bed.

Since they were to lead craftsmen's lives, crossing boundaries of all kinds, part of their informal training was in self-defense. Teleo had lost the appearance of hard outdoor life and so at first he was taken as an easy mark. It was fun to prove otherwise, for he was an adept wrestler, strong and agile, and had a fine archer's eye and arm from his time in Lydia. It took a hardy body to live the minstrel's life. No one weak and sickly could perform for three or four hours at a stretch, singing intelligently.

They were all irreverent tricksters. Thaddeus, a boy of Teos, was the great womanizer. "Menelaos—that wimp—gained everlasting life because he slept with Helen. I too want to find a divine woman and live forever. So far I have been looking day and night, and they all seem like goddesses to me." He was pleased with the general laughter and his reputation. It was also Thaddeus who composed the best song about a curious event that they were all witness to.

A man showed up in Kolophon one day who had been lost for so many years that his family had long since performed the funeral rites and gone about their business. He had to go through the ritual of hysteropotmoi, a reliving of babyhood and childhood, being dressed in swaddling clothes and suckled, before he could be himself again. What dignity he could salvage from his situation was past imagining to the school boys, and many a song was sung about his fate, Thaddeus' being the most scandalous. Everyone in Kolophon learned it, and they felt only a little bad when the man disappeared again, to the great relief of his heirs.

That could have happened to Odysseus, he reflected, or to me. And he began to consider asking the oracle his great question.

***

Teleokairos Maionides had not sought the answer to his parentage while Maion was alive. Now he was alone again, preparing to make his way in an Ionian world, and the oracle of Apollo at

Klaros lay within a two hours' walk. He no longer hesitated; he would go to the sanctuary after the festival. The oracle spoke only at night, and this was the most numinous time of the year.

The festival month was upon them, and poets from everywhere had come to compete at Kolophon in composing songs to be sung in the ceremonies. Theophilos insisted that his boys compete. They also always took part in the chorus of girls and boys who would sing the winning hymns as they led the long festival parade from hilly Kolophon to Klaros on the plain, a distance of five miles. The procession was the climax of the holy month, a dazzling experience of sound and color under the light of the sun. The chorus would accompany the Theopropos, one of the special officials who managed the affairs of both city and sanctuary. Teleo was to be affected deeply by the glory of the sun god on that day, the god who shared the powers of music with Hermes.

This year he was different. His mind was on the oracle instead of the competition, and yet he knew that he must give his best gift to the god. It was a great struggle, but both he and Thaddeus composed winning hymns, and Theophilos, who was official bard of the city and among the judges, was immensely proud.

The song of Thaddeus was lovely and delicate:

Phoebus, even the swan's cries and the music of his beating wings sing of you as he alights by the bank of the swirling river; just as the sweet-voiced bard and the music of his well-tuned lyre always sing of you first and last. Hail to you, lord! I seek your favor with this song. (The Homeric Hymns)

Teleo's song was to Artemis, who shared the shrine with her brother:

Sing O Muse of Artemis, sister of the far-shooter, who, raised with Apollo, also loves archery. She waters her horses in reedy Meles, then quickly drives her golden chariot through Smyrna to vine-bearing Klaros, where Apollo of the silver bow, waits for his far-shooting sister. (The Homeric Hymns)

The day was one of the most memorable he would ever know, full of music and delight, and the choruses sang their songs with heavenly voices. He knew the night would be memorable, too, and the edge of excitement drew him through the long afternoon. At twilight, when the revelers had turned back to the city, he stayed behind, and Theophilos lingered, anxious for his prize student, tender in his concern.

"Do you want me to stay with you?"

"No. Thank you for your kindness, but you have duties now. Thaddeus is somewhere in the outskirts—" they looked at each other and smiled "—and I'll walk back with him in the morning. I think this is best done alone."

The approach to the oracle was not elaborate or unusual, though he passed through halls from which corridors branched away. These led to sanctums dealing with initiations which were not his concern. He declared his intent to the priest and then was led aside for meditation and purification.

After a simple sacrifice, he entered a narrow passageway which led to stairs descending into the earth. Along a symbolic corridor, turning in seven directions, he walked until it opened into a large echoing grotto. In the center stood an omphalos which he was instructed to acknowledge, and then he saw at the end of the room a gate, behind which was a veiled doorway. The prophetes sat in a chair beside the gate to the sacred chamber and as Teleo approached, he rose.

Teleo strained to see through the curtain into the room of prophecy, where the Thespiod—descendant of Teiresias through Manto and Mopsus—would drink of the prophetic water and then speak for the god. Terror at the thought of such power flooded his brain and he stood dumbfounded.

The prophetes spoke.

"What would you ask of the god Apollo?"

"I beseech him to tell me who I am."

His voice sounded meek and toneless to him, as if it were a child's. He did not recognize it. The air was electric around him, and small points of light danced before his eyes.

Silence reigned. They waited, listening for sounds from the inner sanctum. Nothing. His heart seemed to thunder within him.

Then through the rush of blood he heard a distant music, thin and high. He could not tell where it came from. As it grew, all around him, he heard within it a pure human cry, eerie and yet lovely, full of yearning. It transformed itself from moment to moment into indescribable music, the suggestion of language present yet absent. And as it had come, it faded away, and silence reigned again.

He was covered with sweat, his heart pounding, his legs unsteady beneath him. He fell to his knees and then lay prostrate before the priest. Apollo had spoken, and he was afraid to know the god's response.

The priest's voice came to him from so far away that it seemed to have emanated from behind the veil, strong and musical, a tone of sound he had never heard before:

"It is good to know who you are but better to know yourself, by far. You will know your father and your blest birthplace when the blind bard of rocky Chios sees my face."

Such joy swept over Teleokairos then that his voice failed completely. He understood nothing yet, except that the god had answered him. Gradually he recovered. Politely he bowed before the priest and then he gestured his gratitude. Before he left the sanctuary he went before the high altar and sang with his heart a hymn to gracious Apollo. As he ended, that god's chariot rolled over the eastern horizon, and he saluted it with a glad shout.

He and Thaddeus laughed and sang all the way to Kolophon. Nobody knew of a blind bard from Chios, but they would look into it.

✻✻✻

The songs of the epic tradition the boys were learning had their origin, according to Theophilos, in the Greek courts of the Mycenaean age (13th and 12th centuries B.C.E.). Many myths of the gods took form there, and the tales of men and their wars were about the royal houses of this place and time. The majority of songs that had survived concerned two heroic ages of these people: the first was at Thebes and chronicled its fall through two violent generations. The second told the tale of Pelops' line, who dispossessed the Perseids at Mycenae and led the Greeks into the fatal war with Troy. And of course there were tales of individual heroes like Jason and Heracles. Contemporary bards had celebrated the deeds of these gods and heroes, singing in the lavish Mycenaen courts of Thebes and Mycenae, Tiryns and Orchomenos, Argos and Pylos, playing the same instruments as he did, as well as some since lost. When the age crumbled and people left the cities, the songs went with them, important both as ties to the past and as explanations of the present.

In the 500 years since, many lines and phrases had changed, but the rules for composing and performing remained standard. Audiences were no longer made up of a warrior class; today's bards sang for the aristoi and villagers, composing in the dialect of their own day and keeping only significant or unfamiliar words as they first heard them. Homer's great epics would contain some elements from ancient Mycenae, but most lines would also have the mixture of Ionic-Aiolian dialect current in the Ionia of Smyrna and Chios.

So what he was learning was both very rigid and very flexible. Rigid in metrical boundaries and the aesthetics of performance, rigid in basic plot line and proper names, for it was vital to remember names and places with scrupulous accuracy. Flexible in wording and number of lines, flexible in the poetry of the line and its sound and association, flexible in the addition of simile. And this made all the difference between a good bard and a poor one. There were formulas every poet knew—sets of words metrically accurate for certain places in the line—which he dropped in where they were suitable. These were usually traditional formulas, but a bard could invent new ones of his own.

If there were this pleasure of the familiar that led to the retelling of epic, he was to find that the more familiar the tale was to the audience, the more he could do with refining his performance—with sound and characterization—especially in long speeches by characters. The more he could do with simile. No serious singer could keep performing the same songs over without changing them for the better, modulating sound by changing wording, trying out ways to give fresh delight. But he had to be careful. People would not tolerate basic change in the story itself, even those who had a high appreciation for the refinements of meaning that he could suggest through sound and the juxtaposition of incident. It was not long in fact before nearly every bard would find meaning and characters undergoing a metamorphosis. During the singing he would find that an accidental word choice or omission would cause him to see new meaning. And whenever a significant change "just happened" as he sang, he believed the Muse had made him sing it that way.

"When you get good enough, that will happen," Theophilos would say. "The Muse will sing through you. You always invoke her at the start of your song. But sometimes she will be there and it will become her song."

✼✼✼

In Ionia everyday ears were keen. They were not used to hearing the sound of metal often; they had never heard glass clink or break. The ear did not need four sounds at once when one was lovely and in a delightful relationship to the next. The din of warfare, sword on sword, was shocking to the ear; the metal forge was thunderous. And memory could hold a long sequence of sound as well as it could a story. Metrical speech was a gift of the gods. Along with the phorminx, a bard's song could bring the life of the village to a halt, and the listening minds would remember so well, so truly, just what the bard sang that many would recall some portions of his story from one hearing. It was easy to believe that all the creatures of nature could understand the song that Orpheus could sing, for they would have truly heard it.

The skillful bard was indeed the child of the Muse and under the protection of the gods, for his art was fraught with meaning. The rich admiration he received raised the rewards of training enough to entice singers whose choice of profession was not motivated by love of the art, but few who did not love it could survive its demands.

Who is to say why a man does what he does? For most, their way of life is chosen for them. So it was with most of the boys, and few had actively chosen to be singers; their father or grandfather had been an aoidos, a singer, and they would be, too, being privy to the secrets of the craft. That is not to say that their fathers lived by the profession alone. Most were shepherds or craftsmen who sang during the winter feasting and annual festivals, sometimes singing out of town. None of the boys Tel knew had fathers who were truly itinerant, living exclusively by their song at various cities, though the cities had now some very talented bards. For one thing, the cities had not had the wealth, until this generation, to support the kind of aristocratic patronage such singers would require.

Theophilos was adamant that bards be craftsmen, though few would have disagreed. Much time was spent making and repairing instruments. Wood had to be old and seasoned. The resonator had to be carefully shaped, made when the air was dry so that it would not contract at a drier time, for that would pull the instrument apart. Curved pieces were made by heating and pressing in a frame, and large portions of instruments were often made by gluing many small pieces of wood together. Hermes was the god of such craftsmen.

"Hermes is the god of singers," Theophilos would say. " He is the god of language, the bringer of words; he crosses the boundaries between gods and men to bring messages, and every song is a gift from the divinities. Your heart is open to the gods. But it is Hermes who made the instrument and the language—even the new alphabet, I have heard. He is the god of the way, as you travel between cities. Every epic singer is in a sense his priest."

Theophilos could never have determined which came first, the conception of the dactyl meter or the conception of the tetrachord; to be sure, few thought to ask him. Both were based on the number four, the sacred number of Hermes. Perhaps the strings of the phorminx had determined it, but it was said the phorminx once had only three strings. "Dactyl" meant "finger," so Tel had decided the name of the basic epic meter was tied in some early Mycenaean mind to the plucking of the strings. He experimented with the idea, playing as many variations as he could. It seemed likely to him that the fact of formulas of words that fit the closing half of the hexameter line and the fact of formulas of notes in music bore some relation to each other. He may even have believed that formulaic composition was rooted in repeated musical phrasing.

✳✳✳

Singers played the aulos too, of course—for the warships—and the Pan pipes, but so did many others. The aulos was not a flute but a double oboe, making a sound akin to that of bagpipes of a later era. The sound was shrill and exciting to hear, but very hard to produce. In order to hold the pipes to the mouth, the player wore a phorbeia, a leather band, across his mouth into which they fit; the band tied at the back of the head and was attached also to a strap over the top of the head. The cheeks, which acted like bellows, puffed and distorted the face—so much so that legend says Athena abandoned the pipes because playing them made her look ugly.

The Pan pipes, or syrinx of the shepherds, was a favorite of everyone, a four to seven tube instrument, with tubes of graduating length, each giving one note of the scale, having no fingerholes and stopped at the ends. All one had to do was breathe into the line of holes at the top, moving the instrument back and forth across his mouth. The tubes were attached to a rectangular raft , rather than the later angular shape following the tube lengths. A syrinx was usually made of reeds, but some were wood, clay, and even bronze. Every child had made a syrinx and played upon it in the long winters, remembering the sweet, bright days when the reeds were gathered.

Other old instruments had special uses. Trumpets were for war and ceremony, drums and clappers and cymbals for women in the ecstatic cults of Dionysos and the Great Mother. But the boys of Kolophon played the auolos and the syrinx and the wonderful concert phorminx, and made themselves tortoise shell lyres in their pursuit of golden Aphrodite.

Bells had been and still were cult objects. In pre-Mycenaean times they were made of clay, but bronze had long since displaced them, for bronze had the power to drive away menacing spirits, and so strings of small bronze bells were hung in sanctuaries and over tombs. Aiolian bells, which swing in the wind, hung in the sanctuary of Zeus at Dodona, and Solomon had hung bells from the temple roof at Jerusalem 200 years before. The old bells were beehive-shaped, but the new ones were hemispheres.

***

Well. When all is said and done, when the bard is asked to sing, he is asked to tell a certain story. And the art of narrative is another miraculous thing that was only now beginning to come into his head. He tried to express to his fellow students what he was struggling to know, but he hadn't the words for it and they did not know what he wanted. If Theophilos did, he did not volunteer it. How a story was told—structure—was in the tradition, and endless repetition of episodes had created units of action appropriate to the conditions of presentation. But how did one know where to begin and end? What constituted an effective ending in a cycle of tales which the audience knew and for which they knew subsequent episodes?

"I think people like to hear twice-told tales," one boy volunteered—he was older and embittered and always thought the worst of matters—"because they know what will happen and they sit there like gods, knowing the fate of the characters. That is what they like best. Power."

Theophilos nodded. " Yes. It is true, and in my opinion a good thing. It is as close to being like gods as they will come." He laughed contagiously. "But it does not breed vanity for they, like the gods, can do nothing to change the ultimate fate of the hero. They will begin to be wise, eh? And there is a pleasure in reciting troubles when the troubles are past. And a pleasure in reciting the troubles of another generation." He laughed again and broke the mood. "And there is a pleasure in giving pleasure. Do not beat men over the head with your own virtue and wisdom. Do not make a story only for yourself. There are many gifts of the gods. If a woman is given beauty, for example, the world will love to gaze at her and life will be full of sweet opportunity. But beauty is best accepted and forgotten, for then she shares it and the world loves her. But if she looks into the world's eyes and sees only her own reflection, they will know that she does not see them. They will use her and turn away."

The sour one challenged Theophilos again. "It is a mystery to me why men want to hear songs of blood and death when they are feasting. Why doesn't it ruin their supper? How can I sing of death while men pick over bones and eat sausages full of blood and fat?"

Theophilos was thoughtful, setting down his phorminx and lounging into a seat, groping slowly with words toward the unspoken part of his question.

"Death is not really your subject. You do not have to be a warrior to know the horror of death. Many of your listeners will have killed, and some will have fought in battle. Every detail of a battle in the traditional song should be kept as spare and explicit as the tradition makes it. Every death is unique. And, after it, the friend must cook his supper and go on living. The tradition is good." Teleo accepted the tradition. He had learned to fight. He had assisted at sacrifices and slaughtered animals for feasts, bound wounds, and buried the dead. He knew the color of blood bright and black.

In fact, he had killed a man once, soon after coming to Kolophon, and had never regretted it. He had come upon him in the mountains standing over the body of an old man he had robbed and butchered. It was cold and his sword was still steaming with hot blood. The brigand had swung round at Teleo, who had an armload of wood. A large piece fell naturally into Teleo's hand at his shoulder and, holding it, he had swiveled completely around and slammed it against the side of the murderer's head with such force that his neck was split and his jaw torn away. He tumbled down the ravine like a boulder and came to rest in a thicket of thorns.

It was over in a moment. The memory filled him with disgust even now. There was no glory for anyone, except that he had probably saved his own life. He hadn't saved the old man. He had taken the robber's sword, and he and his friends had come back and thrown dirt on the bodies. No one thought very much about it.

This seemed somehow to be a different death than that of the battlefield. This death had nothing to do with his stories.

✳✳✳

Some epic traditions had ceased to explain themselves, and Theophilos had to instruct the boys about them: "Some things cannot be discarded—for example, the repetitions of address and ritual behavior—for they teach what is proper to each generation of men. How to prepare a sacrifice, how to welcome strangers and speed them on their way—this behavior retains its numinosity in every man's life when he hears it over and over in the song of the aoidos.

"The epithet, the identifying phrase—swiftfooted Achilles, the wine-dark sea—derives from old patterns of speech that were common when kings were truly divine. Courtesy is the benevolent exercise of power. In divine councils gods rise when the great god enters. Seats are offered to guests, both human and divine.

"There is something else about repeating some important passages, true to every word, that your audience may not be aware of, but many of you will be official rememberers and know its importance. When messages are sent between kings in our cities, you as messenger know that you must repeat within the answers you bring back the original wording, verbatim, of the questions in order to assure that the right question was given and understood by each party. The identical words, all of them in order. This form must appear also in your songs of great heroes as a mark of respect for the receiver and an indication of the quality of mind of the speaking character. Use exact word repetition of spoken orders when the order is enacted, and have the enactors say the exact words again when telling others what they have done. Such stock passages honor civilized relationships by their very inclusion. They will be admired by men of understanding."

Theophilos agreed with such a valuation of right language. "The song of Troy includes battles of words more fateful than the clash of arms, and we are warned of the dark side of the power of speech. Every time we sing of Nestor or Odysseus and then of Thersites, whose mean-spirited language no one can tolerate, we remind our audience that the song itself is celebrated, embodying the highest stage of our language, the harmony between thought and action. And the song is as necessary as the original action. There were wise men before Nestor and brave ones before Jason. But we only know of those that the bard has saved for us."

Teleo grasped his meaning, deeply. The great palaces were gone, the cities burned, the people long since dead, but the words of the singer told of their complex lives. His village had a great wall, but the people who lived there now in simple houses did not know why it was there; no bard had told the story and the walls stood mute. He felt that absence in his heart.

And he had doubts. He asked Theophilos. "How do you know that the heroes themselves had the feelings we sing of? Are they not the words of the bard only, tempered by his own understanding of what a hero could have thought? The words each generation has added in the light of its own understanding?"

"A fair question. Of course I do not know. But I can look to the language, and where I find words for feelings I know the feelings existed. There are ideas current now that are looking for new words to convey them, but if a word exists in the old forms, something of the feeling did as well. And bards always use the safer words, the words that everyone can understand.

"Greeks give their language much attention. Even the shepherd names his dog with care. It must have a name appropriate to the nature of the dog, but will have two syllables which carry well and can be clearly articulated, different enough from natural sounds and the names of other dogs in the village so that one call is enough. It is a courtesy that defines our people, a courtesy to our dogs and horses." He smiled, adding, "and it should be a name that is pleasant to say and for the whole valley to hear."

"I know a man," one student said, "who hated his vicious mother-in-law so much that he named his dog for her, and he would beat it regularly, reviling it before the whole village. So the dog became like the mother-in-law and there were two to plague him."

"I know a man who loved women to distraction," Thaddeus began. "He would call his dog by the name of the woman he wanted to seduce and, in her company, would stroke and caress his dog, half-whispering lovetalk and moving his hands so that the woman would leap upon him in a great passion."

"Dream on," they hooted, calling his dog Polynome, the many-named, from that day on.

***

Even though the population of Ionia at that time was about 100,000 and every village had its aoidoi, Theophilos could hear a boy sing one song and know what bards he had heard. He was absorbed with Teleo because he was so different, and he sought him out in the late evenings. "You either sing after someone I don't know or your ear is too much your own."

" I have sung a lot of songs with my uncle and with Phrygian singers in Lydia. And I know the stories of Smyrna, of course."

"You remind me a little of a bard named Laocoon," Theophilos said. "Did you know him?"

Tel's heart filled with joy. "I heard him sing in the summer when I was eight. It is no wonder, then, for I have tried to remember how he sang. Nothing could please me more than to think that his Muse would sing through me. Of course, you know I was a lost child. Nobody knows my name."

A long pause.

"I sometimes think I have a shadowy memory of singers. Perhaps because I want to think so. I cannot think why I know the stories so well, but I do, and I trust myself in it.

"The first song I sang to myself I made up out of a dream. I was an aoidos singing in the palace of Proteus under the sea. I was wearing my scarf from Samothrace. As long as I was singing, that lovely place surrounded me, but when I ceased I was on the sandy shore of a grey sea alone in a north and bitter wind. I tried to sing as long as I could, to hold the room and the soft eyes of the naiads in the floating motion of the feast before me. Maybe I want to bring back a time that is gone, for me and for Greeks. I only know I am free of the moment when I am singing."

"What do you mean, free of the moment?"

"I really don't know. I just said it."

"Your dream, " Theophilos began. "What was that about Samothrace?"

"I was found at sea wrapped in a scarf like Samothracian initiates wear. When I was a baby. Why?"

"I've heard of that place. Arctinos, the singer of Miletos, had a song about that island."

His heart leaped. So unexpected. So important.

"Sing it, " he said hoarsely.

"I can't. I've never heard it. But others have said he had such a song. Something about Dardanos."

"Had? Is he dead?"

"Oh yes. Several years now. But some of his family will know it. Look them up some time." He stopped short, moved by the look on the boy's· face. "If you're wondering if you sound like him, you don't. Sorry. But Arctinos was a great bard. Someone will know how he came to sing of Samothrace." He changed the subject. "Antimachos of Teos will come next spring. I want him to hear you, Teleo. Maybe he can place your style."

***

Performance began to dominate his time and thoughts as Teleokairos became better known. Rarely was a singer insulted by an audience, but inattention could be just as devastating, as could distraction and interruptions. He had to learn to take it all in stride. It was hard to follow a fine singer for someone even as good as he, and he learned to use humor after lamentation. There was an order of emotion in every audience, and the best singers would learn to lead them through their feelings with small adjustments to sound and story.

He learned to pile simile on simile until the tension was right, and then release them into a new mood. He learned to include expected episodes when everyone needed a rest; he learned to use patterns—battles, assemblies, recognitions—to lead the audience to accept the inevitable and yet be surprised when it carne. He became adept at 'ring' composition.

He began to realize that story-telling was a patterned order profoundly different from the experience of everyday living, which it supposedly described. Much later someone would ask him, "Do you think that narrative form is imitative of life?" and he would say it was story-tellers who had convinced men to see life in narrative form.

Living at Kolophon with Theophilos, then, was not so much the experience of learning a great deal of new material, though that did happen. It was that high keen emotion of discovering that he knew, of being given the terms and patterns to abstract himself, to set before himself in another frame of language what he knew. It was to externalize into a discipline a profoundly internal experience. And this was what, ultimately, Theophilos had said. It was to make himself real, to meet himself in others. To begin to be self-conscious. There were no words in Greek yet for what was happening to him. It did not simplify his learning, nor did it make him a more skillful singer. In fact, the un-conscious singer—someone who just sang—was far better to a certain level of performance, doing what he had learned to do well and for no reason other than that it was to be done.

***

Teleo sought out Theophilos one day. "You said you knew Laocoon," he began. "Tell me about him."

Theophilos nodded, wary. "Yes. I did know him. We talked together several times." He paused. "It isn't wise to discuss him, even now."

"I know that. At least, I sense that. But tell me about him anyway."

"You have the gift, my boy. Not many do, you know. Laocoon had it, in full measure. As great as Orpheus or Musaeus."

"Tell me about him, Theophilos."

The older man looked at him sharply.

"Well. So it is like that, is it? You heard him sing. You know he was different. He was daring. Powerful. That kind of thing doesn't come from an ordinary heart.

"He told me he had known a man once. Someone, he said, who had changed the world. Had changed him. When he was just a boy."

"I don't understand."

"Laocoon never talked about himself. But he talked to me once about someone he called Phanes the Poet. A man he met at Al-Mina, I think, though he thought he was an Ionian by birth. The man who created the new Greek alphabet."

Theophilos paused. "'What genius!' Laocoon told me. 'Imagine the genius and courage! Only a poet could have done it! ' "

Tel was puzzled. "I don't understand."

The old singer's caution had dissolved and he now spoke earnestly, intensely. "Don't you see? There have been all kinds of writing systems for thousands of years, all so complicated that only trained scribes could make use of them. Thousands of pictures or syllabic symbols. Surrounded by power and mystery. Especially power.

"This man—Phanes the Poet—conceived an idea absolutely new. Absolutely daring. That, by the way, is only a bardic name—it means Revealer. Who knows who he really was? Anyway, these ancient and elaborate writing systems had never allowed the sacred vowels to be isolated in their pure power and divinity. They were too numinous, too sacred. The seven vowels and the silence around them carry mystic meaning. The key to language. The key to poetry! to thought! The Revealer dared to isolate all the sounds and put them in an alphabet. For all to see. Everyone. To use."

Theophilos rested, wiping his brow which had been covered with fine beads of sweat. His face was flushed. "He took the Phoenician alphabet as a base, a very modern and simplified set of consonant sounds. Mundane sounds. Then he changed five Phoenician consonants not used in Greek to stand for five vowels, and he invented signs for the others.

"Imagine! The simplicity and incredible daring of such a scheme. Instead of thousands of symbols and the absence of the essential and numinous vowels, Phanes the Poet's new alphabet had 26 signs only, then 24—the vowels of eternity and the consonants of time—all made literal. Secularized.

"Revolutionary! Now subtle poetry can be written down with no loss of movement—accurately, rhythmically. Written language is no longer holy. It is secular! Writing is no longer the province of the selected few, of the king's scribes and the merchants keeping records. That is why Phanes did it, according to Laocoon."

Teleo's heart was heavy. "Then Laocoon—and the Revealer—did break the sacred custom. They did defy the gods."

Theophilos stopped, sobered by his reaction, wary again. A long silence.

"Well. Laocoon has paid the price for that, hasn't he? Perhaps Phanes did as well; I never heard. Or perhaps there are places in Ionia, or where the Greek and Phoenician cultures coincide, where men dare to change the old prohibitions, or where they have lost their meaning. Or where the old gods are dying."

The master singer spoke boldly now. "But it has been, for many, a gift from the gods, this incredibly simple—and secularized—alphabet. Very Ionian. Independent. Literal. It will bring vitality and ease to the lives of men. Of poets, too."

"Then why isn't the great man who invented this alphabet known and honored?"

"Danger. Fear. Perhaps revenge. Some would protect him, others deny him. The person is already lost to time. What he did is not, though. That can happen, you know. It could even happen to you, that people will sing your songs after you are dead, not knowing who shaped them so nicely. Just as you have done with others in the long tradition. Is it important who does wonderful things, after all, just as long as they are done?"

Theophilos relaxed, laughing, shaking his head. "Men already say that Hermes gave us the alphabet! They always find a way when it is to their advantage. The troubles attending the spread of the new alphabet will be buried with its inventor. No one will remember that he was a dangerous innovator, that he stole religious secrets and gave them to the common man. Isn't that what Gilgamesh did, after all? No one will even think twice that he must have been a poet, and a fine one, at that. Phanes did it for poetry's sake, that is what poor Laocoon told me. You know the curse of the first fruits. The innovator is the sacrifice to the gods. Laocoon must have known, and yet he persisted."

Teleo was thoughtful. "In this alphabet, only the words can be written? What about the music? Is that in the alphabet too? I don't see how writing has anything to do with singing."

Theophilos sighed. "I don't know. I know the symbols. Most of us do. Frankly, I use the idea of the separate vowels in my instruction on song. That's all. But I do know that in the old complicated writing systems stories were written by the scribes. I know it was done in Hatti. The old stones call scribing "the mother of recitation." The readers of the tablets say they begin, 'The singer of the land of Hurri sings as follows.' And they begin with 'I will sing,' just as we begin our epic songs, telling the subject first."

Tel was suspicious and incredulous. How could the stone sing? Marks on stone did not tell the music or the mode or the pace. They may record an act or a prayer, but all the music would be lost—what did that have to do with what he did when he performed? And besides, how could there be an audience which could share the story? There could be no common experience, an important part of epic.

No, a list would help him remember place names and men, and the rememberers were definitely men of the past, but epic singers would not be materially affected by the new writing. Who would enjoy a song if he had to sound it out all alone for himself, with no music? Would they make letters for music too? Maybe Gilgamesh had gone back to Uruk and written what he knew on stones, but there were no stones that sang to the delight of a feasting villager.

Still, in Teleo's youth there were men on the coast who were learning to write, and recording stories. Even Theophilos wrote down the winning hymns that eventful day. They had begun to write on grave amphorae, though it was not done in Smyrna until the turn of the century. The singers wondered if having writing would make more stories known. Most felt it was useful for trade and government to have such a marvelous new system. The innovators had paid the price; the sacrifice of the first fruits had been made.

What would happen would come in his lifetime, though he could not know it then. The mind that could read and write began to lose its capacity to compose long formulaic poems during performance. Perhaps it was because there was no need. More likely it was the shift in mind, in conception: to see a word mentally in letters instead of hearing it as a palpable sound winging through the air broke the old training or complicated it to a point where it failed.

There were already three stages of development for a bard, or perhaps three kinds of bards, since at any moment there were men going through each stage. The first were the learners still singing their songs as they had heard them. There were many in every city who sang that way; in every family perhaps someone could recite most of the old songs.

The second stage was his now, when the intricacies of the craft were his, and he himself composed with confidence and true creative flair, adding the grace of language as he sang the traditional tales. Then there was the third, which often was the falling-off of age, when true creativeness in some became dulled by repetition and familiarity, and the bard simply became a reciter—a rhapsode—keeping old forms and wordings, making changes only inadvertently. Such a rhapsode was valuable but he was a performer, not a composer.

The person who was literate became a rhapsode and finally became a writer-down of epic. And the music was gone for the reader. Phanes the Poet, the first bold blossom of the Ionian genius, would have grieved at such a loss, would have felt the terrible irony. It would be left to Homer to redeem the time.

INTERLOCUTORY:

The Voice of Letha Gooding

This is hardly a good introduction to a great love story. But you have to understand the bone-wrenching power of the Great Goddess; she is still alive in all of us.

I had to struggle this out, and I found Joseph Campbell and Erich Neumann just in time. May you be more fortunate. Read The Masks of God first. I don't see how any woman can survive today without some knowledge of myth. In fact, everyone needs a good course in myth at puberty. If you want to be happy in this world, you will have to understand the mythic use of sex and learn to separate the individuals you live among from the archetypes in your heart. That would do more for society than a million sex education classes of the literalists. It would have been a boon to women who, through the ages, have been victims of this terrible transference.

Simply put- -and I mean very simply—in myth feminine image is always tied to substance, to the earth, regardless of the idea cluster it represents, for good or ill. The feminine represents the nourishing/smothering unconscious, intuitive side of being. The mountain. The moon. Night.

Contrariwise, the mythic male image is tied to human consciousness, to ideational, insubstantial fire and thunder, to light and hence to Reason. The male image, the hero, dominates because light is what we all struggle toward, scorning the irrational (feminine) in ourselves, especially if it is powerful and threatens to overwhelm rationality. The simple fact is that these are mythic figures, archetypes, that are still in our minds whether culturally or biologically based.

The sea god, for example, is ambiguously fluid and substantial, earth-water, and hence a conscious figure of the unconscious. Oblivion is the recognized natural enemy of rational heroes. I agree with those who believe that Greek myth tells the story of the mortal struggle towards consciousness out of a fertile and undifferentiated pre-conscious state. It also seems to record the evolution of social and religious ritual from an earth-based worship (matriarchal, lunar) to a sky -oriented one (patriarchal, solar). Robert Graves explores that thoroughly in his The Greek Myths where you can pick up a thread from the index and weave your own garments, endlessly. Fascinating.

Now. Because every human has both conscious and unconscious life, both male and female mythic images live in every person. And when an image shifts from female to male—as Lamia to Dracula, for example—it means we have moved the content of the image into consciousness.

The trouble starts when you project onto some helpless individual person your own feelings toward a mythic image. There is no problem in regarding an individual man as reasonable; even when he isn't, you have done him no harm. But every individual woman becomes the mythic unconscious. Even to women, because the mortal woman is as much a mixture of conscious and unconscious forces as man, and fears the same oblivion. When will we free ourselves of this curious trap? You rightly suspect that I am not optimistic.

What has this to do with Homer? Much. He shows sympathy with women that is just not present in most western literature. Did you know that in the last century Samuel Butler maintained that the Odyssey must have been written by a woman because of its feeling for and knowledge of women's world? Just who did you say was the blind man???

It is ironic that Homer's readers have so thoroughly accepted the patriarchal values and institutions he draws so well without keeping his deep understanding of women. Maybe we can open this subject more fully where it appears so centrally in Homer, in the Kingdom of the Dead.

If you're wondering, Gooding is my husband's family name. He and I share it with our children. I like its implications, the continuance of good. May it be so. We are one, the two of us. Still, I did write the Affirmative Action plan for my university.

CHAPTER 4

Love and Death

734 B.C.E. Sardis

In late winter Theophilos caught cold. It deepened into pneumonia and, while it didn't carry him away, it left him feeble and facing a long convalescence. There had been no word from Maion, and Melesigenes dreaded going to Smyrna, so he decided to visit Ardys again. It had been over seven years since his summer in Lydia and, though Theophilos hinted that he would like for Tel to keep him company, he left for Sardis with a light heart and high expectations.

He crossed the plain north towards the gulf and turned east to the Black Pass. Smyrna lay at a distance across the water and against the foothills, which were glittering and bare in an early morning frost. Today it seemed as remote in his heart. He did not stop. Bundled in long woolen chiton and mantel, his legs laced in high fur-lined boots, he strode comfortably along, his phorminx and pipes in a shoulder bag with a few other possessions. Singers learned how to travel modestly, and he stepped lightly from rock to rock along the tumbling streams and strode the crisp grasses of the meadowlands, happy to be free of duty, anticipating the pleased surprise of Ardys. He stopped two nights at wayside shelters, building a fire among the rocks, piling up a blanket of leaves and grasses to cut the cold while he slept. He met no other travelers, fortunately, for it was dangerous to encounter others when traveling alone. On the last night out of Sardis he found a remote campsite, a small cave off the road, high in the foothills northwest of Mt. Tmolus and away from the bank of the Pactolas.

He settled behind his fire, shivering from the cold and unable to sleep, thinking of all the people who had come down the ancient ways, armies and merchants, craftsmen and refugees, and wondered how it would be, this life he had chosen. He wanted to see the wide world. Normally a bard would travel with a group, for minstrels were welcome on long journeys. On this trip he had been accompanied only by ghosts and memories.

He thought long about the countryside around him, of the mountains and the gods and the men, about all the armies and lost cities of his songs, all of the ruins around him, and the spirit-haunted heights. His brain chilled at the thought of a city being thrown into a chasm, its very ruins lost to sight under a mountain tarn. Of all of the lost people. What songs could possibly be sung at the banquets of their gods? He fell into a troubled doze.

Something pricked his mind and he was suddenly alert. There had been movement near the fire. He felt eyes upon him and slowly leveled his head to find himself looking across the embers into the steady gaze of a black panther. The animal's eyes held him as time dissolved.

He was not afraid. Something in the animal's shoulders told him he was safe. As he stared everything in his vision melted into a uniform blackness except for the luminous green eyes that drew his heart out of him. They were lightly flecked with brown and flattened into disks like copper washed with tin when the firelight caught them. But the greenness was their essence, implacably inhuman.

When he recovered the panther was gone. He felt that he had seen a god. But he had somehow known she was dying even before he found her body the next morning on the ledge below the cave. She had left a cub behind for him to care for. To have this wild baby given to him left him trembling with echoes of his own beginnings. What goddess was this who knew where he was and what he was thinking in the caves of the wild country at the approach of spring?

He had brought his long woolen birthscarf with him to show to his uncle. Now he had a practical need for it. So he pulled it from his carryall and wrapped it jauntily, almost mockingly, around his little panther and his own tousled hair and beard, tying the cub securely around his shoulders for warmth and keeping his arms free for the strenuous stretch ahead. He sang as he traveled. He looked like Hermes carrying a ram to sacrifice as he came at last to the gate of his uncle's home. He stood on the threshold, legs apart and arms akimbo, calling heartily and singing a line of greeting to those within:

"Pour a libation and drink to the powerful god of the wild. Welcome the journeying stranger who carries the goddess' child. Pour a libation and drink to the mountain goddess with grace. Welcome the meeting of loved ones at last coming face to face."

Flame-lit faces by the altar-hearth turned to see him, familiar movements came toward him, the wonderful touch of beloved flesh engulfed him.

His uncle had not aged, though Teleo himself had lived a lifetime since they last had met. Ardys still looked like one of the immortals, wiry and dark-haired, elegantly groomed, clear-eyed and gracious, as he remembered him.

"You do not seem very surprised at my coming," Teleo said, smiling broadly, returning his embrace.

"Do you really think a purple -scarfed man with a panther on his back and songs to the morning can scramble into Sardis without being noticed? We are happy it was you." His uncle could hardly conceal his pleasure. "We must give you a proper welcome."

In the Greek style he was welcomed first to the bath, usually presided over by a young woman of the family. Water was heated in the copper cauldrons to be poured over him in the lovely tub, a bright stone vessel shaped for the body to rest and waterproofed in blue and red designs. A familiar voice spoke behind him, familiar yet different. "My lion cub is gone. Is yours?"

He turned and there she was, Amygdale, his playmate, his cousin Amy. She alone of the family had changed. At almost fourteen she had a woman's form. Her face was triangular, with a broad forehead and low brow, high cheekbones and wide-set dark eyes, almond-shaped. Her mouth was full and straight, her body slender and narrow waisted. She had the large hands and feet so admired by Greeks and Lydians, graceful long fingers, and she smiled divinely.

"Yes." He beamed at her. "Hello. Sacrificed by my family."

"So was mine. I still dream about him."

"Well. I have brought you another, Amy." And he told her about the cub. "Don't you think it was meant for you?"

"Yes." She was delighted, both at the prospect of having the cub and the fact that he had remembered their friendship. "Though the panther is sacred, I will not let him be a sacrifice as our lions were." She turned to take up the toweling so he could dry and dress. The line of her body was easy.

He rose from the tub and stepped into her toweled arms. The water dripped from his eyebrows and beard. His legs are delicious, she thought. His arches high, and his fingers very long, their ends calloused from playing his music. She looked at his manhood with frank admiration and watched as he combed his hair and beard with practiced fingers. She reached for the flagon of oil on the table and touched him with the fragrant balm. They each started, and he began to oil himself. "Here, let me," he said, not looking at her though her fingers lingered in his senses. She was flushed at her neck and temples. "Your body feels very hot," she said. "Be careful not to catch a cold. Dress warmly." She had regained her composure and become hostess once again.

"What shall I call my panther? You must give him a name for me."

"Theodore. Gift of the God. He is a gift of the goddess of Mt. Tmolus. May he guard you for the goddess." And so they were friends again, and she led him into the megaron for the feast. The housemaids had covered the polished chairs with cushions and placed tables of meat and bread around the hearthside seats. They poured the wine from pitchers of silver, Cypriot vessels chased in gold and black enamel. Ardys and his guests poured the drops to the gods and fell to feasting. Teleo sank into comfort, with a sense of true belonging as the hum of human company surrounded him. And after all the guests had left, the hearth fire had been banked, and shadows filled the great hall, he and his uncle Ardys talked together long into the night.

When Teleo had come before, at ten and with an ailing man to care for, he saw little of the city life of Sardis. But now he sought it out. The Lydian settlement on the river had flourished since his last visit. Goldsmiths, who had come from Babylon, now were transforming the city. It lay scattered from the acropolis to the junction of the Hermos and Pactolas, three miles away. Ardys had built a larger and richer home, and others had as well.

There were not strong defenses around the houses on the plain, because the acropolis of Sardis was impregnable. The plain was a busy commercial and residential area, with the busiest part at the river junction where the great bazaars would bloom in the next century. The smiths were starting up along the Pactolas' east bank.

There was more shabby housing apparent here than in the Greek cities; some houses were built of reeds and some of reeds and wattle. Ardys had a home with a base and half-wall of fieldstone with higher courses of fine mud brick, situated on a tributary stream northeast of the sacred precinct of Artemis, the goddess of the city. Lydians were not building yet with marble. Some thresholds, though, were graced with steps of polished bluestone and a few homes had elaborate terracing and split-level room designs. What the prosperous Lydians lacked in housing they made up for in moveable luxuries. Their floors were covered with rugs from Persia, their rooms divided by hanging tapestries, and they had long collected the finest pottery, some pieces saved through the centuries from Mycenaean times.

The tumble of life was louder here. Feasting and music, and its attendant passions, were important to Lydian taste. They mixed their wine with nectar, making a combination of wine, honey, and flowers. The breads of the city, in variety and flavor, were famous; and the Lydian chestnut was a delicacy others envied. Lydian figs, called "blood-figs" because of their red hue, were equaled only by those of Paros, and the meats and sauces were famous aphrodisiacs, especially karyki gravy. No one would give away its secret.

Kandaulos, a stew of boiled meat, bread crumbs, and Phrygian cheese, with broth and a sauce made with honey, eggs, and flour, could equal the barley cakes of Teos in awaking the passions. The Lydian was a gourmet at heart and a romantic, and in flourishing Sardis the civilized arts—even the exotic—were beloved. Lydian music was soft and beguiling, conducive to sensuality and emotion even then—or perhaps it seemed so after the music of Ionia.

At any rate, when word spread that Teleo was back and had been singing at Kolophon, everyone wanted to hear him, and he began a round of feasting that was almost constant. He was the toast of both Greek and Lydian Sardis. Fairer and taller than they, his eyes as blue-green and luminous as the seas around the lush southern islands, his tawny hair and beard modified, out of courtesy, to the local fashion, he was a visual sensation. His strong voice and Doric musical mode made him spectacularly different, virile and invigorating, while the ease of his performance and his youthful pleasure in giving pleasure bridged any distance between. They called him the Lion of Smyrna. The ruling Greek families welcomed him royally and bestowed rich gifts on him for his singing, including the beds of their loveliest women. He was overwhelmed.

"Watch out," his uncle warned him. "They take lions for trophies. When a new singer arrives, they will forget the old one."

And they did, soon; though he was still invited with regularity, he was no longer lionized. But he had learned by his experience, and he listened more carefully now to the songs of others. A lot of his wit had been lost on the Lydians who could not play games in his dialect. He became a better critic of his own work, being able to see weaknesses brought out by singing to people not really close to his tradition, however Greek they considered themselves to be.

The Lydian attitude toward women was interesting, for women here had much more freedom and authority than any woman of Smyrna. Some family lines still were matriarchal, but it was more than that. Women were treated like people, and it made them confident, even brazen. They had great freedom of movement. They would look him in the eye, and were honored by their families, and they even attended the feasts and other public functions open only to men in Smyrna.

"It is because of the Great Goddess," Ardys would say. "Our people honor the Great Goddess, Kybele the Mountain Mother, whose shrines are on Mt. Tmolus. The Greeks call her Artemis and have the sanctuary in the valley where I also worship, but Kybele and Artemis are the same here, aspects of the same ancient power; Artemis as girl, Kybele as mother. They share the same rites and festivals. Kybele does have her son/consort—Baki—who is like Dionysos. They are ecstatic gods, powerful and terrible if you cross them."

Ardys was suddenly sober and looked away into the distance. "I have honored them all of my life. It was Artemis who saved me in my travail when I was abandoned and dying. It will soon be time for me to pay my debt." Tel looked at him, waiting for an explanation, but Ardys shifted the subject.

He brought out the birthscarf to show to his uncle. Ardys examined it closely, turning it over and over in his hands. Finally he looked into his nephew's eyes.

"I don't know. But it looks to me like a scarf of Samothrace. The length, first of all. It is clearly a sash to be worn, to be wrapped about the body and tucked or tied. What makes me think it is

Samothracian is its special color. It is not quite Tyrian purple, is it? It is some other dye, too. Maybe another animal dye. Oh, Tel. What a heritage you may have, after all."

Puzzled, Teleo stared at him as he handled the scarf.

"Since you were here, I have looked into this when I could. The scarf is worn only by those who have been initiated into the mysteries at Samothrace. It seems there are two degrees of initiation, as there frequently are in mystery cults. However, at Samothrace very few people attain the second degree. And the scarf is awarded only to those few. "

"Anyone? It may not have been a sailor?"

"It may not have been a man, either. Women and children, slaves and kings, people of any race, can apply for initiation. I don't know who the select few of the second stage may be. Certainly they are unusual people."

"How did you find out about this?"

"I have been to the coast several times since seeing you and talked to seamen. Frequently to Kyme and twice to Mytilene on Lesbos. The Lesbians have settlements in the Troad, and Samothrace is visible from that coast. Mytilene has resettled Troy."

His heart leaped. "You mean it? Troy is being rebuilt?"

"Well. Not that. It is only beginning, but they are holding their own, and the country is fertile and still perfect for raising horses. The old city of Troy, they said, sat on a gulf when it was first built. Then the gulf became a swamp, and the swamp became a plain. Now the plain is very wide. Even in Mycenaean times the plain was there below the city where once there was a bay. Some day the same thing could happen to Miletos and to Smyrna or Ephesos. But it will be many generations from now, and Earthshaker is less than predictable when he wants to help a city—or destroy it."

✾✾✾

The spring and summer days were flying by, and Melesigenes spent them happily, singing and feasting, riding in the country, often in the company of Amy and family friends. Theodore the panther would go with them, keeping a distance from the horses. Ardys' sons had sons of their own now, old enough to explore the countryside as Teleo had done so long before at Smyrna. They ranged west across the Pactolas to the hills of the necropolis where the rockcut tombs of their ancestors lay. The Hermos was wide and fairly serene in the summer, and they would cross over and ride north to the bank of the Gygaian lake, about seven miles from the river. It was a beautiful place. The kings of the Lydians had burial mounds as large as a city acropolis on that route, situated between Lake Gyges and the Hermos, marvelous to contemplate. Under the smooth grass-covered hills marked by pillars, semata, were elaborate burial chambers, usually not in the center of the hill but hidden by many false tunnels in a labyrinthine maze, so that looters and conquerors could not desecrate the bodies and carry away the treasure. Tel was reminded of the tomb of Tantalos and reflected on the glory of kings and cities. Was a tomb as good as an epic?

Amy and he became fast friends and constant companions. They shared a wildness of spirit, an exhileration that they felt most when they were together, something defiant and beautiful, barely controlled, like Theodore. Her freedom was great even for a Sardian woman because her father indulged the child of his return. Teleo was teaching her songs now. Amy played the Phrygian flute and the triangle, as everyone here did, but she was also learning the paktis and magadis. The paktis was a high-pitched lyre of Lydian invention, and the magadis a low, strumming lyre, soothing in its tones. The girls of Sardis who took part in the festivals of Artemis had to know these instruments, and the priests of the goddess taught them from childhood. Amy was not really patient enough to be a fine musician. She said so herself and admired his skill immensely.

Teleokairos did not like the priests and priestesses of Kybele and Artemis. The priests were eunuchs, castrated during the orgiastic worship of the goddesses and now elaborately dressed, their long hair worn in perfumed locks. Unlike the priests and priestesses of Smyrna, who lived normal lives and had other livelihoods besides their festival duties, these priests were only that. They were subordinate to the head priestesses, living off the temple receipts. The priestesses were powerful, members of leading families, learned and skilled in politics. While kings would come and go, the worship of the Great Goddess in her two forms shaped the lives of the citizenry. Kybele/Artemis had many names in the area; she was Cabebe to the Phrygians and Kubaba to the Lewians of the southern coast. At Sardis she rode a lion. At the ancient Hittite capital city of Bogazkoy there was a famous carving of her as the youthful Goddess of the Wild Animals, shown in her naked divinity on a pair of panthers, holding another small panther in each hand.

On the "Day of Blood" in the annual festival in March, the chief priests or priestesses would offer blood from their arms as a gesture toward the year's growth, while, to the sound of flutes and cymbals, the priests would whirl madly about, slashing themselves and splattering the altar with fertilizing blood. A pine tree, the sacred symbol, which had been cut and brought to the altar, would be soaked with the restoring blood, a primitive symbol of the union of nature with culture.

Ardys spoke of the great goddess solemnly. "The earliest sanctuary of Kybele is on Mount Dindymos in the Troad where there is a holy rock which is said to have fallen from heaven and has the power to draw the earth to itself. Kybele is as old and essential as the earth. She IS the earth. The cities of men are built of her bones—of rock. The food and clothing of men are the flesh of her plants and animals—the youthful Artemis, goddess of wild life.

"Here in Sardis the festivals of Kybele and Artemis coincide. We have comingled their worship, as was done in ancient times. Both goddesses remind us that the wild and natural world is fundamentally indifferent to humans. Kybele is mother to more than man and woman—the hind and the panther, the lion and the lamb, the oak and the pine. Artemis leads all the young living things—the nymphs of the sacred rivers and springs and all the young girls—in their initiation into fruitful womanhood.

"Imagine yourself as the child being nourished, held to the bosom of a fruitful and sheltering mother. The high altar of earth is the mountain itself, with all of its bounties. It rises up before us as if to remind us of her power. In the old wars of the gods, even the floods did not conquer the mountain, nor did the storm god of the skies. Though the Greeks say she is defeated, she is not. Kybele is Demeter, too, the mother of the vine god Baki/Dionysos who makes her fruitful, whose essence is zoe, the force of life itself. While she is eternally the same, her son dies with each year's vegetation and is reborn in the spring. Through the mystery of life he is both the son and lover of the mountain goddess. Her image is of a woman half human, with many breasts and eggs, bees and birds, plants and beasts carved into the pillar that is her body. And Artemis is Kybele as a young girl, full of her savage promise." Teleo wondered at all this, but said nothing, for the city belonged to the Great Goddess.

***

One afternoon Teleo and Amy had left the house and followed the creek to the Pactolas to look for gold. Most of it was in the form of dust in the sediment, laboriously panned and sifted, but sometimes nuggets gleamed in the rushing waters. Amy directed them to a spot well upriver from the settlement where the torrent plunged with great force into a quiet pool, washing much gold down from the holy mountain, leaving it gleaming quietly on the shallow floor of stone. In an eddying pool near the top of the falls Amy reached into the water. She held up a nugget which shone warmly between her golden fingers.

"A gift of Artemis," she said as she came toward him. "and of the river god. Use it well." And she placed the precious substance in his hand. "I will. I will," he laughed, and they began to descend along the edge of the waterfall. "It will make beads on a golden girdle, like that of Aphrodite herself. Whoever wears the girdle captures all the passion of the man who sees it. Here. Let me help you." He turned back to reach for her. She took his hand and leaned forward over him, smiling into his sun-stricken face. Then her shadow blocked the light and the weight of her long black hair washed over him and rested on his shoulders.

He was in shock. It was as if the day had disappeared and he was in a dark cave, smothered by her hair, touched by its electricity. It slid away, sparkling. She smiled at him, now in a position on the rock beside him. His body flushed and shook.

She leapt lightly from rock to rock below him, looking like Artemis herself.. When she turned back to him, she knew. The wildness in them, so close below the surface, now erupted. The gold nugget, utterly forgotten, fell back into the river to mark that magical place forever, as they sought and found their own treasure. They claimed each other that very day, in the rushing stream of the Pactolas, washed by the sacred river, abandoning all else. Just as Otrynteus and the Naiad had lain together by the Gygaian Lake, near the fish-giving Hyllos and eddying Hermos, so did Aphrodite loosen their limbs in love.

Then every moment became part of a design to get away from others and share their passion again, insatiable, immediate, thoughtless. They could not remember how to act as if they did not love. But they were not concerned; somehow everyone would understand. They had been so loved and needed they would be forgiven. In the great confidence of the beloved daughter, Amygdale told Teleo that Ardys would take their part. After all, he was not a blood-cousin. All would be well and they would ask to be married.

They came together savagely, impatient with time and its treacheries, making a world bound by the touch of only one other human being. On mountain, by stream, slowly in the tall grass, tenderly in the moonlight grove, they shared their love again and again. Aphrodite and Kybele and Artemis Protector of Children let them live for awhile.

But all would not be well. Teleo went to Ardys about their plans. After an unspeakably cold silence he was ushered away and not permitted to see his uncle for several days. Finally Ardys confronted them both formally, beside the hearth in the megaron. He was softer than before but very contained and distant, full of authority and some great sadness.

"May the gods forgive you. And me. This marriage will never take place. Teleo is a guest in my keeping, and though he has violated the rules of hospitality and the trust of the family, I will not violate the guest laws myself and invite the wrath of the gods. I have enough to answer for." He looked steadily at Teleo and then turned to Amy.

"Amy has always been a special child, as you know. I have indulged her past what is usual even in Sardis. But there is something neither of you have known, that only her parents and the high priestess of Artemis have known, and I must tell you now. When I was alone and dying of malaria, I prayed to Artemis to save me. In my despair—my madness—I vowed that if she saved me I would sacrifice my next daughter to her when she became a young maiden."

A long silence. Agonizing.

He was struggling to speak, his words harsh and cutting. They could not believe what he said, this warm and intelligent father, this wise man.

Stunned, they stood there.

"When I was saved and brought home again and you were born, Amy, I had prayed you would be a boy and I would be released from my vow. But you were a lovely girl. I went to the high priestess and told her I would dedicate you to the temple. I would educate you and train you to be the finest priestess Artemis could boast. I promised to endow the temple with all of my treasure. I have sacrificed hecatombs to Artemis through the years, praying to be released from my vow.

"I have offered myself instead, but she is adamant. Amy was not to know until her ceremony of maidenhood." He added bitterly, "That initiation, the dancing with the bear as we say, Teleo seems to have usurped. He will have to answer to Artemis for that."

He turned to Teleo again. "You know the dangers of being the first. The gods will sacrifice you for taking the first fruits. That is why young girls always dance with the bear in the temple before marriage. Only a fool will sleep with a virgin, even in marriage."

But he was not listening. "How can you tell us this? How could you have done such a thing? Sacrifice your daughter on the altar? That is barbaric! Unthinkable!" And he raged at the stony man before them looking suddenly so old. Amy had stood white-faced and unbelieving.

Finally a terrible cry came out of her and resounded around them. She burst out. "Instead of marriage I am to die? You have known this always? When you kissed me and played with me—you knew this?"

She began to tremble and scream, holding to Teleo in her hysteria.

Ardys waited and then spoke again. "I thought the awful goddess would strike you herself. She is famous for shooting the sharp arrows that bring sudden death to women. Every day I wondered 'will Artemis exact her pledge today?' But I see now that she will hold me to my word and I must go through every bitter moment with you."

Teleo shouted at him. "Why did you ever come back? How can giving the life of a young girl make anything you ever did acceptable to anyone? It cancels everything else you are. It was a coward's act—'I promise to get my child to die in my place'—oh, villainy!" Teleo could have killed him on the spot.

"Yes. If you kill me now I will not curse you. I would happily give my own life, but that would not change Amy's fate. She is the child of Artemis and always has been. We have thought now for a long time that Artemis gave life to her for this purpose."

But there was more to come. Amy was with child. There was grief and consternation everywhere among them. They were amazed every morning to wake up to what they were facing. The love between them had become a desperate thing. They clung to each other now in terrible anguish.

The priestesses of Artemis decided that the child was not to die with her. She would bear it first, placing it in the guardianship of the temple to be brought up in its service, and only then would the sacrifice of Amy be carried out. Teleo would not officially be the father; it would be the child of the river-god Pactolas, and, as a divine child, would also be a sacrifice should troubles come to the city.

Teleo was beside himself. To lose Amy and the child both to a savage goddess was past enduring. He refused to leave Sardis, even though he was no longer welcome in his uncle's home. He worked hard in the fields at harvest, exhausting himself at whatever work was given him and tried to sing for his supper, receiving kindnesses from other young people who sympathized with his plight, for everyone knew of it. Many were outraged at the coming sacrifice, but their fear of the great goddess kept them quiet.

Teleo managed to see Amy from time to time, for he was desperate and the guards would look the other way. But now Amygdale had been dedicated and was living with the priestesses, learning her service and wearing their robes of saffron and scarlet. She had not chosen this goddess and her first sense of outrage and betrayal was terrible to witness. All that saved her was her love for Teleo-kairos Maionides.

Their belief in their love was stronger than ever for awhile. They knew they were participants in life, living its deepest principles. But as time passed and her instruction at the temple continued, as her body turned matronly, Amy seemed abstracted and her silences increased.

She seemed to be falling under a spell. He wondered if they were drugging her. Theodore had apparently disappeared, slipping away into the mountains. Teleo had been urging her to run away with him ever since their fate had become clear. "You have got to come with me soon, or we will have to wait until the baby comes. That would be more dangerous. We will go south to Cilicia and get a ship to Cyprus. I will find where my true parents lived and we will go to my people."

Amy would sigh. "My father is better known in Cyprus than yours, whoever he may be. Besides, we would not be running away from my father. It is Artemis we cannot escape. Sometimes I believe that, if I am loyal to her, she cannot possibly let me die; she will rescue me as she did Iphigenia."

They smiled sadly at some of the ways others were dealing with their tragedy. "One of the priests is trying to convince me that Pactolas really is the father of my child. Maybe a eunuch could believe it." They laughed. "But I have felt your passion and I know better. You are better than the gods." And they would make love one more time.

Ardys' attitude towards Teleo had changed slowly through the waiting, as if his own suffering were bringing him closer. He confessed that he was glad that Amy had known love before her cruel fate engulfed her. He knew that his indulgence had made her dare past other girls and did not blame his grieving nephew, seeing their love affair somehow also fated by the gods.

The baby came, a boy, just as spring was pushing through the ground. Teleo was forbidden to see him, but he contrived to anyway, through a pitying slave, a few hours after the baby's birth. He was small and red and wrinkled, but he was real. Teleo would always know that this was not a dream. He had given life.

Now Amy was denied to them all, sequestered within the temple. After she had been cleansed of the pollution of childbirth, she would be rededicated and sacrificed as soon as possible. It was the month of Artemesion, March and April, and the festival of Artemis was upon them. The town had suffered long enough, and he was told that he should leave, for everyone's sake. But there had been no animosity towards him. It was Artemis' business. Everyone believed the goddess would strike him dead, for he had been the first to know a woman who had been dedicated to the goddess.

He said goodbye to Ardys. Silently, Ardys pressed the stranger's gift into his hand, the parting gift of host to guest. It was his gold enameled ring from Cyprus. "Remember me," he said. But Teleo could not see Amy. He was told she had accepted her fate and now served Artemis willingly. He knew it could be true by now. He hoped it was for her sake. They had no last words.

Numbly, he set out on the fateful festival day. He could not bear to be there, nor could the town tolerate his sorrow. Ardys shut himself away. The town was full of festival, but every mind was at the sacred altar high in the mountains, on the edge of the great chasm into which the sacrifice would plunge.

The sun was bright and all the earth was alive with spring. He struggled down river on the Hermos, hating the mountain towering into the sky behind him. He crossed to the north in an effort to separate himself from its obscene presence. He looked at the earth and retched and could not eat any of her fruits. He thought of the Great Goddess in every rock, every boulder, every bursting bud. Artemis. The goddess of the wild earth and her wild animals- -including men and women. How he hated her. He would never escape her. Even when he died, he would rot in her bosom. He felt like a trapped animal.

High in the crisp sunshine far behind him, Amygdale stood on the altar's edge. Her dark eyes and delicate face were warm with love—for the child she had borne, the gift of their love, for the earth she would fructify soon with her blood. Her figure was slight against the great mountain, like a blossoming almond clinging to life at the edge of a windblown chasm. For a long moment she balanced there, above a world blooming with promise. Then as gracefully as a young panther, she stretched her rich body into the morning, hurtling without a cry down the long silence, to shatter into oblivious matter on the jagged rocks below. The priests and the vultures were appeased.

Long after dark, on the darkest night he had ever known, Teleokairos Maionides Melesigenes struck a fire near the river's edge and threw himself down. It may have been a dream or a wish. He opened his eyes and saw on the other side of the fire the sleek black fur and glowing eyes of the goddess. Next morning as he climbed the valley toward Smyrna, a black panther watched him from high on a blossoming ledge of Mt. Tmolos.

That was the last time he ever went to Sardis, and in his great epics he never mentioned her name, referring to her once by the old name of Hyde. Though he and Ardys were reconciled, they never spoke again, sending infrequent messages through third parties.

Ardys had had a rich life and, he had thought, some degree of wisdom all the while that Amygdale grew. But he had been devastated by his action, and with her death he changed. He was hard now, unapproachable, like the dry shell of an insect under which the life had disappeared. Among the Sardians he became a man whose life had been especially blessed and cursed, which set a distance between him and others.

As the year passed, the summer was especially fruitful and a vein of silver on Mt. Tmolos had shown itself after the spring rains. People said that Artemis was pleased, and life was especially precious, promising, and beautiful. For a time all was well.

When the boy Dionysos—for that was the name the priests had given the child—reached the age of four, he disappeared during a Phrygian raid up the valley, seen for the last time slung over a warrior's grey horse, bloody and clinging to the mane as the man swept north again, leaving the smoking slave quarters of the sanctuary's chief priestess and a sacked treasure room. The treasure had been considerable, since the temple served as a kind of bank for all citizens.

And at that turn of events, the townspeople said that Artemis had been displeased with the boy and taken her revenge. But Ardys was freshly in his grave then, sleeping on the stone bench of his tomb carved out of the soft rock on the west bank of the Pactolas, marked by a fine stele made of red and white marble from the banks of the Gyges. His sons had divided his wealth, and few thought about him further, for no bard sang of his bright deeds.

Teleokairos had returned to Kolophon to find that Theophilos had died during the winter. The old bard had never known why he had not come back in the fall, and in his suffering Teleo had not thought to send word. It was another stroke of his evil fate, he thought, and he returned with resignation to work in Smyrna. Later, when he heard what had happened to his son—his, not the river god's—Teleo was glad, for the boy had been saved from certain sacrifice. He had plotted in his mind about rescuing him, but destiny had taken a hand and he was glad. His own fate had been repeated.

Despite himself, Teleo saw a divine pattern at work and was forced to believe in powers greater than man. The gods' cruelty was indisputable; hence, their existence was as well. He talked with friends about pursuing the Phrygians. They discouraged it. The band was from the distant north and had two months' lead time. He thought of curses and vows of vengeance, of promises to the gods, but only for a moment.

He did not feel like singing, and went back to the fields and the ships to work.

INTERLOCUTORY

The Voice of Letha Gooding

Homer is supposed to have composed <u>The Margites</u>, a poem which Aristotle says was to comedy what epic was to drama. But only a few lines are extant. That poses a problem. We could ignore it, since its dating to Homer's lifetime is open to question. Or we can use it, in which case we must create a work and interpret it. What presumptuousness! But this whole manuscript is a monument to hubris. A humble author is an oxymoron.

The birth of comedy is for too important to me to ignore. Homer is funny, you know. Delightfully comedic. I can believe <u>The Margites</u> came out of his youth, such a youth as this. It is a side to his akrasia. Who could predict where such a grief would lead?

We do know <u>The Margites</u> was a mock epic. It seems to me to have been a satire mocking the power of the Great Goddess of Asia herself! What more propitious subject for our poor bard now. We could not have been more fortunate had we had to invent its existence ourselves. I have taken some chances teaching comedy, especially Aristophanic, absolute, festive comedy. Properly demonstrated it unstructures the classroom and invites chaos. Unless students experience that spirit they have not understood. Read Edith Kern's <u>The Absolute Comic</u>; she believes the twentieth century revived Old Comedy, and there is much evidence lately that she is right, certainly in film..

One more thing, an opinion for the learned debate over the presence or absence of selfconsciousness in Homer: If he composed comedy, <u>The Margites</u> fragments, he had a modern consciousness. But let's get on. As Homer points out several times, after great loss we must still cook supper.

CHAPTER 5

The Margites

733 B.C.E. Smyrna

The ship Maion had promised Teleo was beached for the winter at Smyrna. With reluctance the family agreed to let him captain it for the season. It would be his anyway if word came of Maion's death, and, considering the life he had lived since his return, they would be happy to have him at sea.

He had been working in the fields and on the ship from dawn until the light was gone. Then he would seek out whatever feasting he could find, playing until his voice would crack, and stumble into bed. Such an engaging man as he had ample company, and their high spirits buoyed him up. He did not sing the songs of Kolophon, the epic lays of heroes, quite the same now. He preferred the riddling and bawdy jokes, the parodies, and he lit into them with great zest and savage humor, delighting the young crowd and giving his bitterness an outlet. He sang all of Thaddeus' outrageous songs and invented new ones. The old stories of the heroes and their gods turned to ashes in his mouth.

That was the year when a rare trouble began. At Smyrna the previous winter, rains had been scant and the earth was far too dry. Early spring heat and high winds parched the valley, and the crops were ruined. The following winter was disastrous. Extreme cold came when no moisture protected roots, killing the plants that sustain animal and man. Bears and other savage beasts attacked men recklessly, even coming near the city looking for food. Grain had been short from the parched summer, and horses and dogs became dinner after the cattle were gone. The vines of the gods, of the Praemnian wine, seemed lost. The Greeks, who did not eat fish except under severe need, did so now. Even the fish in the city goddess' sacred pond began to die, and men were more frightened by that than by their own hunger. The goddess' curse—that those who harmed the fish would be eaten by fish—was fulfilled when a family who ate them went mad and threw themselves into the sea.

Everyone turned to appeal to the gods, to the two Nemeseis, ancient goddesses of retribution who had long been among the major deities of Smyrna, having a sacred precinct on Mt. Pagos to the south. They were imagined as riding a cart drawn by winged griffins, their strength and judgment shown in sceptre and rein, and the change of fortune shown by the turning wheels. The great goddess of plenty was barren, and they seemed to say that there had been some offence.

The Aiolians of Smyrna had worshipped the terrible goddess Boubrostis, who was Ravenous Hunger. In their fear the Ionians began to do honor to her power. The sacrifice to her was painful to give, a great black bull completely burnt in the ceremony, hide and all, after having been cut into certain pieces of ritual significance. Her name was the direst curse one could pronounce against an enemy, too awful to think about. But now it was whispered that this Aiolian goddess had been invoked by the local Aiolians to avenge the taking of the city a generation before by the Ionians;

thus suspicion also gnawed at the unhappy people. Some thought it was a divine contest between Boubrostis and Demeter, the Ionian goddess of the earth, which of course it really was. Mortals could only pray.

Teleo in his bitterness was amused at first. He had always been obedient to the gods at Smyrna, this obedience and acknowledgment being the essence of Greek worship. He had observed feast days properly and sacrificed with his family to the gods of the city and countryside, especially to the great sea god Poseidon whom the Lydian sailors and Pelian Ionians so naturally revered. He had learned the stories of the gods of his forefathers and filled his heart with the celebration of their power, had been glad to be alive and to sing of the beings with power over his existence. Now with bitterness in his heart he felt the deprivation around him and its relentlessness.

Sometimes he took a grim pleasure in the silence of the gods. He wished that he could believe that the Great Goddess had been so offended at the sacrifice of Amygdale that she had sent disaster to mortals. But he could not quite believe it. Then he thought it bitter that the terrible sacrifice had brought no good. That was the grimmest thought of all. Perhaps there were gods, but to his mind mortals did not know who they were or how to call upon them. The priests and priestesses, so smug in their rituals, knew nothing. They had no power, and if they did have, they would not have known what was right to do. He was overwhelmed with the pain and pity of it all, disgusted with the arrogance of those who presume to know the gods.

It was in this context and in his terrible sorrow that Melesigenes composed The Margites, a song of hexameters interspersed with trimeters, a mockery of epic. It was a sly song, outrageous and subversive, but wickedly funny and too clever to be obviously what it really was, an attack upon the ancient mountain goddess. There were some who caught his meaning, though; in any case, it was a great success.

Homer maintained when he was old and famous that The Margites was not his song at all, that he had learned it from an old man, a divine singer, who had come to Kolophon when he was an apprentice there; but that has always been the stance of the satirist, the trickster's child. In a sense, it was not his song. For it was so much the fashion that at every singing up and down the coast new comic stories were added and the song took on a life of its own, its original direction becoming blurred and ambiguous.

Margites was a mock hero, a man who knew many things but knew them all badly. He failed in every endeavor. In one tale he knew of a marvelous new grain, a variety of wheat. It was so superior to old strains that all the rest of the seed was neglected and only his was planted. Then for two years running the crop failed, and since there were no other varieties, everyone starved.

In another city he gave a miraculous new knowledge to men, the means to make everything they touched turn to solid gold. But soon that city starved. Margites wanted to hear the Sirens sing, as Odysseus had, for then he would know all there was to know upon the fruitful earth. He put wax in his men's ears and had himself tied to the mast, but when the Sirens sang to him he could not understand the language.

Then Margites learned to fight as a great warrior does and thought himself invincible. He determined to fight a great snake of the east who was ravaging the herd of Mt. Ida. But when he faced his foe the fire of the dragon's breath melted his shield. The hot metal dripping on his toes made him dance in a frenzy, spinning so rapidly that he vanished into thin air. By the time he slowed down from his warrior's dance the monster had eaten the herd and departed. Everyone loved that one.

There were all sorts of Margites stories. One series of tales followed the theme of his brutish laziness—"none would he heed and no work would he do." Others were puns and verbal jokes. In one story Margites visited the tomb of a great singer. To his amazement he heard singing coming up through the earth. He hurried into town to get someone else to listen. "Do you hear it?" he anxiously asked. "Oh, yes," the man said, "but that's odd. He is singing his song backwards!" Margites beamed, satisfied, "Of course. That's because he is decomposing."

Any good joke would do, and everyone had an addition. A lot were hung on the old adages. A popular series of jokes demonstrated that the fox knows many a wile, but the hedge-hog's one trick can beat them all. Now, a lot can be done with such an old saw, and his intent was not the obvious one. All the hedge-hog knows is how to roll up in a ball, and that's all he needs to know to survive.

Margites was a survivor, not the village moron. His songs told of a man so dumb he did not know who bore him, his mother or his father. Teleo trod dangerous ground there, and the priests thought of the stories of Hephaistos, Dionysos, and Athena, those oddly-parented gods, but most often of Demeter.

In another episode Margites would not lie with his wife for fear of what her mother would think. The priests of the great goddess did not laugh at that one, though everyone else did. Margites tried to carve a boat out of stone and carry water in a sieve; there was open mockery there. It was great fun to get even so publicly, so innocently, and to see the same feelings being liberated in others. The deep truth was in his hedgehog. No matter how many wiles the great goddess fox had and how poor her son/consort, it was the hedge-hog that she needed, and if he rolled up with his back to her, she was defeated. And that one confidence would overturn her world.

So the poem rolled around Ionia, sometimes tales of an ignorant peasant too dumb for the new technology, sometimes the too-clever technocrat defeated by natural law, sometimes the man who refused to be civilized, always underneath a mockery of any man who couldn't free himself of the dominance of matriarchal beliefs, of the ancient slavery of castrated service to the Great Goddess of the East. It said to every man's unconscious that to refuse access to the goddess would leave her barren. If Aristotle was right in saying this was the first of comedy, it was rooted in a new attitude toward the festive, a subversiveness that would give men a new courage, even in the face of a natural disaster.

Like most important things, the success of The Margites was too complicated a matter for Teleo or anyone else to understand. The phenomenon of the song had a great impact on Ionia, and there were those whose lives were more affected by this outrageous song than by anything else he ever sang.

Most important perhaps was its healing power for Teleo himself. He had great fun singing it, and he was finally honored at home, helping men laugh as they struggled under the fearful power of the earth's forces. Mocking the epic was fun after all that serious training. The surprise value of its performance was wonderful to experience, the conviviality memorable, and the jokes and stories endless. Men told of their deepest fears and, in doing so, were moved to conquer them. He basked in the approval of his city and sang for the next years along the coast at Teos—where Thaddeus made memorable contributions to his song—at Lebedos, Kolophon, even down to Ephesos. His dexterity in composition grew with his reputation, and his wit responded to that. Puns and preposterous folly filled his imagination.

The wonder of sound beguiled him. The power of humor to heal men's troubles, perhaps even to heal their bodies, gave him pause. He looked around at festivals with a fresh eye.

Festival was a period outside of time. In these days time was calculated so that any discrepancies between the counting of months and the order in the sky was given over to timeless festival days. In order for the lunar and solar years to coincide—the earth goddess' lunar time and the sky god's solar time—considerable adjustment was necessary. And why not celebrate the difference?

There was a mystical rejuvenation in days set aside from time. The mind had to be aware for this rejuvenation to take place, he had thought at first. But did it? Could not a child be told "These are days you do not lose in your mortal allotment" and accept them with delight? On such days the commune ruled and individual identity dissolved. The terrible burden of being oneself was lifted altogether and all were part of each other again in an amorphous recognition of eternal forces. The sacrifice—yes, there was one and always had to be—had long before been decided upon, and the accidental violences of such times ignored. Because it was not personal, just human; when it became individual, that was a different matter, as Teleo's wounded heart could testify. There was great power in such a time, a pull toward death, to be sure, toward loss of hard-won knowledge; but there was also a liberation from self that enhanced its return. Festival days properly lived led to growth. The new comic festival spirit said that man had reached self-consciousness by celebrating its dissolution and return.

There was terror in festival too, since it was an order outside of time and normality, the chance that normal order might not return, that chaos and madness and loss of one's self could engulf the polis. Just as the winter solstice celebrated recognition that the sun would return, before the instant occurred existence lay in the balance. The sun, of course, had always come back, but one knew well enough that civil order might not. At Smyrna theAiolians had lost the city when the Kolophonian refugees had violated the rule of festival and carried their triumph into common time.

It was odd to look into the eyes of festival, he thought. When men and women gave over their responsible identities, their eyes changed. It was hard to say what he saw there. Fever and fear, the pull to do nothing and be nothing, like Margites, the terrible need for license, and even the freedom from that.

The festival masks people wore were ambiguous. Were mortals pretending to be gods,or mocking them, or mocking themselves? Or were they really divine then, living outside of time? Was it a real metamorphosis, the act itself, that they were seeking? Was the moment full of desire or decay? The only real difference between the gods and man was metamorphosis and mortality. If mortality was dissolved by festival, metamorphosis was possible, too.

Slowly Teleokairos healed again. The edge of his anger was blunted, not because he had forgotten but because he had to go on. The follies of mortals continued. The individual died for the group daily and in countless ways. But with time, and his songs, gratefulness at humor and hope spilled over into him and he shared the simple warmth of life among the survivors of a bitter time.

✢✢✢

In these years when he could, Teleo combined seafaring and singing, trading to see the cities of men and singing to know their minds. Once near the end of the sailing season, as he looked to sea from Emporio, he found himself gazing at Samos island lying to the southeast, remembering how Maion had promised to take him there on their next voyage, to see the temple of Hera.

Longing for his missing father gathered to his eyes. It had been over five years, not long enough to lose hope. He would sail south for the winter, looking methodically, carefully, stopping at every port as far as Miletos. He would strike out to the islands if the season allowed, though he did not know those waters. Fear of them sat in his heart, and of the seas west of Cyprus. He would sing his way through the markets and on the beaches until he found a trail.

Of his crew from Smyrna only three agreed to go with him, boys no older than he and ready for adventure. He stopped at Teos and recruited Thaddeus who was happy to join him, though he knew little about sailing a phortus.

"But I am a shrewd trader, my friend. I will pay my way well enough." They laughed together, their youth somehow renewed.

They had little trouble finding a crew, and so they began the quest, stopping at Lebedos and Kolophon and finally Ephesos, lingering in each city to sing and inquire. It was an idyll, sailing along the coast singing to each other, seabirds and dolphins keeping them company. They traded well, and, singing at festivals, usually won the competitions. Handsome, young, amusing, they took the hearts of the villagers. At evening the harbors rang with music, villagers danced by torch and starlight reflected in quiet bays. Some had known of Maion, but they knew nothing now.

***

"I have a pilgrimage to make alone," Teleo told Thaddeus as they left Ephesos behind them. "To the ruins of Melia, near Mycale. Charite thought that was my birthplace."

"What do you expect to find?"

"Memory. Maybe a place, a sound, will nudge my memory. It's possible."

Thaddeus' silence told him what he thought.

"Drop me at Mycale, north of the strait by Samos. Give me two days and come back."

Thaddeus did not understand this obsession with fathers. His had been a profligate, and he knew where he was buried.

Teleo landed near the sanctuary of Poseidon at Mycale and went in search of Melia. It had once been a powerful city of the Carians, but the Greeks of Boeotia, Thebans, had conquered it and established the sanctuary. It had been one of the original twelve of the Panionian alliance.

But no bards sang of its fall. In the terrible political infighting of the century before union, Melia's pride had offended the others, and she had become the sacrifice. All evils were heaped upon her, the sanctuary appropriated. Priene won the priesthood (in 750) and Melia was utterly destroyed, as if the memory of her existence were hateful to the others.

No one was proud of her death; it was better forgotten. No stories were made, and the silence of the place was as profound as that of the bards. Teleo tramped the hills, alone except for passing herders who could point to ruins. He sifted through the cold ashes. No special outline, no wall or blackened hearth, no grove or curving shoreline stirred the slightest memory. He had not been here. It was not his. He could make no song for this doomed city.

He returned to the shrine of Poseidon on Mt. Mycale, where he would meet his ship. The

Temenos of Poseidon Heliconian lay on the top of a hill facing north, the council's meeting place situated at a lower point to the southwest. Between them was a huge cave which only the priests of the sanctuary, a family of nearby Priene, were allowed to enter. Samos and Priene had fought royally for the priesthood, and the mainlanders had won. He arranged with the priests there for a sacrifice to be done in the afternoon.

Teleo stood long, looking at the beach below the Temenos. Laocoon had been murdered here, torn apart by Phoenician priests. Or the god. His gorge rose at the thought. For   written sounds? Because he taught children sounds written in the sand?   He struggled to grasp the fateful import of that action. If it were so momentous a thing to do, Laocoon had been a new Prometheus, bringing divine power to mortals. His gift of one conception—that the music of language had been named and isolated into separate sounds—that gift had already become part of bardic training. Of his training. It had already occurred to him that a special knowledge of vowels may have had much to do with the power of Laocoon's song. So much greater a song than anything else he had ever heard. Except the sea. The sea sound lived in his body. In the beat of his heart and the pulse of his passion.

He gazed at that vast blueness and thought of the eyes of Laocoon. Here at the shrine of Poseidon was the site of his ritual murder. He blinked and looked away. His mind was whirling.

That afternoon Teleo made solemn sacrifice there, staying long after the rite was done and everyone had left, unwilling to end his pilgrimage. He wanted a sign. Some strange emotion began to possess him. He deserved to have a sign from the god. He would wait.

The hours passed and night came. Laocoon's music sang in his head. Maion's rescue and the years of patient ministerings passed like a warm golden chain along his memory. The flames of Melia burned behind him, a city sacrificed to the god of Helicon and Ionia, the god of the fish-giving sea.

Night passed into dawn. No sign came. More hours went by. At last Teleokairos began to recognize the strange emotion that had come, a fury too deep to define. He stood, with great effort, and addressed the altar of the sea god whose immense domain washed indifferently against the shore below him.

"You took Maion from me," he said. "Was it because he saved me? Saved me from the mighty Poseidon?" His voice was rising, out of his control. "You have your way. He is gone!"

Did he mean Maion, he thought, as if in another part of him. Or that Melia was lost to him at last? Hopeless tears welled in his eyes. He looked down to see them fall away and spatter on the terrace stones at his feet, making a wet place there.

"How in the name of all that lives could you burn Melia? What happened to its people? They worshipped you. God! I hate you!" and he paled at his blasphemy.

"Strike me now! End it! Did you have to take them all?" Then suddenly he blurted out, "Laocoon who died at your feet! Was he my father too? Speak to me! Was he?"

He had said it. He had not known he thought it. Shocked, he fled the sanctuary and, heedless of danger, scrambled down the face of the bluff to fall in an exhausted heap on the beach where Laocoon had died. Curious seabirds wheeled above him, and a gentle surf touched his arm and fell away again.

⁂

They went to Samos, directly to the Imbros river, to ground which had been sacred for two thousand years. Hera had been born here near a sacred bush, and she had married Zeus here, so it was doubly hallowed. Her magnificent temple held an aniconic image of wood, found there when the Ionians had come 250 years ago. It was said to be like the palladion, the image of Athena at Troy. Teleokairos felt awe at the thought of it.

Thaddeus and the crew went with him to see this famous building, unique in the Greek world. Maion would always stop and sacrifice, and marvel at its beauty. It was a true building, 100 feet long, not like the small shelters in the open temenoi of most villages; it was the earliest in all Greece to have wooden columns on all sides, the famous peripteral style. Its grandeur, the harmony of the conception, was such that he knew Maion had been right: something new had entered into man's conception of the gods.

"What is it?" He asked Thaddeus as they sacrificed at the altar, standing in the paved terrace before the temple.

"A temple. What do you mean?"

"What makes me feel that this is a temple to men?" He felt he had blasphemed again.

"Yes. Something." Thaddeus looked at it with a keen eye. "It's the columns. She is in a cage of columns." Teleo smiled at his friend's insight. A highly ambiguous sacred grove indeed. "We needn't have invented Margites, after all," he said.

How different she was from the Niobe and Kybele. For the first time in many years an image rose in his mind of a carving at the mouth of a cave on Mt. Pagos. It was of the Mountain Mother, in a strange style, with features unlike any people on the coast now. Perhaps the same people who had carved the lost camps of the mountain expeditions of his childhood. She rose out of the ground at the cave opening, bosom and shoulders and enormous head, the earth itself the rest of her body. Her elaborate headdress was the growth of the mountain itself, her expression serene and all-powerful. He had come upon it alone and unsuspecting, and he had never told anyone about it. The cave gaped beside her face, and the bones of cattle lay on the rock shelf before her, an overgrown temenos. It had filled his dreams on many a night.

He shook himself and smiled at Hera, the new Greek goddess tamed by Zeus.

And there he did hear of Maion at last. The priests remembered he had come by there on his fateful journey. He had told them he had decided to go to Cyprus and had left heading south for Miletos with a fleet. So little, but they were pleased. They would not have to cross to the islands after all. And Maion knew that route well. Perhaps he was safe. They left rich gifts with the new Hera.

✼✼✼

It was with a joyful heart that Teleokairos and Thaddeus and their musical crew sailed into twin-harbored Miletos just ahead of the first storm of the season. They beached the ship in the crowded harbor and joined the "season of forty songs" where they sang and heard singers all through the winter.

Miletos was a city with "children." For 75 years she had been colonizing and thriving in every case. In the Black Sea she had Trapezus and Sinope, and, with Phokaia, Aniesus. The Propontis was even more lucrative. Cyzicus was the center of a wool and electrum trade. The ports of Miletos were choked with busy traders, and the houses of the city always needed a bard.

Arctinos' songs were sung by his family and other Milesians, but Teleo heard only snatches of the Samothrace song. It had been about the birthing of Dardanos and a flood, but no one knew much of it. Arctinos was long since dead, having flourished at the time of the fourth Olympiad. But a song of his youth, a song of Troy, was well remembered as well as his Aethiopis, composed when Tel was a boy. He had heard these and the great Titanomachia while he was in Kolophon, but to hear them again by the bard's own relatives was a revelation to him.

No one knew of a blind bard of Chios.

Antimachos of Teos was there, and Teleo came to know him well at last. He was old now and could barely sing one sitting from his renowned version of the Epigoni, and others helped him when he tired. "There are fine bards everywhere today, " Antimachos confided. "We get around better that we did, and everyone has a broader repertoire. I've heard more versions of the Jason and the Odysseus than you can shake a stick at. It's been great fun. I just wish I were twenty again, like you and Thaddeus."

"Youth has its problems too."

"They tell me you are the rascal behind Margites." And he sang a scurrilous song of his own to add to the canon. He smiled with delight. "Only an orphan would have taken the chances." They laughed heartily over their songs and spent many a happy hour together.

It was Thaddeus who first heard word of Maion. The fleet had left Rhodes for Salamis in Cyprus, but a storm had scattered it far and wide. Some said he had been taken hostage by Phoenicians in the struggle for cities on the south coast and killed when he was not ransomed. Others said he had gone down on the west coast of Cyprus. The darkest tale said that they had seen his ship, his stempost of two horses running together; it was reported sacking the coast near Al-Mina, its crew of bloodthirsty Greeks led by a Lydian corsair. But that was a tale by a Phoenician in sympathy with the Phoenician struggle for towns on Cyprus. He would never believe it. But he would go no further this season. He had blasphemed the gods and must sacrifice to them.

The bards of Miletos held him, too, and he was the best among them.

Bitterness and loss seemed old to him now. Dear Thaddeus had been his brother and close companion, and the attention he got from his audiences was heady nourishment after such a long famine of the heart. The world of rock and ocean became beautiful once more, and he found comfort in seeking out Maion's friends and sharing memories of him. They urged him to go home again, promising to give him news from the crossroads ports of the Aegean.

There was much talk among the singers about the festivals at Delos. They thought about going, on the way home—Delos was 100 miles directly west of Miletos—but he had to get his ship to Smyrna. With Thaddeus, he started north at the first sign of Persephone's return, still fatherless, but with many memories of fathers. For him, for now, the search was over. His voyage had not been the voyage of Telemachos. It was time to pick up his phorminx and sing of such things, the voyages and the returns of heroes.

✳✳✳

Why his anger with the Great Goddess lessened as he resolved his search for his fathers on the long way home he would never have understood. From the deepest well of feeling he wanted to believe that he would see them all again in the Underworld, even Amygdale and Dionysos. He realized with an ache that at the instant of that thought he had accepted their loss and laid the past to rest. He had mentally set a bowl of honey in the sun to honor his dead.

When he came back to Smyrna, Teleo sought a place outside the city where he could sing alone, where he could work his poems out for himself. Much of life took place on the surface, of course; so much of what people were was really of the moment, unreflected, spontaneous. But Teleo had lost the belief that surfaces would do. He was not content with narratives that did not suggest the human cost of the action. He needed a private place to compose.

The place he finally found was perhaps an image of the search he was beginning. He thought of the oracle of Klaros when he found it, a small cave hidden away on acropolis hill beside the river Meles near where it rose to travel its short and lovely course into the bay. It was a place of birthing, an inner place, a womb, a mind, a fruitful darkness with a fine resonance. In later years it was said he did all of his composing here, but that was far from true. That he was led to find it by a swarm of bees was literally not true, either, or may have been one of his witticisms. But there is no doubt that here he felt at home again.

CHAPTER 6

The Sibyl

727 B.C.E. Smyrna

Smyrna watched intently as Gannon of Erythrai, commander of the expedition, drew with a stick in the soft dirt. They were preparing to attack Phoinikous, the Phoenician settlement on Mimas peninsula, to recover a hijacked vessel.

It was all a result of the time of famine, when the Greeks had no grain or oil to sell and the Phoenicians, who depended on neighbors to trade for food, had been cut off by the winter seas from their own cities. Times had been hard, and incidents of theft and violence hung between Phoinikous and the Greek villages. Now a young firebrand, Josephus, who nursed a hatred of Phokaia, had impulsively taken a Phokaian trader as it had passed through the Chian straits and had taken shelter at Phoinikous, intent on selling passengers and crew into slavery farther north. One Silenus had fallen, wounded, into the sea during the boarding, then had swum ashore near Erythrai and raised the alarm. Five Smyrnans had been aboard.

The Erythrians signaled Chios Town across the strait, who also passed the signal to the Smyrna watch at Mt. Pagos. Within hours Smyrna and Phokaia, as well as some Klazomenians of that gulf village had marshalled their men, and now a land force was meeting at Mimas pass near Erythrai. A dozen men from Kolophon had just joined them.

Gannon, a heavy, awkward man in his late forties, was still a forceful fighter and strategist, and he knew all of Mimas.

"Speed. Speed is the only answer if we are to get our people back. And the ship, of course. The strait must be safe."

He spoke soberly. "The Phoenicians would prefer to fight at sea. We can't let that happen. We must hit by land and then escape by sea with help from our own fleets. Later we will send the talkers to make peace.

"I have already sent runners to Teos and Lebedos to the south. They will bring ships to the mouth of the bay at Erythrai and join the attack by sea from the south. The Phokaians with four war galleys will lie around the north headland out of sight. But Chios will place the entire fleet of ships they have—traders and war galleys and fishing boats—behind Oineus island, directly opposite Phoinikous." He was marking their positiions in the dirt as he talked.

"The Phoenicians are expert seamen," one man said. "Won't they see all this going on?"

"Perhaps some of it. But they may be expecting an embassy, or ships from Phokaia from the north. Silenus is sure they took him for dead. They won't expect a raid so soon. At first light tomorrow we attack by land while the Phoenicians are watching the approach of the fleet from three directions. In and out. Fast."

He looked at the men for reactions. They nodded and listened. Gannon went on.

"The south cove—the city lies on this neck of land with good beaches on either side—south is where the war galleys are usually beached, and traders too if there are any in port. We've seen two going north in the past few days. The north beach should have six or eight local fishing boats. I'd guess the pirated ship is in the south bay."

"Land defense?" another man asked.

"Weaker than most, since they are the only city on Mimas except for us. I don't think they expected this. Or wanted it. The drought is long past. This must be settled decisively and quickly. The traffic through the strait is as important to them as to us."

"Why don't we send an embassy then?" someone said.

"Negotiations cost, always. And while they go on, the village will arm. We have to be quick. There is the danger too that Josephus will sail on with his captives. Phoenicians often sail at night, by the stars—he could even be trying to slip out tonight."

Everyone looked grim at the thought and hands went to weapons. "How long since he got there?"

"A night and a day. We don't have much time." Gannon smoothed his hair back and squared his shoulders. "We have to be ready to attack at dawn tomorrow.

"It's twelve to fourteen miles from here, maybe a little more," he estimated. "There are 62 of us—we will move steadily along the mountain in groups of six; we should be there by midnight. They will probably see some of us but let's hope they think we are scouts. Surprise. We need to surprise them."

Gannon quickly laid out the plan of action. A third of his men would take the north beach and secure small vessels for the escape, stoving in or dragging out and capsizing those they don't need. "Disable. Don't destroy," he said.

"Fifteen of our best will give land support at the south beach if it is possible or go on into the town. The rest—25—will go into the village and rescue our people."

"Is there a sea gate? Who knows the village?" one man asked crisply.

"Yes." Gannon was drawing again. "If the captives are not on the vessel—and by now that is unlikely—they will be in a storage house by the sea wall. There were women and children aboard—some of you didn't know that"—he glanced around with a careful look—"so it may not be so easy to get away. But we'll have to see some of these things when we get there. What else?"

Silence.

"Then let's get up there as fast as we can. Eight hours of light left. But be careful. They will be expecting something to happen. Cover your weapons with dirt. But keep them handy."

Teleo was excited and appalled together. This was a raid, not noble warfare. But he was attacking a city. It had just happened that he was not assigned to the war galley, and he regretted it. That would have been a noble fight. The Phoenicians were worthy sea fighters. Here he was sneaking along a ridge in leather vest. No clanging armor had been brought along.

The men moved swiftly now, twenty from Smyrna, almost as many from Kolophon, a dozen or so each from Klazomenai and Erythrai. The terrain was rough, but they were all used to rocky trails and long hours of work, so they went easily through the shadowed forests and across the barren slopes, working their way through the long evening and dark night.

✳✳✳

By two a.m. they lay against a high rock behind Phoinikous. The sea was clear of ships, though he knew that by now fleets were hidden around the headlands. Nightbirds called, and he knew all had arrived. He wondered if the Phoenicians knew as well.

Someone stirred behind him. It was Gannon, giving orders, assigning duties quietly.

"You go over the wall to the storage house with Eteoklos and my son Philomelus," he said to Teleo. "Wake up the hostages and run with them for the seagate. Our group will be opening it. Then get them to the north beach as fast as you can. The captured crew will help you. The ships corning round the north headland will come in and pick you up. Can you do it?" Teleo said a quiet yes.

"One thing," Gannon added. "You will have to cross the causeway, the neck of land out to the wall, before the rest of us. You must be ready to go over the wall when we start across. The guards will probably see some of us. Too many to hope otherwise. If they do, we'll have to shoot towards you," he touched his bow. "Good luck."

Tel knew how three men scale a wall. He was worried about how they would get across the causeway, now high with grasses, grass that was easily read. He began to sweat. Fear rode on his shoulders. He felt his knife and sword again, and hefted the small thick ash club in a sling at his hip. He didn't really want to kill a citizen defending his city. Nor did he want to die. Sea fighting was more noble, less personal somehow.

Fear and the night cold kept him awake. He knew the Phoenicians navigated by the stars, and he wondered why the ship was still there. He would have left, given the situation. He guessed the villagers were still reacting to events, perhaps disagreeing on what to do, for the Phoenicians were ruled by councils, too. But a city was at the mercy of its rashest element, he thought, no matter how wise the leaders may be. He wished the Greeks had sent an embassy first, then remembered his own bitterness at the time of hunger. He felt for the man who still hated. And he respected the Phoenicians.

He knew they had not always been seamen. They too had suffered in the great disintegration of 500 years ago when the migrating Mycenaeans and Minoans had sacked and burned their coast cities. Maion had told him about it many years ago. But the Phoenicians had held on, had absorbed the refugees and learned their sea skills so that within 200 years they had begun to dominate the seas themselves. They were survivors, having clung to that coast east of Egypt for a millenium after coming out of Assyria. He had admired their enterprise and independence, and their reasonable settlements among other peoples. Most of the time. When they were not pirates. As traders no one could equal them.

"They have to overcome in everyone the fear of foreign goods, that somehow things contain magical powers, that somehow a person may be captured by things," Maion had told his crew.

"But in a way that may be true," one man had said. "If they need what I have, then I have captured them."

So much the more astute they are then, Tel thought. How sad that it had come to this because of one man's hatred. Phoinikous had been there long before the Greeks had come, and he had no desire to destroy it. Yet five Smyrnans lay captive in the hut below, and he must rescue them.

Now it was time to move. Gannon touched his shoulder—"If anything goes wrong, head for the forest and home. May the gods be with you"—and he faded into the trees. Teleo and his companions moved very slowly, inching their way through the tall grass, making no noise, stirring the long stems as little as possible. A light wind helped by touching the grasses, heavy with seed, moving them ever so little, rustling them all. He said a silent thanks.

It was an eternity before they reached the wall and turned to give the signal. Then they sprang into action, on shoulders and up the wall. Miraculously he found himself going over quick as a thought and racing on light feet toward the storage building. Philomelus jumped one sentry and he and Eteoklos grappled the other to the ground and burst into the hostage quarters just as the cry went up.

"Men on the causeway!"

An instant later a hue and cry came from the watch in the south harbor.

"Ships!"

The fleet had been sighted.

**

Then everything happened at once. He ran into the storage hut with every sense alert. He could only see dimly the tangle of people waking up and fighting confusedly, not knowing they were being rescued. As soon as they understood, half of the seventeen prisoners rallied to get the hostages out to the gates. Tel ran forward to help move the heavy timbers lying across the gateway.

That was where he encountered the fighting. Amid shouting and the sounds of struggle, two men overwhelmed him, throwing him to the ground. He rolled away and rose on one knee, ready to slash the throat of any attacker. By that time the rest of the Greeks as well as the rescued crew had caught up, and the struggle at the gate began in earnest. He fought savagely, stabbing one attacker, stunning another with his ash club. Then the gate was opened and he shouted to the captives to run—needlessly, for they were streaming through the exit. He shook himself free and followed.

There was confusion everywhere. The Chiote ships from behind Oineus were close in now, heading for the south bay where two trading ships lay beside three war galleys. Some of the traders were reaching their ships and scrambling to the oars, ready to get underway. A fighting ship was already moving toward the Greeks, its ram gleaming wickedly in the pale light. They would engage within minutes.

A shout flew across the water as the small craft from Erythrai and Teos came into view around the southern point. The sea seemed to be covered with them, and they continued to come, roaring defiance to intimidate their enemies. On the north the land force had reached the local fishing boats and the rear guard were fighting off the townsmen at the watergate who were alert to their strategy by now.

The struggle at the north beach was brief, for the townsmen were distracted by the sea full of Greek ships heading for the south bay. Tel helped to move the small boats out, ready to cast off, as the captives scurried down the beach and into the shallows to clamber aboard. It was a long way in the absence of surprises. A few seemed to be wounded, being helped along. Two men were being dragged bodily and were trailing blood along the rocks. One woman was frantic, screaming and looking back as they carried her to the boat. The attackers had dragged half the small boats out into the water and capsized them, to prevent pursuit. As the remainder pulled away four great Phokaian warships and the galley from Smyrna came into view around the north headland and turned landward to come to the aid of the fleeing hostages. He knew then that the raid was a success. He cheered and threw his arms up with all the rest and turned to take his seat at the oars.

As he did he saw someone on the beach behind them. It seemed to be a small child, pattering frantically down to the water and along the shore, calling after them as the woman behind him screamed again. His heart lurched. Before he could think he was in the water swimming back. Only after he surfaced did he even think of the Phoenicians. Now he saw two men going after the child. I can handle two of them, he thought. All attention was focused on the fight in the southern bay and the approach of the Phokaian ships.

By the time Teleo reached land the men had picked the child up and started toward the hill near the causeway. They had not seen him, apparently angry at the sunken boats and awed by the great fleet in the waters of the strait. The child was crying and they handled him roughly, only glancing casually about as they hurried, intent on the sea battle.

Teleo was infuriated. He came upon them from behind with an oar, levelling the man on the right and hitting the buttocks of the man carrying the child. The man went down and Tel beat him savagely. But the Phoenician reached his knife and sank it into Tel's left arm just as Tel's fist smashed into his skull.

He snatched the boy up in one arm and looked seaward. No boat had waited for him. He could never make it now to the ships. Tel ran for the woods, the closest cover he could find. If he had been seen, the observers were too far away now to stop him. Well into the woods he sank down to look at his bleeding arm. Only then did he realize that the blood was not all his. The boy had been struck too by the Phoenician's knife. Tel could not remember how or when.

He looked at the child with horror. He was pale and bleeding at the left shoulder, perhaps three years old and not big enough to comprehend their perilous situation. He began to cry. Tel packed their wounds with periwinkle leaves and fled sosuthward as fast as he could to get out of earshot of the village.

He did not stop till noon. Fear and pain kept him moving, stumbling, staggering southward below the ridge. He knew he was slow now. He thought that if he stayed close to the sea he might hail a Greek ship and be picked up. He knew his path would be easy for pursuers to follow, but he counted on some delay. Pursuers seeing the blood would feel confident he could not travel fast.

He sank down by a cold stream to wash their wounds. He did not try to stifle the boy's cries, for it was futile. Sweat poured from him as he worked. The sea was clear, without a boat in sight. He could not understand that. He had no idea how far he had come. They drank and rested and dozed.

Something startled him awake. There were voices on the mountain behind him. Quickly he tied the boy in a sling across his shoulders, using their clothing and his leather knife belt. In a panic he began to run again. He tried to think what he would do if he were hunting, but he did not know the number of his prey. No. He was the prey. He had no idea where he was now, but it must have been far enough south to strike inland through the pass. It was only 650 feet high. There was no likelihood of rescue by sea now. If he missed the pass he would go to Erythrai.

The ground rose steadily. Time passed. He was weak and the boy moaning and feverish. There were still sounds of pursuit behind him, closer and lower, carrying more clearly. Then, when he was most desperate, they stopped.

It was too good to be true. He sank against the rocks exhausted. When nothing happened for a quarter of an hour, he put the boy down and scaled a tree to reach an overhanging ledge. He heard his pursuers again, moving down the mountain. They were leaving!

He could not believe it. They were safe, at least for the moment. He went back to the tree and shinnied down. When he turned to get the boy, she was there.

Beside the rumpled and bloody child there stood gazing at him the oldest woman he had ever seen. It was her eyes that were old; actually, she was straight and tall, her robe the color of the mountain. He knew she was a goddess and stood dumb, and light-headed, not sure she wasn't a dream. Her voice carne to him from a great distance.

"They have gone. They will not come near me."

Then she was a goddess. He began to tremble. "Help the boy. He is dying."

"No, he isn't. Sit down and rest awhile. Then we will go." She was matter-of-fact, speaking with great authority. Teleo looked with relief at the boy. He was lying as he had before, listless, perspiring, in bloody rags, but now he wasn't worried. He knelt beside him, taking his little body up and cradling it against him. The eyes burned up at him without visible sense. Tel rocked and sang to him, comforting him. "It will be all right," he said, meaning for them both.

She radiated power, but Teleo was not afraid of her. As they sat, she simply waited, like a tree, under the shade of the ledge, blending with the rock. He thought of the ancient carving by Mt. Pagos, the placid face and shoulders growing out of and merging with the mountain.

"You are Kybele."

She didn't answer. Then she moved toward them. "Let me take him. We must walk awhile now."

Tel followed her, quite forgetting his wound until he saw bloody drops behind him on the stony ground. Only then did he reflect that this was his phorminx arm, this arm that meant his living. The fingers moved stiffly, gory with crusted blood. He could not lift his arm; it had grown numb. It seemed unimportant now anyway, and he followed meekly, wearily, climbing even higher.

"Where are we? I have lost my direction," he told her as they entered pine forest.

"Behind Erythrai. You must have missed the pass. It is only a little further now." She peered at him and then went on, moving easily over the roughest ground. He thought of how blue her clothing was, the same color as the limestone mountain. A static of fear crossed his neck suddenly, and he wondered whether he was really safe here. But he knew now who she was. Everyone knew the sibyl's caves were behind Erythrai, high in the forest. She was Herophile the Sibyl.

She was not a goddess but the next thing to it, one of a family of women endowed with extraordinary powers and especially long-lived. The story went that when Troy fell certain sacred writings were brought here and hidden. Some women of the family had migrated to Kyme and thence to Cumae. They were the foremost diviners of their time, some say greater than those of Delos and Delphi. And she had said the boy would not die.

They reached the great cave where the sibyl Herophile lived. Homer would describe it in the Odyssey as the cave of Calypso

It was hidden among alder and aspen and fragrant cypress trees where birds came for shelter, soaring in after fishing the waters below. Grapevines hung around the mouth of the cave, clear brooks wound through the glade, and in the high meadows were violets and wild celery. Inside, the large cave rooms were warmed by sweet smelling logs of juniper and cedar, ablaze on the hearth. (Odyssey Book 5)

She seemed to live there alone, and he asked her.

"There are many caves. This one is mine." They went about the task of caring for the boy. He washed him in the clear cold water while she went to her herb pots standing on a polished sideboard. Working deftly, ritually, she prepared a poultice. She applied it, then she forced a clear liquid, pale green and fragrant, down the boy's throat from a gourd ladle, elaborately incised, and gently rolled the poor child into her arms to cuddle.

"This is nice." Her eyes twinkled toward Teleo by the light of the hearth fire. "Haven't held a babe for two hundred years. Something you don't forget." She chuckled with pleasure. When he seemed to relax into sleep she lay him with great tenderness in a basket of soft skins and looked at Teleo. "Let's see your arm." It looked terrible to him, but he knew he had not lost a lot of blood. "The important thing is to keep you clean. There doesn't seem to be much damage here."

The wound was two inches below the elbow on his inner arm, a tender spot now badly bruised. Herophile lay a concoction on it that quickly put the nerves to sleep. Then she cleaned it and glued it together with a healing paste. She gave him herbal drinks that made the cave seem light and airy. She seemed to be growing younger.

"Now you'll sleep. Don't worry about your phorminx. You'll be able to play again." She smiled gently.

"How did you know that? You must be a goddess!" he exclaimed. He was astounded and dizzy from exhaustion, and everything seemed miraculous to him.

"The callouses! On your fingers, dummy. It doesn't take a goddess to know you are a bard." Her laughter rang in the cave. She rose to go to the hearth and came back chuckling, carrying an applewood bowl full of steaming broth. Teleo drank hungrily and almost instantly dozed away.

He remembered, after that, tossing about in the dim cave for indefinite times, hearing harp playing and the child crying fitfully, but most often hearing singing. The songs were wild and primitive, measured and stately, dissonant, plaintive, whirling, mournful. He tried so hard to know them, but the memory would slip away. He could remember nothing except that he had heard much singing. Once he sensed several presences around him, leaning over him curiously and discussing him. He smiled crookedly at them but like a baby could not speak. They were delighted. There was dancing and singing before they melted away.

Teleo finally came back to himself. He woke in the mouth of the cave in the morning sunlight, lying on a pallet of skins. "Is this a hint for me to leave?" he asked Herophile as she brought him refreshing drink.

"You can't stay here forever, that's true. But the sun is your time keeper and it did bring you around." He stumbled to his feet. The day was glorious. He was stiff, and so he moved about, gradually becoming strong and beginning to relax. "Where's the boy?"

"Sleeping. He's fine. We've been having a good time."

"I remember hearing laughter and singing. How come?"

She looked surprised. "Did you think being a sibyl and living in a cave didn't have its advantages? We have a great time. But it has taken a long time to learn to be old, longer than most mortals have."

He looked at the sibyl in the clear light of day. She was wearing a long dress of pale linen and a cape edged with ties of silk, fashioned to make loops and intricate fastenings. A narrow band of fine embroidery was worked all around the hem. Her face was familiar now and serene.

"I have seen you before somewhere."

"No doubt. We like to get out every now and then at festival. Clean up now. We have a lot to do."

Teleokairos had never had so much fun in his life. Herophile told him hilarious stories about what really happened at the taking of Smyrna, of Helen's escapades in Mycenae and Egypt, about the strange sex games of the Scythians. "People are crazy." She shook her head. "And full of tricks. You can expect anything." She told him how an ancient priestess she knew had helped the Ionians take Erythrai from the Cretans.

It was a famous local tradition. An oracle told Knopus, the Ionian leader of the famous family of Athenian Kodrus, that he should bring a priestess from Enodia in Thessaly to aid them. Chrysame came, skilled in herbal magic; she prepared a bull for sacrifice, adorning him lavishly. Then she mixed in his food a potent poison that would drive him or anyone eating his flesh into madness. The bull, maddened, escaped from the sacrificial procession into the watching enemy camp where he was seen as a good omen, captured, and eaten. When the fits of madness had taken hold of the Cretans, the Ionians took the city and had held it ever since. The priestess was greatly honored, and she joined the sibyl on the mountain. Some said she was still alive.

"Is she?" asked Teleo.

"No."

He asked her how long she was going to live. "God knows," she laughed. "I plan to enjoy every minute. Might as well, right? I do know enough of the past and future to know I will die eventually." She paused. "You know what is the most fun in life? Sex! It is warm and exciting. And close to another life. The gods know it, too, and keep interfering in our lives, messing up the distinction between mortals and gods. I was one of those caught in the middle."

**

There followed a time he could only remember in snatches, brief, jewel-like moments, each of them set forth singly and sparkling.

"Tell me about the future," he said.

"Yours?" She was being evasive. He waited. "Well, people will be born and they will die. Cities will grow and be destroyed or abandoned, leaving only ruins. Boys will grow up and kill each other. Girls will grow up and do the essential things and be forgotten. You don't want to know how many times Smyrna will die and be reborn." She laughed in a high, ironic, detached way.

"Men will struggle toward being reasonable but passions will always rule. Rivers of blood will run into the sea over whose god is the best god. To give up miraculous life for gods who never have to die will be the criterion of goodness." She laughed uproariously, then sobered. "Then one day it will all be over."

"What do you mean?"

"Ares won't win—that's the good thing. But indifference and ignorance will. A little middle-aged tired ordinary person will make a mistake and BOOM! For no purpose. No reason. Not even for passion. All this lovely place."

"Do you mean all of Mimas and Smyrna too? They will—explode?" He could not imagine a greater destruction. Like a volcano.

She looked toward him across the embers, her eyes burning, her face as craggy as the mountain. "Melesigenes, for once I will be serious, though you may wish I would not. On the morning the world dies, there will be many mortals who still will know your songs." She smiled, irrepressibly. "They won't know who you were or why you did what you did"—she was delighted with the thought—"but they will love your songs. Believe it."

"Then the world will die in my grandchildren's time? Or their children's?" He was pressing earnestly to grasp her meaning.

"Oh no. A hundred thousand ships have sunk in the Aegean since man learned to make them. And a hundred generations will sing the sea song you will make."

But the world will live then, he thought. One hundred generations is enough. Long enough for mortals to learn to be like gods.

"I cannot imagine that," he said. She was shimmering in the rising heat and light of the hearth, almost disembodied, radiating amusement and affection.

"I know," she said. "Let's drink to that and have a dance. It's going to be a long time before I have such illustrious company again."

"When the world dies, the gods will too? Then they are not immortal."

"If immortality means living in the minds of men, their days are numbered, yes."

"Can gods live on when no one believes in them? Can there be gods no one yet knows about? Gods not yet born?"

"No. Yes. I guess we will see." She shifted the subject. "Men will learn how to do many things. Like this"—she suspended a heavy iron ball in the air between plates she held in her hands; she sent crackling lightning across the room. "And they will find much in my herbs"—she gestured toward the elaborate sideboard. Her eyes glittered and she added, "I think they will even fly to the moon and circle the earth much faster than the sun." And they laughed uproariously.

Then they will be gods. He felt a huge satisfaction. "When will I die?" he asked Herophile.

"Ah singer. Do you really want to know? Death is always an interruption." She paused, giving him a sidelong look. "Well then. Beware of the riddle you hear from two boys fishing: 'What we catch we leave behind; what we don't, we carry with us.'

"You are good at riddling. But when you have truly solved that one, death will not be far away."

A part of Teleo's mind contracted, making a place for her words, not letting them touch his senses. Making a cautious place. He felt a thrill, a shattering, an undoing.

"You should not have told me."

"I know."

"There will be a lot of trouble when writing becomes common among men." They had been speaking of words and singers.

"What will happen? I don't see writing as important except to put a few rememberers out of work."

"Ah, that's where you're wrong, my boy. There will be more consequences from the Greek alphabet than anything since the word itself. The Great Alchemist distilled the music out—the vowels have become separate conceptions. The new man will know his words not as winged words, as globes of sound that fly forth and toward his hearer; he will see them in his head, as symbolic ciphers."

"See them in his head? How?" He was incredulous. "Words are in my throat and ears. How will I find them? Will they fly from my brain without speech? When men become gods will they hear such words?"

"That is another problem altogether." When he asked her about his parentage, she turned him aside, saying sharply, "You have that answer already.

"Teleokairos Maionides, before you go, I have one request to make of you. When you go home, do not talk about your stay here or the things that we have said. It will be misunderstood, and the boy's mother will be distraught. If he tells stories of the cave, say that he was delirious or dreaming, and they may believe he has been visited by the gods. It's nice up here, and I don't want every shepherd and his sheep asking for favors. Those who can screw up the courage now, thinking of me with dread, probably need the help. Let's keep it that way."

"You make me think of Circe and Calypso in the songs of the returns."

"That's no surprise. I know them well. They are my cousins." She laughed. He could never tell when she was serious, and this time he felt certain she was mocking him. "Sorry. I have a slight advantage over you."

"Will you be alive when the world dies?"

"No. That will be another generation."

"Let me ask you this, though I don't quite know how. Considering how old you are and your sisters and all—when do you have children? Who are their fathers? I mean, how does it all work?"

The light in her eyes came up. "A fair question. Don't worry—I'm not going to enthrall you. A bard's child would give away secrets to the most ordinary men. Not that I'm not tempted, though. Your legs are marvelous." She smiled at his embarrassment.

"Well, the gods erred in our case. We come before Zeus' generation and operate on a different level. My childbearing days are almost over, but they last so long for us that that is no tragedy. Can you imagine a mortal woman bearing for so many generations? She'd be sick to death of children. It's amazing how few children Zeus has, when you consider his life span. He's a wimp. Don't look so shocked. So's his wife.

"You think I have a bad attitude. I can see that. Gods and sibyls have to be dignified and serious? My god, how can anybody in my place survive unless she can laugh? Unless she enjoys irony and trickery and amazing people? I love the dreary seriousness of the good hard worker; it is the fabric of mortality. Not of the gods. I must see too much of that pain to live that way myself and not go mad. Laughter is liberating, it liberates me from over-long life and frees me to see beauty." Her voice had begun in a scold. But she had softened into inaudibility and now sat gazing over the mountain, through the heavy arbor and dappled shade to the screaming blue of the channel.

"You would do well to go back some time, in a few months—and make peace with Phoinikous."

"Why?" he asked angrily. "They started it. They wounded us and tried to kill us. They would have sold the boy as a slave. The apology lies the other way."

"I didn't say apologize. I said make peace. You lack my sense of time—men always do—and these cities need to get along, in terms of generations. Do what you can to keep the contacts open. It is the terrible silences that kill."

"Sorry. Even a sibyl can ask too much."

"I have no stranger's gift for you, Melesigenes. Objects get lost in the world. And objects with power, in the wrong hands, are dangerous. My gift to you will have to be the complete healing of the wound to your phorminx arm, which would have made a difference. And the healing of the boy."

He looked with astonishment under the bandages on his arm. There was no scar, no soreness. A slight redness remained. "Don't be too impressed. The body is inclined to heal itself. It's all in knowing how to help." She jerked her head toward the medicine table. "Some of you mortals know a lot already about the healing power all around you."

***

Teleo left the sibyl's cave with no notion of how much time had passed. Herophile had cleaned their clothes and given them figs and pears for their traveling. He told her he would be back many times, but she said sternly, "Make no such promise to me. Let the world take its course." But he knew she regretted his going. She watched them, waving sadly at the last.

It was hard to get his bearings; he went down until he saw Erythrai to the southwest and then turned inland through the pass into the gulf. He moved patiently with his small friend (whose name was Sarpedon), carrying him most of the time, singing and telling stories. They ate the figs and pears and picked raspberries along the narrow lowland coast. It was with a glad heart that they finally saw Smyrna gleaming in the sun beneath its red mountain slopes far across the gulf.

He went to the baths of Agamemnon, the hot sulphur springs along the south shore below the peaks of the Two Brothers. Someone would pass. He told the boy how all of Smyrna looked toward those peaks daily, for they foretold Smyrna's weather. He reached the springs, a small stream in a shallow ravine surrounded by low shrubs, and let them wearily over the edge, sitting down among the rocks to take off his shoes. Sarpedon was already in the stream playing happily. Teleo eased himself into the steaming water, welcoming its pungent odor and healing heat. He lay down in midstream to let the water flow around and over his body, to feel the current pull gently on his beard and around his ankles, run through his fingers and massage his loins. He could understand Agamemnon's joy at stopping there after battle.

They rested long at the hot springs, bathing and recovering their strength. Finally a boat came and they got a ride home. When they could be seen approaching, the city populace came running along the wall and down the beach and out into the water. It was the most wonderful welcome he had ever had to Smyrna.

The boy's family lived in Phokaia. Signals went up immediately, and a boat was dispatched, carrying him home. They said fond goodbyes, and Teleo promised to come to see him. The boatman was told to tell the family they had been hiding from pursuers and did not know how many days had passed. In fact, he didn't, and it seemed strange that it was only seven; he felt he had lived a lifetime.

Some time later the family—parents and two older children along with the boy Sarpedon—

came to honor Teleo in the city. They brought a pan of bronze and a bow for hunting, baskets of figs and apricots and a fine aulos from Pergamon. Sarpedon and Tel had a nice reunion; he did not remember the cave of the sibyl. Teleo composed songs instead about the rescue at Phoinikous. There had been deaths on both sides: when a Greek ship was rammed, two Chians were lost, and the Phoenicians lost three at sea and one in the defense of the city. One of the seamen was the only brother of Josephus the firebrand. As for that man, they exiled him. His anger was still terrible, and the coastal cities knew he would bring trouble if he lived. On his way down the coast to Cyprus he disappeared.

✳✳✳

Teleokairos Maionides finally did consider the sibyl's advice, and on one of his jaunts to sing in Chios he stopped for the night at Phoinikous. It seemed very natural on the quay that night to sing in the city he had attacked only a few months before. He wondered who would come to listen, and few did. But it was there that he met two men his age who were to become his friends, twins whose parents had come only recently to the settlement. They spoke Greek fluently, as most seamen of the coast did, but they had been born in Cyprus and their greater family was from Tyre.

The boys were Hiram and David, named for two famous kings who had been friends 200 years before. Hiram was the Sidonian king who had lived at Tyre, a great city on the coast east of Egypt and south of Byblos and Sidon. The second Hiram ruled there now. The king David of 200 years before was the king of Israel, a small nation, also Semitic, which bordered Tyre. The reason Teleo found all this out was that David, the twin, was a fine musician, and when he heard Teleo playing, he fetched his own lyre and they sang all night under the cold stars, exchanging songs. David played his lyre with a plectron, or pick, when he sang, but when he did not sing, he plucked with his hand. He also had a zither, rectangular in shape, with ten strings running parallel to the short side and not centered. He sang the song of the friendship of David and Hiram, so beloved by his own father that he had given their names to his sons.

"How do your people feel about twins?" Tel had asked them. "Which of you was born first?"

"I was," said David. "Does it matter?"

"We have an old belief in Smyrna that the first born is the child of a god."

David laughed. "Don't I wish. I could be my own bard." The song of friendship of the two kings was beautiful. It told how David of Israel had led a bitter fight against the Philistines and finally broken their power (in 975 B.C.E.) the Philistines being the remnants of Cretans, Mycenaeans and other sea peoples displaced by the age of turmoil. Much of the Philistines' power had been maritime, and King Hiram was grateful to David for helping to alter the balance of power on the seas because his people held only a small territory and were dependent on trade for their existence. Now Phoenicia flourished, in amity with David and his country. In return, Hiram had granted David use of his fine seaport and ships, and the two nations opened ancient trade routes inland through their territories.

The present day Hiram and David told Teleo about Ugarit, the beautiful old city which had been their Troy. It had been sacked and burned by the sea peoples a generation before Troy and never rebuilt. Ugarit had shone like a jewel, trading with Mycenae and Crete, with Cyprus and Rhodes, even harboring a mix of residents who could write the old scripts of Mycenae and the eastern cities. It had known the bardic traditions of the Hittites, Sumerians, Egyptians—all of them.

Before they were destroyed, the people of Ugarit learned the secret of making a deep red dye from the murex sea snail—that shade called purple by so many. The secreted fluid was so expensive, there being such small amounts in each creature, that only royalty could afford it. Securing snails from the waters around Mimas and the gulf one time, the boys let a tiny snail crawl on Hiram's chiton, secreting a narrow trail of yellow fluid. Then they sprinkled the cloth with lemon juice and set it in the sun. The cloth turned a brilliant white, while the trail of the snail turned from yellow to blue, then to red, and finally to a deep, rich magnificent red. It was a wonder to behold.

David commented. "Some say the Phoenicians were named by the Greeks from their production of this crimson cloth, for Phoenicia means red man. It is only a version of the name of our people. We are from Canaan. The Akkadians called us kinahhu, the red people or people from the red lands. Here our village is Phoinikous, the city of the red men. So in the Aegean we have a Greek name, but it means we are Canaanites."

Teleo was a seaman at heart and admired the Phoenician skills on water. He wanted more of that story. When the Philistine power had crumbled under David's attacks, the Phoenicians were ready to control the sea. They had learned from the sea peoples two enormously important things about sailing. The first was to row facing aft instead of forward, this simple expedient increasing control and speed. The second was to use the keel design of the north rather than the flat bottom of the Egyptian river boat used heretofore, which allowed more control in holding course against the waters.

They were resourceful and independent. The Phoenician cities had also learned to organize their ships into fleets with royal commissions and to divide their profits.

Teleo did not know how important an influence the Phoenician idea of a city would be in the shaping of the famous Greek polis—in both its physical positioning and in its combination of political and religious rule. But he knew well the story of the great city of Tyre, his friends' ancestral home.

Hiram had been an innovator. When he became king (around 1000 B.C.E.) the city of Tyre lay on the edge of the coast with a fortified island 650 yards offshore, consisting of two flat and rocky ledges covered with seaweed. Hiram had the narrows between the ledges filled with rock and debris from the mainland. With the help of the old Cretans and Mycenaeans, who knew much about summer palaces and city walls, he built into the sea to the north and south of a causeway two magnificent harbors, with quays and jetties, filling and shaping them. On the lower land of the two original ledges—the fort was the higher one—he had a beautiful civic structure built and called it Sar, Rocks, a place of great beauty and power. Nonnos the epic poet was to describe Tyre as a young girl bathing in the sea, feet resting on the shore and arms stretching out on either side.

The other Phoenician cities—Byblos, Aradus, Sidon, Berytus—admired Tyre, and Aradus followed Hiram's plan, as the Greek cities had.

"But what did they do about water? You can't build a city in the sea without drinking water. Such a city need only be captured at the shoreline."

"You may well wonder, and I will tell you. There are freshwater springs that bubble up in the shallows under the salt sea on this coast. Hiram and the kings fashioned leather hoses and attached them to heavy clay or stone funnels. Then, turning the funnels over the emerging fresh water of the bottoms, they recovered the fresh water, the force of its running pushing it through the hoses and out into the cisterns." The Phoenicians at Sidon had used the sea in another ingenious way, according to David. Silting up of their southeastern harbors was a continual problem until they built and maintained a network of canals and basins so the prevailing winds would drive surface water inland while trapping the sand-carrying water in a strong outbound channel, thus contriving to have the tides work to keep the harbor clear. David added, "We have talked about the silting up of the Hermaian gulf here. There is a natural current clearing it at its southern toes because of the four streams of the plain, but the harbor mouth near the pebble-carrying Hermos is definitely silting up."

Teleo had frankly never thought about all of these things, and was surprised how the Phoenicians had learned from Mycenaean Greeks and Cretans. They tried to get the best—and give it—in their contacts with other peoples.

The Phoenician attitude toward the sea was so different from the Greek. Working in the sea, the constant vigilance, the patience and the strength to carve harbors and to live more wary of the land and man than of the sea—all were marks of a different people indeed. But even he knew that the old Mycenaean pattern of city-building was gone, and Greek cities now seemed to be following the lead of the Phoenicians.

David told a wonderful tale about the building of the temple of Solomon, king after David. That king asked Hiram to send special craftsman to design and construct the shrine. Production of the holy objects of Solomon's great temple at Jerusalem was supervised by Huram-abi, whose mother was Hebrew and father Phoenician. The building itself was after the Phoenician style. A large outer court led to a central door to the temple, and inside the building was of three parts: a vestibule, a rectangular hall, and a small sacred area where only the high priest could enter. In Solomon's temple in the outer courtyard was a great bronze container filled with water. Two huge pillars flanked the entrance. The rectangular room held an altar of gold and the room itself was of shining Phoenician cedar. The curtain to the inner sanctum, which held the Ark of the Covenant and the Ten Commandments, was entirely of Tyrian purple, the work of the murex snail. No sound of building was ever heard at the temple site, for all of its preparation was done elsewhere. It was a masterpiece.

And then there was a delightful trick at the end of the account. The cost of Solomon's temple had been so great that he could not levy taxes sufficient to pay for it, and so deeded twenty coastal villages to Tyre. Still, difficulties with payment persisted until the two wise sovereigns Hiram and Solomon contrived a way to settle the debt with honor. They bet each other great sums of money in riddling games. Each managed to win and lose appropriate sums to the other, loudly proclaiming abroad the wisdom of his opponent, and since Solomon owed the money and could not pay, he was seen to be the wisest. Eventually the confusion became so great that the debt was declared resolved. Such was the wisdom of the two leaders.

Then David sang some songs, strange and beautiful, that David the king was said to have composed himself. He had been a bard who played a magnificent kithara of cypress wood with inlays of amber and gold and precious woods. A close friendship grew from that night of music on the quay, and the men visited often after that. If anyone remembered Teleo from the dawn raid, it was never mentioned.

PART TWO

Axiokersa, Eros, is Desire,/ Who touches Earth and makes consuming Fire.

Interlocutory: The Voice of Letha Gooding

Ah, we are near the heart of it now, having shaped our man of clay.

The spark of Homer 's genius will ignite at Samothrace. Only when consummate skill encounters profound insight can anything as extraordinary, and extraordinarily different, as the Iliad come into being. I believe that happened when Homer was initiated into the mysteries. But you do not know about this sacred island. The world has forgotten Samothrace. Maps in otherwise excellent books of history and criticism fail to identify it or, worse, even to include it. Many a lengthy index contains no reference to it. Yet Livy calls Samothrace as holy as Delphi.

The parents of Alexander the Great met and fell in love at the mysteries there. In the Iliad Poseidon himself sat on the highest peak of Samothrace watching the war on the plain of Troy. And the Romans declared the sacred icons of their city were none other than those of the Great Gods brought from Samothrace by Aeneas. Heracles, Orpheus, Jason, Odysseus, Aeneas- -all were considered initiates. More importantly, Herodotus. Yet the world has forgotten! Can I even consider that such an initiation would have no impact on my life? On any of these lives?? To believe so would only be evidence of my own spiritual sterility.

We know that it was death to reveal the mysteries, and have assumed that that special knowledge was forever lost. But it is one of the delicious ironies of intellectual history that every time we have sung the Odyssey we have in our wonderful ignorance preserved it! Incredible! Truth may indeed be the Daughter of Time, albeit a neglected step-child. I have wondered, though I haven't used it in the story, whether there were some life-saving device in the Samothracian scarf, to save men, literally, at sea. Dardanos in the myth wraps himself in a wineskin and floats to the Troad. Friedrich Schelling's Treatise on the Deities of Samothrace and myth criticism provide the ideational base for these initiation ceremonies, and the archaeological expeditions of Karl and Phyllis Lehmann, whose publications on the work at Samothrace continue with the next generation of scholars, provide the physical evidence and the reconstructions of the sanctuary. I honor them with all my heart. While I take full responsibility for errors of interpretation, we are all in debt to the people whose scrupulous care and unstinting labor have brought the past to light. They have lived the truly richest of lives, their study the profoundest form of worship.

I have taken two liberties in this narrative, for which I can only say that they seem necessary to the clear telling of the tale. Ironically, such compromise, however slight, will bother only those fine spirits I have just honored, the scholars in the field, those I would least want to offend. So I explain. First, the words of the initiation rites would have been far more potent, more dramatic, more mythic than I have drawn them in my simple explanatory mode, but we probably could not have understood them, had we access to them. The altars, described as they exist on the oldest levels, would I feel certain have functioned substantially as I have shown.

Second, I have used the initiation halls of a later time because they provide us with the most accurate evidence of the rites. Few sacred buildings existed at the time we are describing, here or in other Greek holy sites; elaborate rituals were held in the open air, or perhaps in a cave, such as the one I invent for the noonday rite.

I also realize full well that the rites would have been elaborated through time, but, given the nature of this worship, you will see that its basic form could never have diverged far from what I have described, even though the rites of the Great Gods of Samothrace stretched from the stone age—its myths include the Flood and tbe founding of Troy in the fourth milennium B.C.E.—to A.D. 391 when Emperor Theodosius decreed the closing of all non-Christian sanctuaries, their presence announced by tbe Winged Victory balanced into the sea-winds of that stormy coast. After that the magnificent marbles would stand abondoned for another two hundred years until a prosaic earthquake would finally topple them all, for Poseidon was dead, of course, long since.

What was it that held the world's devotion so long, which caused great cities to send official representatives to its Mid-Summer festival for almost a thousand years? What role did it play in the slow civilizing of humankind? For it would initiate anyone free of pollution into its first degree- - king, slave, child, woman, Greek and barbarian. Anyone. The Samothracian mysteries were said to promise safety at sea and to make people morally better.

We must set aside modern religious contempt for pagans and look with open hearts at such a rite. Schelling thought Samothrace a remarkable place, with a worship which he considered to presage Christianity. He felt the second initiation foreshadowed the Christian church—another reason why I have chosen to describe it. Whether or not he was right is not within my power to say: Up along the long aisle, smothered in water and earth, who is revealed in the summer's accidents? Perhaps it was necessary to prepare human consciousness for the Christ to come.

CHAPTER 7

Shipwreck

725 B.C.E.

He was in Mytilene singing for the winter. Although it was close to home, on the lee side of Lesbos, he had not been there before and, when an invitation came from the prominent Aiolian city, he had accepted gladly; Teleokairos was 27 now and wanted new audiences and new tales. All had gone well; he had ranged through the island villages even in the chill of the season, listened for stories, for old words in new cadences, for new twists to old stories, perhaps too for words of love and companionship. Just as his interest began to flag, a ship was leaving for Lemnos with a profitable cargo to trade for metals, and he was urged to go along. The shipmaster's people lived there, and he wanted them to hear this bard.

"It's a beautiful island, Lemnos, quite unlike any in Ionia," Nikos the captain told Teleo. "We are the children of Hephaistos, an ancient people, with secrets of metallurgy which we have shared with others, and a beautiful language of our own. But I want them to hear you sing—the best of the Greeks. There is no poetry equal to yours. Winter with me. I promise we will provide rich gifts, things you have never dreamed of before."

And so they set out. It was late in the year for sailing, but the weather had been mild and they hadn't far to go. They traveled with a skeleton crew of four, having dropped off the regulars at the last two ports for wintering with their families. Teleo helped out, being an accomplished sailor himself, and they made port at Methymna from Mytilene in one day. The next morning they crossed the channel early and made the thirty miles to Tenedos in a bright crisp ocean.

Just one night from home, the captain, who was a short thickset man with an aquiline nose, was full of good cheer. He raised a toast to his island home. "You will love Lemnos. It is much larger than this"—he gestured toward Temenos. "Here we are offshore just three miles and the island's only fifteen miles square. Lemnos is fifteen times that and four times the length, with a neat waistline, cut by two wide bays on the north and south shores. My village is on the east." His eyes remembered it. "Lemnos is volcanic but the land lies low and is very fertile from old lava flows. We grow figs and grapes, grains and nuts. Sheep abound on our hillsides. But we are most famous, after our metalwork, for the Lemnian earth."

Lemnian earth was a powdery clay rich in iron, a deep russet-golden brown in color, used in poultices. It was a fine astringent, constricting body tissues and checking the discharge of mucous in running sores, as the bard would know soon enough. But this bole as well as a local dye plant had a strong smell, Nikos said, that clings to the skin of those who work them, primarily the native women. He laughed when he saw Tel's expression.

"Ha! Yes, the Lemnian women do stink! But they smell just fine to Lemnian men, who think it's great to keep all the Greek adventurers out of their beds."

Tel looked at him in mock horror. "Did you think I planned to sleep alone all winter? Now you tell me this. Well. Actually, I was thinking about Philoctetes," he said. "I sing about the Greeks abandoning him at Lemnos because his wound had putrified so they couldn't stand the smell of it. Now you're telling me they probably put him ashore to have his wound treated by the Lemnian bole!

The captain grinned. "Who tells the tale makes the meaning. But you know that."

His companion cocked his eyebrows. "But who is this Lemnian who puts out stories to keep the Greeks away?"

Nikos laughed."My enemy, you may be sure." He paused to drink again, his eyes happy. "We will show you the forges and the work of our craftsmen. And take you to the sanctuary of the Cabiri, who are the special deities of our people. Well, it will be a profitable winter for you and a good one for my village." He was expansive, and they drank late, sleeping on board.

Next morning they shipped out before dawn under an overcast. With a land breeze and the shelter of Imbros, they struck out northwest, knowing the wind would carry them southwest slowly onto the shore of Lemnos, but dawn brought heavy skies. A sea crow flying toward them dipped straight into the water. Only the captain's determination to get home kept them from reading the signs and turning back as the seas rose.

Suddenly from east behind Imbros a great wind swirled down and they were driven wildly between wind and wave. They watched helplessly as Lemnos swept by on the left, out of reach except for its extreme northeast peninsula. They tried to make for it, but the breakers were savage against the rocks and there was no shelter. Gusts from south of Imbros propelled them past the Lemnian headland as they tried in vain to seek shelter along a receding northern coast. Sea followed heavy sea. Rain, changing to sleet, obscured the land. Though it could not yet be noon, it was dark as night, the black storm hanging just above a furious ocean.

Great tracks of lightning split the skies and thunder crashed around them as if it had been midsummer. They bailed in silent panic as the ship moved from crest to crest, sliding across enormous seas. Then it seemed to smash itself against a wall of black and foaming water and, with a great shudder, it pitched them headfirst into the Aegean.

Teleo felt himself being tumbled and crushed in a downward current. It was strangely silent after the shrieking of the storm, and his body was warmer than when he had struggled in the icy wind. He fought for the air that would save him. Objects bumped against him in the turbulence, a tangle of rope grabbing his leg, pulling him down. Finally he wrenched free and shot upward, stroking with every ounce of his powerful will.

He broke surface near the wreck and fell across a piece of mast, spitting the bitter brine out of his mouth, his heart pounding. He shook the salt water from his streaming hair and called in vain for those he hoped to help. He shouted over and over, and then shouted again. And again. Finally he lay quiet for a while, remembering that he had been like this before. Not that it was in his memory, the storm and wreck so long ago; that belonged to Maion. He began to call his name and realized again that all the years since Kolophon he had been searching for him. Now he needed to be rescued again. Maionides cried out for him, filling his memory with that ancient rescue, and he called out to the gods of Samothrace for help in the midst of his peril.

A light began to glow in the darkness to his left, a bright blue flickering light, hovering and bobbing, slowly coming nearer. He was transfixed. Some god of the storm had sent a sign. He shouted from his raw and aching lungs—to Aiolus! Hephaistos! Prometheus! The gods of wind and fire, of life, his voice instantly snatched away in the salty spume. The blue glow grew into shimmering flame, moving closer over the water. And then he could see it was playing around a moving center, a pole riding in the wind. It was minutes before he realized a vessel lay below the strange apparition and now could be seen steering in his direction. Rough hands hauled him aboard, faces stared into his.

"He's alive. Look to his leg. Bind it." Then, "The others. How many?" This last was addressed to him. The speaker was Aiolian.

Teleo gasped with the pain in his leg, something he had not been aware of before the cold air hit him. He retched and shook with horror and relief. At least he was not going to drown. "Nikos. A Lemnian…making for home…two more…called and called…gold in their pockets…two years work." He hung his head.

"We'll find them if they're here," the captain said and turned back to his duties. The vessel was large and well manned. Even so, the crew struggled to keep it under control. Gradually the wind moderated and the sky became lighter. Teleo was astonished to see the day return and remembered with anguish their morning departure. There would be no homecoming for Nikos. They circled repeatedly and found nothing but pitiful debris.

Noting their location from points off the islands now visible around them, the captain finally put into a bay on Lemnos' northern coast. They built a great fire on the beach in a hollow carved out of the volcanic tufa long ago, a high place to shelter boats and full of dry firewood. This captain knew the coast, Teleo thought in his misery. He tried to speculate about his rescuer, whether he was a pirate or a merchant, but he was too weak to care. He heard the captain give news of shipwreck to someone, saw shadowy faces look at him and shake their heads and go away. Welcome sleep overwhelmed him.

❖❖❖

He woke to pain and a glaring sun. The captain was dressing his leg. He had been bundled unconscious into the stern of a boat and, from the sun's position, they were headed due north. Standing on the horizon ahead of him was a spectacular sight, the highest mountain he had ever seen. Even in the clearing sky the peaks disappeared into cloud cover high above them. He looked a question at the captain.

"Samothrace," he said.

Teleo's heart lunged. It was then he noticed that, under the woolen chiton and heavy cape of the captain was a deep purple woolen scarf, bound in a girdle about his loins.

Samothrace. He could hardly breathe. He fixed his eyes on it greedily, as if he would take it into himself. He felt dizzy and empty, hungry and weak. Desperately weak. He began to shake.

"What is it? What's the matter?" the captain mistook his anxiety for illness. "Lie down. We'll be there soon and you can rest. Keep warm."

He watched tensely. It was a forbidding coastline. His practiced eye could see no landing place, no flocks of sheep or habitations of men, no smoke rising from houses. Firs covered the elevations to the timber line, thick and dark below the snow-patched peaks. On the lower ridges a winter sun washed the leafless woods a golden brown against the sharp blue sky. Sheer cliffs below were like bronze walls rising from the wine-dark sea. Dwarfed by this rough grandeur the tiny ship bobbed along in a cold white spray as the bow plunged and rose in a freshening wind.

They rounded the western coast. He saw one beach, but they did not pull ashore. Further westward and somewhat north of their position was a more inviting island, but they turned east into a broad channel that separated Samothrace from the mainland, that barbarous Thracian coast he had sung about so often. The northern shore of Samothrace looked as inaccessible as the rest, but soon they turned toward shore. As they approached he could see a high fall of water tumbling from a ledge far above, a broad river cascading into the channel. East of it was a small harbor with a sandy beach, their destination. It was still a hard landing in a choppy sea, and the snow began to flurry as clouds moved in. Teleo felt dreadfully sick, and by the time they had beached the ship safely out of reach of the boistrous surf, he was shivering and feverish. He reeled and fell as the men handed him out of the boat. He heard calls from the cliffs above, and in his delirium he thought the Great Gods of Samothrace were coming down to welcome him. As he slipped from consciousness he wondered why they had saved him twice and brought him here.

***

In the struggle to get free of the wreckage, the bard's leg had been torn by fish hooks. They were made of bone and had splintered off under the skin, causing infection in his left thigh, and the bone of his leg was broken. Rope had peeled a strip of skin off, from shin to ankle. He lay under poultices, weak and heavily sedated, as the days and nights ran together. Finally when it was clear that he was recovering, a man came into the small room in which he lay and seated himself beside the bed.

"Life is yours again. Hello. I am Prax."

"Prax?" Teleo raised his eyebrows at such abruptness. "That's it?"

"An old family name. It means 'doer.' My father was Kedalion, 'he who takes charge of sailors,' and I'd put you in his hands if I could. He would know what to do with you." He spoke slowly, not unkindly, with a sober deliberation entirely suitable to his banter. He was lean and weathered, somewhat taller than average and balding.

"Teleokairos Maionides of Smyrna. Yes. Ionian. Well, if you are a doer, then bring me the crew that saved me. I want to thank them all."

"They're gone. They'll be back later, in the summer. You can thank them then. It will be a while before you can travel very far. And everywhere is far from here!" He shifted tone. "Are you a merchant sailor?"

"My family are merchants. I was going to Lemnos to visit for the winter."

"Your friends are lost. I'm sorry. You must not know the north Aegean, being out at this time of year. I came to welcome you to my home. We are hospitable people and will take care of you, even of an Ionian from Smyrna." He smiled and left.

The women that attended Teleo did their work well. They plied him with concoctions, decoctions, infusions, purgations—an endless stream of strange medications and the magical Lemnian earth. Finally, provided with a staff of ash wood, he could move stiffly about the room. It was finely finished with white plaster and with floor blocks of a stone unknown to him, black and dull and very hard. The stool had been replaced by a sturdy chair, oiled and shining, with a soft linen lining to keep his battered leg from further damage. A low bronze tripod furnished light and heat, a small table held water and wine, and in the corner by the door a weathered sea chest contained an extra chiton and a goatskin cape in anticipation of his return to the outside world. He began to wish for it. They finally began to take him down to the hot sulphur springs on the coast nearby, and he became a well man.

He was in the Greek village above the port. It sat on a promontory which formed the end of a north-south craggy ridge, detached from the high mountain; an acropolis sat at the top of this lower peak, shared by all the islanders, wherever their homes were. The latest inhabitants, Greeks, lived in this small settlement and had been there only a generation. He was to find that most of them were Aiolians but not of the same cities, a mixed immigrant group with many tales to tell. Adjoining their village and also below the acropolis, almost making one continuous settlement, was the ancient native town, and it was hard to know how old it was. The island had been inhabited long before the age of bronze. Most of the present residents said they were Thracians, or Phrygians, or Pelasgians, and most of them spoke a time-honored and unfamiliar tongue. The diverse peoples of these two villages, apparently the only settlements on this lonely mountain, lived together reasonably well, perhaps drawn to each other by their very isolation. No protective walls stood between the towns, though there was talk of building a wall down the steep hillside from the acropolis to the beach. The cliffs of the island's perimeter seemed to Teleo more than enough to ensure their safety from outside attack except at that vulnerable spot.

Prax was a leader of his genos and basileus of the Greek village. His house was a village center, larger but not richer than the others. Teleo Maionides lived in one of several rooms that ranged around the outside edge of a courtyard and was opposite the megaron, the common room, where the family hearth was situated. The children of the house and close dependents lived in rooms like his, and the apartment of Prax's wife Phyllis was above the megaron. The altar to the household gods stood as usual in the open courtyard. It was the common island village, somewhat more scattered than those confined by walls. Athena was the goddess of the polis.

Spring was well advanced before Teleo could walk distances; there was little flat terrain. In his days of recovery he had earned his keep at the innumerable winter duties concerning houses and boats, sheep and goats, and assisting the men at the sacrifices. They knew he was a singer, but the village had its own bards and he let them sing. Now he began to make a phorminx to play again, sitting in the mild spring sunshine, the children watching and full of questions.

He noticed two of them, a brother and sister ten and eleven years of age, who wore certain rings. These sacred rings were all about him in the adult population of both towns, but it seemed strange that children might have been entered in the mysteries. He decided it was time to talk to Prax.

"Show me the island," he told him. "I am completely myself again but in a strange place, despite your hospitality. And it is time I told you something. I think I am here at the will of the gods."

"Of course. Aren't we all. And your name means the initiate. Remarkable."

"No. I mean more than that. Sit down. It's a long story."

At the end Teleo said quietly, "The scarf I have is still in Smyrna. I have never believed that it was mine to use, even though it saved me. Do you think, if I had brought it, it could have saved Nikos? Could it have saved my father? Should I have given it to him? I don't understand all this, or what I am to do now." His agitated voice trailed away into silence.

After a few moments Prax stood up. "Let's go for a walk." And he took him to the sanctuary of the Great Gods.

***

"You have waited a long time to see this. It is open for everyone to enter, except for the places of initiation."

The sacred ground lay immediately west of the Greek village. But it had not been visible because town and holy ground were separated by a rushing stream on the west bank of which rose a steep and wooded bluff. This high bluff, upon which the sacred area began, sloped westward and faced northwest across the channel. It was bounded by water on its western boundary too, a small tributary which joined the eastern stream to form the north point of the sanctuary. Still another river, farther west, joined the stream to plunge into the ocean, the river he had seen from the boat. He had been looking even then at the sacred ground and didn't know it, he thought. Here at last it lay before him. He looked around, but there was little for him to see but a series of rock altars of various colors, some in low enclosures. There were two simple buildings, only one of which he could enter. He went in. There were benches along the wall and a circular speaker's stand before them. Nothing else.

"That's all? That's all?"

"What did you expect?"

"But this isn't even as civilized as Samos. Or even Sardis. It's just rocks. It's just more bloody sacrificial rocks!" His old anger began to swell up and sting in his eyes.

Prax turned to him without emotion. "Did you expect an epiphany? Were the Great Gods to be sitting here waiting for you, with ambrosia and imperishable robes?" He spoke evenly, matter-of-factly. "You can come here any time you like. We go this way."

And he led the way inland up the mountain to the south. They passed the necropolis, on the rise overlooking the sanctuary. A fresh grave strewn with wilted wreaths lay in their path and Prax reached over to clean away the debris and smooth the grainy earth, already sprouting green. Then he stood erect and strode up the steep hill southward. Teleo could not speak to him.

***

They walked all over the island during the following days, at first subdued but with a growing delight as spring was coming to the mountainside. Snow had left the icy peaks of Saiion and everywhere silver freshets ran toward the sea. The island, a rough oval shape, was about 13 miles from east to west and seven wide. Its location, in a strategic sea lane, should have made the site important. But the winters were bitter, the storms frequent, the seas violent, the winds eternal, the soil poor, the coast like a bronze wall. It could never sustain a large population, Prax pointed out, certainly not with only one or two usable beaches. But the gods had chosen it for their own, he added, and they walked on.

They tramped about in growing good spirits. The time came when they sat atop the island's highest peak, Moon Mountain, looking all around over 70 square miles of island tumbling 5200 feet below them to the sea. The air was thin and sweet, the pale clear gold of spring mornings in the Aegean. Prax stretched, throwing his arms vigorously upward, and laughed into the sky, a great, exuberant laugh. Surprised, Teleo laughed too; then he lay against the rocks, spreading himself to the sun, listening to their human voices in such a place as this. Prax scrambled about the peaks, with sweeping gestures directing his gaze to the sights before them.

The coast of Thrace stretched across the northern horizon, thirty miles away. On its edge a little eastward a great river mouth gaped toward Samothrace, as if in wonder at its height. It was Hebros, the river of Orpheus. A song began to rise in his throat, even at the thought of that famed singer. Of course. It was Orpheus who insisted the Argonauts be initiated here before setting out for the golden fleece. And it was from this very river mouth that Orpheus' head had floated after his murder. All the way to Lesbos. He imagined the direction of the current and reckoned that it could have been to Samothrace instead.

Prax got his attention again. "The island close by the Thracian coast over to our left is Thasos, rich in gold. The Thracians and Phoenicians struggle there, but I think it will soon be Greek." Its peaks were almost as high as their vantage point.

He swung west and south indicating Lemnos. "You came this way from the south." They gazed at the seas between, where Nikos and his cargo lay on the ocean floor. It seemed a wide ocean to Teleo here, though it was no farther than Thrace. But he had struggled for his life in those waters and the north Aegean here was a living enemy to him, Lemnos very far away.

Prax was talking to him. "Speaking of sanctuaries, one of ours, to the Cabiri, lies there on the coast of Lemnos looking toward the northwest. You can see their fires from Samothrace on festival nights. And they are frequent visitors here." He gazed for a long moment into the distances.

"That is Imbros"—he indicated a low-lying island about half the distance to Lemnos, lying southeast. "We have a sister sanctuary there as well." Then he looked north again to Thracian Hebros. The coast swept east from there into a deep gulf ending in a promontory behind Imbros. "The Hellespont," said Prax. "Now look past the ridge on Imbros. There lies Troy."

Troy! It lay on the horizon, barely visible, but imagination supplied it. Teleo felt fragile, as if the gods had lifted him high into their windy skies, in this delicate morning, and taken him back in time. He saw the plains and the cliffs behind, the bluffs where the city lay. He stood unblinking until he heard the clash of arms. Slowly he began to sing. The wind took his words and carried them away down the mountainside. It was the same wind which had gusted through the ranks of fighters, kicking up sand and dust among the chariot wheels. He sang of the fighting at the ships and of the flames of a burning city, living memories of this very wind. He sang until his voice, cracked and shredded, stopped of itself, and he sank in silence against the great stone mountain.

At first Prax had stood astonished, listening as the battle song raged, immobile as a boulder, staring at the horizon. When the singing ended and Teleo looked for him, he was a distance away, sunk on a rubble of stones, his head covered with his cloak.

"The first Prax," he said as they made their way down, "was a great grandson of Achilles." He had gathered himself from the dust and risen, without words, his eyes swollen, but now he seemed softened and hospitable, almost confidential. "Where did you learn to sing like that? I have never heard such passion."

"Nor have I. I don't know what came over me." He was as surprised as his companion. "I have been making a phorminx." And they talked about manageable things.

✳✳✳

Teleokairos asked Prax about his lineage again at their next meeting. It was this first Prax who had established a sanctuary north of Sparta in honor of Achilles. That was eleven generations ago, he said, and the descendants of Achilles had scattered through the world. But the line was strong in the northern regions of the mainland. There were legends about him too all through Thrace and along the northern shores of the Black Sea. Other descendants were on the northwestern coast of the peninsula. "I am proud of my descent, of course, but I am no Achilles, nor was meant to be. What do you know about Samothrace and the Trojans?" Prax asked him.

"Nothing," Teleo replied. "I guess the two had contact through all the time they flourished. The city of Troy goes back into the age of stone, according to my Lydian uncle, and so do the islanders, to listen to some of them."

"It is a much closer thing than that. The legend goes that Dardanos, the founder of Troy, was born here on Samothrace, and that he emigrated in the first boat after the great flood. So when Troy fell, some of the survivors came back here, seeing it as their ancient home. Some of the Old Village consider themselves to be of Trojan stock."

"That makes sense to me. What songs do they sing about the Trojan war?"

"I can't really say. I have not exactly advertised that my ancestor was Achilles to Dardanians. You understand." He smiled wryly. "But maybe it is time to talk—to sing—about it. I want you to sing for all of us as soon as you are ready. Just don't emphasize the Troy matter too much at first. You know how some Aiolians still feel about Ionians from Smyrna."

"No. But I'm learning."

So Maionides began to sing again. He was out of practice and had to mellow his new phorminx, but it seemed to him that he sang better than ever. He loved some of the Aiolian expressions, and it was stimulating, sometimes even uncomfortable, to sing Ionian songs to these people. He found his own viewpoint tempered by the temperances he made. But he knew, here among Aiolians, Thessalians, Thracians, Phrygians, Pelasgians—and old Greeks and Trojans tied together by the memories of death—that he was not really like any of them. And, though his own heritage was Ionian, he had been tossed ashore there as much as here. So, as his interest in the old stories deepened, in his own way he felt curiously free. He was a traveler in the world, a boundary-crosser, an observer of men, and he touched surprise within himself that he could love equally the men of opposing traditions. His whole life seemed to him to have fallen into such circumstances that he was never squarely on one side or the other. He was not really Smyrnan, not really of a bardic family tradition, not quite a merchant, not exactly a worshipper of Ionian Poseidon. The only thing certain in his life was that the scarf of Samothrace had saved him, not once but twice. Perhaps this was to be his home. It was not his favorite place, lacking the abundance and warmth of sunny Smyrna. But the gods wanted him here. He was convinced of that.

✳✳✳

If he were to be Samothrax, he wanted to know of the name and the island's stories. Had the confusion been deliberate, it could not have been more complete. The island had had a number of names in the past. Originally it had been Leucosia, or Leucania, either because it appeared to be white or because that was the name of the white goddess, Ino. White could refer to the moon goddess, whose name still was used for the peak—or even to the sun. It also used to be called Electris, for here Zeus married Electra, the daughter of Atlas. Or Melite, no one knew why. Others said the island was the home of the Saii, an ancient race—hence, Saoce; or that Samos means "sacred island" in an ancient language. The story that it was settled by Greek Samians 200 years after the fall of Troy was patently false because they had not even got to Ionian Samos so soon. Or it was named for Saon, the law-bringer who was a son of Zeus and a nymph, or the son of Hermes and Rhene. That a mountain was called "samoi" was true, and he privately decided Samos came from that, the mountain of Thrace. There were several Samoses, just as there were several Olymposes.

But by far the most popular early name was connected to a legend he came to know very well. The island, this tale said, was ancient Dardania, named for one of the sons of Zeus and Electra, Dardanus. After Saon had established law there, Electra and Zeus bore two sons and a daughter on Samothrace, twins Iasion and Dardanus and their sister Harmonia. Iasion was killed by a thunderbolt because, enamored of the goddess Demeter, he attempted to have intercourse with her. Grieved at his death, Dardanus built the first raft of hides, for boats had not been invented, wrapped himself tightly in a wineskin, and floated to the Troad. Teucer the Cretan reigned there then, and Dardanus wed his daughter Bateia—or Arisbe—and founded the city of Dardania. After the death of Teucer the region became his, and he established the gods of Samothrace at Troy.

At this turn in the story the bard's interest quickened. This was entirely new to him, learning the old tales of the Trojans, free of much of the Greek perspective.

But that was only the beginning of a great tangle of tales. Dardanus' son Idaeus brought the Samothracian gods to Mt. Ida and into Phrygia, where they were now dominant. Some said that Iasius did not die but ruled all of Thrace while Dardanus left and went to rule in Phrygia. Thus Dardanus founded Ilium, and Iasius ruled over Thrace. Some said Iasius had ruled in Samothrace. Another version of the story held that Harmonia, their sister, married the great Kadmos of Thebes who sent Dardanus off to Asia to Teucer the Trojan, part of a whole cycle of stories about Kadmos and Harmonia, the one that Arctinus had apparently heard.

But this bard was absorbed with the connection between Troy and Samothrace. Remarkable. Sensible. Unsettling. One story said that the Palladion, the sacred wooden cult statue of Athena in Troy, had been brought to the city from Samothrace. Another version said Dardanus had stolen it from an altar of Athena in an unnamed place, that he, his sister, and brother had taken it to Samothrace and he had then taken it to Troy. Still another story indicated that, after the fall of Troy, Aeneas the Dardanian went first of all to Samothrace, took their gods, and carried them with him to Italy. Or that he stopped at Samothrace as he left Troy, to honor the shrines from which the Palladion had come.

Another layer of stories celebrated Samothrace and a Flood, one before Deucalion's, which caused the Hellespont to burst out of the lake of Pontus. It flooded much coast land that has since been covered by the sea, and they said fishermen even now brought stones from ancient cities up in their nets from the seafloor between Samothrace and Imbros. The Samothracians, seeing the waters rising about them, fled up the great mountain, praying to the gods. Their lives spared, they set boundary stones all around the island at water level and still offer sacrifices on their altars to the gods who saved them from the Flood.

It was after the Flood that Saon established the law under which the children of Zeus were born. In this version Dardanus became an ambitious and inventive man, the first to make his way to Asia on a raft. Another said that he prepared the raft to escape the flood and that, when the Flood subsided, Dardanus founded his city, placing it higher than the later Troy so as to avoid floods to come. Teleo remembered Ardys' story that Troy had been built on a bay that now was a plain. Still another version of the story said that Dardanus had only been passing through Samothrace when the flood occurred, that after being carried to Mt. Ida in the Troad on his raft, he was told by his father Zeus to found a city where he landed, at Dardania.

Other stories began elsewhere, placing Dardanus and his family in Arcadia. When the Flood came, some of his people were supposed to have stayed there, while his group became part of a large fleet which wandered the coasts of the Aegean looking for safety. High Samothrace became their haven, but its poor soil and violent sea caused many of them to move on to Asia under Dardanus. And a recent version of that tale had the Latins of the west claiming that Dardanus emigrated from their country or the land of the Etruscans. There was even a story that had him coming originally from Crete. Teleo smiled at this; every hero story he had ever heard had a version that began in Crete—an old joke among the bards.

So the worship there was ancient, going back to the Flood, and the people before Dardanus supposedly sprang from the earth itself, another way of saying their origin was lost to time. One popular tale recounted that when the Amazon Queen Myrina had conquered Asia Minor, she set out to conquer the Aegean islands too. But caught in a storm—he understood only too well—she prayed to the Great Mother and was carried to this island which was then uninhabited and name-less. Here she had a vision in a dream which told her to make the whole island sacred to her goddess, call it Samothrace, and declare it a sanctuary for all peoples. Teleo remembered the Amazon tales of Ionia and thought somewhat bitterly that the worship would have to have changed considerably not to be savage indeed. The Amazons seemed to have been all over Anatolia. But that was a long time ago.

∗∗∗

As he was absorbing all these stories, the curious bard from Smyrna would roam about the island, looking seaward, examine the many boundary altars, and go again and listen. He was not the only Troy-watcher. There was an old man he saw every day when he walked over the island. He was weathered and toothless, but his silhouette against the sky was erect and alert. He scrambled deft-ly along the arete, looking about, scrutinizing every prospect and—after squinting, deliberating, nodding—moving on. They called him the Old Trojan. His family claimed descent from Trojan refugees and, in his youth, somehow he had taken to heart that the Greeks had come again. He had opposed their being in Samothrace, but, when Greeks began to resettle Troy, he was very distraught. He would climb to the top of the Mountain of the Moon and watch the Trojan shoreline. He was there constantly, and then gradually he began to pace the perimeter of the heights facing Troy, on the lookout for—it was never exactly clear what—perhaps landing parties.

By his late fifties he was arming and on watch from the walls of Troy, his grieving family ac-cepting his madness as a divine visitation. He was a living rebuke to the Greek villagers, one that they respected without comment. The boys of both villages laughed at him, played tricks on him, imitating his vigilance, making games of his tragedy. But he was preoccupied with his work, a man of few words. Teleo expected him to be a taleteller, but a sentinel develops habits of silence. To come upon him napping innocently in the sun, on the bench before his door, was one thing; to encounter him unexpectedly on the mountain, rising suddenly out of the mist, his eyes burning and empty of recognition, was to believe that Hector's ghost could walk. The demons of his soul spoke only with dead heroes.

Teleo realized he himself really did not seek a single truth about Troy and Samothrace. He was simply sorting out the tales of what was clearly a mixed tradition. Wonderful tales. The stories of Harmonia seemed to be a favorite topic of Prax. When Teleo had said he had heard of Kadmos the Egyptian, Prax corrected him. Kadmos was Phoenician, he was sure; Tel conceded, not thinking it especially important. Kadmos had come to Samothrace looking for his sister, who was trying to escape Zeus' lust. When he arrived he fell violently in love with Harmonia, and they were married in elaborate ceremonies here on the island. These were repeated every Mid-Summer Day since then at the island sanctuary. Tel would have to come to the festival, Prax said.

After the marriage, Kadmos and Harmonia had gone to Thebes, where Harmonia named one of the city's seven gates for her beloved mother Electra. They had carried the mystery cult of the Cabiri there, where it had flourished, even after the destruction of the Mycenaean citadel.

Teleo heard all of this from the islanders of every age and description, but especially from the singers, for they are the memory of every civilized community. He began to learn the songs sung in Greek, most of them in Aiolian Greek, but the native Samothracian tongue was entirely strange to him. He heard few songs about the Amazons, fearing the world they represented, an early savage time before men's primacy. He still sang infrequently for others, though they clamored for him; they enjoyed his Margites. Among the Samothracians Achilles was the best of the Achaeans in spite of his folly, the Atreus brothers of the Peloponnesos no better than they should be. There was little interest in Odysseus and Nestor.

Hector was the best of the Trojans, though there were other heroes and other stories, even moving stories about the Trojan women. A later rumor that Homer invented the man Hector, naming him for the famous king of Chios, may be true; there may be some tribal connection. Chios had the same people as Troy as early as Troy I, as well as many Aiolians in its northern mountains, which may account for the Aiolian name of the greatest Trojan hero.

The bard also began to listen to more mundane versions of what had happened at Troy from the descendants of the Trojans. In that time, they said, the Hatti people to the east of Ilium controlled all of the land for thirty days' journey inland from the coast, outright or by tribute. The great Hittite king considered the king of Troy to be his ally; if Troy did not pay tribute to Hattushish, the Hittite king, he gave mutual respect.

When the Achaeans—the Mycenaean Greeks—began to seek footholds on this Anatolian coast, the Hittite king expected the Trojan king to oppose the expansion policies of these Mycenaeans, even though they traded together and were descendants of the same distant ancestors, speaking a dialect of Greek. The Mycenaeans had been very bold, establishing flourishing colonies at Miletos and Emporio and in the islands, and trading with Troy. Their raiding parties were harassing the whole coastline, and any these traditions confirmed what any Smyrnan knew, that Agamemnon had confronted the Mysians on the Kaistros to gain a foothold in that fertile valley, even going so far as Smyrna and the baths. A favorite habit of these aggressive Mycenaeans, according to the Trojan tradition, was the carrying off of women for slaves and profit, often the women of important families who were usually of good stock and highly skilled in crafts and management.

According to the Thracian islanders, Alexandros of Ilion—Paris of Troy—was sent by his city to Mycenae and Sparta in an effort to stabilize the political situation in the Troad. This man was flamboyant and charming, an experienced fighter albeit in his forties, and he made a diplomatic stop in Sparta to assure himself that Troy was not on the agenda for acquisition by the Greeks.

He had first gone to golden Mycenae to negotiate with Agamemnon who was loath to give his word without consulting his brother Menelaos; at least that is what he told Alexandros. But Agamemnon sent word secretly to Menelaos that the Trojan prince was on his way hoping to force a peace pledge from them. Menelaos was in a touchy situation himself: he was an aristoi from Mycenae, not of the race or even native to the locale of the city he ruled. He had built a fine new palace for Helen his bride, and had extracted much wealth from the people. And he and his brother's Achaeans maintained such a lavish standard of living that the only way to keep their retinues prosperous was through the booty of war.

So he had to play on his brother's pride and foster Greek aggressions for his own political safety. In order to avoid having to promise the Trojan that he would not fight in the Troad, Menelaos contrived to be out of town on a sudden emergency. When Alexandros arrived for his state visit only to confront diplomatic insult, he had no intention of accepting such a loss of face. So he kidnapped the queen and her retinue, in the fashion of the times, and brought them as hostages to Troy.

Alexandros, sadly, was not a good judge of men, and he brought disaster on his city. The brothers, finding the tricksters tricked, rallied their forces to move against their old allies and ancient brothers, and the feeling on both sides was bitter because of old friendship violated and hospitality mocked. The Hittite king was safe for the moment, while old friends destroyed each other. How Helen looked and how she felt was quite beside the point, according to the Samothracians.

Teleo got a huge kick out of all this, imagining how such a song would play in Ionia. Who tells the tale makes the meaning, as poor Nikos had said. Troy had spilt all the blood of its nobility in Helen's name, and the blood of their Hittite-dependent allies, even his dear Maionians.

Unfortunately for the Hittite kings, after Troy fell the marauding continued, less rather than more civil, more rather than less frequently. Then drought and famine hit Anatolia, and whole tribes were on the move. The system of tribute which had enabled the Hittite empire to flourish fell into great disorder. The Greeks returned to a disintegrating world at home as Dorians invaded from the north, and within a generation the great cities were ablaze and the old warriors were pirates, the major Achaean base being Tiryns of the mighty walls.

So the surviving Trojans had told it to their children. Teleo thought of Tantalos and the guards of the Black Pass near Smyrna. What story would the bards of Hattushish and the Maionians have sung, he wondered.

Whenever he sang about Achilles, Prax and the Greek villagers would beam with pride. Achilles was Aiolian, after all; he spoke their dialect and was a man of the mainland, not the Argolid. He had saved the Achaeans often and shone like a star in the firmament. He was the heart of their fighting force, and all the legends knew it. Had there been no Homer, Achilles would have lived as long as there were Greek singers.

Teleo began to think deeply about this Aiolian hero who even the Ionians celebrated—the golden goddess-born boy, his life as brief as youth. Even the Trojan descendants loved such a warrior, especially since he had been so gloriously doomed. It was Odysseus they despised.

CHAPTER 8

Initiation

724 B.C.E. Samothrace

Prax had never volunteered that he was an initiate of the mysteries. Teleeo knew it because he wore the ring. "You know I must join in this worship, if only to honor the men who saved my life," he told Prax one day as they rested from planting. "When? At the summer festival?"

Prax looked over at him thoughtfully and then smiled. "You can be initiated any time you like. There are two degrees, but you don't have to wait for the festival or for a year between degrees. You may be initiated into both degrees one after the other. But there is a test to pass for entrance into the higher degree, and not many qualify. Everyone is welcome—children, slaves, women, barbarians. How about in three day's time? There are other candidates then. You can be with them."

Such a mystery did not require that belief come first, but that the mind be open to the experience.

No great wall enclosed the sanctuary because its natural boundaries were so clearly defined. One road led to it, not directly from the villages as it would later; it crossed a low saddle of the hill and entered the sanctuary from across the stream at a point almost in the center of the slope. The Temenos, a small walled area where the public festivals were held, was immediately ahead and uphill slightly to the right. In his walks around the island he had come across the road, but he had not entered the sacred ground since that day with Prax.

Four of them, with seven priests in attendance—all men and women he knew—assembled for the initiation at twilight on the bank where the road crossed into the branch. The night would be clear and warm, and the winds, ever present in the day, had died to almost nothing. Teleo wondered what the initiation would hold, and thought about his rescuers. He wanted to honor them, to remember them, to be like them. He made an effort to empty his mind, to be ready to receive.

First the initiates prepared by entering the stream, discarding their garments and bathing in the water, cold from the heights even in early summer. They stepped from the stream onto sacred ground, up a soft bank, to skim oil over their flesh and put on long white robes. Fillets were placed on their heads, circles of curiously wrought leaves and vines woven in a pattern; light veils of transparent cloth, tasseled at the end, were draped over their filleted heads.

There was no talking, and by now it had become dark. Torches were burning here and there along the slope, winking through the foliage and lighting the entrance to each enclosure and building. Each of the four mystes, initiates, was given a lamp to carry, and each one lit it solemnly from a brand held by one of the priests. Cups of wine were given them, from which they poured drops to the Great Gods at the point where they had entered from the stream.

Each was asked to give an oath of secrecy, repeated aloud, individually. The head priest intoned the punishment of swift death, should the oath be violated. Then they drank the fragrant cups and, walking in solemn procession, followed the presiding priest. A single flute sounded from the middle distance, in a Phrygian mode. Teleo was instantly alert. If this were Sardis again, he would run away, in spite of everything.

They entered a small terraced area and stopped. A sheer cliff rose on the right. A high bank ahead of them was walled with cyclopean blocks, huge and carefully dressed and joined, an ancient groundwork older than anything he had seen on the island. Then he was amused at his own thought: rocks are as old as the earth; what can be older than they?

The head priest had turned left and walked up a stairway of large fieldstones, stuccoed over, to stand above them by a shoulder height. He faced them from a surface formed by one huge outcropping of porphyry. Old as the earth itself.

"Yours is not a long and complicated trial by suffering. Many mysteries are, as some of you may know. We consider our entire island to be holy. No person still guilty of pollution may set foot on this island, and you are, as initiates, charged with seeing that it does not happen, regardless of circumstance.

"We are not oracular, as Delphi, nor political, as Delos, nor"—he hesitated—"Greek. The ceremonies are shared among all peoples. The holy language, symbols of which you will see, is a very ancient one."

He stepped forward.

"Every man, woman, or child, of any station in life or any tongue, is welcome here to learn of the Great Gods and receive their blessing—a condition unique in the world. So that these gods will know you, we will visit each altar and present our sacrifices before the initiation itself." He paused several moments, withdrawing into himself, shifting his level of thought and discourse. Then he began again. "This is the altar of the first of the Great Gods, Axieros. Many stories belong to her. She is the sacred mountain." He gestured to the polished porphyry glistening below him. Its groundmass looked like night itself in the darkness, and the flickering lamps caught crystal reflections, like stars in the blackness.

"The stories we will tell later of the Great Earth begin with this altar. Pour a libation and pray now to Axieros."

Each of them prayed and then saluted Axieros with libations from cups provided by the priests and poured into a small channel along the southwestern edge of the polished rock. The liquid slipped away silently into the darkness.

The procession moved along the terrace to a space between the Temenos and terrace, southwest of the altar of Axieros.

They entered an enclosure walled to a height of six feet with elegant red porphyry blocks. The ground was paved with fine yellow tufa around a high rock of blue-green porphyry, all the colors very intense in his consciousness now. They seemed most remarkable.

The priest had stationed himself on a small stand flanking the sacred altar on its northeast side. It was of the same dazzling blue-green but flattened and polished, and the light from his lamp sparkled with the metallic glint of the mountain. The Great Mothers of Asia, he thought, were not half so beautiful as this, and he recognized in the feldspar the rich iron deposits of the sacred island. The priest, alone this time, poured a libation across the high blue mass, and it ran quickly through a pipe between the altar and the stone on which he stood.

"Here we stand before the altar of Axiokersa, the great daughter of Axieros. It is she whose being, whose loss and return, we celebrate in the public rites before Mid-Summer Eve, who in truth is the same being as Axieros but in a transformed state. She is the fruit-bearing daughter of Earth, in her positive aspect the Greek's Persephone. Do honor by placing fruiting vine from your fillets upon her altar.

In her negative aspect the Greek will honor her as Cerynean Hecate to whom dogs are sacrificed."

While the fillets were being handled, each initiate helping the other, he noticed figures moving at the edge of the light, other islanders, the initiated, coming to join the procession. The priest sang a hymn in Samothracian unquestionably to Persephone Axiokersa, as they made their gifts to the goddess.

Leaving this enclosure they went to the terrace at its southern end and grouped around a pit which was dug into the earth. At first it seemed to be of dirt. Then he could see that it was an oven, a circular container made of small stones embedded in clay. At its northern rim was a shaft which ran deep into the earth—20 feet at least—, the bottom of which was a marble stone, scrubbed but still stained from centuries of sacrifice. The shaft was lined with panels of funereal cypress.

"Axiokersos is king of the nether world, a god whose nature is revealed in this pit and its sacrifice." A black pig was brought forward and placed on the small altar, head down as always in chthonic ritual. After the handwash, drink offerings of honey and milk, then wine, and finally water, were made, the barley sprinkled and prayers of dedication made. Hairs were cut and cast into the fire. The pig's throat was cut, and the red blood poured out. The meat was spitted and a small portion placed in the oven. The rest was carried away to the Temenos where the initiated prepared for the feasting when the ceremonies were complete.

"We honor two more altars before we enter the secret rooms." The priest moved swiftly now into a deep glade south below the terrace; the northern-most corner of the Temenos was high above it, the woods were thick around it, an indication of its great age, since trees would not be cut in such a sacred area. There was no need for an enclosure, for the area was bounded by the cliff to the south and the foundation and bedrock under the Temenos ranging southeast. A curving ledge of bedrock formed the rest of the limits, and they stepped down from it and moved before the altar.

But here, where the bedrock could easily have been the altar, it was not. The flattened rock instead was floor for a dressed and polished cube of granite, rather like a herm but squatter. Foundation steps surrounded it, and a wider square stone stood at the eastern corner upon which the priest had stationed himself. A spring flowed through the glade near the cliff wall, its quiet face catching the gleam of lamp and torch. Fieldstone and black sand glistened along its bottom before it ducked into the undergrowth somewhere behind them.

"This is the sacrificial altar of Kadmilos, the fourth of the Great Gods. His nature is not easy to grasp. It is he rather than Kadmos who marries Harmonia in the Mid-Summer festival—or should we say Kadmilos is the secret identity of Kadmos. Kadmilos is both god and hero; his altar is not of the living rock, as those of Axieros and Axiokersa, nor is it the pit of the netherworld deity Axiokersos. His altar is this square, hewn, which rests symbolically upon the living rock below it. This is the altar upon which we sacrifice a ram, placing his head down and then up, to indicate a double nature. It is Kadmilos as god and man, as god in man, the transformative agent, that we honor."

Until this point Teleo had seen nothing new, nothing to challenge his thought, but now he did. He watched the ritual but grasped nothing except the double nature of the god. Be patient, he thought.

After the carcass had been taken to the Temenos, they poured libations on the altar of Kadmilos and set off to the last altar. It lay at a distance, south past the Temenos and almost at the point where the tributary stream came toward them from a curve southeastward under the necropolis. This region was steeply banked at the water's edge. There was a spot here that was naturally below the level of the largest boulders, a flat kind of promontory with no enclosure. Here, surrounded by torches staked in the ground, was an enormous outcropping of red porphyry rock, solid, perhaps 100 square feet of it. On it sat great green porphyry boulders, some over ten feet high and not ten yards from the bank of the tumbling stream. On the eastern edge of the rock mass sat a brown cube of stone about three feet square, its top channeled for libation and sacrifice—the whole area a rugged and dazzling climax in the series of sacred altars.

They sacrificed a goat at the Great Altar, one of the rotae, the wild goats of Samothrace sacred to the Great Gods. The initiates' attention fastened on the chief priest who was completely absorbed by this altar, his intensity extreme. No music was heard here except the rush of water on their right. It seemed almost to be below them and made them aware of time and motion, of continuous movement, of endlessness.

"You stand before the altar of the Great Gods together. Its size and complexity then should be no surprise to you. To honor the gods all together is not the same at all as honoring them separately. We have named only the first four; there are others here. This altar is especially dedicated to the Cabiri. As we think on this, we go to the hall where the secrets of initiation truly begin."

✳✳✳

After the outside, where torchlight had only increased the surrounding darkness, the Anaktoron, initiation hall, seemed like day. All in the procession set aside their own lamps as they entered, blinking, and were conducted to the lustration basin in the southeast corner. Teleo looked about him, adjusting his eyes to the unaccustomed brilliance.

The hall was rectangular and plain. They had entered through doors cut in the middle of the long west wall. The only other doors were double ones at the top of a bank of steps on the north side. Benches lined the long east wall, and he realized that they were filled with people, robed and quietly waiting. A round platform stood before the benches, holding a single empty seat. Huge torches, in wall sconces and floor stones, flamed all around the room. After lustration the ceremony began.

"The stories of our public festival lie at the core of our belief. They are true and are to be revered. They are like divine stories everywhere—having a literal meaning and also embodying other layers of image and concept. The uninitiated hear a story for the tale alone and experience delight. They are led toward acceptance. The initiated experience the deep structure of the tale, and a delight that is inexpressible to others. It speaks to them of their own nature and of the design of all living things. We will reveal here the nature of the gods you have acknowledged—and who now acknowledge you—and then we will tell and retell the sacred stories. You have come to see what is revealed here and in the secret chamber"—he gestured toward the doors at the top of the steps—"and to join us.

"Whatever names we give to the gods depends on our birth, for the gods are everywhere. The ancient names used here are important for us to keep because they are not familiar to your cities and so can embody more than a name already laden with associations. But the clusters of powers which these names represent are familiar to you. Axieros for the Greek mainlander has much the same power as Demeter, or Kybele for the Ionian"—he glanced toward Teleo—" or for others. She may be a savage goddess in many places; do not be scornful, for in her rawest, earliest form she <u>should</u> be that. For she is NOT the greatest god; she is the FIRST god. She is the FIRST god from which a world is begun. Axiokersa, the second, whom she seeks and finds, is her own transformation into fruitfulness."

He picked up the torch blazing beside him and held it above his head. "In this second form earth becomes FIRE." As he flung up his other hand in a gesture of epiphany, he let loose a handful of matter, and the torch roared into a ball of exploding flame, then died back to burn, a steady fire, fierce and red. "For when Axieros becomes two, she becomes herself and other, and duality begins."

He spoke again, more slowly. "The heat of divine Axiokersa, seeking union, is so great that she must be banked, by WATER, the essence of Axiokersos, their marriage both a unity and a paradox. Such a divinity is qualified by banking, by subduing, by death. Axiokersos in this sense is the god of the netherworld, the promise of death, the twin and inevitable opposite of life. The tears of mourners are signs of this meaning.

"But Axiokersos is not the only god of the underworld. He has a positive nature as ecstatic as his consort's, his own other side. He is the father of the life she generates in nature and, transformed by desire, he is his own child and hers, as she was both her mother and her mother's child. And so he is his own second birth, as Dionysos is to the Greeks. There are many songs to Axiokersos and his double nature. The underlying harmony of these two can be obscure, a mystery, as is the harmony between Axiokersa and Axiokersos, between Axieros and Axiokersa, as well as all dualities, or opposites. The symbol of the principle of opposites is the Kabiri, the twins of Samothrace. As the Dioscuri—their Greek equivalent—they are not identical, but they are a unity which returns harmony into being."

He told all the old stories over again, beautifully, against the mimed actions of dancers; to the music of flute, of phorminx, bull-roarer, drum, or tambourine. The story of creation, of the fall into opposites and the coming of death, of the harmony of which each living creature and all non-living elements of nature are a part. And as he spoke the bard from Smyrna listened in peace and admiration.

The spiraling dancers, weaving and unweaving existence, subsided, and the priest spoke in the echoing hall.

"The fourth deity, Kadmilos, is known publicly as the servant of the gods, a hero-divinity. But the Great Gods are an evolving sequence, each in a sense embodying the others and becoming more. As Zeus, for example, in swallowing Metis, took all she was into himself and made her part of his nature, as separation, union and metamorphosis take place, the last god is the highest god and embodies all unities and opposites before him. He is higher and more complex than they. The fourth god Kadmilos is like the Greek god Hermes; his name means 'herald of the coming god.' To herald greater things is not to be a servant; Kadmilos is that complex agent which brings the human spirit into the world, which brings awareness of one's self to each of us, which is consciousness itself. The spirit is air, is thought. It transforms the world. Hence he is the profoundest god for humanity but not the first in time, for the first three gods create our world and mortal bodies.

"Kadmilos is herald, herald of all the gods and the promise of all that human beings can come to understand. That is why he is the creator of language and music, of communication. In the purest sense he is the great boundary-crosser between all dualities. The gods that have followed him and will follow him—for there are many gods and goddesses to come—will be gods of the consciousness, of intellect, of action, of the city, of the higher range of human accomplishment in all its forms and concepts. So we on this island welcome <u>all</u> gods of <u>all</u> societies that they be worshipped with understanding and respect for their powers, and be given honor by human kind.

"By the nature of duality, each power can be both destroyer and creator as long as opposites exist in the world. We anticipate the higher gods to come, without fear, and not forgetting the ancient deities.

"The Pattern, the great secret of Samothrace, is yours now. Let us reveal the sacred objects which show forth our belief."

The ritual priests and mystes, initiates, walked to the step and waited at the foot while the priest ascended and turned to face them. "You enter now the most sacred place in Samothrace. Go into the door of mystes, the suppliant." He indicated the door on the right. "When you leave that other room, you will be initiates. However often you come into this building, you may never use this door again, for it is the entrance into knowing. An old world, of old conceptions, will be left behind when you close it. I must go through this other door, the portal you will use hereafter. Each of you must enter separately, opening and closing the door thoughtfully for yourself, repeating aloud the vow of secrecy."

It was such a simple action, to open a door, and yet to Teleokairos it was momentous. All actions are truly this important, he told himself as he watched his arm reach forward. His touch was alert to every texture in the elaborate knob. The look of the doorpost burned into his memory. He opened the door, and closed it on all that was behind him.

✻✻✻

Inside, a long table stood against the far wall, flanked by many pots of greenery. No bloody sacrifice, no libation cups, no music. His body loosened. The table held a number of objects. At the center was a highly polished black herm, squared and exquisitely proportioned. On either side were golden pillars around each of which a snake of green malachite was coiled. Before it lay a polished tortoise shell larger than any he had ever seen and translucent, as if lit from inside.

On the left, where the mystes were stationed, was a row of metal plates—gold and silver, copper, tin, and iron. The priest spoke. "All, in the form of ore, can represent the power of the Great Mother who bore them. Then, forged by the fire of Hephaistos, they are melted down and made separate, each with its own true nature transformed into liquid. With the fire of the gods they may be mated together and transformed into new natures useful to humanity. The purest nature, gold, is combined with silver to form Elektra, the mother of Harmonia, harmony between earth and sun. The plain ore of iron, separated by fire united with fire-transformed living matter of wood or bone, and tempered by water, is transmuted into steel. Or touched by the power of the Great Mother—Magnetite—it can draw all other iron to it and impart its power to that iron. The herm which you see before you has that magnetic power. It is shaped from the sky-stone which fell from heaven, and it shares the power with other lodestones across this sacred island.

"The lodestone has been squared, to indicate the four directions and the power of the fourth god Kadmilos who now gives his secret to mortals. He is the god, like Hermes, of this concrete and conscious world of being. A fragment of lodestone will point your way to the four corners of the earth, for it always points in the same direction. To the north. I will demonstrate."

He stepped to the center of the room with a thin bar of iron suspended on a golden chain; he spun it several times, and each time the arrow came to rest pointing to the north. "The arrow always points to the polestar at night. You will never be lost again, on land or on the trackless sea, for sky and earth will guide you in harmony. This is the stone of the ring of Samothrace."

Next he stepped before the tortoise shell and asked the initiates to join him. Teleo looked closely to see the shell, dotted with twinkling points of light, apparently made by light shining through tiny holes bored in the surface. The sections of shell had been outlined in silver, as had figures in each section of the carapace. "This tortoise shell represents the night sky and the stars of the constellations. The priests of Samothrace do not prophesy, but they can read the seasons of the earth in the heavens and help the wanderer home. The Pattern they know is in the shapes of the constellations, in the myths they represent, telling the secret of earthly powers in the heavens." Carefully, patiently he instructed them on the meaning of the constellations and the harmonies in nature that each represents. "You will find the Pattern everywhere, even on the tortoise as it crawls upon the earth." He explained the divisions of the day into 24, and the divisions of the starry sky into the 24 sidereal graces. The 24 of time and timelessness. The Pattern.

"The tortoise shell also becomes, in the hands of Hermes Kadmilos, the sounding box of the lyre which through its sacred nature gives to the hands of man hymns to the gods, harmony made manifest in music and number." And he sang a hymn to Kadmilos, his voice as clear as a bird's song, a lyrical pattern of sound in a melodious unknown language. The bard from Smyrna wept; he did not know why. He wished Theophilos could hear.

They were told how the harmony between earth and sky rests in two sets of symbols, the snakes of the earth and the stars of the sky carved on the silver ring of the priest. "There is power all around you in the earth and its living creatures, to be released by knowledge of the higher gods. Hard-won knowledge men must struggle to find. Plants with god-like powers surround you—here are some of them which even now the priests can use for healing." He gestured at the display of greenery and carefully, patiently, he instructed them.

"All these numinosities represent the harmony between gods and mortals, earth and sky, planets and stars. And the ring of Samothrace, made of the sacred lodestone, is your symbol and protector." He held the ring forward for all to see.

"How deeply you comprehend the secrets only you can know, for you are bound to silence, even among yourselves. It is permitted to talk with priests, and you may attend initiations for this degree here or at other cult sites of the Great Gods if you wish to deepen your understanding. The ring you will receive will be your entrance sign."

As Teleo closed the door behind himself and stepped into the assembly room as initiate, he was greeted with dancing and singing. Hands reached up to take away the veil from over his forehead, and he was led as a king to the circular stage and enthroned in the midst of song. The high priest placed the sacred ring with its magnetic stone upon his finger and led him, now symbolically united with the gods and in harmony with all being, down into the circling dancers to join in the welcome of those initiates after him. Then they all swept out of the hall and up to the Temenos where the feasting began. In the midst of the high revelry, he saw in the eyes of others—or thought he did—a communion of knowledge, and he knew he would never really be alone again. What beauty he saw in the gods now.

As the last cups were toasted to the new initiates, he knew the sacred herbs were in his portion, and he welcomed them. He left the sanctuary, his head blooming with visions of the creation of the world, of the Great Gods of Samothrace, of the highest and sweetest deeds of nature and humanity. His eyes could see in the darkest night as if it were day, and, without having to find his way, he raced into the forests of Samothrace, up to the very heights, singing passionate music to his gods.

CHAPTER 9

Making the Iliad

724 B.C.E. Samothrace

If there were a time when he could say the Iliad began it was then. Dawn was coming when he roused himself and looked around. He was sprawled across a large outcropping of feldspar, rust-colored and glittering, almost at the top of Moon Mountain looking up into the face of a rosy sky, as pearled as Aphrodite's shell. The dawn held him as it grew. Only gradually did he become aware that he was looking toward the crust of continent to the southeast, its dark line cutting across the horizon between the sky and milky sea. He was looking at Troy, at Ilium, from the peak of Samothrace just as if he were one of the gods. This is how it must be for them, he thought. How remote the anguish from such a seat as this.

How long he gazed he did not know, his sharp memory reliving every instant of the night, always circling back to the Pattern. The pattern held him, like the lodestone, like the stars and the snakes of Hermes.

Dawn faded into day. The red sun rose over the Hellespont and climbed into a brassy sky. He bestirred himself only when the heat began to scorch him. With aching bones, his clothes sodden from the dews of night now steaming under the sun, light-headed from the height and the revelry, he started down the path with a stiffness alien to him. Gradually it left, and he felt like a disembodied spirit moving across the face of the mountain.

No one else was near. He paused to listen, but in the strangely quiet air nothing moved except the wrinkled sea below him. Glittering on the distant coast was the bluff of Troy. He stopped again and again to look. Then without eyes he found a smooth seat in the rocks, shaded from the sun, and sank into a timeless reverie, his mind open and alive, his vision on Troy. He imagined it all, all the songs he knew in all the versions he had remembered. The embassies and landings, the catalog of ships, the savage turmoil on the plains below this most magnificent citadel, expeditions under cover of night, the immense effort of the Horse, the final fire. And the gods watched from such an eminence. Why, what kind of gods were these?

He thought of Smyrna, out of sight down the coast, seen from such a prospect. The great glory of his grandfather, taking the city by stealth and, under the guise of the satyr, using the women in their beds. He tried to sort out how these women must have felt, the same old Aiolian women that he knew. Their children had Ionian fathers, and he realized for the first time what had happened to their older Aiolian sons. He remembered the endless accommodations of the Lydians, the stone warriors of the Hittites still standing in fruitless vigil, even while he was here, thinking on this island of all of the Great Gods.

Troy became real to him. Greeks and Trojans, certain of their honor, of their gods, committed to their instants of time and full of love for their generations, fought for Ilium in the full sight of their gods, and they are gone, in the wind. His aching heart swelled to overflowing. The tears began slowly, then flooding down his cheeks and spattering on his clothing, saturated his chest and loins. He wept

as a woman weeps, her arms folded about a loved husband who has fallen with his people, fighting to keep ruin from city and family; as he suffers and dies she wails aloud as the enemy beats her with their spears, dragging her off into slavery where grief and toil will mark her face as long as she lives. (Odyssey Book 8)

At last blessed sleep overcame him.

The cold woke him up. Stars were wheeling through the sky. He felt as if he had aged a generation since the initiation. As he stirred he looked toward Troy, but there was only darkness. The wind of the heights could not reach him here and he decided to wait until the moon rose, for the photosensitive drug of the previous night had worn off.

When the outer eye cannot see what is before it, the inner eye awakes. Men were as unique as gods, and both were limited, but mortality was the only tragedy, the limit of time and space, the limit of man. The choice to limit that strength to youth and fame the noblest folly of all. The only hero everyone on Samothrace wept for was Achilles, his tragedy and beauty greater than any wisdom. And most dangerous. For his wrath was the spirit of Ares, elemental as the water of Axiokersos. Of Scamander the river. Of violent death. The enemy of the Greeks. The enemy of harmonious action.

Exhaustion hung in his flesh, his eyes ached, his body throbbed from listening with every pore, every sinew. Slowly he sensed a strange harmony, a pattern he let into himself, that pattern his soul had been seeking for so long. Parts of him were distinct and independent, visible in and of themselves, but they were functioning within a pattern, whatever name the priests had given it.

Teleo dozed again and woke. Shimmering into his mind out of sleep came TheophiIos of Kolophon. What had he said about Hermes? He strained to remember. It was Kadmilos he meant, the number Four. The number of consciousness. Then Hermes sent the singer a thought that would change all of the time to come.

Out of nowhere, Teleokairos Maionides trembled with a new recognition: the epic hexameter was another manifestation of the divine harmony! His song was part of the mystery! Theophilos said that once the epic utterance had been only four feet, each of four-beat duration. It had combined much later with a dactylic dimeter to make the present form! He had thought nothing of this at the time, but now it was fraught with meaning. The basic truth, the reason-for-being of the epic hexameter, the six-feet utterance, was the 24 beats, the same 24 as the temporal hours, the same 24 as the sidereal graces of the stars. The same 24, he thought incredulously, as the 24 letters of the alphabet without the digamma and koppa! The new style! The alphabet of Hermes. Hermes the boundary-crosser. Knowledge had risen from sleep to his feverish brain.

His heart was pounding. How could he have become a master of the epos without understanding why its rhythm existed in the form it did? He had been a child, imitating without understanding. He had sung and not known what he did. The harmony of the basic fours in music and poesie, the beats that transmuted them to the 24 of the utterance, were part The Pattern. How beautiful. How gloriously simple.

He began to laugh aloud for the sheer joy of it, the delight of knowing. Suddenly too he knew what he would do. And so good a thing to do. He would compose a song of 24 parts, each corresponding to the 24 of the hexameter utterance, to the temporal and eternal sky studded with its majestic constellations. He would pattern a glorious song to the harmony of the cosmos. It would tell a tale of harmony lost and restored. Not of Troy and its doom—he could imagine he saw it lying out there in the darkness. No. It would be about Achilles, the favorite of Samothrace.

Men of later ages would attribute the break into 24 books to the Alexandrian scholar and librarian, the first Homeric critic, Aristarchus. He may indeed have done so, but he was not the first. And, of course, Aristarchus was from Samothrace.

Teleo, who had been soaked in sweat, now became chilled to the bone. A shiver ran through his body. He thrilled at-what? His boldness? Dare he change the old songs? Who would listen?

The Samothracians would. But such a long song would be impossible. How could he sing it? The Pattern was the issue. He knew he could never sing again as before. The enormity of what had happened to him began to rise with the moon, as his old self as singer fell away into shadow. The island lay below him washed in silver and black.

The Muse would help him. And the Samothracians. They were dear to him and they loved Achilles. Rash, glorious, wrathful, tragic Achilles. It would be a song of his life, not his death. Of his wrath and his recovery from it. The song could not end in death, however present it was.

***

When Prax found him at home the next morning, he felt great relief. He had missed the bard after the feast and searched for him, then and during the day. It was not unusual for an initiate to disappear onto the mountain for a day or two. Nevertheless, each of them was relieved to see the other doing simple morning chores. Not to talk of the mysteries was painfully unnatural but they had sworn an oath. They understood each would avoid the other for a few days and let the mundane world steady them again. Teleo packed his bag with food and wine and went with his phorminx onto the mountain, not returning until after nightfall.

Prax was busy preparing for the Mid-Summer festival. Sacrificial animals had to be penned and fed special diets, the sacred area cleansed and sprinkled daily. Boats came often now to the small port: the islanders were importing food and drink enough to supply the festival visitors, though the regulars knew to bring their own. Camping areas were staked out for the overflow, but many came to stay with relatives in houses bursting at the seams.

Teleo was sharing his room with three others, two nephews of Prax from Macedonia and a priest from Lemnos. The boys were refreshing to see. So young, he thought. He enjoyed the new faces. The stimulation of fresh audiences every night demanding songs, some of them his, seemed wonderful to him. His mind was teeming with the composing he was doing daily on the mountain, but the festive atmosphere of the villages pulled him back to the present. The festival was upon them, and he wanted to experience it all.

It was like so many mid-summer holy times beginning at nightfall two days before the solstice, the crowds assembled at the Temenos. The first night was a re-enactment of the search of Demeter/Axieros for Persephone/Axiokersa. There was miming after the narrative, and everyone searched the mountains, by torchlight, participating in the public ritual themselves. Dancing and feasting followed until dawn. Everyone slept most of the next day, reassembling for the Dionysian rites of the second night. Ecstatic, orgiastic, like the public festivals everywhere, revelry resounded over the mountain as the dying and resurrected god was acknowledged. There was nothing remarkable in Samothrace, as far as the public rituals were concerned, and in his state of mind Teleo had expected more. But the celebrated marriage of Harmonia and Kadmos would end the festival the next day. He had been instructed to meet for it with the initiated, who held a secret ceremony of their own.

At mid-morning almost everyone succeeded in arriving at the acropolis where the wedding procession would begin an hour before noon. The youngest virgin past puberty among the island's families was dressed to represent Harmonia; one of the heads of the native families, this year Halys the Phrygian, was Kadmos. After making offerings to the city shrines on the acropolis, the couple led the wedding procession down the spur of mountain, along the familiar pathway now strewn with flowers, towards the sanctuary. Crowds of celebrants, accompanied by flute and harp, sang the marriage songs that celebrate the union of earth and sky and praise the sun, bringer of fertility.

They would arrive at the Temenos precisely in time for the ceremony of marriage to take place at high noon on the day of solstice, when the sun stands still and time is conquered. The initiated followed at the end of the procession until a certain place, where they turned aside into the over-hanging trees and disappeared. Teleo followed with them into a deep ravine and thence to a cavern, so different from the brilliance and color he had just left that it was a shock to him.

Led by a priest, joining hands to keep their bearings, for there was no light, they walked in the black, echoing cave. It resounded with their steps. No word was spoken. The revelers should have reached the Temenos by now, and he wondered what he could experience here that could be equal to the harmonious union taking place below them. The darkness was absolute.

Suddenly a shaft of light shot down from above, making a brilliant circle of light before them. It came through a slit in the ceiling at the instant of high noon and struck an altar of plain black rock upon which stood two metal statues of Kadmos and Harmonia. They were decked in shining wedding finery and crowned, Kadmos with the gold of the sun and Harmonia with the moon's silver.

The statues rose majestically and hung before them in the air, suspended between invisible forces of the lodestone and the rock that fell from the sky, together united in an unbreakable union. Millions of dots of light sparkled in the alcove all around them, what seemed to be a great crystal chamber of stars. As suddenly as the eye had grasped these dramatic images, just as suddenly the light was gone and they were plunged into blackness again. The instant when the sun stood still before reversing its direction, timelessness in time, was past.

Now they could hear music swelling. The flame of torches came from behind them. They left the chamber and, following a short tunnel, burst suddenly out onto the rise above the Temenos, to find the gay celebration spread out before them. They were pulled into the festive crowd and were soon dancing and feasting, breathing the sweet air of high summer.

***

It was at this same festival that a new passion came to Teleokairos Maionides, and his life on Samothrace was changed. How much the Iliad had to do with it, or it the Iliad, even he would never be able to say.

She came on a ship from Thasos, the woman of the bard Ligyros who had come to sing at the festival. He first saw her on Midsummer afternoon, dancing at the Temenos. Why the flash of her white arms and the pale blondeness of her hair, moving in rhythm in the lambent air, were a miracle to him he did not know. He could remember thinking of the love goddesses Ardys had told him of, the ivory and gold of their statues come to life before him. It was something in how she moved. She could not have been fifteen, yet her carriage and the fullness of her body sang of man's touch and her joyful knowledge of it. He forgot everything and, as if alone, followed after her through the throng trying to see her face. She was Kylein of Thasos.

When Ligyros sang, Teleo did not listen to him through his own senses. He watched the face of Kylein and saw the music there. She astonished him. Her eyes, as deep a blue as the summer sky above the mountain, were naive and generous, indifferent yet warm to all the attention that she drew. She listened completely, with her whole being, and he envied Ligyros that she looked at him. Under her gaze, Ligyros sang divinely.

That evening when Teleo began to sing he hoped she would be there, but she was not. He felt he lacked an audience, though the courtyard was packed with listeners. Out of his longing he chose a hymn to Aphrodite, smiling to himself at the irony. But as he sang it grew for him. He was singing it with passion he seldom felt for it, closing his eyes as if he prayed to the goddess in his song, as if he prayed intensely. When he turned again to the audience, she had come in and her gaze was turned toward him like the full moon on the water, falling like a blessing on his music. She was listening as completely as she had that afternoon, and his song rose to meet her. His song began to soar as the long evening fell. He had never sung so sweetly. A dove settled on the wall beside him. He felt the warmth of the torches' flame. And as he sang to her a blush washed over the face of Kylein, warming the flesh of her neck and bosom. She did not look at Ligyros again.

After midnight, as Teleo lay on his bed awake, a shadow moved into the moonlight at his open door. Without words Kylein came to him, slipping her silken chiton to the floor, waiting for his hands to touch her, her blue eyes deep as the wine-dark sea, a soft smile on her swelling lips. The hymn he had sung to her echoed in his blood all night as she sang the fleshly song of Aphrodite, full of her pleasure and her passion for him. Kylein had found a worshipper who could reflect her own passion, her own beauty, and she took him without a backward glance. Ligyros went back to Thasos alone.

✳✳✳

The pattern of the monumental tale Teleokairos was planning was based on the hexameter line, each foot having four beats' duration—one long, two short beats. The diaresis of the line—when both foot and word end together at a pause—was one of the traditional places of emphasis within the utterance. It occurred also at the end of the ancient epic foot of four; consequently, bards would place the most important event there. Deciding what that event would be required a careful plotting of all the song. If his theme were the deepest loss of harmony in Achilles and among the Greek armies, it would have to fall at the death of Patroclus and, ironically, at the highest point of success for the Trojans. The greatest distortion of everyone's true fate. Yes. That death would sting Achilles to action, to superhuman action. He would become like another Ares, reaching almost to his god side. The change would come at Patroclus's death, at the end of the sixteenth song, the end of the ancient fourth foot, at the bucolic diaeresis of his monumental poem.

Now he thought about the caesura of the epic line, which would have to fall after the first or second syllable of the third foot, in other words, at the ninth unit of his song. The point of Achilles' deepest error which would bring about this great disharmony. The Embassy. The capitulation of Agamemnon and the beginning of Achilles' truly isolating anger. The suit for peace—for harmony restored—would gain pathos in such a position.

Most important, he could not end his poem with Achilles' death. That was another subject. It had to end in harmony. And he must end the utterance with a spondee, two syllables of equal value. Well. He would give one syllable to the Greeks and the other to the Trojans. Two funerals. Of course. The two funerals that the wrath of Achilles had caused—the price of his anger. The funeral of Patroclus. And then what? That of Hector. Another funeral? No. That would be too close a repetition. No one would listen. His last syllable could include the funeral; but it had to be the return to dignity, even in death, of Hector and a wiser Achilles. No; Achilles could not be wise. An Achilles able to be human.

As the weeks passed into months Teleo began to sense how the song should move. He would sing it in four-part units, each with its own interior four-part design but linked to the harmony of the whole. He wondered if the Muse would help him, if she had been with him on the mountain at mid-summer. Had Hermes released the plan into his head, his own Muse might be jealous and might not help him sing. The terrible danger was that he was asserting himself in this song, not opening himself to the Muse's inspiration as he had always done before. He trembled to think of the risks he took.

The wildness in him, the akrasia, rose up in his defense. He knew he could do it. Here on the sacred island, for the Samothracians. Some of them would understand what he was doing. It would be his gift to the Great Gods.

The Iliad of course had begun a long time before, with the first song of Troy. The tales were so numerous that to sing them all was a lifetime's work, and he already knew a great many. In the Greek cities of Ionia, perched on the edge of a vast and alien continent, the Trojan—the Other— was to be feared and hated, but in this mixed island, the tales had to include the Trojan sympathetically, and the Aiolian too. But, more than that, his initiation had brought him to the place where the multitudinous lays of Troy were much more than entertainment. Here the fashioning of language in old forms was no longer his over-ruling passion. Men had changed since Mycenaean times. The great tales still tied immigrant to homeland, but not to the worship of the past. Implicit in the epic heroes were the seeds of their destruction and that of their culture. Implicit in Achilles was his change from god to man.

The Great Gods had taught both Tel and his audience—for most were initiates—that men are responsible for their acts, that they can no longer blame the gods for every flawed action of their own. He suffered through a process of seeing the need to make this clear. That did not mean his characters would be distorted. Nor the events. But the audience's way of seeing them would. Who tells the tale makes the meaning. He knew that the songs needed now to reflect not only the flaws that brought down the old time, but signs of the qualities his own times needed to value. And the lay was too short, just too short, to do something so complex. So he found reasons in his head for daring in his heart to make a new kind of lengthy epic poem. Who tells the tale makes the meaning.

✲✲✲

To live as he had all of his life, surrounded by as many shrines and gods as there were people, overwhelmed by their variety and particularity, was the common experience of his time. Out of all of the gods, each polis had officially recognized certain ones and honored them with festival, bonding their civic life in a loose order of sacrifice. Still, every mountain and river had its own deities. In the face of such abundance was great confusion. Families had their own gods, too. But here in Samothrace there was a great clarity born of generosity and intellect, not of rejection and conformity. There was room in the world for all of the expressions of deity, but there was also a Pattern, one that looked forward, a struggle toward something new. One that demanded effort. He knew that here he could not glorify Mycenaean tradition as an ideal in his songs. Neither here nor in Ionia were people like the Mycenaeans any more. Nor were their gods.

In the Iliad he had no need to sing of Demeter, Persephone, Hades/Dionysos, for they were the Great Gods who come before the cities. Their worship was certain, so basic to simple survival that their cults would flourish everywhere. In the Iliad he was interested in these higher gods, these Olympians of the Greeks, the constructs after Hermes. Were they still fragile things in the minds of men?

Perhaps Hephaistos was not. He was a maker of things, as Hestia was the maker of the hearth fire. But Hephaistos was in a radical state of change, with the rapidly spreading iron technology and the commerce he was generating. What secrets, what new gifts would this god think of next? He was the child of Hera alone, of the earth alone, but Zeus had adopted him because of his spirit and cleverness. He was ugly and lame, not Olympian in appearance. It was important to show that. One foot seemed to be of metal or stone, or perhaps diseased from too much labor with copper and arsenic. The Olympians were not really comfortable with him. He was a god of material metamorphosis, a transformer of one thing into another useful to man. A close friend of Hermes.

It seemed to Teleo that when he looked at the gods past Hermes, the cluster of powers and inventions they provided were so concrete, so tied to the functions of daily life in the city, that the gods were inevitably drawn to human actions themselves. Just as the gods of the pastures were shepherds, a goddess who invented weaving was a weaver. Hephaistos was a craftsman and Hermes crossed boundaries. They became activists themselves. They became people and visited among men. I will sing of them as people then, he thought. Not the great creation deities before consciousness, nor the god of the irrational—Dionysos—for they are all too numinous and inexact. But the gods of the city and warfare: The inventors, the ship-builders and traders, the singers and athletes, the fighters and sailors are there looking over our shoulders and coaching us. If I play better, the Muse sings through me, and Hermes made my phorminx. It is easy to think that the man who stops at a forge to suggest a new design can be Hephaistos himself, especially if he is an old coppersmith suffering an arsenic infection.

The culture gods can be like men and women; they must be imagined in that way if their true nature is to be understood. And I am free, he thought happily, to present them that way to an audience in Samothrace who know as I do that they are evolving forms, real, but imagined in the ways we need to imagine them now. Poseidon and Zeus are difficult: not creation gods, not necessarily civilized. Powerful. Natural forces, even vital enemies. The works of Olympian city gods go down before thunder and flood, earthquake and tidal wave, just as those of mortals do. They are destroyers of cities, just as mortals are. Poseidon Seabluehair is in a class alone. Certainly to me he is, thought the castaway poet.

As the summer wore on and the Iliad took shape, the gods of the cities of men became to him gods of freedom and beauty, identical to the men they watched over in every respect except two: They were shape-shifters and mortals were not. And they were immortal. That made all the difference. The gods could not change fate. Yet individual gods could act in opposition to that fate for individual mortals. There has to be a pattern of hope for us, he thought, a duality between immoveable fate and moveable gods. In honoring them, we become more noble ourselves, perhaps more noble than they—because there is no risk in their choices. They pay no price and thus must seem to have a certain divine indifference to suffering.

It would be fun to sing his gods to the Samothracians. He could not remember exactly when he realized how very long a song he was making. It seemed to happen naturally. By late summer he had gone back to perfecting short episodes, but every day the pattern of his monumental poem possessed his mind.

The Iliad was not a spontaneous song which fell unconsciously from the lips of a trained tale-spinner, unchanged for centuries in its meaning. Its length alone would betray its unique purpose. Its design, its pattern, was an important part of its meaning. It was a song for the Trojan as well as the Greek of a new age, its spirit that of the new spirit, its themes disharmony, and the fatal flaw of being mortal.

He remembered the Gilgamesh story, told at Kolophon and Sardis and everywhere in Anatolia. In it the goddess' son is doomed to death, too. It tells of the tender friendship between Gligamesh and the nature-man Enkidu and their brotherly exploits together. The terrible lamentation of Gilgamesh when Enkidu dies, after dreaming the council of the gods, his search and the acceptance of his own death that brings him back to the city of man. Was this the tale of every people? The council of the gods and a mother who is a goddess were ultimately of no more use to Achilles than to Gilgamesh. And that story was old when Troy was flourishing.

***

Never had he such a summer, nor would he ever again. His daring to make such a new kind of song seemed to him to have been rewarded by the gods with the gift of a Kylein, whose body turned to him like a flower to the sun whenever he came near her, whose gaze accepted all his music as her own reflection. "You are my Muse," he told her wonderingly, smoothing her tangled hair as it lay against his arm. "When I sing, your eyes hold me in thrall. Has my old Muse abandoned me and sent you instead? Or are you my Helen?"

Kylein kissed his calloused fingers and leaned over him, baring her breasts. "You are the one who needs to sing. I am the one who needs to hear. It is simple," she smiled as she welcomed him into her body. He sang divinely that summer, even as he began to discover that he could not really think out his patterns under the gaze of his enchantress. He had to do that planning by himself, that arranging and sounding out. He had first to make his song of Achilles alone. He found himself wishing for his cave on the Meles, and seeking out the wilds of the island again.

He sang the Iliad everywhere on Samothrace: in the caves, often on the mountain looking toward the poor lost city. As mountain dwellers see a stable natural world that changes in time, as sailors perceive a timeless one that is always in motion, he sang as one on a mountain surrounded by water. He threw his voice into the eternally windy skies. He created a world and wept for it. Under the fire of Helios, out of the implacable reflection of the moon on the mountain, by sheet lightning on the horizon, firelight, and the blue memory of the mastfires of his saviors, he planned the pattern and sang it. On the black sands that stuck to his robes, the red and green porphyry, the light and smoky tufa and heavy grey limestone, by the altars of the Great Gods, he composed. By dark cave and sacred stream he struggled with his conceptions. They rushed through his mind like the mountain torrents, glittered in the rock like feldspar, flashed like the wings of seabirds in the sun and soared above the crags on columns of air. They burned in the wind that had fanned the flames of Troy. He was living with the people of Achilles now, Aiolians. With the founders and refugees of Dardania. And they watched him work from the bottom of their hearts.

INTERLOCUTORY

The Voice of Letha Gooding

A word with you now about the Greek gods, especially the Olympians, the family of the Iliad. The surprising thing is how sensible and complete the Olympians, as a description of a culture, turn out to be.

You would accept my statement that there is physical energy present in all perceivable phenomena, either latent or actively being expended. But you wouldn't accept my statement that this energy is "divine," a congregation of spirits capable of taking on human and other forms? That is the basic difference between you and Homer. If you think, by the way, thet you can ignore or discount this energy, that it does not affect you, then you are the one who has the poorer understanding.

But back to the Olympians. The "inherited conglomerate" of gods by Homer's time was immense, of many species, classes, generations, people: creation gods, underworld gods, daemons of localities and families, adopted and adapted gods, demi-gods and heroes, and of course Olympians. City deities, seasonal, developmental, healing generetions of gods of all kinds of people.

A Bureaucracy of Divinities! Jealous of their space, arbitrary in their exercise of power, these very qualities assertions of their strength. I like that term, "inherited conglomerate" (a bow to Gilbert Murray). It predisposes you to the natural complexity of any belief.

That Homer was devout no one seriously questions. The Conglomerate permeates his world and he lets it speak for itself in every tale he tells. It is his Olympians, his culture gods of the Iliad, that are so memorable, so human. Maybe they become human when they become political; they are certainly that, in the epic and the world that followed it.

Maybe they become human at their pleasure in the competitive sport of warfare, where they sit like fat cats in the press box on Sunday afternoon calling the plays. That pleasure echoes in the games of the great festivals.

But back to ourselves. If deity is power, then worship is the acknowledgement of that power. It seems to me that the Olympians plus Dionysus make a satisfactory pantheon of all the social and psychological forces of the Greek city. Remember that the Olympians are not creation deities; they are second and third generations of consciousness, most having to do with human activity and the forces that affect human activity. Each god represents both constructive and destructive manifestations of some power, and each god rules over a complex cluster of ideas associated with that power.

Of the dozen or so Olympians, six are children of Kronos and six or seven are their children, the next generation. Of the oldest generation the three men are much more powerful than their sisters; in fact, they divide the cosmos between them: Hades the underworld, Poseidon the sea, Zeus the sky, sharing the earth. Demeter retains only certain agricultural functions. Hestia, guardian of the sacred hearth, becomes a passive if potent force. Hera alone in Homer achieves a fully human personality among the women, colored with the machinations of the disenfranchised, retaining only the power of prophecy; the sisters are the Great Goddess divided and conquered. The oldest myths say that the most powerful god, Zeus, is the youngest, the one who restores life to the others who are now in his debt. Homer makes him the eldest. These are the natural forces upon which human society depends.

It is the children who reveal the Greek's self-portrait: Aphrodite and Ares are elemental, often interactive passions in a society—sexuality and physical violence. The culture gods hate Ares, but blood-lust exists in every human nature, to be acknowledged and hence controlled.

If you were a pagan Greek, in your worship you would acknowledge these powers and recall their usages through story and sacrifice: You would honor Aphrodite to acknowledge the power of sexuality, for good or ill; Athena for intuitive wisdom, the sense that creates ands runs cities, ships, battles, manufacture; Apollo for abstract reason and the disciplines of the arts, medicine and mathematics which it generates; Dionysos for sensuality and irrational impulse, a part of every psyche. You would acknowledge in Artemis the goddess of ecological balance, the protectress of continuity and the young in nature—the cultural Other of her twin, the educated, artistic, civilized Apollo. In attending the festival of Hermes you would honor the great agent of consciousness itself, the boundary-crossing faculty between living and dead, of communication and realized experience, with his tools of language, music, commerce. Homer would include Hephaistos, the lame step-child of Olympos born parthenogenetically of Hera, the craftsman of substance, the metallurgist with the wealth of the earth at his hand.

What I'm saying is that if you put all these Olympians together in their positive aspects, you have a design of the cultural values of the Greek polis, both external and psychic values. In their negative aspects you have a design of those forces they would most fear. The stories of their triumphs and conflicts are truly human. Any god ignored will distort the psyche and the polis. Lovely? Absolutely. I just had a great idea for the reorganization of the university:

The College of Aphrodite—sexuality. Note: every student majors in it after hours.—why not count it honestly as a double major?

The College of Apollo—mathematics, philosophy, fine arts, PE, medicine

The College of Ares—criminology, martial arts

The College of Artemis- -natural sciences, especially ecology and veterinary medicine, nursing, elementary and secondary education

The College of Athena—political science, industry, law, military strategy

The College of Demeter—agriculture

The College of Dionysos—psychology, religion, the performing arts

The College of Hades- -theology

The College of Hephaistos—architecture, engineering, applied arts

The College of Hermes—languages and literature, communications, commerce, history, inter-disciplinary studies

The College of Hestia—home economics and sociology

The College of Poseidon- -physical sciences. Zeus would have his tenure here, lecturing in geography, meteorology, astronomy

You may have noticed there is no College of Hera, for she is the ghost of the Great Goddess whose original powers have all been divided among the rest, leaving her only a jealous (read powerless) but desirable (when she borrows from Aphrodite—read powerless) woman. Nowadays she would rule over a small program in Women's History and Pre-Consciousness.

Your worship would be study. Your duties would be instruction. The essential sacrifice? Would of course be you. The myths of this university would describe the growth and interaction of the colleges and would define the society at large. Where education has been failing today, the ancient Greek would tell us, is in graduating a student from one college only. The Greek, the humanist, if you will, would point out that the gods will get you for that!

Of course, these are not the Great Gods. Homer cannot tell you that great secret.

CHAPTER 10

Singing the Iliad

724 B.C.E. Samothrace

At the approach of autumn, as the year matured, love with Kylein was still an early summer, answering for Teleo all his akrasia, the seeking for a satiety that lay on the edge of endurance, a fulfillment that—even so—needed to promise more. When he performed she listened with her whole being. She did not need to talk to him about it, accepting his songs wholly. "Doesn't my tale of war appall you?" he had asked her once.

"Oh, not your tale. It is a war, after all, caused by Aphrodite. Fought for Helen's sake." She looked at him clear-eyed and sure.

He glanced away. "Born of the discord of Zeus' making Thetis couple with a mortal she did not desire."

"Yes." She brightened. "The discord is Achilles. He was the child of that marriage. It was natural then."

He looked up at her sharply. "What a curious wisdom you have, after all."

"Me?" Kylein laughed, delighted. "No. It's just that all the songs are about power. Power gives access to beauty."

"Then beauty is the best man's reward?" He looked away again.

"Of course." Kylein added, "When will you sing of Achilles' loves? And of Pasiphae? That I long to hear."

The bard began to feel a strange ache in his heart.

***

The pattern of separation and return was an old one in epic, and he defined the fates of all the warriors in the Iliad with that in mind. Simply put, they either killed or were killed, never to return home. Anything in between—wounding or escape—was part of the plot of divine intervention. The lives of the women were also defined by separation and return; in fact, the return of Helen, Breseis, and Chryses was the motive of all of the action.

The great change that the Iliad made lay in the transformations that took place in the lives of the men, not of the women. His whole epic existed to trace the transformation of Achilles into a mortal. The half-divine Helen would deepen and suffer, but she could never change, going in passion to the bed of Paris at his least admirable moment, never dying.

Still, Troy was the city of Ares and Aphrodite more than of Apollo. The women of Troy, though potential prizes, had feelings that the audience would hear of, and their peril would provide a motive for action on both sides. Heroes both Greek and Trojan spoke of women as prizes, his Achilles greedy for such spoils and proud that he had sacked two dozen cities to get them.

***

It was Prax to whom Teleo came for comfort when he first heard of it. The goldsmith, a Pelasgian of the old village, had made an armlet for Kylein, a spiraling golden serpent with green eyes, and she had gone to his workshop and lain with him to thank him. "He's a scrofulous old buzzard!" he raged in his anger and disbelief. "How could she do it? I'll kill him!"

Prax gentled him, soberly. "For making something beautiful for Beauty? She cast her spell on him. How is he any different from you, my friend? Did you think Kylein was not generous to her worshippers?"

She came to him that evening, as usual, to hear his song and enjoy his passion. He never spoke to her about the goldsmith, knowing now that Aphrodite led her by the hand. Gradually, as others gave her miraculous gifts, she bestowed her body like a blessing on them all, and then came back to listen to the bard. Every man began to envy him, and his heart began to warm to Menelaos. But she was not Helen, for Helen understood. This woman gave him, along with her joy, a sadness he could not throw off, and his song took on a melancholy strain.

It was with the first frost that a small fleet of warships out of the Black Sea dropped anchor at the beach under the sanctuary. Cimmerians on an exploratory expedition, they were resplendent with furs and glittering jewels and shining steel weapons, marvelously wrought. They had heard of the Great Gods from the Thracians and had come to be initiated before returning home, for they desired protection on the sea. Heaping treasure on the sanctuary, they brought to the last night's feasting their own golden cups and exotic singers.

It had been at the dancing that the Cimmerian prince Xandros had caught sight of Kylein of Thasos, her white arms flashing, her pale golden hair floating in the lambent air. She could not have been sixteen, yet her carriage and the fullness of her body sang of man's touch and her joyful knowledge of it. He forgot everything and, as if alone, followed her through the throng trying to see her face.

At the farewell feasting while his bards sang, Xandros, full of passion, presented Kylein with a golden necklace hung with lapis and carnelian and filigreed with doves. She listened to his suit with her whole being, and a blush washed over her face and across her neck and bosom. She did not come to Teleo's bed that night, going instead to the black Cimmerian flagship where her pale and tangled tresses fell like a blessing along the leopard skins and shaggy arms of a prince who would conquer Phrygia, deep in her passion and pleasure without a backward glance. By daybreak they were standing out to sea.

The men of the villages mourned her going, for their own sakes and in sorrow for the bard who fed on her attention. It was with misgiving that they gathered that night, uncertain whether he would appear. A ripple of relief spread through the room when they saw his familiar figure in the doorway, when they saw he smiled and hung his phorminx on the pillar, to feast and drink as usual. And his song delighted them: he sang of the loves of Ares and Aphrodite:

Let me tell you of the first time Ares made love to flower-decked Aphrodite. It was in secret, in her marriage bed after he had showered her with many precious gifts. But few secrets are kept in Olympos—Helios, post-haste, told Hephaistos he had seen them making love in Hephaistos' own bed.

Cuckolded and wounded, the god of crafts fashioned his revenge. He spun a net of chains, so fine no one could see it, not even a god. Then limping home, he hooked it on the ceiling over the bed, ready to drop at his command. Announcing he was off to Lemnos, his favorite place on earth, he left. Ares, on fire with love, fell into the trap, hurrying to see Aphrodite, who had just come home from visiting her father Zeus. Without a thought they hopped into bed to enjoy each other, and the trap was sprung. Tightening the invisible chains so that there was no escape, Hephaistos held them there and invited all the gods to come and see the spectacle. He cried to Zeus to return his bridal price for such a shameless wife.

Of course, the gods came swarming to the scene, except for the prudent women. Poseidon and Hermes came, and Apollo and all the others, gleeful about the cunning trap and how the crippled god had fooled the strong one. Apollo turned to Hermes, asking, "Tell me, boundary-crosser, if you were shackled in a bed like that, would you sleep with golden Aphrodite?" And Hermes cried at once, "O Apollo, would that I could! Triple the chains, let all the gods and goddesses look on, and I would love to sleep with golden Aphrodite!" (Odyssey Book 8)

When the song died away there was an instant of silence. And then laughter and applause began and would not stop. For only a moment the bard watched them wonderingly, and then he joined in their laughter. It was a marvelous evening. Many a man on Samothrace went to bed that night convinced that he had slept with Aphrodite, smiling broadly at the memory, and Teleokairos Maionides was one among them.

✳✳✳

Winter came swiftly then. Killing winds shrieked through the sanctuary. The ravines were smothered in snow. A cold, grey, impossible ocean churned around the island. On the rare sunny days village life struggled on, but it was soon clear that this would be a winter spent in the caves. Just as people in the southern islands retreated into cool caves in August, the Samothracians lived in the caves in severe weather, going to the villages only for necessities. There was one particular cavern, well drained and spacious, where the villagers feasted together. A great fire was built, well back from the tunneled entrance, flaming brightly, fed by air from stream channels far in the mountain. Signs of habitation were here—no one knew how old—ledges along the walls, fire platforms, sconces for torches in the flooring. The temperature was constant and well above freezing. Life became communal in this dark and frozen time. The altars to the Great Gods, despite the threat of food shortages later, burned often with sacrifices, and the Samothracians feasted while they could.

It was here, in that furious winter, that the Iliad was first sung in its entirety, in a rough pattern at first of a song or two each night. In later years, the many times he sang the Iliad in marble megarons, standing on patterned mosaics in the full light of summer sunsets flooding the world with color, Homer would remember how it began the night of the winter solstice, a night that was longer than the day. In the great cave, with all the island's people now full and content after feasting, with the animals settled for the night and most of the children asleep on their pallets or their mothers' bosoms, Teleo had taken his phorminx up and stood for a moment watching the firelit faces turned up to him. It would be a terrible winter, and though they did not fight on the plains of

Troy, not all of them would live to see spring again. With a somber flourish of strings he began: "I sing of the wrath of Achilles..."

The song opened, as it would close, with an old man coming as suppliant to a great warrior to beg for the return of his child. The first would be refused and last would be granted his sad wish. That first irrational refusal would be echoed in another refusal, when Achilles would deny Agamemnon's embassy. The tragedy of the two refusals would bring the death of Achilles' dearest friend Patroclos and the death of Hector, leading finally to that last granted plea when Achilles would release the body of Hector to Priam. So this first refusal and the argument among the Greek heroes was bitter and ominous.

But the gods in this opening song brought absolute delight to his listeners. The great Apollo, angry at the mistreatment of his priest, came down from Olympos to wreak vengeance with a plague. When Teleo sang of great Apollo kneeling down and shooting—heroes? no, the mules and dogs—surprise and amusement welled into the faces around him. As he sang of Athena snatching Achilles by the hair to keep him from great stupidity, there were chuckles of delight. At Hephaistos hobbling around mocking Hebe at the banquet of the gods laughter rang through the cave. These gods would be entertaining, relieved of the sober business of trying to stay alive.

Their antics made bearable—or more unbearable?—the terrible folly of the Greeks' assembly. As the fatal argument between the best of the Achaeans developed, Teleo saw in the faces around him their suffering at Agamemnon's blind vanity and Achilles' noble but childlike anger. That anger would lead his goddess mother to exact a promise from Zeus, to give hardship to the Greeks who had scorned him, a hardship the consequences of which Achilles would bitterly regret.

The magic of the bard took every imagination out to that familiar beach. Now shrouded in ice and torn by the tempest's fury, for them it twinkled with the glow of campfires beside the black ships, moored stern to the land below the walled city. When he finished the first song—such a mixture of discord and delight—they would not let him go. They would not sleep, wanting to hear more. It was only then that he understood how he could indeed sing his whole story to the islanders. The gods had sent the time.

A surge of energy caught him, and he began the second song, opening with Zeus' charge to the Bad Dream to go to Agamemnon and deceive him. He sang dramatically, half playfully, leaning in imitation over the body of a sleeping man as he sang the words of the Bad Dream leaning over Agamemnon: "You are asleep, son of Atreus, lord of many horses!" Laughter danced around him, waking the sleeper as he blinked up at the bard. As he sang of the waking of Nestor and of the gathering, he added a simile dear to their hearts—"They were like a great swarm of bees, coming endlessly out of a cave and hovering, droning, in clusters over the flowering fields." (Iliad Book 2)

The similes he dropped into his song reminded them of life again, of other seasons and other seas—the Icarian sea in a sudden squall, the west wind over a wheatfield. But he reminded them of this world too, the noise of the sea when breakers thunder against the rocks, the loneliness of a man away from his wife for a month unable to get home because of the tumultuous winter ocean. He reminded them of the leaves and flowers in tens of thousands, of the swarms of flies over pails of milk in the springtime, and they smiled when he sang of the wildfowl over the Kaistros, turning to the woman among them who had been born there.

Here where the descendants of both sides sat around the fire, he told of both Greek and Trojan.

He sang of Nestor advising each Greek tribe to fight as units but together, tribe supporting tribe. After that he formally introduced the familiar catalog of Greek forces, the long and glorious listing of the fighters and their strength. It was the same old list as always, describing the forces in the order of concentric geographic circles; each man listened carefully to be sure it was true and complete as he had heard it, and of course it could not be.

But then he surprised them with the marshalling of the Trojans, an addition he had learned much of after coming to Samothrace. When he began with Dardanian Aeneas, a shout went up among the old villagers, and as the name of each ally was sung, it was echoed by a voice or a brandished cup or weapon. When he came to the Maionians, to the Gygian Lake and Mt. Tmolus, he honored them with a sweep of strings and dropped a tear in their memory. As the catalog ended, every soul in that cavern had been captured by the new song of the bard. No one wanted to hear more that night. Instead each went to his sleep full of the dreams of an ancient home.

❀❀❀

Teleokairos Maionides rested his voice the following night, but the next he sang his third song and his fourth, very different from the first two but following the same emotional pattern, and his intricate plan of balances.

He began with the armies advancing in great clouds of dust "as thick as a mountain mist creeping from the south." People huddled closer, remembering as he sang that "shepherds fear it, robbers love it better than night; a man can't see a stone's throw ahead." They expected a battle next but found instead Menelaos and Alexandros/Paris face to face in single combat. Alexandros recoiled, and his brother Hector berated him for cowardice, saying the Trojans should have stoned him long ago for enthralling Helen. When he sang Alexandros' reply, excusing himself because "You can't throw away a god's gifts, offered unasked, which none could win by wishing," many eyes smiled with the memory of Kylein still fresh among them.

The hope that the single combat between Helen's two men would end the war brought Helen herself into the song. Teleo sang of her trip to the walls to watch the duel and her hope that Menelaos would win. Here he dropped in the traditional descriptions of the Greek heroes as Helen identified them to Priam the Trojan king, giving physical presences to them to complete the psychological portraits of the nights before.

He developed the combat through the first exchange of weapons, so skillfully that suspense sat in every eye, and the wistful hope even now that the war could have ended honorably there. But Aphrodite intervened again, spiriting Alexandros away to the bedroom of Helen where the goddess charged Helen to accept him in love. Helen, at first anger, asked the goddess, "Will you spirit me away somewhere even further off, to some city of Phrygia or Maionia, where you have another friend among mortal men?" Teleo wondered as he sang of those familiar places why he had thought of them. It was to a Cimmerian that Aphrodite had given Kylein, and he could not have known that very prince would conquer Phrygia and Maionia. But the Muse had given him his words and knew things the bard would never know.

He ended the song with Menelaos striding angrily through the ranks of red-faced Trojans, while Alexandros raged with passion among the hills and valleys of the exquisite Helen. Then he sang Agamemnon's boast, "Take notice, Trojans and Dardanians and allies! Victory lies with my brother...and all the Achaians raised a cheer." Whoops of hilarity rang through the cave, cheers and whistles and laughter. Everybody loved it. A time of dancing began and couples disappeared into the darkness, reminded by the song.

It was well past midnight before they settled again to hear the second song of the evening, already used to the expectations of a serial song. This fourth song was a sober change from the earlier one, opening with the gods drinking and watching the battlefield from their golden palace. Teleo was bringing his audience back to the serious matter of warfare, reminding them that Hera and Athena favored the Greeks, reminding them that Zeus had promised Achilles' mother that he would make the Greeks suffer for Achilles' sake, reminding them that Zeus must manipulate Hera and Athena into some folly. He dropped into Hera's speech a grim reminder that Argos and Sparta and broad-avenued Mycenae would be sacked, cities dear to her just as Troy was dear to Zeus. Reminding his listeners of how much indeed this war would cost them all. And Athena was ordered to break the truce.

In mockery of the true hero's weapon, Teleo described the history of the bow of Pandaros, the Trojan who now broke the truce at the urging of Athena. Pandaros was persuaded to try to kill Menelaos for personal rewards from Alexandros. In elaborate detail, he recounted the treacherous act, the placing of the iron-tipped arrow, the well-placed shot which did not kill because of the intervention of this same Athena, the reaction of Menelaos and his kingly brother to the wounding, the summoning of the doctor.

At this point in his song suspense was high: the only fighting—the abortive exchange between Alexandros and Menelaos—had been framed by the shots of Apollo's plague bow and the treacherous shot of Pandaros. He was readying his audience to hear true warfare, exciting them with foreplay, disgusting them with the "long-distance champion" who fought with the bow instead of the sword. In all this song, with its fine description of arming and wounding, of brotherly concern and medical treatment, he dropped in two similes from his own life, the memory of Herophile sweeping a fly away from the sleeping boy, and the memory of the stained ivory cheekpiece for horses that Ardys had treasured. And now he could feel the tension mounting in his audience. They were ready for a battlescene, and he would give it to them now. Almost now.

First he roused them by singing of how Agamemnon passed among his troops, challenging his leaders to warfare—first Cretan Idomeneus, then the Ajaxes, mindless, already bristling for a fight, and Nestor the wise man, who was arranging his armies tactically, sensibly. Odysseus, whom Agamemnon slyly insulted, responded in anger. Diomedes listened patiently while Agamemnon goaded him with his father's exploits. Sthenelos, however, was angry and cried, "We are better men than our fathers" who had died of their own rash folly. Diomedes then put it another way, reminding Sthenelos that victory or defeat would be at the feet of Agamemnon, thus reminding Agamemnon of his own responsibility, a neat and calculated reproof the point of which Agamemnon never understood.

And now the audience and the Greek army were ready for the slaughter. Long similes of massive movements and the terrible sounds of war rumbled and crashed through the cavern. The terror of killing, each man's individual death, burst into the mind of each listener as he heard of his own mortality:

Antilochos struck first, killing a Trojan champion in the first rank, Echepolos Thalysiades. He struck the man on his plume of horsehair, and the bronze spearpoint ran through his skull; darkness moved across his eyes, and he fell like a tower in the confusion. When he fell Elephenor caught him by the feet, Elephenor Chalcodontiades captain of the Abantians, trying to drag him away to strip him of his armor; but not for long, because his own side was uncovered as he stooped, and so Agenor ran him through with a spear. Thus did Elephenor lose his life, and over his body there was a savage war, Trojans and Achaians leaping like wild animals, struggling with each other.

Then Telemonian Ajax struck down Simoeisios Anthemionides, just a youngster. They called him Simoeisos because he was born beside the river Simoeis, while his mother was on the way from Ida with her parents, tending their flocks. He would never repay a son's debt to the parents, for he died as he stepped out in front of Ajax, struck on the right breast at the nipple, the shaft running all the way through his shoulder. (Iliad Book 4).

He sang of the death of Leucos, friend of Odysseus, struck in the groin, and the retaliatory action of Odysseus, who killed Democoon—"The spear pierced the man's temple clear through, and darkness spread over his eyes; he fell heavily, crashing down in his armor." The Trojans gave ground, and Apollo rallied them, while Athena rallied the Greeks. Diores Amarynceidos was struck by a jagged stone thrown by Thracian Peiros Imbrasides:

The cruel stone smashed his right shin entirely at the ankle and he fell backwards in the dust, reaching out both hands to his companions as he breathed his last, for Peiros ran up and speared him through; his bowels gushed out and darkness spread over his eyes. But as he sprang back, Aetolian Thoas cast his spear, piercing the lung. Thoas ran up and pulled out the spear, then drew his sword and sent a fatal thrust into his belly. But he could not strip the armor, for the other Thracians swarmed round him, topknots bobbing and threatening pikes at the ready. They drove him back, staggering, and reeling and falling. And these two lay in the dust together, Thracian captain beside the Epian as many others died around them. (Iliad Book 4)

The hush after his song ended was a profound one. They had had their taste of blood. All went to their beds late that night, their minds full of death, Trojan and Achaian sleeping now in the same cavern as the snows relentless and silent fell in the deep night of winter.

***

What can be said of that singing? Those who still love the Iliad do not need to know more of that miraculous epic in another's words. Those that do not know it have something astonishing to look forward to. Not just in the work itself. The bard could not know that through the centuries wonderful commentaries would grow up about it, written by the best of minds in polished, engaging, civilized discourse. A lifetime of pleasure would exist in reading the words of these men and women, the world's best company of spirits. They would celebrate the bard's skill in formulaic composition, in the deep patterning of character, in voicing the exquisite joy and pain of life, of struggle and death. They would explain the subtle patterns of ring composition that give shape to the units of song and weave parts of the whole to each other. They would find infinite pleasures in the sound and sense of his poem, in the sure, brief strokes with which he could create a life. As he did with Patroclos. A line from his boyhood explained him, for he had accidentally killed a dear friend in sudden wrath; what dimensions, then, became present in his death? Teleo could tell of each death with a detail that suggested a life that could have been lived had it not been taken by war. How many lives and lost generations did the wrath of Achilles suggest to the Samothracians?

And when the song was over Teleokairos had transformed the glorious war tale of Troy into the profoundest plea for harmony, the most clear-eyed sense of the tragedy of mortality, the most terrible recounting of the paradox of human consciousness that anyone would ever hear.

**

And so the Iliad came into being. All winter they talked of it, sang it in pieces, argued about it. All the singers learned it, adding their own traditions. The language was rich and clear and direct, the syntax simple, the similes lovely and part of their lives. Hot arguments raged about battle tactics, especially the use of chariots—but no one felt obligated to resolve them. What they didn't understand in the tradition they kept, thinking someone would know why it was there. The ragged cruelties of the old epics became softened a little, for after all, times had changed and men were more civilized than in the heroic age. Still the war was brutal and grim, and it purged the listeners' aggressions even as the dust of fame settled on the armor of dead heroes.

By the time the snows began to melt, the Iliad was old news. It belonged to every Samothracian. As spring came to the mountain, every soul climbed the peak to look again at Troy. And so the day carne when Teleo, with other singers to spell him, sang the whole Iliad at the spring festival, dividing it—at the Embassy and the death of Patroclos as he had envisioned from the start—into three days singing.

The effect of the singing of the Iliad on the Old Trojan was memorable. In the cramped quarters of winter he had stayed close to Teleo, listening intensely, nodding, interrupting, weeping. Now with life returned to normal, he began to follow the bard. He left his post frequently now and would sit by his side as he practiced. He began to walk along with him, not speaking, just being somewhere nearby—to the village, to the sanctuary, to the hot springs and rivers, to the gardens and the port, up the mountain—everywhere. Sometimes he could be heard singing for himself. He would chuckle to himself over some private amusement. But his eyes were wild inside.

" That crazy old man is driving me nuts," Teleo told Prax. "What am I going to do?"

"I don't think there is any harm in him. He loves you. But be careful. You are Greek, after all."

"Do you think he is crazier for hearing my song?"

"Who knows? Your song inflames his feelings and that could be dangerous. But the fact that all of us now talk about his favorite subject makes him feel closer, I think. Not so alone. I think he's happier. And the children keep him company now, treating him like an old warrior. I just don't know."

Once a messenger came running to Prax. "Help! The Old Trojan is below the sanctuary fighting the river. He thinks he is Achilles."

"Achilles!" They were astonished. "A Greek?" The men laughed at the vision. But Prax jumped up and in one fluid motion was racing down the path. "Don't let him kill the sacred fish. Stop him!"

But it was too late. When they arrived he had already found the pond and, knife drawn, had plunged into the enclosure, stabbing at the startled fish. They flicked around him frantically, flashing, while he staggered and slashed, raving in red-faced fury.

Never had Prax moved more swiftly. He had reached the raging man before anyone else was even in the water and he hurried them all out, his face ashen. The old man was exploding with anger, his throat arched and his head flung back, his mouth agape, possessed by hysteria. He had seized a fish and crushed it against his naked thigh, shaking and screaming unintelligibly. Prax grasped his arms from behind and flung the fish loose and onto the ground where it lay stunned and gasping, its head split.

"Stop! Don't touch it!" Prax shouted as Teleo had leaned forward toward the fish. "It's sacrilege!" and he flung the babbling man aside and stepped between them and the fish. "To touch him is death."

"All right. All right. I won't." He looked at the dying fish. It was a red mullet.

"The fish has been polluted and must die. The pool must be cleansed and rededicated. We must offer a sacrifice to the Great Gods. Take him and leave. I have work to do." He spoke quietly, drained by his efforts.

The Old Trojan was unmanageable, rolling around on the rocky hillside. As they struggled to get him up, he broke away and began racing at breakneck speed through the sanctuary and into the woods above. They tried to follow, but he was running at incredible speed, dodging obstacles and jumping over low scrub at a rate that defied them. He disappeared from view, but they could hear him raving in the forests above. Prax said, "Let him calm himself. He will be all right unless the gods want to punish him. If they do, you cannot help him."

The old man came back a few days later, apparently much as before but quite a bit happier. He said that Hermes met him on the mountain and gave him a root that would protect him from danger. And that the gods had decreed the fall of Troy, therefore the Greeks could take little credit for it. He did not go out on guard duty for quite a while after that.

Teleo looked thoughtfully at Prax. "I was like that once. The night of the initiation. The night before the Iliad came to me on the mountain."

"Yes." Prax looked into his eyes. "Only the Gods know what their touch will release in a mortal."

"It was the red mullet."

Prax said quietly, "It was the tale, Teleo. The mystery is the tale that we tell."

"Who tells the tale makes the meaning. That's what Nikos said."

"Exactly."

CHAPTER II

The Scarf

723 B.C.E. Samothrace

Autumn came before Maionides asked for initiation into the second degree.

The rites began at sundown with the sacrifice of a ram on the boulder altar before the Hieron. The Hieron was a long narrow building with a porch of columns, a recessed entrance, and a curved short wall opposite the entrance, a peculiar-looking structure of mud brick and very old. Teleo and three others were directed to wait at the Temenos to be called forward individually.

A Corinthian trader was taken first. After twenty minutes or so, what seemed to be an eternity, Teleo was tapped on the shoulder and told to follow. The priest was Prax. Teleo moved quietly behind the robed figure, watching the heels and the proud and level shoulders of his wise friend, thinking it would be painful not only to fail to be accepted but also to be diminished in the eyes of a loved one, for he did love this man.

They came on the east side of the Hieron to the Bathras, the place of testing. Two flat square stones lay near the east wall, a large torch burning between them. The torch was seated in a stone in the ground and had carved on its shaft the twining snakes of Samothrace. The Corinthian captain was not there.

Prax turned to him and exacted the oath of truth; as always, when one took position on the bathras stone as witness or accused in a public trial or ceremony, he pledged to speak the truth. Then the priest would invoke the presence of the Great Gods. Teleo mounted one stone and Prax stepped onto the other.

"It is required of you, if you wish initiation into the epopteia at Samothrace, that you answer satisfactorily to certain questions. First, have you received initiation into the first degree of the cult of the Great Gods?" This formally, perfunctorily.

"Yes. "

"Next, have you sworn solemnly never to reveal the mysteries you have learned?"

"Yes."

"Who are the gods we have invoked here?"

He paused for only a moment. "I have sworn never to reveal them."

The eyes of the priest danced for a brief second. "But I am a priest and I know. You can tell me."

"Then you do not need for me to tell you. I have given my word to the gods."

"Why do you desire this initiation?"

"Because there are things I do not understand. I have heard that men who have seen the mysteries are better men afterwards, and I would be a better man."

"Do you believe that knowledge will make you better?"

"I do not know. I believe that not knowing will not make me better. Perhaps this mystery is not about learning..." He had talked too much and fell silent.

"Are you a pious man now?"

"In the eyes of the gods who can say. I believe I am as pious as a man like me can be." He had sounded complacent rather than honest and he regretted it instantly.

"What is the greatest misdeed you have ever done?" An answer spilled to his lips and fell back again. Amy, of course. Or Theophilos. His father. He mumbled,"That is hard to answer."

"The gods demand an answer."

"I fathered a divine child and have lost him. He was stolen by Phrygians and I have not looked for him." Teleo began to burn with shame, surprised at how he felt and that what he said was so near the surface. There was silence and expectation. "In my youth I mocked my Lydian foster-father to my Ionian friends, for their approval." Further silence. "I did not get home before my foster-mother died, and I know I broke her heart." His heart ached as the words tumbled out of him. "I left my mentor Theophilos while he was sick and wanted me to stay. I came out into the world to seek a lost father when I had three good men who had taken his place—three who I have criticized and not properly mourned for."

He stopped a moment, then struggled on. "I know that I am the best singer of all, and I am proud of it. I do not think it is wrong to be proud. But I caused the deaths of Lemnian sailors which I might have prevented had my thoughts not been filled with gifts and pleasures and the desire for praise." He paused a long time. "And I have thought to myself that the gods brought me here on purpose, I have gazed about me imperiously, I have looked down on other initiates—the slaves and women—thinking myself more valued by the gods."

He was speaking slowly, quietly now, his hand to his head. He began to step down, saying, "Let me go."

"Stay where you are," the priest commanded. He stopped, frozen to the spot, afraid he had offended the gods, anguished, utterly depressed. There was a stir behind him, but he did not look.

Prax again. "Of all your dark and thoughtless deeds, which is the worst?" It was the same question. He had not answered it.

He tried to decide in his misery, but he could not. "Only the gods know that, and they will punish me soon enough, for I have stood before them and told them." He drew inward and stood numbly looking at the torch's flame.

Shadows materialized into two marshals who led him around to the front of the building. It was flanked by torches set in the ground. Prax had not looked at him again, but had moved instead out along the path to the initiates at the Temenos. His heart went out to them as he walked slowly up the steps of the entryway.

At the double door he repeated his name and requested entrance, as he had been directed to do. Only when the doors stood open was their inner frame exposed to view, an elaborate meander pattern of ivory inlaid in the dark wood, a pattern he had seen many times but never thought about. He stared at it intently and then passed between the doorposts. An anteroom lay inside where priests awaited him. They led him through a narrow grille made entirely of precious iron which separated the area from the naos beyond, down a broad step, and paused as if to present him to the room of initiation.

Here, under bright torches there were twenty or thirty people arrayed on benches on both sides of the long walls. They wore the purple scarf and short chitons, their heads crowned with fillets. At the far end of the naos was a curtained area higher than the floor, with a curtained center area flanked by the now-familiar snake-wound torches. A bema, a large granite stone, projected from the curtained area, and steps led between the two levels. There were doors in the long walls between the bema and the benches.

The group was not all the same as in the first initiation. There were several young men and women, but most were older, and there were no children. Recent visitors on the island were here— the Egyptian, the black Ethiope, the Dorian with blond flowing hair. A stranger, red as a Cretan fresco, caught his eye.

The priests led him sharply right toward a basin in the floor by the outside wall, for the purification rite. One priest prepared to pour the holy water from a pitcher, a great silver container chased with golden figures. From the bench nearby another lifted the end of a purple cloth which extended along the seat and out of his vision among the spectator-initiates. It was the porphyris, the scarf of Samothrace.

The priest spoke. "This band has been cut at the end"—he held it up before Teleo—" to make the porphyris for the person who was last initiated. As you can see, the sash had no end, for it is continually being created at its other end. It is the life-bestowing power of divinity, which is endless. At the point of beginning one thread joins another, from point, to line, to fabric, coming into being from a pattern that extends infinitely in both directions. You will cut off that portion which is yours, which you will wear and keep. Those initiated before you have done so, as those will following you. The scarf is always the same, as this world is, though your section of the pattern may age and crumble, even as your flesh. It is the color of life, and a symbol that life is unending. It will not fade, as the pattern we celebrate here will always be pure and true. Now you will cut your portion, discard your mundane clothing and, after purification, in the holy water, you will wear the porphyris of the Great Gods."

Stepping forward with a steel knife, the priest handed it to Teleokairos. The handle was wrought in electra and marked with curious symbols. He quickly severed the material at the point where two priests, holding it stretched before him, indicated. Then he discarded his old robe, the priests still holding his sash and loosely screening his nudity from the company of initiates. The warm waters of his lustration poured over his head, streaming over his face and shoulders. The priests anointed him with oil and, rubbing him with soft stuffs, twisted the sacred scarf of Samothrace about his loins. The investiture was complete.

He was next led to a small eschara, or hearth, which lay in the center of the naos floor a little forward of the entrance arch. It was a hero's altar, dedicated to Iaison or Aetion, the divine guardian of his oath and the hero-founder of the cult, the first man to allow strangers to become initiates— the first initiate. In the ancient language of the cult his name was Adam. A morsel of the sacred bird of the sanctuary, the shearwater, was given him to dedicate to the sanctuary founder. Then he was led to sit upon the foremost bench on the left to wait for the others. The Corinthian was not there. He wished the others better fortune.

One did join him, the outcast from Sparta who was brutally scarred, having a distorted cheek and jaw; he was dark and cruelly ugly. Teleo knew that such a man in Smyrna would have been a sacrifice, a pharmakos to be dragged out of the city, flailed on the genitals and burned alive. Here he was a brother, sitting on the bench beside him in the porphyris of the Great Gods. He felt uneasy.

The curtain between the torches opened to reveal the high priest. He advanced to the bema from which he presided. Among other things, he said, "Sky and earth are one harmonious whole. You have learned this from the stories of creation. You have the means to travel the earth by using her lodestone which is ever pointing at her counterpart in the sky, the polestar. Let us reveal to you now that there is another level of truth in the story of sky and earth and the stories of the heroes; they are the stories of creation not alone of the physical world but also of yourself.

"All of the parts of you are a harmony, too. You are born from darkness into light, from un-awareness into awareness, and the principle of opposites exists for you not only in the world but inside you always. Knowing both darkness and light, you must yourself unite them harmoniously within. When you can acknowledge the darkness within yourself—as you did in the confession on the stones outside, recognizing that you and not the gods are responsible for most of your acts—you have then reached true consciousness, awareness of yourself, the level of Four, of the hero, in the pantheon of Samothracian gods. The darkness is both good and bad, good because it contains all potentials. If you pursue the Pattern of separation into dualities and return to unity, you will grow with all the gods to come. A person knowing that his inner harmony and that of the physical world are one—for you are also part of this harmony—is ready to hear our initiation narrative, the hieros logos."

And the priest told the congregation the story of a voyage. It appeared at first to be the story of Kadmos or of Dardanos again, but the voyager had no name, many names, and was himself. Winds blew him from place to place until he chose his own way. When he did this, he was saved from the sea by the scarf of Samothrace's gods and, after confession, found himself miraculously home. The voyage had been full of difficulties, but as he made friends of animals and used the efficacy of plants, accepting these gifts of the gods, he had learned to control himself and free himself of the control of others. The turning point in his voyage had been a trip into himself, a labyrinth, in which he saw those whom he had destroyed and sufferers with his own nature. It was the trip to the underworld, from which he was reborn, just as Iasion/Aetion who in uniting with Demeter/Axieros, was "struck by lightning" and—not killed—but reborn.

"These stories are your story, the story you have already told on the confession stone. It is the death of the old and a rebirth into harmony. You are the hero beloved of the god. But this knowl-edge is not truly yours until you have experienced it."

Teleo was led up the steps and behind the curtain with the high priest into the sacred abaton. It was shaped like a hemisphere, a ledge of bare ground surrounding a large circular sacred pit at the bottom of which the holy rock of gray and green porphyry lay. Above this symbolic cave was a domed ceiling upon which the skies at mid-summer were represented. With a dignity that he would recall on many a sleepless night and blackened day to come Teleokairos Maionides was led through the ritual of rebirth: he descended into the depths of the crypt where he died and was revived and came joyfully out to the world again. The priest handed him a small unlit torch. It smelled of sul-phur. He was told to light it from the great torch blazing by the bema and then to douse it in the basin of water which was nearby. He did so, and was amazed to see the torch, when he raised it from the water, burst into flame again. The congregation sang a joyful song. His torch was ensconced by the benches and he was led, crowned with laurel, to his seat.

After the Spartan had been reborn, the priest stood again on the bema. "Which gods lead you on your voyage depends upon you and the voyages you make. For we hope you will make many voyages.

"Now the greatest secret of Samothrace can be suggested." He stopped for a significant pause. "Because we are mortals—of all kinds and appearances and countries—voyaging under the guidance of the gods to understanding—there is only one answer to the riddle of the gods. The Great Gods of Samothrace, as they evolve, created by us as powers of our world, are many forms, always changing,of one god, one power; they can have no names, for they are One. One infinitely transformed and unfolding, partially perceived, completely powerful—One.

"There is, then, a new meaning you will know when men say those initiated into the mysteries of Samothrace are safe at sea. They truly are. For the mariner—guided to God by the pattern of harmony, always revealed in earth and sky and manifest within—is you."

Teleokairos took it into himself, carefully, to hold and not let it be touched, so precious and so new a thing as this. It was not his yet; so strange; he needed to hold it awhile.

Then he was disturbed into action. The two initiates were summoned to the lower steps for the showing of the sacred objects.

The first was the meander pattern he had seen at the door, symbolic of the search, with its obstructed directions suggesting a maze and the obscurity encountered in the search for revelation, symbolic of both its endlessness and endless promise, symbolic of its inner-ness, the labyrinth, the underworld.

The double snakes twining up the columns flanking the abaton torches were in fact the caduceus of Hermes, the signs of duality, of earth and sky transformed by flame, the sign of the boundary-crosser.

The priest spoke to them of patterns of number in image. The pattern of three, the triad symbol, had many forms and myths, two of the most familiar being the twin brothers and their sister—the Dioscuri and Helen—or Aphrodite, Phanes, and Phaeton. The twin brothers as dualities, mortal and immortal, were legion in myth and copied as dual kingships in the states of men. He spoke of the civilized gods that follow Hermes, Athena of the city and Hephaistos, who transforms earth with fire in the worship of beauty. He pounded a plain piece of iron with the tools of Hephaistos until it had the power of a lodestone. He then spoke in great detail about the divine pattern in numbers.

The mysteries of the creative gods that set the limits of mortal existence are seen in the first three gods and their numbers. All of them added are the marriage number, six, of earthly harmony. This triad, four times over, are the number 12, the number of the solar year, and for earth and sky the marriage number. The number of seven represents the union of three and four, reflected in the number of planets in the sky which do not move with the fixed stars. The sun moves against the divisions of the sky, the Greek horai, and makes the number of 24, which is the number of the signs in the Greek alphabet. Then he spoke of the numbers in music and poetry in harmony with the mystery of the pattern evident in nature's sounds as well as in the bodies of men, animals, and plants. The musical instruments follow the law of the numbers of the pattern. He spoke of the patterns in plants and animals which reveal the harmony of seasons. He spoke of the harmony of craftsmen and the buildings they make following the sacred pattern of numbers. He explained the constellations and their stories as secrets to guide and anticipate man's growing and sailing seasons. He explained that the priests would give them the next day all specific sailing directions—distance, sea-gates, landfalls, names of winds—for the Aegean and the sea to the west, for they knew these things from the initiates who had returned.

The bard from Smyrna was overwhelmed. He had foreseen the mystic numbers of mousike! He struggled to grasp the vision of this ceremony while he was delighted with its directions and practicality. He had the desperate feeling he was missing a lot. It was too much at once. He saw all the cult members still listening intently.

"One last matter here, though by no means the last of our ceremony." The priest held up a root before him. "This is a symbol of our awareness. It is moly, a Samothracian onion that grows here in the autumn. It will demonstrate our openness to you, though many of our operating secrets are in the priests' hands only because they are too powerful and invite misuse. You must have realized that in our initiation rites we use herbs that condition the mind and body to receive secrets of a mystic nature. We need them especially for leading large groups into difficult subjects. The gods provide them for this purpose. If you have recognized them, you know their danger, if used without the gods' presence. Moly is sacred to our cult because it is a control, an antidote to the powerful visionary drugs of other cults which sometimes lead to madness. You must study it and know it and make use of it when necessary. Let us now prepare for feasting."

The instruction had been long and solemn, but now the mood shifted. Everyone rose and assisted, as tables were brought in, welcomes were offered the new initiates, and festive cloths were set on the long benches. He was anointed again with subtle oils and led to a seat of honor in the naos amid tables and festival. He was served first, with the Spartan, a special portion of the sacrifice. There was noise and jollity all about him, of dishes and laughter, and the voices of many people. Libations were dedicated, and the wine flowed freely. There was bread, and the smell of fragrant herbs in the air; and each person was served a special platter of fish. The priest approached with a portion for him.

"This is a dish of cult significance. You will take it from me, and eat at the center so as to see the bottom of the dish." He did so.

"What do you see?"

"A symbol. A mark on the dish. It is in red and black. A circle with a line across the center, not quite touching its sides. And two other signs, A and lambda."

"It is the written sign of our cult in Greek letters, the theta for the gods. The other letters are the same, in the language of the island. When you see it written down, remember the secrets that have just been revealed to you. You will see it many times used by men for other meanings, but for you this meaning will always be uppermost. When you have finished your portion of fish—for it must all be eaten—bring the dish before the eschara and dash it into pieces, for it may not be used again."

Teleo ate with absorption, never so aware before of the taste of fish flesh. It was the pompillius fish, the red mullet, the kind so plenteous in the Aegean and that follows the ships of men, drawn to their light at night. It was the goat-fish, he realized with a start, the constellation! Another sign of something he had missed.

He rose and carried the dish with its theta symbol forward to the hearth, sad to destroy it. The colors glowed, the image burning in his brain. He cast it on the floor, where the shards scattered into the shadows under the lip.

The bard of the feast was called for. To his astonishment it was Prax, singing so sweetly that it melted his heart. He had never sung in all their time together. He was fine, disciplined, clever in his performance. Teleo felt foolish but delighted with the song.

He could hear himself laughing at a distance, giddy, as if it were another man he heard. He tipped his cup to Prax and drank again. As the song was ended, he realized that the room was filling with light. It dazzled his eyes, as if he were looking into the sun. The priest's voice sounded nearby, but in the light he could not see him clearly; he seemed to have lost his outline. "The God has blessed you with secrets of the pattern of harmony. There is a harmony between men and gods as well, and, for those who can understand, there is a life of the spirit that is joyful after the death of the body. You are now seeing that this is so."

In that light brighter than day he felt suspended in air and alive as a soul, loved and released, part of the earth and the stars and more. There was distant music and he felt himself dance to it, as lightly as a wisp of fennel blown by the wind. He was a god.

***

He woke to the clear light of a beautiful Aegean morning. It sparkled, but after the experience of the night before, it was strangely ordinary—and at the same time blessed because of that.

He felt wonderful. But as the day wore on, his frustration grew. He could speak of his initiation to no one. Why did the gods not want him to share it? A vision of the harmony, of joy, of specific knowledge, of useful things the world sorely needs. He felt a vague anger at the initiates he had known for so long and who had held the secret. He wanted so to talk about it. A man could not really live until he knew these things. He felt that he himself was still gleaming, and he looked a dozen times an hour at his new porphyris.

Then he encountered, on the road out of the village, the Corinthian trader who had preceded him but had apparently failed the test and who now approached him eagerly.

"They took you." He looked at the scarf. "What do you have to say to pass that test?"

"You know I can't tell you that." He tried to sound casual in the face of obvious disappointment.

"I don't understand. I grasp all the concepts of the first degree. I know I do. And I am truly anxious to know the second. I can't believe I am not qualified for admittance. What could I have said wrong?"

"I really cannot imagine, my friend. Maybe they don't ask everyone the same thing, and of course you cannot tell me what they asked."

"Is there some hint you could give me, just a guess as to how you passed? Because I will try every time we sail by here until I make it. You could save me time and effort if you'd help me—I could make it worth your while with much gold. Which you, of course, could give to the cult. I would not bribe you," he added hastily.

"Then it would seem that the gods may want you to keep visiting them," Teleo said slyly. "No mortal can read their minds. If you think long enough, the answer will surely come to you."

"Well." He was mollified but sullen. "It is very important to me to have the full protection of the gods at sea. I am expanding my fleet. I have my ring, anyway. That's a lot."

He turned away without courtesy and scampered down the rocks to the quay. Soon he was barking orders to his crew and preparing to cast off into the windy channel. He would be back, Teleo knew. He wondered what it would take to move a mind from one state to another. More than he wanted to think about now, having been moved himself.

But he did think about it, nevertheless. Each of the two initiations had affected him quite differently. The first had enlivened his sense of the world around him and the patterns between man in his world and that of the gods. It had produced the Iliad. But the second was and would be different. It would take a long time to absorb the second. With the memory of a bard he went back over every word, every action, every detail of the holy precinct. He tried to hear them in his head for he could not utter them. He had given his oath to the gods. To the coming gods, too. The one god—well, that was still beyond his imagining. But it was not the Great Goddess. She was only the first, and he had finally understood her place.

***

During the long winter Melesigenes considered becoming a priest. He would stay in Samothrace the rest of his life. After the first initiation he had almost assumed he would stay, consumed with the Iliad. It was summer and life was good. The dark gods had receded and his Iliad gods were as brilliant and physical and implacable as the summer sun, active, amusing, and—except for Ares—the gods of civilization.

Now in the winter he had retreated into the cave. He dreamed of sunny Smyrna and the lush plain before it, of the cave by the river Meles, of the Ionian sound of Greek. His heart told him he was a traveler in the world, a boundary-crosser.

Finally, Prax told him to go. "You weren't meant to stay here. You must sing the Iliad in Ionia and the islands, even on the Greek mainland some day. It is a monument to the new times and an honor to the old. If you stay here it will not spread, being tied too closely to the secrecy of a sacred island. It will become suspect among the cults of cities. But, most of all, you are not what priests are made of. You love the feast, the commerce of the world. Go home and fit into the pattern. I would marry you to my daughter if I could, but you need to go home."

So Teleo decided to go home. But he would visit Troy first.

He left Samothrace with the next ship going to Troy. The new settlement there—most of the families from Lesbos—was small and very vulnerable. There were horses being bred, just as in the ancient city, and fine pottery and textiles would come in time. He wandered in the ruins, to the Scaian gate and the great sloping walls. He looked in vain for the palace of Priam. His head echoed with the words of the songs he had heard since he was born as he stood in the unceasing wind of this haunting earthly place. He looked toward Samothrace and seemed to see the gods sitting on its peaks, brilliant and laughing in the clear air. When he turned to Mt. Ida the shadows of the old powers of earth were palpable to him and he thought "Celestial footprint and turtle rattle hover in the chilly shade of Spring. And I think I will have to doubt that for two reasons."

Nothing was really there in Troy any more except the gods. He was surprised to find himself so sure of that. The men were gone, dead, and the women's dismal fate long since resolved. He picked up a stone from the gateway and rolled it thoughtfully in his hand. The bones of the mother. It bore scars across its flat face, and a dark and ashy grit was ground into its surface, as if chariot wheels had pummeled it against bedrock. Dragged by the great Horse icon? Burned with it? He placed it carefully in his secret hem. Later, in Smyrna he hollowed a place for it on the sound box of his phorminx and placed the stone in it so he could feel it under his palm as he sang the Iliad. He was to lose it again, this time amidst so many blackened rocks that, could he have seen them, he still would not have recovered it.

The other article he picked from the Trojan ruins was a small filigree ball of gold, delicate and sweet. He was to set it in a tortoise-shell pin and give it to his bride. It, too, would die again in Smyrna.

While Teleo was in Troy a familiar figure came up the beach to the city. It was The Old Trojan, who had followed him. The bard explained to the settlers about him, and they set him to patrolling what was left of the walls. But these were not his people, and trouble was not long in coming. He steadfastly refused to allow horses past the old city walls, stationing himself at the gate. He killed a few, lovely animals, ripping their bellies out with his sword. When he became obsessed with the fate of Astyanax, they began to fear he would throw a child from the wall, so they took him back to his family in Samothrace. He came back to Troy twice; finally they held a formal court, declared him an exile, and sent him back a third time. Broken-hearted, betrayed, he leaped into the sea.

CHAPTER 12

Zoe

723-715 B.C.E. Smyrna

Teleokairos Maionides came back to Smyrna like one returning from the underworld. Word that Nikos' ship had sunk with all hands had sent Smyrna into mourning. But here he was! Come to life again, shambling into town dusty from travel, carrying a new phorminx, smiling wearily, happy to be home at last.

Everyone stood still, astonished. "It's Tel!" they shouted. "Where have you been?" "What happened?"

Word spread like wildfire. "Where in the world have you been?" They looked at him curiously, seeing changes besides his thinness and his scarred leg, something in his blue-green eyes, in his no longer youthful voice. He needed to rest and recover, they said, and then tell them all about it, in his songs.

Smyrna had changed, too. It sprawled everywhere, overflowing its walls, houses perching in the foothills up almost as far as the acropolis. Ships crowded the bay, and toddling children, strangers to him, were in every courtyard. The goddesses Nemeses, however, were still pursuing Maion's family. Of his foster brothers, only Iannos, the youngest one, remained. The oldest had died in a pirate attack. Leonidas, now on his death bed, did not recognize Teleo. Sophie, old and care-ridden before her time, was glad to see him.

"There are two of us left, Teleo," Iannos told him when Leonidas died, " and I need you. I have plenty of land and I give you a good portion—and your ship, of course. We have been sailing it." He smiled. "But you must have land. It was Maion's before it was Greek, anyway."

Iannos still had the attitudes he had grown up with as a second son, an empathy for others, and a conviction that land was essential for Ionian aristos. His welcoming of Teleo, though, was rooted in his childhood admiration for this foster brother who sang to him and traveled all over the world in his big black ship.

"You don't have to be a bard anymore, you know," he told Tel. "Stay here and farm with me, and we will sail together in the summer and let the workers do the hot work. I am a good manager and trader. I am almost seventeen. I am a man, you know."

Tel smiled slowly and embraced his kind young brother, now as tall as he was but darkly handsome like his father."I know." Then he laughed heartily and threw his arm around his shoulder. "But give up my singing? Never? I cannot! It is too glorious, too central to my soul. Ah, what I have been singing, Ianni! It will amaze you. You will have to settle for a noisy companion—every night, every morning, every feast day all day, you will hear me!" He grinned. "Can you take it?"

"Yes. Happily." And Tel and Iannos became brothers for the first time.

❊❊❊

Smyrna expected Tel to have some new songs for them, but the Iliad filled them with wonder. It was so different, so dramatic, it confounded them. And so long.

"Why is it so long?" they would ask. "Why don't you include the death of Achilles?" " Why so much about the Trojans?" And so on.

Some people, especially other singers, did not like the new song at all. Tel was really good, they said, but he had lost his head among all those northerners. He had spent too much time among Aiolians. But, god, that was powerful singing. Every night, for all those nights, his audiences were spellbound. They did not know what to make of it.

The old bards harrumphed, but they acknowledged his virtuosity. There was no such singer as he anywhere, but they were sorry he had lost the old ways. The world was changing too fast these days—out of control. Still, his Iliad moved them to tears.

Tel and Iannos worked hard. They spent spring in the fields and as Iannos had suggested, hired workers to toil in the fields while they sailed the coastal cities. Smyrna had smiled at their reunion at first but soon began to offer advice. There were no children in the house. It was time for them to marry, have the help of wives, have children to inherit the land. Tel was over thirty and could become a bad influence on his fine young brother.

"They're right, you know, Ianni," Tel told him as they slept in the great room all alone in their beds. "The Assyrians say every man should have a son, plant a tree, and compose a poem before he dies."

Iannos answered sleepily from his corner. "You've done all that already, haven't you? Haven't you a boy among the Phrygians?"

Tel sobered. "Yes. Perhaps. He would be twelve by now. If he lives and sees the light of the sun. And maybe others, if the truth were known. But you know what I mean. A family, Ianni. You can wait a while—you have time. But I was thinking about it all the way home. Now you have given me prosperity. Maybe the gods are telling me to plant and sing and have many sons. The Pattern of life, full of natural harmony. Another kind of music."

Long silence.

Iannos spoke. "There is a woman I want. She has always been in my heart. The daughter of Xylas. Irene."

"My god, Ianni! She is just a baby!" Tel sat up and stared at Iannos. "She can't run a household."

"That is not why I want her, Tel ," Ianni replied. "Irene or no one. I've made up my mind."

"You sound so sure. Maybe Sophie can help her into householding. Well. I'm the one who is beginning to need marriage, but I haven't anyone in mind. I've known so many women. Loved some of them. But not for this life…"

"Get the genos to help. Think about it. Lots of women want you—I heard them talk when you were away."

"What woman can marry a traveler? Can stay home and be faithful?'

Iannos laughed. "Since when has distance anything to do with fidelity? Some wives are true, some aren't. I think most here are, except of course at festival time, and that doesn't count."

Tel was persistent. "Still. I want a special marriage. Like the marriage of earth and sky. Like the sun and moon—"

Ianni laughed and turned over to sleep. "The union of sun and moon comes once in twenty years! That's not the marriage I want! I'm starting out at every twenty minutes!"

Iannos and Irene were married soon after. Just children, thought Tel, and his heart warmed to watch them. He would ask the genos for help. Who would want to marry his daughter to an aging vagabond, an orphan of the sea with a reputation as long as the coastline? Who could he love enough to want to come home to her?

But the gods were kind.

There was a woman of their genos who drew him to her now. She was younger than he—16 to his 29—old to be unmarried; an earlier marriage agreement had failed when her fiance had died of snakebite.

Her name was Zoe. It became important that she look at him, and sight of her made his blood surge. Her eyes were large and smokey, blue-grey with flecks of amber, and her hair was a dark honey color streaked with brown. She had a way of gazing at him, slowly, that held him wordless. Her skin might have been fine and marble-like, but she worked in the gardens with the women and was tan and strong and as tall as he was. She was said to be a shrewd trader and a fine weaver. All told, the genos considered her an appropriate wife, except for one thing.

"I am bad luck, you know," Zoe told him right away. "Snakebite killed a man and scared the others off. A snake sacred to the Great Goddess. Aren't you afraid?"

"No," he answered. "I've made my peace with her power. You do seem to have some of it, now that you mention it."

She did not understand what he meant.

Zoe did not like his courtship, she said later, when they had agreed to be married. "You were too professional about it—getting someone to tell me you wanted me, singing to me, moving very close and spinning miraculous webs of words all around my head. I could imagine you doing it to a thousand other women. It seemed false." He was surprised and half defensive.

"Well. Seduction is an old bardic habit. A tradition." He tried to make light of it. "But I will not need those women now."

"I truly hope not. But don't promise something you can't know." She was looking at him evenly. "I marry you for just who you are. We will probably change each other as time passes. But if one of us ever tries to make the other over—into someone else—well. That will be the end for me."

"What do you mean?"

"I will live as I please then. I mean it. I see all around me people who fight and cripple each other because one insists that the other change into somebody more convenient for him—or her—somebody more this way or that way. Just be yourself. Always. Take me as myself. Then we will be happy."

"That is what I want, too. And I am old enough to know that fidelity is the core of marriage. The Pattern. It is important to me now."

"I believe you." She laughed and turned toward him. "Show me again how you do it, bard." And he did.

So they were married. Zoe arrived at his house in a wagon, and the axle was then burnt, signifying she would not return to her previous home. The nuts and dried fruits showered upon them during the marriage feast were happy signs of a fruitful union.

❊❊❊

When Tel had returned from Samothrace and decided to marry, he had gone to Phoinikous to invite Hiram and David to his wedding. Theirs was a joyful reunion, and he met their new families, for they had married now and had children. David had told him almost immediately that they were emigrating.

"The world is beckoning westward. There is too much trouble brewing in the southern seas. The Assyrians are pressing the old country. But we have settlements a day's sail apart all the way to the great ocean which lies past the pillars of Heracles. Carthage is on the south, and beautiful islands are off the northern coast."

"I will never see you again then." His heart ached at the thought.

"Probably not. But Phoenicians are travelers. We will get word to you."

They planned to go to Tartessus in Iberia, a city founded by the Phoenicians 400 years before, that many centuries later would be called Cadiz. The land was rich and well-watered. Tin and other metals were abundant, and the country was ideal for cattle-raising. "We have grown to want some land," said Hiram. I guess we have been corrupted by the Greeks! By the way, Greeks and Etruscans are moving into this area too. There are many fine bays and locations for villages."

"I cannot lose such good friends. They are rare in the world. Why not go to Thasos? Phoenicians have found gold there. And it is so much nearer."

"And colder. No. But we would love to have a Greek bard and his bride aboard to sing us to the promised land." Tel sighed. "If I had talked to you before—I might have gone. The world is large. And beautiful. Incredibly beautiful." He felt a faint regret. "But no. Zoe and I belong here."

They promised to come early to the wedding and threatened to stay late. There would be some time to say goodbye.

"Good. Bring all your families too. We will sing all the old songs together." They did. And they parted while everyone was youthful and happy.

Teleo had needed a woman like Zoe. She was comfortable, warm, independent, relaxed. She would lead him to meals when he was preoccupied, to the dance when he thought he was too weary for it. She was matter-of-fact, a woman of special words and frank gestures. She let him know when she needed him, and she never refused him. When they made love they seldom pulled their heads back and closed their eyes, imagining they were gods. They loved each other face to face hungrily, amiably, kindly, even riotously. He thought his was what a marriage should be, what Odysseus would think it was, that man who longed for home.

Zoe was as rich and supple as a young pear tree and suitable for bearing him many fine children. She dropped them like a mare in the fields, naturally, easily, joyously, and turned to nurture them. There was room in her spirit for life for them all. She built a regime that he could comfortably leave and that she could comfortably rule. He loved her deeply and saw her grow heavier and stronger as the children came and their wealth accumulated, but her vitality did not diminish. Zoe was fond of saying that Teleo was fire and air and that she was earth and water, and he thought well of that. There was a surprising delicacy in her senses. He did not at first appreciate how much Zoe did understand, and perhaps it was the living with him that cultivated her understanding. And so they grew closer through the years. In conflicts she silently used her own existence to end them. Zoe was adamant about observances, her beliefs traditional. She was a solid place from which he launched his movement. She did not expect him to be like her.

He wasn't. But he loved her with great passion and she became to him an image of the great mother in all her forms—Kore, Demeter, Hecate and Aphrodite. He knew that she was mother and wife and daughter at the same instant, and, curiously, she awakened echoes of these same feminine aspects within himself. In some way, through the mystic union with her, he thought that once or twice he knew what she was. But being mortal, he would never know.

Most of his songs, as the Iliad was, as life was, were soaked in blood, but Zoe knew what the world was made of. She had washed and wrapped the bodies of the dead, parents and kinsmen, and would live to see four of her nine children die. Although men prepared the sacrificial meat, Zoe knew well the touch of feathers, scales, hides, and entrails. She tended the mountains of offal that humans and animals produce and knew well the routes that life takes to nourish other life. The smell of sickness and decay was as real to her as the burning of sulphur which took it away. And yet she delighted in planting and would not miss the rituals that assured fertility. Death was an event of life and life was as indestructible as death.

In these first years five children were born to Tel and Zoe. The first was Kristos, (in 722) named for the good in the life they had now. Two years later came Lydia, and (in 719) twin boys they named Ardys and Maion. In (715) Iannos was born, a boy named for Tel's brother and beloved friend.

***

For six years Teleokairos Maionides farmed his land. He made frequent singing trips as his fame spread, but he kept fairly close to home. While other men patiently waited for crops, he would earn rich gifts by singing, and he delighted in bringing things home to his faithful—and usually pregnant—Zoe. He still enjoyed traveling the coasts, feasting, and seeing the cities of men.

There were three ways to get to Teos when he decided to go south: one was to walk 30 miles over some rough country, but it was low, not over 300 feet. Another way was to sail, north out of the gulf, doubling back hugging the coast, close to 100 miles. The last was to sail to the extreme southwest corner of the gulf, beach the boat near Klazomenai and walk the seven miles overland across the narrow neck of land connecting the massive peninsula to the mainland, coming out a few miles west of Teos. He much preferred the last way when he was alone, and the sea route when he felt sociable, and in the sailing season. He would usually go to Lebedos and Kolophon, and a few times went as far as Ephesos. On the sailing route he would stop by Emporio and Chios Town and then cross the channel to Erythrai. He thought sometimes of visiting the sibyl again, and once he sought her cave, but she did not want to be found. He knew there was something in Zoe that made him remember Herophile.

Lebedos was a small village on a low peninsula with the acropolis on the main ridge behind, just as Smyrna was. The nearby thermal springs on the seacoast west of the town made it a popular coastal stop, but the city had not really flourished yet, even though it had been founded by Andropompos, a son of the Athenian king Kodros. But Teos had prospered. It had the usual double harbors north and south and was protected from storms by Mimas peninsula. It was also a logical overnight stop between Ephesos and Erythrai. He would always enjoy Teos because Thaddeus was there.

After his marriage, Teleo had had a phorminx made by Mannos, the finest craftsman in Smyrna, a master of stemposts and woodwork. It was the instrument he loved better than any others, and he would always take it with him on his travels for company. As the feasting ended and the bard was called to play, he would pull the precious instrument from its soft bag of lambswool, polishing it carefully and tuning it familiarly, holding it aslant, intent as if he were alone. As his eyes dreamed into the song he sang, all other eyes were drawn to his phorminx. It was stunning, heavy and small with a bulging body and rounded bottom. It was made of cherry wood—body, arms, and sounding board—polished and oiled, gleaming in the light of the braziers. Around the margin of the sound-board and up the arms to the yoke this craftsman equal to Hephaistos himself had wrought in ivory, silver, and ebony a delicate inlaid pattern at once familiar and unidentifiable. The bard would never tell what the design signified, saying his Muse had given it to him in a dream one night upon a mountain. There was set into the soundboard a small flat stone, scarred and blackened. He told the children it held the power of his song; he told others it held the curse of the gods upon anyone who touched it. He was to own a number of instruments, but this was his favorite, the one he took most often to the cave at the rising of the Meles where he met the Muse.

***

"The flower must drink the nature of the soil / Before it can put forth its blossoming"—John Keats on Spenser. Now the nurturing was done and the man moved into legend. Whether it was marriage that completed him, or fatherhood, his own sense that at last the Pattern was manifest in his own life, only the gods can say.

All mortals can say is that in these years the great flowering came. Ionians sat open-mouthed at the refining of the Iliad, unable to grasp how it was happening or why. And no wonder. Suddenly among them was a force of language and intelligence that would not be equalled until Dante or Shakespeare, if then. A hugeness of spirit dwelt in him—he said it was the Muse—that drove him as a vessel before the wind. It took all of his seamanship to give himself direction, to man the sails, as he felt the wind and the pull of the sea against the hull and watched his audience, like dolphins arching and flashing beside him, caught in the eternal motion of his song.

Every singing brought new insights like a river of gold streaming through the cities laden with wealth enough for a lifetime of listening. Just as a father stands gazing at his glorious son being crowned in Olympia after a flawless performance, remembering the child of before, so Smyrna stood gazing at Teleokairos Maionides. Just as a bridegroom delights in his new wife, buxom and laughing and fertile as the wind, so Ionia delighted in its sweet singer.

Just as a mourner mourns for himself in the death of his friend, they mourned for Achilles. And for the first time they mourned for the Trojans. How much of what the Iliad was had come from thiry-five years of life and how much from the Muse? His miraculous rescue, the music of tales, his training, sacrifice, search for fathers, hatred and fear of mothers finally resolved but never understood? Initiation and return? Perhaps nothing more than the miracle of birth itself.

It was the times, too, full of turbulence, optimism, affluence, and change. They made an audience willing to listen to new voices without forgetting the tradition. For that was the key to the Iliad: an audience knowledgeable about the tradition but willing to let its singers change it and sensitive enough to language to know something of the miracle before them.

The singer knew well his own power and was overwhelmed at what was possible when the

Muse is a friend. But he was a man who lived amid his audience, a warm man with an earthy life to live, acceptable, if not ordinary company, to the ordinary people of an unusual time.

***

Teleo found himself invited to Aiolian cities too, as word of his new Iliad spread. Especially to Kyme. Kyme sat on the sea north of the Hermaian gulf, facing northwest towards Lesbos. It spread over two hills now and was by far the largest and most prosperous city in the Aiolian league, proud and industrious, its spirit part of the rising sea trade. Kyme could be reached easily from Smyrna by an overland route of about 40 miles. He took the coast road west around Sipylos to a tiny village called Menemen, crossed the Hermos about three miles northwest and stopped at Larissa to sing a night or two. Then he took the straight road through the pass east of Phokaia to Kyme on the sea.

The Aiolians had founded Kyme in the age of the great migrations when they were already firmly established in the area. First they had taken Larissa from the Pelasgian natives and settled right at the mouth of the Hermos. But when they found the sheltered cove on the coast ten miles northwest and accessible through the low and fertile plain that lay upriver, many settlers moved from Larissa, still keeping close ties between the two. There were other small settlements near Larissa to the east—Neonteikhos four miles away on the slopes of the Hermos and Temnos just four miles east of that. There is a story that an armorer named Tychios housed Tel at Neonteikhos, and the citizens would show a poplar tree under which the poet used to sing. So Tel would make a circuit of Sipylos, east or west, eastward following the coast to Menemen, Larissa and Kyme, then back through Larissa to Neonteikhos, Temnos, south across the Hermos to Magnesia-near-Sipylos, then down the hill behind Smyrna to his home.

He would almost never include a visit to Phokaia on this trip, though it lay parallel to Larissa and only thirteen miles west. Phokaia was easier to reach by sea, only 23 miles upcoast. It lay in its own lovely harbor in a bay at the mouth of the Hermaian gulf.

Its history, in fact, was similar to Smyrna's. Apparently it was first settled several hundred years before by Aiolians on land given to the immigrants by Kyme. But it was taken very early by Ionians from Teos and Erythrai; some said by immigrants directly from Phokis in Greece. So it was Ionian as Smyrna was now. Phokaia's spirit was modern, pragmatic, a city famous for its ships and sailors, some equal to the Phoenicians. It claimed the finest Tyrian dye of all the coastal cities, and Tel would bring gifts of cloth to Zoe, for when he sang he was well rewarded. He was still a hero here for the rescue of Sarpedon after the raid at Phoinikous.

When the bard sang in Phokaia it was sea songs and the returns of heroes, the voyages of the Argo and Odysseus, that his audience would crave, and many a late night argument raged over landfalls and wind directions in the poems. This is where he went when he was hungry for news of far-flung cities. His grandsons would live to see Phokaia found Marseilles, and settlements on the Black Sea; he would not have been surprised, for the spirit was stirring even then. Phokaia, then, was a separate northern trip not only because it was Ionian, but because it looked outward intensely, its back to the Aiolians and Lydians, and to the Sardian plain where Mt. Tmolus and the Great Goddess still held the souls of men. The rocky platform facing the sea at the very end of the peninsula, the most prominent part of the city, was the temenos of Athena, the goddess of the city, of the boats and of the cities to come. She was a new Athena, unlike that of ancient Troy and barely kin to the Hera of Samos or the Artemis of Ephesos or Sardis.

***

These years were good ones for Teleo and Zoe, full of hard work and deep feeling. Their first son's birth was a miracle to them and there was no music equal to the sounds of Kristos' childish voice. When Lydia was born they were delighted. She was a golden child but in her twelfth month the fever struck Smyrna and carried her away. Zoe was with child when it happened, and all feared for her survival. But tradition served her well; there were things expected to be done, and Zoe did them. She washed the small body and dressed her fair child in white, tenderly placing a crown of flowers on her head. The prothesis, or mourning, was brief, and then the expleora, the burial procession, was begun. With her face bare to the heavens Lydia was carried to the rock-cut tomb on the necropolis, her head foremost so that her small spirit could find the way home again on the Feast of Souls. With her were buried her terracotta horse on wheels which Teleo had brought from Emporio. Zoe removed from her own arm the golden bracelet Lydia had loved to play with, now dented with small teethmarks, and placed it on her daughter's arm. After the simple interment, feasting followed and the giving away of the meager treasure of worldly goods the deceased had collected.

Offerings would be made at the tomb on the third and ninth days and each anniversary of the death as well as at the Anthesteria in the spring. At that time the families would entertain the dead, and on the third day of the Anthesteria the ghosts of the dead would leave again. Zoe would bid goodbye again each year to her lost daughter. It was bitter at first, but as time passed and relatives and friends joined her, it was easier to have her go away, back with them to the land of the dead. The next day would find Zoe zealously cleaning the pitch from around the doorposts, put there ceremonially the week before to keep the spirits of evil from crossing her threshhold while they were abroad in the world again. After all, there was nothing unusual in the death of a child.

The twins came as a surprise to Tel and Zoe, and they could laugh again. "Which god was it?" he teased her. "They are all a bunch of rascals, getting even with a poor bard who mocks them now and then." "Only Apollo has legs as good as yours," Zoe told him.

The farming thrived, and their land was as fruitful as Zoe. It was the spring when Iannos was due that a Cypriot ship sailed into the gulf and made for Smyrna. When the village boy came running into the fields where he was plowing, Tel thought he came to tell him he was a father again. He had stopped with the other men for lunch under the shade of a plane tree, and so he jumped up with a shout to run to meet the messenger. All of his companions, fathers themselves, were grinning with expectation. From the messenger's face he could tell it was good news.

"He is here! Ha?" he roared and threw his face to the blue heavens in his joy.

"No." The boy stopped in confusion, realizing what had happened. "A ship is in the city from Athens, a Cypriot ship. It has come for you."

The sun was burning his shoulders, and his head felt like air. What could reach his feelings at a time like this?

"What?"

"The Archon of Athens wants you to come. They will explain."

The wine to toast a new birth was in the cups of his companions and laughter was on their lips. Now there was a pause between them. Now they felt his difference from them rather than a bond. But only for an instant. He sent word he would come soon, then drank with his companions and danced in the field to celebrate his good fortune, loudly and freely one of them for the last time. When he came back to Smyrna he had become a name.

The embassy explained that they had been to all the cities of Ionia to invite its finest singer to come to Athens as the Archon's guest for two years. Everywhere they had stopped Teleokairos' name had sprung to the lips of the citizens, and so they had come to Smyrna.

Zoe was in labor when he reached the house. He could not tell her now, and he left her with the women and went to find the men. Everyone understood his dilemma and felt the gods were blessing him; in fact, such an abundance of blessing made them uneasy. While Zoe and he were well wedded, no one expected that he decline the honor or delay until he could take his family with him. In fact, the head of the genos would officially give his consent, for the genos would have to arrange for the working of his land and the support of his family while he was away. The head of the genos, a man named Dionysos, spoke.

"Considering the last time you were in a Cypriot ship, we did not dream you would set foot in one again, Tel," he chided. "Are you sure you want to do this?" He watched carefully, sympathetic to the high emotions of the day, inviting Tel into a calmer state of mind. Tel could not speak, so he did, smoothly and formally to those assembled.

"We are honored that our Athenian brothers, whose blood flows in so many of us, recognize the accomplishments of our Ionian confederacy and that in all the cities of our coast where men live the name of Teleokairos Maionides is first to be praised among singers. We must let him go to sing in Athens the songs of its descendants. We will miss his sweet music, his merry ways, his vigor which brings joy to the feast. It is right that Smyrna share such pleasure with the world. Let all the city families meet to plan gifts to send for festival and for the leaders of Athens. Tel will take these with him. Our greatest gift will be the singer who will melt their hearts and make their days happy."

There was rousing approval and the feasting began. Men offered their help to his family, especially Iannos. Some suggested songs he should sing to the Athenians. Others had messages for him to deliver and inquiries about relatives and land in Attica, some wanting news of friends, whether or not they still lived and saw the light of the sun. All felt pity for the new child arriving as his father left. Some believed there was a god in Olympos who was not a friend of this sweet singer.

Soon word came that Zoe was delivered of a ten-pound son. "Iannos! For my dear brother!" Tel led the toast and disappeared in the general hilarity. He sprinted for home, his heart pounding, flushed with wine, bouncing between the narrow passages, careening off the walls. He could not leave Zoe now. Another beautiful boy. Was he all right?

He rushed into the room and stopped. Zoe was holding the babe, cleaning the birth mucous from his tiny throat. He was still gasping for his breath and clearing his lungs, very naturally, as he would for the first hours. His color was good. The midwife was cutting the umbilical cord and tying it off.

He looked at Zoe and she smiled. For that instant they were the creators and they had bestowed the gift of life. He enfolded mother and child in his arms, holding the universe. It was a long time before he remembered the invitation from Athens, and he did not tell her until the next morning. They just talked quietly that night, and, lying against her sleeping body, he and the child fell asleep together.

Zoe seemed not to hear him at first when he told her about Athens. Two years was too long an absence and she had to struggle. He did not think he could leave her, either. He doubted that he could even sing. They suffered over it for three weeks while the embassy waited.

And in the end he went.

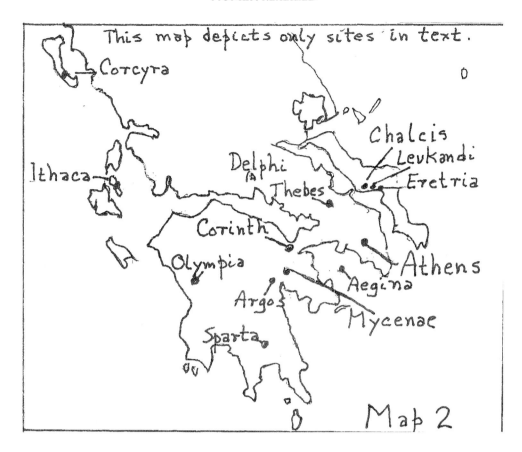

Map 2

This map depicts only sites in text.

PART THREE

Water, foe to Fire, that fertile suffocates,/ That teaches Death in Life,/ That cools, that levels, shapes,/ That modifies with salt the blood of Fame./ Axiokersos is his name.

Interlocutory: The Voice of Letha Gooding

When does the poet learn that his song has a life that others will give it? That his words winging into the hearts of others take their own direction there?

Early. He knows this early. He hears his lines modified in the next singing by another and muses about it. And he knows that he has done the same thing, all of his life. We are not speaking of a time, anyway, when copyright and piracy were important.

The Margites should have shown too that a song changes. It became another almost instantly, inviting parody and providing katharsis. It was the first success identified with Homer's name. But the Iliad is another thing—a work of such magnitude and concentrated action that few would have consciously tried to change it, not quite understanding its difference, yet feeling its power. It was as a thing apart that only a brash novice would have dared to tamper with.

It is The Uses of This World that we come to now. Not only the uses of a work but the uses of a famous bard. What now? How does the world behave toward such phenomenon? What does the maker have to do with the disposal of his creation? Can he or should he control it? Where does he go with himself after his triumph?

Fire is the primary agent of metamorphosis, altering irrevocably everything it touches. Uncontrolled it is divine power, genius. In a dualistic mortal world it must have an opposite; Fire is banked by Water. Homer says as much when Achilles in his god state blazes across the Trojan plain after fighting the Scamander, his only enemy the divine river itself pursuing him. Where Fire is God/Life, Water is Mortal/Death. Is the river Styx. Is Hades. Is Axiokersos. Yet Axiokersos has his own duality, his nourishing rebirth.

So this section of the monomyth is about voyaging, traveling over water, the tempering of genius by the times and the uses of a mortal world for his immortal song , just as, after loss, we must all cook supper and even give ourselves over to fearful sleep. So the Muse's song is inevitably subject to the mundane uses of the day. Of course it is.

The political mind will love that. Politicians are not creators; they are the street-smart users of ideas. Anything as divine as the Iliad in its divinity must have instantly been useful to the users. It should have been, of course. But I have always wondered what that means to the maker. How does an artist feel about the ways in which he is understood? No one who has ever written song or story thinks he has ever been heard exactly, and surely he hasn't.

There is an old story that Homer and Hesiod were in a song competition, a delightful game, demonstrating Homer's great wit in responding to Hesiod's clever traps. At the end each was asked to sing his favorite passage from his own works. The prize was awarded to Hesiod because Homer chose a passage about the horrible glory and pity of battle, while Hesiod chose one about farming. The people chose Homer, but the king chose Hesiod because his subject was peaceful. What irony lies in that anecdote.

So we voyage across waters of the physical earth, the waters of Poseidon. How will they bank the fires of genius? It is in small part only the voyage of Telemachos to see the world. It is the voyage from Achilles to Odysseus, from stubborn youth to accommodating ruler, from individuality to individuation, from inspiration to survival, from the heroic act to patience and endurance. The Odyssey that comes out of this man is a far different story than you have been led to expect.

CHAPTER 13

In the Court of the Archon

715 B.C.E. Athens

Ionia's great singer approached Athens from the sea in the gold of a late spring morning. Above the wine-dark waters rose the high ground of gleaming acropolis hill six miles inland, that ancient citadel that had not been sacked by the Dorians, survivor from the Mycenaean Age.

Synoikia was a festival special to Athens, this occasion for which Teleokairos Melesigenes had been invited to represent the singers of Ionia-in-Asia-Minor. It began in the middle of the month of Hecatombian, with the new moon before the summer solstice, and celebrated the combining of the people of Attica into one political unit under the protection of the city goddess Athena. So it was political as well as religious, one of several state celebrations for the month of Athena's birthday at the beginning of the new solar year.

Teleo came ashore at the port city of Phaleros, for Piraeus was not yet the city's harbor, walked inland under a warm noon sun and climbed up the blue limestone hill, entering the acropolis through the gate of a Mycenaean tower, pausing with his companions to see the flourishing city outside, now spread a mile or so from its center spilling southward toward the sea, houses and shrines sparkling in the glorious clear air.

He arrived at the threshhold of the archon Medon's home at a propitious time. The archon's son Glaucos had just been married and festivities were well underway. Medon, a large and active man, greeted him firmly and pleasantly, saying, "If you are not too weary, we would want you to sing for this happy occasion. You are most welcome to."

Teleo took a seat, poured drops to the gods, and quaffed the festive wine with relish; his body loosened with fatigue and the wine sang in his head. Strangers were all around him, whirling in intricate dances, laughing in the sunshine. As time passed, he felt himself sliding and began to doze.

He was looking for his phorminx and couldn't find it. The audience was waiting and he was not sure where they were. He was alone and his fingers were cold. In a panic, he kept looking into houses, but he knew that the audience would be gone when he arrived. He struggled to wake up.

"How about a lullaby? Our minstrel seems not to be interested in weddings."

"The only arms he sleeps in are the arms of Morpheus." Laughter close by. He was disoriented. Several young men stood before him, looking down at him sprawled in his seat against the column. One was fiddling with the strap of the phorminx slung over a peg on the column. They were happily drunk, looking for amusement. "Sing us a song, bard."

"I know a good tale for your instrument." Uproarious laughter.

"Let's hope it's not too long."

"Does it have to be long to be good?"

"I'm hardly the one to asskk!" They were chuckling over their cups, dazzled with their own wit.

"One at a time, boys." A gust of howls then.

They went to get more wine, clustering close around a young maid-servant, smiling into her bosom and making shameless suggestions. She colored and lowered her head, her nipples rigid under her chiton. Teleo thought of Zoe. A voice spoke above him.

"Have you rested enough to play for us? Do not feel you must."

The bard stood up respectfully. He was a confusion of feelings, aroused but sleepy, the edge taken off his arrival. What was Zoe doing now? What was he doing here helping strangers into a new bed? He wished he were home again. He wished his head were clear. He looked toward the bride and groom to get his bearings. They were shining in the beauty of the day, and he was instantly renewed.

"Ah yes," said Teleo, and he sang of the wedding of Kadmos and Harmonia for the first time since his own marriage, with joy and reverence and a profound longing.

The wedding guests were spellbound. There in the midst of their revelry was a striking new voice. Even the archon was watching him intently, his guests forgotten. Each person seemed to be listening apart, except for those who reached to touch someone else close by as if to say the song was shared between them. The rest of the evening was spent in introductions and warm compliments. Another singer, from Megara, asked him his father's name. Teleo was puzzled. "Do you know my father?" His mind raced ahead. "Where is he?"

"No. I mean your patronymic. And your real name. You know. Bards who travel the world do not use their real names. There is no reason to. I thought you had chosen Teleo."

"We don't do that in Smyrna."

"Well. All the big names do it. Those that do not live at home. Think about it. Just shows you're still a child in the world, that's all."

He smiled wryly to himself about it as he went to bed. Teleokairos would do as a bard's name until a better one came along. He was 37. Too old to worry about fashion. Still, maybe too young to ignore it. He wondered why he had come so far to be attendant on a ruler in a strange land. He wanted Zoe. He wanted to be true to Zoe.

***

Medon was 45, in the middle of his second term as head archon and at the height of his political life. He had been first elected in 732 as a war hero in the fight with Aegina and had proven since to be a skillful and civilized administrator. Political life in Athens was unique, Medon explained to Teleo as they strolled next day on the acropolis where Medon's house stood, together with those of other officials.

"From what you have said, you make much of us as survivors. So do I. We always have been. Many people have come to Attica—the land with long shores. Under Kekrops we became a twelve-village confederation. Look around you. We are still that, but the villages have grown together. Under Theseus six hundred years ago we attained a truly unified political existence.

"This wall you see"—he gestured toward the cyclopean defenses of the acropolis—"is said to have been built by the native Pelasgians centuries ago. I think it had much to do with our remaining unconquered when the Dorians engulfed everyone else. Of course the hill alone is a marvelous defensive site, isolated as it is on the plain and ringed with rivers and a protecting chain of mountains."

He looked around him at the city he ruled. "You can see why we used to be called Cranaa—Rock City—by the Pelasgians."

His Ionian guest asked, "Why archons, though? Theseus is a king according to the tales we sing."

"Theseus' family still held kingship when the great flood of refugees began 500 years ago. We welcomed them and they helped strengthen us. Some of them were powerful people who learned to exercise power here, too. Your people, the Ionians who left to settle on the coast of Asia Minor, began to migrate during the reign of Melanthos, a man of Messenian extraction. His son, Kodros, was the last king of Athens."

"What happened?"

"It's a curious tale now. I expect he was a scapegoat. It was when the Dorians were approaching Athens, after Corinth had fallen, that the oracle told Kodros the city would not be taken if the king were slain. Kodros disguised himself, so the story goes, and sought out Dorian troops. He started a brawl and was killed, which frightened the Dorians away because they believed the oracle. In his honor Athens abolished kingship in favor of an archon elected for life."

"Is that what really happened?"

"Yes, it happened. But, like most tales, it is only an outline. Who knows what the political realities were, or the true nature of a man who acted thus?" He looked keenly at Teleo.

"Go on." Teleo said. "Kodros' line is much revered in Ionia."

"I am glad. The first archon Medon was Kodros' son, ruling while the emigrations continued. The archonship was reduced to a ten-year term only 37 years ago. The ruling archon was re-elected but died in '37, was replaced briefly by his son, and then by me.

"I have been lucky. A generation had passed under the ten-year rule, just long enough for bitter opposition to have died. Literally. Long enough for me to have read the mistakes of my predecessor."

Teleo smiled. "You really are a king, whatever you call yourself."

"No, far from it," Medon said firmly. "There are nine other archons, you know. Like an executive board, all of us responsible to the assembled citizenry. One is polemarkos, the war commander. The others are called thesmothetai, decision makers. So this is my city, my Ionian friend," he concluded, smiling with the pleasure of it all. "There is none like it anywhere."

Medon could not know that during Teleo's lifetime, (in 683) the terms of service of all archons would be reduced to one year and a council of the Areopagus added, made up of all past archons. The Athenian political spirit was an active one, remembering shared powers among villagers, but forced by the pressures of growth and economics to new patterns.

***

They walked from the private houses toward the official areas of the acropolis. On the northern rim the old Mycenaean palace of the ancient royalty still stood, home of the men of Kekrops and Erechtheus. In the Erechtheion were the ancient sanctuary of the local daimon-hero Erechtheus and Athena's temple, a small building housing her time-honored image of wood. The owls of the acropolis nested everywhere in the rocks around her temple, making their messages known in the twilight of the evening. Sacred snakes had free access to her temple.

The tomb of Kekrops was there, as were the salt spring of Poseidon and the mark of his trident near the olive tree of Athena. Teleo remembered the story, how Athena and Poseidon vied for control of Athens, each challenged to give the best gift to the city. Poseidon struck the earth and made the spring, but Athena won through her gift of the blessed olive. The relics of the contest were still worshipped on this high and protected place.

As he gazed at the hills and valleys of Athens, Teleo was overwhelmed by the sheer presence of humanity. He was not used to so many people in one place. It was not oppressive—the prospects were lovely—but so many people! The city seemed to be loosely spread but everywhere.

"Think of us as almost continuous villages," said the archon, "and you will be more comfortable. You might as well know our hottest political issue here lies before your very eyes. The simple fact is that in this century Athens has grown beyond belief. Seven times the population of only 100 years ago. SEVEN TIMES! And tripled in your lifetime."

Teleo was really taken by such a phenomenon. "But why?"

"I'm not sure I know. Only a portion of them are immigrants, and that is the most significant of all. They are US, the people of the city and plains, suddenly repopulating our world." He laughed and shook his head, turning to look again over the city spreading toward the sea. "Sometimes when I stand here all I can see is a giant headache. You will learn soon enough that Athenian politics are unique. It is not a dull life."

And the city did seem to grow before his very eyes. Ordinarily when he learned his way about a new place, the scenes were almost instantly familiar and distances seemed to collapse into short and habitual routes. But here he found fresh perspectives at each walk, as he found also every stage of human habitation. It was exciting and disturbing at once.

✻✻✻

His host the first few days in Athens was the archon himself, but soon the press of affairs drew Medon away, and his eldest son Tesebulos took over the entertainment and management of visiting dignitaries. The archon and his wife had two sons, as different as night and day. Tesebulos, now half his father's age, was clearly being groomed to take his father's place in the polis.

The second son was Glaucos, only a year younger but already preparing to find his living in the new commerce; there was a pragmatism about him that would serve him well. He had learned, as second children do, that there are indirect means to a goal. He cared too much about position because he did not have it. He was never especially loved, for that protection went to the bright-haired baby that had died. But he was accepted. He had a place, albeit unnoticed and unremarkable, and had become a materialist who studied with an eye to profit.

Tesebulos was a different matter. He seemed to be blest by the gods, touched with a divine beauty and intelligence that made him the cynosure of all eyes. He was like a torrent of pure water tearing down the mountain in the spring, splashing its bounty lavishly and roughly over everything nearby, loving and shredding the tender wild plants, oblivious to time, thinking that being a waterfall was the common state of being. He was in a hurry to do everything, a believer in everything good. No one, he thought, given the chance to do a good act, would let it go undone. There was infinite energy where there was infinite desire.

His laughter was legendary. Since his childhood people had paused at their distances and smiled inside when they heard his hearty laugh ring out and trail away. His was not so much laughter as high delight in action and perception. It was not a musical sound; it was a wordless assertion of his presence. Some thoughtful people heard it change as he reached manhood and learned to use it, for that is what it came to. He would be a man to reckon with, and all the families knew it.

He took an instant liking to Teleo, probably at first because he was new and naturally sociable, but most deeply because Tes knew and admired excellence. He knew, too, as he pointed out immediately to Teleo, that if he were to live in the minds of men, he needed a bard for a friend. "So you're my ideal companion, bard. Too good to need much from me, too vulnerable to do without me, too old and too foreign to provoke political jealousy. Let's be friends." And his quick laugh and generous mind would take them off in another direction. So they enjoyed the days before the synoikia. It was then that Teleo would sing the Iliad.

The celebration of the synoikia was annual, but every other year the event covered both the 15th and 16th of Hecatombaion and involved elaborate sacrifices in the names of the Phylobasileis, the ancient kings of the four Ionic tribes. Medon had decided to use it as an important political gesture in wooing the Ionian cities of Asia Minor.

On the 28th of the month, Athena's birthday would be celebrated with great pomp and public expense, although the games and the Panathenaia would not begin until much later, (in 566/565). Homer would have been overwhelmed to know that Peisistratos of Athens would create a competition at the Panathenaia for recitation of the Iliad and the Odyssey, an event that later men would consider significant in the preservation of the bard's work. This first time Teleo would sing the Iliad during the days between Hecatombaion and Athena's birthday, two songs each day. It would be a marathon performance.

The birthday of Athena was very important. The Pannychis, a dancing ceremony, began at sunset on the 27th, with young men and women circling about the temple on the acropolis all during the night. Later there was the Pyrrhic dance, by eight men in full armor, imitating the dance Athena had done when the Titans were defeated.

The central event of the 28th was a parade, a procession to present a new peplos to the goddess, a glorious dress begun on the last day of Pyanepsion at the Festival of the Craftsmen—nine months before. It was of traditional wool, with brightly colored designs woven into it, a miraculous work of the Ergastinai, a group of maidens chosen from the aristocracy.

***

The Iliad set Athens afire. No Greek horse was pulled into the citadel; the wrath of Achilles consumed it. All the heroes lived and died again in this other city of Athena. While little of Athenian valor was mentioned in the poem, the catalog of the old citadels, the knowledge of their present states of ruin, heaps of stones sheltering the ghosts of the past, resurrected in men's minds the singular unified effort of the Achaeans and the long aftermath when Athens gave succor to the survivors.

That they had survived now amazed them. They mentally polished the poor burnt stones and took their own ancestors to heart again. The Ionian kings of Athens had been descendants of the refugees, and old family loyalties were reborn.

That was the first reaction.

The unusual length of the epic astonished conventional minds, but the exhilaration at such a great accomplishment swept through a city already proud of its festival. That there was no Athenian center to the song allowed room for all the genetti to praise their own heroes. Achilles had no descendants here, that flawed and tragic warrior. In Athens there were few friends of Dorian Corinth to be found, and no Dorians in this tale.

After the first enthusiasms, some felt the song dealt too sympathetically with the Trojans, and Teleo let them complain. His defenders argued that an enemy must be worthy of such a costly war; there is no glory in killing so many wolves in a sheepfold. And Hector surely did bring about his own death. As for the city's cults, the priests of Athena were proudest. Each cult forgave the humanizing of divinity because the utter power of divinity shone forth so fiercely, so implacably, that the result was a reawakening of religious fervor in the citizenry. If such a poem increased religious attendance and sacrifice, then the end effect could only be positive. For Teleokairos the most important personal result of the singing of the Iliad was the effect on two very different friendships.

Deep in the night after the last lines of the Iliad had died away, there was a knock on his door. He had been lying sleepless, still unwinding from his performance. There in the doorway stood Medon with a wineskin and two golden cups. "Come out into the moonlight and talk to me," he said, and he led the way to the sacred olive of Athena. He sank down by it and poured a libation, with ceremony and solemn dignity, and handed it to Tel. They poured the drops to Athena, which disappeared darkly into the thin and powdery soil, and Medon raised his cup to Teleo and stared into his face.

"You have been crying," Teleo said quietly.

"Not exactly. I have been too moved to know why. The story of Troy was no different from any other versions that I know. Your sound I already knew was equal to the language of the gods. But Teleo! Your Achilles! Your people! Look at what you've done!" He fell into silence, staring again into the moonwashed face of the poet.

"Men are changing, Teleo." He looked away to the silvered fields, across the roofs of the sleeping city which lay in his trust. "Your song tells me you know this, too. But look at what you've done! You have put the past to rest at long last. Now our song is finally sung, celebrating and weeping for our forefathers who destroyed their world. Such brave and wonderful and terrible destructors. We have been lost children until now, here in Greece."

He paused a while. "Athens does not need to be important in the Iliad. In fact, I'd rather she weren't. She is the lesson, you see. The survivor city was not important in an age of glorious deaths."

The poet nodded. "Ionians of the east know they are survivors, too." He drained his cup.

"Now Athens learns from you. Sheltered here awhile, your people left and found a new Ionia. Your song tells me you too have put the past behind you while remembering. Athena defeats Ares. The power of the mother is broken and the motherless daughter leads men. Kybele can do little with the rising consciousness. We are readying a new age. A better age."

Out of a long silence Teleo said, "I'm not sure of that. I do not think the men who hear me sing really hear my song. War excites them."

"Each man hears what he needs to hear. Some hear only the roar of battle and funeral lamentation. The despair of old men left without their sons crawls through your verses everywhere. For me." He spoke these words sadly and Tel knew they meant something close to him. Medon went on.

"How many generations does it take to rebuild a world of civility once it is gone? To give substance to a people whose noblest sons die with their potential undisclosed? For five hundred years we have lived among roads and walls and tombs we no longer know how to build, amid pots we cannot reproduce, amid fertile fields begging to be used but devoid of people to till them or the knowledge of how to do it. Now we have people again, and the fields are busy, and your poem comes along to help us. Nostalgia is good. We see the past as the past and we are free of it—free, that is, to use it rather than be used by it."

His face was happier now and he reached over to place his hand on Tel's shoulder. "There is such power in your voice, my friend, and many will see a people's triumph where there is actually the triumph of one spirit. In a fleeting moment of time. To sing as you have. What Muse lives in your heart."

Teleo smiled ruefully, then more brightly. "Yes. Well, it goes with the job. Let them enjoy it. A man's supper must not be ruined by too much thought. I am an entertainer, after all."

They laughed together at that and raised their cups to the moonlit acropolis, knowing how rare it was to be understood.

✵✵✵

The effect of the Iliad on Tes was electric. He saw himself in every hero, or more accurately, something of every hero in himself. He struggled with it, living it all over again in terms of Athenian self-interest. "I don't like what you've done to Achilles, but you've awakened Athens to its heritage, reminded us of power and majesty again. You've reminded us of what it takes to be great and of what can defeat us." And he began to speak to Teleo of his growing impatience with the world around him.

"My father and his generation are just like the leaders in the Iliad. It is the old men who ruin everything with their politics and greed. Nothing can be done straight out and above board. Nothing is pure and noble. Everything is caution. Eat before you fight. Caution! Caution. The times call for bold strokes and the old men sit in council."

It was true that, whatever the archon had been in his youth, he was now deliberate, quiet, capable of compromise, a clever strategist, a careful man. Tes was not any of these. Strong, competitive, quick-spirited to the point of rashness, his sharp intelligence led him to act immediately and, since he was so often right, gave him a reputation as the star of the rising generation. Teleo shared the excitement of Tes' friendship; he was everywhere, learning, fighting, debating, practicing, listening in his own way, getting ready to lead the city. He wanted to be polemarkos first, the leader of fighters.

Tes and his father finally reached a stage where they disagreed on everything in the area of public policy, to an extent that made private discussion stormy and public discussion between them impolitic. That they loved each other was unquestionable, but they could not talk ten minutes without conflict. Medon would burst out:

"Why can't you be more rational? You think with your guts. You want everything done yesterday. You think no one over 30 is to be trusted because at 30 a man may take public office. You think by then all men are cowardly and avaricious. Where is the beautiful and brilliant child I have raised to rule Athens when I am gone? You will be the pawn of every clever man who can turn your rashness to his own advantage."

And Tes would try to explain. "I love you as my father. I do accept my family and public duties.

I just cannot accept that my own father is leading Athens to disaster! You will listen to everyone but me. You never hear me. Or anybody else under 30, because they are not yet in the game. We can't even talk any more. It's hopeless ."

It may have been hopeless, but they did continue to argue. There were two points upon which they could agree: the times demanded conscious long-range policy, and the exploding population was the blessing and the curse of the times. Traditional city government was splintering apart under the pressures of growth and there was no clear answer. Each had different fears and different solutions.

Tes would rage at Medon. "Don't just believe me. Look around you! Just look at Corinth! Or should I say look out for Corinth. Practically at our doorstep. We're losing to her and it's time we did something. In ten years she has stolen a part of our metal trade and completely usurped our position as potters. Teleo says Corinth even trades with Sardis—a barbaric town in the middle of nowhere! Ever since Mycenae fell, Athens has shone as the center of pottery making and export. For centuries we have traded with Rhodes and Cyprus and the Phoenicians—the Phoenicians even founded our port city. Through the long meager years everyone looked to us for contact with the world. But now in one short generation—(since 730)—everyone has begun turning to Corinth. And Aegina, too. The damned Dorians! A city of the Peloponnesos. Late-comers no better than barbarians! How can you let that happen? And they've solved their population explosion to the admiration of all. They have flourishing colonies. Why can't we? God knows we need to. People are literally springing up out of the ground on every garden plot."

Medon would ask, "Since when have Athenians turned to Dorians for answers? We're the only city they could not destroy. I will think for myself. Athenians are not Corinthians."

"They soon will be. Every skilled craftsman is heading for Corinth to build ships and armor and goods for the adventurers. The heroes of our time. Eumelos their epic bard is of the royal house itself and has composed an epic poem of the history of the city. And then gone off to help found Syracuse. They are alive and full of action. Their new armor is the talk of the Aegean. And what do you do? You piddle around in the plains of Attica teaching people how to <u>farm</u>, for god's sake!"

"Because first things must come first, Tes." Medon spoke sharply now. "It doesn't make sense for Athens to behave as Corinth does. We need to keep our most valuable assets with us. And I maintain that they are the people themselves. And the land around us. All around us. I want to continue the consolidation of Attica that Theseus began. And to be successful we must learn to use the land well. We have forgotten. It is good land if we know what to do with it."

"So is the land in Corinth. In fact, it is richer than Attica."

"Then they should learn to use it well, too. What is so wonderful about colonies?" Medon began a new path of argument, calmly, even-voiced. "When the land can no longer support the people or when second-born sons of aristos can find no livelihood, cities have sent expeditions, with fire from the sacred hearth of the founder, to settle new areas. Fine. But we have a homogeneous population here that has not yet begun to use the land well, in fact, is only now reclaiming pasture and orchard not used since the heroic age. We need social reorganization that will accommodate the best of our people—second and third sons, and fourth—and keep the best with us here at home. It may not be apparent now, but we will be better off in the next generations if we build a great city centered in this vast and easily defended province. We have a tradition of combining and assimilating villages already. You do not think of the possibilities here."

Tes snorted. "No. Just keep on doing what we've been doing. That's what it sounds like to me."

Medon shook his head. "Just look at the Trojan debacle. That whole movement to colonize Asia Minor failed disastrously. It was an effort to find new areas of settlement and profit for the too-numerous sons of a war-like and booty-mad nobility, men from the overcrowded cities of the Mycenaean age, brought up to be fighters." Tes countered, "That was different. Everybody wanted to be a chief. And war was a means to control them. We need colonies." "No." Medon's voice was angry.

And they were back to cities again.

"Commerce comes first." He was interrupted by Glaucos. "We have potter's clay of the finest kind and lots of it. Aegina is outstripping us, and Corinth too now, and we must lead again. Our mountains have the finest limestone and marble and silver. We need more ships to bring more artisans here. Craft generates wealth. Colonization is subtraction, however you figure it."

The archon spoke. "Men change in many ways, but they will not control their loins or their greed. You know this as well as I do. We look about us at the ruins and will not learn." He sounded grim.

"Let us look not at ourselves but at this place, this fortunate location, and respond to it. Here where the very dryness of the air invigorates us. There are only 35 days a year when Helios does not shine and six times that number of days that are completely cloudless. Yet our plains are well watered. Our heads are clear to think and our bodies healthy to work. Though our soil is not deep, it is good. The Attic plain is the best in the world for fig trees, and the soil is excellent for the olive. The foothills are wonderful for vine cultivation and the mountains for sheep. Hymettus and its purple flowers serve us the finest honey in the world. We are not plagued with malaria and tropic disease, nor with the chilling weather of the north. Why do you want to go anywhere else? Let ships come to us. Let them carry away the work of our potters and bring ivory and amber to us. We have fine silver in our mountains. But most of all, our people are homogeneous now. Let us unite those who see us as a family of men, and drive out—exterminate, if necessary—those who won't join us. We will probably have to buy wheat, but we have plenty of everything else and the wealth to acquire it. Life is brief and has risks enough. I know a good thing when I see it. Athens is the best place in the world to be. Let's stay here."

Tes sat silent and angry, not willing to confront his father at the feast but perilously close to doing so. He ticked his head aside, a small gesture of impatience that he had. Theseus was in his mind, the warrior, not the politician.

❖❖❖

That Athena's gift to the city was the cultivation of the olive had a significance not lost upon the aristo-business man. The return on olive cultivation and harvest was very high compared to the effort in growing the crop. Glaucos explained to Teleo, "An olive grove supports without enslaving. It allows man leisure for other things. For sport, for thought, for action and talk. All the work can be done by women and children." And he and the archon would talk about agriculture.

"There are whole tribes who live off of trees," they would tell him. "In the high mountains it is the hard fruits, the acorns and chestnuts, that feed man and beast. In the foothills the soft fruits—apple, cherry, pear and fig, olive and the carob. Vegetables and grains, cheese and milk and bread, horse-breeding and cattle are for the lowlands, the grasslands."

Men, of course, were required as herders. Goat-herders, half-nomads, were not regarded as stable or civilized. The keeper of pigs, though, who stayed in one place and raised a profitable and intelligent animal, was a respected person. The distinctions, he concluded, were the same as in Smyrna, the same as they were in the epics he sang. He recalled that when Menelaos had offered a horse as a gift to Telemachos, Telemachos politely refused it. And properly so. The incident was in the epic to point out the character of Menelaos, who believed that the finest gift of his country was necessarily the finest for everyone. He was a man who had traveled widely—he had just told Telmachos so—but who had not learned very much from his experience.

Teleo the bard was a grasslands product, unashamedly happy with beef and cheese, bread and sun-soaked vegetables, with clothes of linen softened and shining from fine oils, with sweet wine and song in the light of the hearth and the torches. He enjoyed life in aristocratic Athens. He listened a great deal, in part because he was a visitor learning, and in part to save his own voice for the inevitable performance. He loved the feast, every part of it, right down to the beggar at the doorpost.

The Greek city beggars were not the products of poverty. Begging was a profession, a necessary adjunct to the feast. Teleo observed with interest the man who frequented the archon's home most often. He saw him everywhere on the acropolis, coming into the megarons and sitting on the floor by the door or pillar. His uniform was that of all beggars—rags, a stick, a sack for food. For he was officially a wanderer. Sooner or later he would be driven out by another beggar.

Most cities were small and had only one city beggar, but Athens had several, each keeping a kind of territory. The acropolis beggar was still very young and exceptionally strong. His great appetite was itself a legend, and guests would lay bets to see how much he could eat. He had his critics who said his gluttony was getting in the way of his job, which was to invite abuse as well as generosity. That was true, to a point, but then he would do something vile or outrageously ugly that would prompt the feasters to mock him and to throw the stool. He was called Mother Pig.

Mother was a great brawler, too, and had defeated every man who had tried to establish himself as official beggar in his stead. Such challenges were staged as banquet amusement. All the men would tumble jovially out of the hall into the courtyard to watch the contest. No holds were barred. Mother Pig knew all the wrestling holds and spectacular throws that would please the audience. He made it a vivid entertainment. It was a game he had to win as long as he could. Some night Mother Pig would drink too much and lose. He knew it, and every fight was truly a wrestle with the gods.

Mother Pig laughed when Teleo confronted him with his risky game one night. "It's the only game in town, bard. You should understand me better than most." He looked slyly into Teleo's eyes and relaxed.

"There is really no difference between me and the priest except the respect of men. I am the scapegoat celebrated of old. Men need someone to abuse, to look down on. More than that. My huge devouring mouth fills them with horror, as it should. Every living thing is afraid of being eaten." This said with appropriate mime, chewing his words up. "Men express in their contempt for me their contempt for themselves as eaters of other living things. For their own gluttony and mewling obeisance to authority. They need to show their superiority at the same time. And their genuine generosity. They need to feel more fortunate."

He paused and chuckled. "There has to be somebody who can take all that shit. I am that other side of religion, the dark side of the priesthood. I am as necessary as any priest. God help the city with all priests and no beggars."

He laughed and ate a great mouthful of tasty bread.

"Were you so wise when you took this way of life? It is unlikely that all that was explained to you in a family of beggars."

"No. Absolutely not, though there may be such things in the wide world. Well, I will tell you then, since you want to know." And he tore off a great piece of meat to savor and swallow while he thought for a moment.

"I had wanted to be a priest of Apollo at Delphi," he began. "From my earliest moments. I had loved the gods more than man. I felt their spirit everywhere, in the marshes and mountains. The city goddess was not at first my favorite, for I felt closer to the country spirits, with natural forces rather than the powers inside city man. I even sensed that I could prophesy, given the proper initiation.

"Then one day, while my brother and I were in the hills hunting, he took me for a wolf and by accident shot me with his sharp arrow. It pierced my lungs and ravaged my chest, but I survived and the wound healed almost miraculously fast. I lived for many nights in the sanctuary of Aesclepios—from what I've seen, I could practice healing too.

"My poor fate began when I found that now I could not be a priest. A priest of Apollo must be physically perfect and, while the wound seemed to me to be healed, it was a deformity. And so my brother was chosen instead. When that happened, in my rage I could have killed him. He who had deprived me of my only desire had won it for himself.

"I confronted him. I even accused him of meaning to mar me. He wept, and said that he must have been the god's choice, it had all been the god's doing. I could not believe it. And there was something so smug, so final in his righteousness. I was torn apart at the idea that he could be what the god wanted in a priest. I thought, it is easy to blame the gods when you perform a forbidden act that you want to do with all your heart. It is, in fact, the same thing and free of guilt."

His anger peaked and he added with soft irony, "But who knows what is in a man's heart? He said only what any priest would say—the gods made me do it.

"My life was ruined. I didn't want to do anything else, and my god had rejected me. I began to find a great solace in drinking and especially in eating. One cannot party too often when love leaves his life. I realized I do love the festive board and the company of people—not the people, just their company. Maybe it is for me a parody of the feasts of the gods. I fell into being a beggar of the town. After giving a prayer to Zeus that he continue his blessings on the host for his generosity, I eat and drink continuously, forgetting about the fights to come, immune to the taunts of men."

Teleokairos had not expected such a tale. Beggars had always been simple louts to him, often disturbing his performances, dirty and disconcerting. Mother Pig let out a belch and fell to his greasy meal again. Then his voice took on a steady intensity.

"No one here knows my real name even now. That should tell you something, Mr. Bard-who-chooses-a-name. I am already only the function I serve. Everyone knows my days are numbered. I say: So what? So are theirs, but they shift their mortality on to me. They hate me for it. I am a crumb of a man, reviled and abused, and finally sacrificed. Well, if you think about it, they need that in a god, too. There is some satisfaction to flesh in knowing that a god has suffered as you have. If he hasn't, what has he in common with you? How can there be any comprehension and love?

"I will be a good beggar as long as I can understand. When the day dawns that I become truly more pitiful than they, I will lose the next fight. That is when I am driven out—and should be. It will happen. Perhaps the arrow was sent by Apollo, after all. I have found my calling and it is harder than a priest's." He paused and added, "When the time comes, I will not go to another city."

"What do you mean?"

"There are ways a glutton can eat himself to death."

There was a long silence. "My god," Tel drained his cup. "I had not realized being a beggar was so complicated."

Mother Pig grinned. "Everything is complicated, my man. Very complicated. Tell me you didn't know that. You with your abracadabra stories." He reached over and slapped his greasy hands on the sound board of Teleo's phorminx. Teleo flared at him in shock and rose, gathering his things together. They tried to stare each other down. Teleo lost.

"Here, have the rest of my bread," he said. As he left, he flung his stool as hard as he could. Mother Pig collapsed in laughter.

✳✳✳

As Teleo had been told, the city beggar, who was so carefully well fed, had nothing to do with poverty and hunger. Real poverty and hunger were everywhere, even in Athens. There were no guarantees.

Teleo talked to Tes about the beggar, among other things. "Only a fool takes people on appearances, after all. That beggar is wise enough to have been Hermes in disguise—which is probably what men think when they meet a wise beggar."

"On the contrary ," said Tes. "People are what they appear to be. If they are noble, it shows in their carriage and speech. Their dress, however plain or fine, indicates their attitude towards themselves and others. Only the meanest do not wash, those ignorant or mean in spirit, for the gods demand it."

"No. Two men who seem to look exactly alike may be quite different. One may have ransomed his land to appear thus, and the other may have wealth untold hidden in his orchard. One is full of bravado and the other full of caution, yet they look the same."

"You are misunderstanding me. I would say even this, that as far as the polis is concerned, both men are of equal value—dubious value. For the one is unstable and the other ungenerous, both likely to go to ground in a crisis. Not the kind of man I want."

"Which would you take the time to cultivate?"

"There is the difference between my father and myself. He would reason with the conservator, and probably get his guarded cooperation. I would always pick the man who risks it all. He is the man of the future. He may lose, but his actions will eventually bring change."

"Times always change. These men have little to do with how."

"Yes, but we of all people must see again that change is good. Rapid change. Our spirit is a heroic one. We must regain it. The Achaeans will rise again. It is the aggressor that brings prosperity. Athena must show us the paths of the sea as much as the cultivation of the olive."

✳✳✳

At about this time Glaucos determined to move to Aegina, that prosperous island in the Saronic gulf within sight of the Athenian acropolis. His reasons were sound ones, though Medon

172

argued hotly with him. Land was still available to enterprising men there, but the basis of wealth was now mercantile. His desire was to begin a shipping family branch there, useful to Athens, and at the same time to be a landholder like his brother would be. Glaucos was an exceptional man, too. His conversation inevitably drew what men knew about the world out of their heads and into his. He had reacted to the Iliad in practical ways: "It is a ten-day sail to Ithaca from Troy, Thessaly is just across the water and Corinth is three days' sail. I can't believe these men never went home in ten years."

Teleo had countered with tales of their love of adventuring and looting. And while Glaucos did not know the delights of Ares, he could understand wealth well enough. He had said little of his own beliefs but clearly cared as much about Athenian policy as his father and brother. He sided with Tes on commerce questions, but he felt Aegina should be made Athenian, a concept closer to his father's than he knew. Personally he longed for land because he was the second son. His heart was with the new trade, but he needed to be landed, for that was what defined position.

Land had been a secondary concern on Aegina as long as anyone could remember. Located equidistant from Attica and the Peloponnesos on the sea lane to Corinth, Aegina was a natural overnight stop for all ships in-and outward- bound. It had suffered collapse with the Mycenaean cities, but people had lived there since the fourth milennium and, of the Thessalians who had settled there on Mt. Elia in late Mycenaean times, the few who remained were joined by settlers from Epidauros and life went on. Traders were the most important citizens in Aegina, and Glaucos liked that. He built a fine home of the local yellow limestone, full of seashells, and began a trade in pottery and bronze from both Athens and Corinth. He spent a good deal of his time trading on the mainland, getting goods cheaply in the countryside and trading them to incoming ships in Aegina, often saving them the trouble of a trip to Megara or Corinth and profiting for his trouble. He had his eye on the ivory trade and was interested in a combination of iron-and bronzework for women's jewelery and expensive weaponry. He quizzed Teleo closely about Lydia, especially Sardis. He had heard that the Anatolians traded in gold pellets of uniform weight. "No," he said, "though that sounds like a good idea. Maybe in foreign trade or gifts to sanctuaries they do that. I have heard that in Ephesos rings of a uniform weight are made and traded. But I don't see anything curious or special about it."

Teleo was far more interested in what Glaucos told of an eastern art he called chryselephantine, what Ardys had tried to explain so many years before.

It was used to overlay sacred wooden icons to make them appear to be alive, Glaucos said, and he sought craftsmen to bring the art to Athens. It should be profitable. First the statue was carved in the sacred wood. Then it would be entirely overlaid in ivory and gold. The skin of the god or goddess would be ivory, and the hair, clothing, sandals—everything but the eyes—would be rich gold. Rock crystal was set in to make the eyes, though Glaucos had heard of lapis lazuli for rare blue-eyed goddesses like Athena. Or like Kylein, Teleo thought, with a sudden pang.

The gilding of wood was a well-known process, but ivory was difficult and new to him. It was softened by heating and shaped in small plates to fit the contour of the wood. The plates were carved and beveled to lie smoothly against each other, and ornamental design was used to conceal the joinings. Ivory had to be oiled often so as not to buckle or yellow as it aged.

An artisan had told the bard, "You see the meaning. The use of living substance with the incorruptible immortality of gold. The combination creates the illusion of life in matter. Nothing is like it. Nothing. Except man." He would not live to see what the Greek sanctuaries would do with such a medium of religious expression, given under the great hands of Phidias the power to create belief in the gods in the breasts of godless men. The gulf between Glaucos and Phidias was the deepest man would ever know, and the most permanent.

CHAPTER 14

Sons or Fathers

714 B.C.E. Athens

Teleokairos Maionides had not reckoned with the combined consequences of fame and official status in the household of the archon. With adulation and respect came demands. It was only a matter of days after the singing of the Iliad that he had become a commodity as much as a child of the Muse. He was in demand at every feast, and protocol exacted an appropriate order of response, something he understood as a phenomenon but was not equipped politically to judge.

Medon, pleased, arranged everything, or his lieutenants did. The Herald Mentor was responsible for Teleo and his performances, and, while Mentor was a fine person, Teleo was 37 and used to being responsible for himself. These were complications he had not foreseen, flattering as they were. It was an uneasy time.

Then, in the wake of the Iliad's success, someone remembered <u>The Margites</u> and its resurrection created another sensation. Athens responded as Ionia had, instantly transforming it to political satire, and every mother's son had a version. Medon was less pleased with this, disgusted at the easy politicization of his Hellenic bard, vulnerable to the criticisms of his policy by conservative supporters who suffered most from the ready wit of Tes' friends as well as the street-wise opposition. For a while he wished devoutly that his bard were back in Smyrna, but he let the satire run its course, knowing it softened envy and strengthened him in the end.

There were subtle pressures on the bard too. Every host had a story or a special version of a story that he thought worthy of song. Every patriarch longed to be immortalized. Every host deserved a short complimentary song of excellent quality; composed extempore during the evening, to be repeated by every voice in the agora the next day. This bard excited such ambitions; his muse was vigorous and brilliant, memorable to other bards who were already copying and carping about his style. He was a singer with the daring and capacity to make new heroes.

He found himself living in an atmosphere where he was expected to give greatness but was not free to choose either subject or strategy because of the constraints between host and guest, citizen and bard-from-elsewhere. He grumbled about it. Tes laughed and told him straight out what he wanted from him. "Fame, my friend. Fame. You must stay and immortalize me when I become polemarkos. Give me a little time."

Tes wanted an epic about Theseus and regaled him with tales of the glories of Athens' past. Medon quite agreed with Tes about Theseus, adding, "I thought Tes would want you to sing of Kodros' sons, the colonizers. That would make good singing, too, but of course that story is not yet done."

✳✳✳

One night as he came to his room Teleo saw a familiar figure propped against the doorpost in the shadows. It was Mother Pig, who loomed up before him as he approached. "I know who stole your ring," he said., uncomfortable in the role of confidante.

"What ring?" Teleo didn't understand.

"With the black stone."

"Who stole it?" He knew his Samothracian ring was safely tied in a pouch at his waist.

"The new armorer Makarios wears it. Boldly, as if he does not fear the house of Medon and the singer of Smyrna. Such arrogance." He snorted with contempt.

"I am in your debt," Tel said simply, giving Mother Pig the wineskin he had at his side, half full. "Sleep with Dionysos tonight. Thank you, friend."

Mother Pig left, feeling close to the bard. Teleo wondered why he had not repaid his confidence with frankness. A Samothracian initiate! He smiled to himself as he drew out his own ring and lay down to sleep.

The next day he walked down to the gate of the Karamikos and found the house of Makarios just inside. In later days the site would be associated with Hermes, containing a gymnasium and shrines to Athena Healer, Memory, Zeus, Apollo and the Muse, including the house of Pulytion where rites of Dionysos Melpomenes were performed, the god of minstrels. Now it was a sunny spot on a gentle slope.

Teleo extended his hand to the smith before him, a sturdy dark man with enormous shoulders and arms, a soft band around his curly head to keep sweat from his eyes. His quick eyes saw the ring immediately.

A wide smile spread across his face and he threw his arm around Teleo's shoulders in greeting, turning him to the bench nearby. "Friend, whoever you say you are. Sit down." And he poured wine for them, drops to the gods and a healthy draft for them.

Tel began quietly. "Are you a native Athenian? I ask because of your ring. Are there others?"

"Lemnos. Beautiful Lemnos is my home. I am here for a while to make armor. The polis recruited me, No. I know of only one other ring in all of Athens, and it is one you will probably never see." Makarios laughed and called out "Melissa!"

Around the corner of the house came a woman, middle-aged but still handsome, her hands covered with flour, "What is it?"

Teleo watched the smith. There was a courtliness in his gesture that belied his station, But the bard knew well that on Lemnos smiths were important people. He had found a noble craftsman, visiting as he was, invited to Athens for his talent. How many of them were there, he wondered. He wondered suddenly if he should even ask Medon such a question.

Melissa was coming toward him smiling. Makarios spoke, "You don't see a ring on those busy fingers, but Melissa has one of her own. She is my housekeeper. You'll notice that here by the forge I am ringless too. Housework is too hard on jewelry." Melissa brushed her hands together, scattering a light film of flour about, like a halo.

"I am Teleokairos Maionides of sunny Smyrna."

Makarios let out a whoop of delight. "The Bard! The twice-born night-singer of the caves! God! I don't believe it!" He was like a man who had happened upon good fortune.

"How do you know me? I didn't see you at Samothrace."

"No, but they haven't forgotten you, you can bet. The singer cast up from the sea. So that was your Iliad!"

"It was ten years ago. When were you there?"

"Often. Every year. Last summer for the festival. They still talk about you. How did you know about me?" He stopped suddenly, struck by the thought. "You are looking for an armorer?"

"No. Someone said you had a ring like mine. That's all."

"Athens and Corinth and Chalcis are looking everywhere for good metal workers. They come often to Lemnos. So I came for awhile, while I'm still young."

"Is Melissa from Lemnos too?" He turned to the silent woman. She was clearly not a slave and certainly more than a servant. Makarios and he helped Melissa put meat and bread out in the courtyard under the trees, and they sat down together for lunch. She was good natured, shrewd and mild-mannered, a widow whose husband had been a freeman on the lands of the aristoi. She made lace and linen for trade and cooked for Makarios for lodging. She and her husband Chremes had been natives of Kyme but because of a murder there were forced to become travelers in the world in their youth. They had stopped at Samothrace in their wanderings and had both been initiates of the second degree.

Melissa was troubled with precognition, coming from an oracular strain in her family, a quality not strong enough to be useful but bothersome enough. She had not let anyone else in Attica know, but she had confessed her trouble to the smith.

"It forced me to leave Kyme. I knew what had happened in that vicious murder, and that we were in danger. Sometimes I will see a scene and know it will be important somehow." She turned her gaze to Teleo: "When I first saw you I thought of a steep hillside, torn and devoid of growth, and a long groove in the red clay. Maybe a landslide or earthquake. And of a burning city."

"I will be careful. I have fallen many a time in the mountains. Haven't we all. But I am more likely to tumble on these confounded pebbled streets than come to harm in a clay gully."

"As for the blazing city, we all know what that is!" Makarios added, laughing. Melissa smiled, "I haven't a care. There would be no point in it anyway. What will be will be. Have some figs."

While they ate they talked about Samothrace at Mid-Summer; about Kyme and Lemnos; a little about Athens. "What songs do men really want to hear?" Melissa asked.

"Always the latest thing, no matter how bad. And then, only later, the old familiar ones."

"Why the Trojan war? Always, always that war? Why not the other great stories—Oedipus and Jason, Prometheus and Heracles?"

"I have sung them, too, one way or another. But it is human narrative that is important now, the tale about men that men want to hear. Heroes, not gods. It is something about narrative itself that we love."

Makarios shifted. "Maybe men like to hear of trouble overcome. But I think this generation really wants to know what went wrong. And they don't want it to happen again. The order of things is up for grabs, and it matters a lot what they do from now on. A lot did go wrong, you know."

Teleo nodded. "I see in the faces of men an intense need to hear good stories. They are like Telemachos, the son of Odysseus, wanting to know about what goes on in the world. Most of them know only their villages, and each village has its good and useful lives. But the best men, the best of the Achaeans, are their primary interest."

He looked up into the leafy trees and down at the table, in dappled shade and sun. "Who lived the truest lives, they asked themselves. One who woke to see the same valley, mountain, and sea every day of his life, who knew where he would be buried, who saw identical lives spent around him, who believed that this was living as the gods meant him to do?"

Teleo looked into their eyes, intently. "Or was it the truest life to know inside you were different, to have an obligation not to accept whatever functioning norm existed around you, and, even though it was comfortable to be accepted, to resist it, not to acknowledge the loneliness, refusing that ease? What was the point of seeing the cities of men and knowing their ways? The gods do demand the sacrifice of the innovator, make no mistake, the victim, the price of change and new knowledge. The first man off the boat at Troy would die. The first man to sing a new kind of epic might also pay the price. But change may indeed have come."

Makarios sighed, remembering fertile Lemnos, remembering his delight with Athens all over again. Teleo paused and began again, gesturing towards Makarios. "We talk of the new iron technology and new kinds of armor. Of learning to write with the new alphabet Where is the fear of the first fruits?"

"Maybe the question should be 'Who will be the sacrifice?'" Makarios answered. "You think a price is paid for every change. The faction Tes and his young firebrands represent says that there doesn't have to be any sacrifice, that a time is coming when men will seek to be the first and will worship new gods who do not demand fruits."

"And most of us do not see those gods on the horizon yet," the woman said soberly. "Tell me, Teleo-the-much-traveled. You have seen the cities of men. If you were to found a city, what would it be like? How would men live there? And women?"

He pondered. "My songs always praise a land of ease in the islands of the blest, where the seasons are friendly and no labor is required. My observation is, though, that many work very hard for the few. For Greeks in Asia, it is the Lydians and Carians who do our hardest labor, or the people of conquered cities. Your question is one I will have to think about. I am a bard and prefer the feast to the fields."

Melissa said, "In the deepest thoughts I have about the polis, I think in the dark of the night, in my heart, that when the Mycenaean cities fell and men were forced to start again, that somehow they should have been able to reorganize, with intelligence and heart. There was no possibility of continuing as they had been. Why didn't they rebuild better?"

"When life itself is in the balance, one doesn't think of the refinements of politics and crafts," the smith said. "Nobody had the time or resources or contacts even to maintain the crafts at the level where they had been."

"But why?" she persisted. "Why didn't men settle in, determined to make a better system work?"

Melissa paused, then flat-voiced and candid, she continued. The future was in her eyes. "And Achilles will be back. This time one of his Macedonian descendants will rage across the whole world." She turned to Teleo. "He will be on fire from your Iliad, my friend, and will conquer the world—all of it. And he too will die young and leave chaos behind him."

They all fell speechless at the prospect. "No," said Teleo and held his head in his hands. "But he will speak Greek," she added quietly, "and be an initiate of Samothrace. A giant of a man. No life can be reduced to one statement. Take heart." They sat in silent admiration with their thoughts.

"But how could my song inspire destruction? That is not its point. Quite the opposite." He was anguished.

"People hear what they want to hear,'" said the smith. "When your words wing to the hearts of others, they take root in whatever soil is there."

***

Pressure built for him to sing a new song. "Always the latest thing," he would complain to Mentor. "I have my hands full with new hospitality hymns." That was his name for the short po- ems of courtesy to hosts. The invocation hymns were always a duty, those few lines to invoke the gods to the feast and to hear his song. He was adept at all of those, and at curses and bawdy jokes and epitaphs. He even sang some love songs in the new Lydian mode, which the older generation considered quite degenerate. At festivals he played for dancing, and there were always festivals. He began to tire.

He began to dream the same dreams over and over, sleeping only fitfully after long nights of performance. In one dream he came to a great palace. It was familiar to him, as if he had been there as a child or had composed it in an old song. It was full of big rooms, one after another, stretching away into shadow where he knew there were even more. The nearest were furnished, often sparsely, sometimes richly, with bedding and chests. He knew there were others, mysterious and dusty, that he wondered why he had not used. But he couldn't for some reason. It was a strange dream, disturb- ing, with promise and some deep fear. He always woke thinking of home. He would build a great new house for Zoe when he returned.

But one dream haunted him as the year went on in Athens. He was hurtling down the road in a beautiful chariot, the horses out of control and running free. Nobody was driving, and he kept trying to reach the reins and control the motion, but he had a terrible time getting into position, stretching and stepping past others who were there and yet he was alone. He could see the road far ahead as he rushed out of control toward the horizon. His heart would be racing when he woke.

And yet, if anyone in the world were completely free to be himself, Teleokairos Maionides was. The world smiled when he entered, and courted his attention. He was the Muse's darling. There were petty jealousies among the bards, and serious disagreements on their craft, too, of course. A lot of them, and most of the audiences, preferred the strictly familiar and traditional. Even the bards who were enthralled by his skill and his new long song eventually fell back to familiar ways. They all together learned new songs and competed good-naturedly at the festivals. And there were always festivals.

Would the world be the same after the Iliad? Of course not. But most of the people alive then didn't know that, and so they went on living in the same context with only an occasional smile at the memory of the great new voice among them.

***

Word came during the winter singing that a bard of Phokaia, an old friend of Teleo named Thestorides, had written down parts of the Iliad, especially the songs of Achilles' shield and the night raid, and was singing them everywhere representing them as his own. Teleo did not react very strongly to the news, but Tes and some of the bards were angry about it and urged him to send his objections. It raised an issue that was entirely new.

"Why should I care that he sings my song? Many people have. They began to do that the day after I first sang it. And I have sung the stories of many men."

Tes argued hotly, "But this is not the same. He wrote it down and then he claimed it."

"People have been writing down songs at Miletos for a generation."

"But they have said who the singer was who made the words, haven't they? This man has said his words are his own and they are not. Don't you see the difference? He is not composing. He is remembering and reciting the song of your Muse! Not his!"

"Then it is as if a man made a piece of armor and another claimed the making of it; I see what you mean. But what do I care if the Muse lets him remember? I expect she will desert him. The gods get even."

No one could arouse his anger yet. This sense of plagiarism did not grow serious until the signing of pots, of works of art, the precise recording of language. And so the elaborate story of his anger at Thestorides' betrayal and his pursuit of him into Chios is made by a later generation of scribal poets with a different sense of honor violated. For Teleo it was a simple matter: the muse of epic poetry was not the muse of memory, Mnemosyne. And that was the end of it. Still, these scribes would not let it rest. There is an old epigram they attribute to Homer which deplores his friend's betrayal: Thestorides, of all the mysteries mortals cannot comprehend,/ None is more unfathomable than the minds of men.

✵✵✵

The gods of the Iliad were a topic of frequent discussion at the feasts on the Acropolis. Once the archon began, "I notice how selective you are in the gods you sing. Only the Olympians, and they are not like the cult figures of the cities. Surely this has caused comment."

"Not really, not from most men. They are used to accepting traditional and limited themes. Few seem to realize I have left most of the earth deities out. But it is a city song of city warriors."

The archon smiled. "The message of the Iliad is that our gods are the Olympians and that wrath is like water and fire. Its madness falls upon friend and foe alike and dooms its victims. To be Ares is to be terrible indeed. But he is conquered by Athena, the goddess of strategy.

"You told us that Hera, the Great Goddess, was a force that is now controlled by Zeus, dangerous but manageable as an Olympian. I think that is the most—important—thing in your poem. Otherwise the gods are simple ones, as understandable as their ancient worshippers."

The archon stared hard at the distinguished company around him and then turned to Teleo. He spoke of the Ionians now, and of the Panionian which he and other Athenians agreed was one of the finest concepts of their century. They agreed that the most important idea, though, was that the polis was based in the official worship of certain cults, as the Panionian was unified under the cult of Poseidon.

"Whatever the motive originally," the archon said, "the Panionian is a politico-religious phenomenon that has enabled you to cooperate and to maintain your heritage. And you are a fine example of the kind of man such a system produces. That is one of the reasons that I've asked you here. I expect you already know of the games at Olympia. They are so successful that there is already talk of expanding the next ones. We are all there together, though the Peloponnesians still dominate it. Here in Athens we will do all we can to promote such a spirit."

A guest, a man named Pilatos, interrupted. "The new writing, a Greek invention in a Greek context, can also foster a pan-Hellenic attitude, and we support it. We will not be mean and isolated as a people ever again. That is why, in spite of my hostility to the archon's party politically,"—he smiled toward Medon—" I understand and support his invitation to you and to other guests. Teleo, your Iliad is magnificent. But it is also what Athens needs right now. We want you to sing it often and to stay in Athens. Everyone does."

Teleo indicated his acceptance of the graceful compliment. The archon smiled at him with great warmth. "My friend, you have intelligence and a good heart. Your Iliad gods are full of power, and they are close to man. They provoke thought and tie the hearer to our past without idealizing either past heroes or gods. But, most important of all, the gods are pan-Hellenes, not the cult gods of specific cities, or the earlier dark gods. They belong to all the cities, Athens included. I would like for you to stay in Athens, too, Teleo. I love you as my friend.

"But your song must go everywhere. Your songs can do for us what nothing else can, what no special, individual city cult god can ever do, unify all the cults of Athena and other Olympians behind a common conception of what they are. Your song will do what writing is doing—make and keep us Greek—but it will do more, for it is both Greek idea and Greek poetry. We are not so much one people racially as we are one people linguistically. And every city of Greek speakers, especially where life is obscure and mean, must hear it."

He had given the charge, publicly, and the bard gracefully acknowledged it with a poem. Later, at home, he said, "I thank you for permission to leave. I want to go home, not be a traveler in the world. It has been too long already."

"Of course it has. Your second year here will soon be done, and you have done well. We will help to spread the song. Perhaps you can visit a few cities on the way home. Perhaps go to Delos. And it is time you adopted a bardic name. It is the Greek tradition."

***

Teleokairos was strangely disappointed to see the archon thinking of his poem as a tool of power, something to serve the present. But since when had that been new? Men always had used narrative for something other than what it appeared to be. He knew that his rascally gods gave a universal flavor to gods that in cult worship were actually quite various. He thought long about it in the next days and decided slowly that his synthesis of gods was right and that the political men of Athens were, too. He would continue to take pains in his singing to mention as many particular places as he could, speaking of them in traditional and accurate epithet. And he would mention the special homes of particular gods. But the gods themselves would be like typically Greek people, welcome and recognizable in all the cities of Greek speakers, never described in terms that would make them look, in the mind's eye, like gods exclusive to a particular tribe or city. The poet as political animal, he thought.

And writers. He knew that writing was promoted as a policy by men like the archon, and so it would be everywhere soon. He thought seriously for the first time about learning to write. He thought sadly of Thestorides, writing down his Iliad. But most importantly, now he saw that others would always use his poem for their own purposes. He had always known that a bard could not control what men thought about the tales he told, and now he realized that even if he wished, a bard could not control how they would use them. The Iliad already had a life of its own apart from his, just as the old tales had always had. Even his great Iliad was his no longer.

Tes, of course, had flared at the bard about the Iliad's gods. Once he had argued, "How can we worship gods who are as capricious as you sing them? Who, more often than not, advise human heroes wrongly? Look at your Agamemnon. Vain and stupid, really. Peloponnesian, of course. Arrogant in his power, like a spoiled child. And still he is superior to a god who sends him a false dream! Can you say that man is less than god there? No! Because he trusts the god and follows his advice. He is obedient!"

"That is true," said Teleo. "But it is the man's arrogance that defeats him. It never occurs to Agamemnon that Zeus would do that to him."

"That's the point. He shouldn't. Your Iliad gods are a bunch of rich aristos, bored and dangerous. Like flies to wanton boys, they kill us for their sport."

"That was well said indeed." He looked at Tes in admiration. "If I am to show Achilles noble, though, isn't he best seen in contrast to them? After all, consider the poor bastards, the Mycenaean gods—deprived of real nobility. The greatest deed, to sacrifice life, is not open to them. What would you have them to be?"

"Wise! Noble. Consistent, omniscient, dammit!"

"And still be close to man? Come on, Tes. If they were, man could not get near them. Like the Anatolians. They are capable of being cruel meddlers when they do interfere in the natural order, and that is something to think about."

"But they are ridiculous! Hopping around the battlefield. Sitting disguised as vultures viewing the carnage from a tree on a dusty plain. Tossing each other about. They make me laugh."

"Great!" Teleo slapped the table in delight. Tes was peeved. "The gods aren't vultures."

"Aren't they? The evidence is otherwise. The gods are what you make them. The god who touches your life is one you half-invented. The one that you never honor is the one you are not aware of yet."

"You become aware all right when the ignored god exacts his vengeance."

"Think so if you will, but it is in your thinking. You in effect say, 'I have neglected Artemis' when you mean 'I have ignored a side of being that must be acknowledged for balance. I must try to make up for my ignorance. It is ignorance, not evil, that the gods punish, I think."

"Or presumption," Tes replied. But he was just making a case. For Tes heroic action was his highest desire. He became obsessed with the New Armor. Under the leadership of Corinth and the Argive cities the Greek fighter's costume had been undergoing radical change in the last quarter century, especially the corselet, helmet and shield. Tes had one of the new Corinthian helmets. It was a savage thing, beautiful to see, shaped low across the neck in back, close to the head all around, with cheek pieces thrust forward and forehead extending down over the nose, leaving a T-shaped slit for eyes, nose, and mouth. Holes punctured in the design around the edge allowed inner padding to be laced on for comfort. The helmet concealed the face as well as the head and was made of one shaped piece of beaten bronze.

"Who's in there?" He peered at Tes. "I can't see a face at all, just a glint in the eye. How can you see?"

"Better than you think. Put it on. It is hot and heavy, that's true. But with modern weapons, it gives the kind of protection that I need. I have been showing it to Athenian craftsmen for a long time now. They are reluctant to make anything Corinthian, but allow that it is a great improvement. Only Makarios the Lemnian will make them. What we are moving toward is a kind of battle uniform that the world has never seen before. Its central strategic pieces are the solid bronze corselet modeled very tightly to fit the individual torso, and the new hoplon, the shield. And, of course, this helmet."

"Isn't the solid torso armor a poor idea? What happens when a man is killed and the family must pay for new armor for the next man? The old armor would be useless."

"If he is killed in battle, his armor will have been someone's prize, anyway. If he lives, he will keep fit—no one wants to wear suffocating armor. If he outgrows it, he can donate it to the temple as an offering. In times past, heroic times, men used it. Not you Asians, of course. It is too hot there. Besides, if the armor is outgrown and left over, it can always be melted down and recast."

"What about the shield? What's new there?" Tes held up what seemed to be a regular round shield, wood with bronze rim and boss. It bore an owl, the identifying symbol of his genos, necessary now that the fighter's face could no longer be seen. Of course, each body corselet, molded so distinctly to each body, also revealed the identity instantly to close companions.

Tes turned the shield over. "Look." He pointed. "It's all in the hold." There was a bronze strip across the concave side, with a leather and linen loop in such a position that Tes slid his left arm into it comfortably up to the elbow. His hand then grasped a leather handle fashioned as a hold on the right backside of the shield. "Total control. See? The weight is comfortably distributed along my arm. It is as if it were a shell attached to my body. There is no telamon." The telamon slung a shield over one's back for use in retreats. "In a retreat you simply throw the shield away. Disposable. Just like a shell." He fell to admiration.

"Why don't you put a tortoise on the front instead of an owl?" Teleo teased lightly, very impressed with the equipment. Tes mocked himself. "Terrible Tes," and danced about, demonstrating its use. "No. This isn't a shield for defense. But it is fine for offense. I can even grasp an extra spear in the left hand and control the shield, too. I love it." His pleasure in it was genuine. "I feel like a new Achilles."

He pointed to the greaves lying nearby, handsomely engraved bronze and tin. "These are individually fitted, too, and very thin. I lace them on my leg over soft cloth. The purpose is primarily to divert a blow and to protect my legs from my own equipment." Tes was back to the shield again, demonstrating its positions during a fight. He caught up a throwing spear, holding it in his shield hand, then tossed it lightly to his right and, finding the throwing thongs on the shaft without his eyes and lifting it to cast position with two fingers, he tossed the weapon so smoothly, so gracefully, that he might have been a dancer. There was love and beauty in the eyes of men, thought Teleo, when they see such extensions of themselves. And lying nearby lay a stirring salpinx, the straight war trumpet, this one made in sections of wood and ivory, the mouth and flared bell made of shining bronze. How could a man own such miraculous things and never use them? He felt an ache in his heart, for he knew he couldn't.

The new armor had been the talk of the city for several years and, since every family was responsible for the training and arming of its quota of soldiers, the matter was everyone's concern. The maneuverability of the new shield made its popularity great, and its defensive weakness was made up for by the heavier body armor and greaves. The Corinthian helmet was less popular, its origin and its mask-like anonimity disturbing to the soldiers' psyche. But its implacability, its very lack of expression, itself could inspire a cold terror. It was a complicated question, because of the interwoven strengths and weaknesses of a combination of weapons.

This was the beginning of the hoplite armor, the panoply which was to revolutionize fighting in the next century and make the Greek warriors' phalanx the terror of the world. But now, though the body armor was being introduced in combination with the maneuverable shield and various helmet styles, men were just beginning to discover its best uses. The warrior still fought as an individual, as he did in the epics Teleo sang. A few minds may have seen the phalanx coming, but it was not yet in use. The beauty of it was the close order of men, each protecting the other, each anonymous, relentless as a muscle in the warrior body, its shields finally wearing only the identifying symbol of the city. But neither he nor Tes thought of such a battle line, though each could sense the panoply would cause men to fight in new ways. "It is glorious," said Tes, "as glorious a thing as anything Hephaistos could have made for Achilles. You must see why I fear Corinth now."

The archon objected to the cost of the new armor. But he had seen the writing on the wall and had brought in the armorers. All the cities were eagerly rearming with it, and he knew sooner or later they would have to use it. "Let the hot heads of some other city test it for us. Then we will see how best to use it. What fighting I want to see now is in Attica, to consolidate our political base and defeat those who will not join us. We are not alone in our strategy, either. I have word that a city to the south is following the very same plan as we are and has finally won. I mean a place named Sparta."

Once Tes spoke of his ambition to be polemarkos. To be war commander. "I will revolutionize our ideas of war on land and sea. Besides the hoplite warrior we should have a cavalry like the Thessalians."

"What are you talking about?"

Tes let out a strained and ironic laughter. "If you want to know, you are the first man in our household who does! Cavalry uses soldiers on horseback, not in chariots. The warrior can ride swiftly right up to the battle and then dismount and fight." There were no so such things as stirrups yet.

Teleo brushed him aside. "Oh, that. Men have been doing that around Miletos for years."

Tes stared. "Now I learn it. I have even heard the Thessalians are bold enough to ride into the battle itself astride their horses. I don't see how they can keep control that way. We are so backward in our doddering old councils here. While everyone else goes out and conquers the world." He was in a passion of despair.

And now word came that, while they had been concerned with Corinth and her successes, neighbors on their north were arming for battle against each other. Both were in Euboea, a large Ionian island north of Attica where the cities of Chalcis and Eretria had flourished for centuries. Each claimed the beautiful valley which lay between them on the south coast, the valley of the Lelanton river. Each had burgeoning populations and had been active in the colonizing movement which Corinth favored and Medon was resisting.

Because the two cities had influence in many areas, the whole Aegean world could be drawn into their quarrel. The truth was that the Euboeans, these Ionians, had been the real leaders of colonization from the earliest part of the century. They had settlements at AI-Mina, and Corcyra north of Ithaca at the mouth of the Adriatic, and at Pithecusae, and (in 759) founded Cumae. Ionian cities in Asia Minor were mixing in the new quarrel too, and Teleokairos wondered just how widely the fighting would spread. He reflected on Medon's pan-Hellenic dream and considered whether it included pan-Hellenic wars. Calchis had as allies already Samos, Corinth, Thessaly, and Erythrai, while Eretria had Miletos, Megara, Chios, and Aegina.

Word came to Athens that the Eretrians and their allies had paraded in a great display of strength 3000 modern infantry with 600 horsemen and 60 fine chariots. The fight for the plain was in preparation. Tes was beside himself. He pressed to send an Athenian force to fight for Eretria, whom he felt had been wronged. His cousins, sons of his mother's sisters, sent word from Eretria that they would be fighting soon.

"No," said his father. "Let them fight. We can send a delegation to the city. They can find out what we want to know. And they can try to keep the war going."

Tes bridled. "What do you mean, keep the war going?"

"Simply that all the wealth of Euboea is being consumed in a costly war. Their allies will pay heavily. It will effectively end any growing power north of us, and any opposition to our consolidation of Attica. It is no tragedy for Athens that the islanders are fighting."

Tes was angry. "Vile counsel. A coward who will not fight for Ionian blood. Vile."

"Which Ionian blood, Tes? That is the point." If the war spread, he would take steps, but now he had to contain Athenian enthusiasms.

"Tes," he said, "'I need a force of men to stretch and define our territory more clearly. Will you lead it? I can arrange it, but only if you agree to my purpose."

Tes sat politely, nodding, his fire banked for the moment.

"While Dorian Corinth moves west and, controlling Delphi, advises every backwater village to colonize, while our early Ionian leaders Chalcis and Eretria destroy each other over a small plain and use up lands a thousand times more important to soak a square mile in blood, we will do neither. We strengthen Delos, and we work tirelessly to convince the Asian Ionians that we are their fatherland. If they are convinced, they are ours without war."

He had said it now, but it was too late to impress Tes. "We must firmly annex all of Attica, this isolated, defensible promontory in the midst of Greece. If the Lelantine war had not come upon us, to weaken and divert others, we would have had to invent it. But we cannot let their refugees stream into our bordering territories and make trouble. That is what I want you to prevent."

Tes was scornful. "There is no glory in fighting villagers and driving away hopeless men. A boy half my age can do it."

"On the contrary. The boy would loot and destroy the land. Do not burn in this operation. Take the land where you need to, but keep it useful. Fight only when you must. Show yourself strong and a defender of a peaceful, prosperous Athens that wants new citizens from the land. You know, we must find ways of expanding our ruling class, to bring in new leaders, sensible noble men dedicated to Athenian power. There is too much to do as it is. As a son of an archon, likely himself to rule Athens for many years, you need this training. It will do more for you with all the people than ten hoplite battles."

But Tes went instead to fight with his cousins. He refused the commission of his father, raised a unit of hoplites, took his chariot and horses and, with six friends of the aristoi and their retinue, bid goodbye to his grieving family and went to Eretria. In the campaign the following spring he cut a glorious figure, clad in bronze, leading into battle with the bright war trumpet, the salpinx, ringing over the Lelantine plain.

Between the warring cities lay another, on the valley floor, rich as it was and beautiful in its vitality, Levkandi. It lay in the path of the armies. What the camping hosts did not corrupt was burnt by battle. Tes and his men for several weeks wore their glorious bronze and did their part in leveling beautiful Levkandi. Then the day came when the mass of Thessalian cavalry rode down from Chalcis and swept the valley clear of its enemies. Tes, who was on the approach to the west gate of Eretria, was amazed at the vision before him, 500 warriors, still astride their war horses, mowing down men as if they were peaceful harvesters. He was not ready for this battle, and he did not survive it. A sword thrust by Dion of Samos pierced his throat, the glorious Corinthian helmet no match for his blazing steel.

His cousins brought Tes home by water as far as Marathon and thence by land to Athens. He was given a hero's funeral. Teleokairos grieved for him and tried to comfort Medon, who suffered from seeing the relief of others that this hot-headed idealist would not inherit Athens after all. "Nothing can console me," Medon said. "He died insisting that I was his foe. He would not be my friend. Even in the underworld he will turn away."

"You are not the only father to have lost a son."

"But I have lost him many times. And he never had the time to discover I was not his enemy,"

"Who knows what he may have learned in those long weeks of battle?" Teleo paused. "Once you were a military hero. Were you ever like Tes?"

A very long pause. "No. I never was."

Soon after Tes had arrived in Eretria his Uncle Damysus, a nobleman of Eretria, had been killed in battle, an event that had heightened Tes' resolve to take up the fight. Moved so recently by the Iliad, it may have been Tes who suggested they honor Damysus with burial and funeral games like those for Patroclos in Teleo's epic song. After the sacrifice of animals, and then of captured warriors, offerings of oil were made, the body was cremated on a pyre, the fire extinguished with wine, and the grave barrow was heaped over the wrapped urn holding his ashes. In time his grave became a hero-shrine, honored with gifts for centuries to come. The bard heard of this from those who brought Tes' body home. He blanched. It was his Iliad's doing, no mistake. He had not intended this, certainly not human sacrifice, and he sought out Medon for comfort. "I cannot comfort anyone," the sad father told him. "At least Tes' funeral did not cost any noble Thessalian an ignoble death. I am sorry that your song, so full of wisdom, can be so savagely misunderstood. Dear, rash Tes' doing. It makes me wonder what is loose in the world. A poem of Hellenic unity? Instead—" Teleo interrupted "—a new age of bloody heroes? The gods have tricked me. That is not what my poem says!"

"True. We still must sing it. Must sing it everywhere." He shook his head sadly. "Literalists. People without understanding. They will always be with us."

Tes was buried in the family plot which he had shown to his friend, south of the Eridanos. "Right here. The graves on the left—my grandparents. Cremated. The eight urns are all babies, three of them theirs. Well, if I should die of reveling, give me an urn with horses and dogs—and hoplite armor. Don't forget that!" He had laughed."Some rich men are using bronze caldrons now instead of pottery amphora. Ostentation."

At the cemetery now was a new trench six feet deep. Within it, at the center, was a round hole deep enough to hold the urn of ashes, its top level with the bottom of the trench. Men were buried in amphorae with handles on the neck, women with handles on the belly of the urn. The hole was covered with a slab and the funeral pyre built in the trench over it. After the funeral, the ashes would be placed in the urn, along with tokens and belongings, and the urn returned to the hole under the slab. Then the grave would be filled, even with the ground, and marked with a stele or urn.

The urn adorning Tes' grave was an amphora in the latest style with many figures, pottery, not bronze. The prothesis, Tes lying in state with his legs extended surrounded by mourners, was painted on a wide band half around the great urn. Completing it was the ekphora, the procession, Tes' body on a wagon accompanied by chariots and hoplites. In another band was the funeral feast. Tiny figures, like the terracotta images broken over a grave by mourners—snakes and birds, mourners tearing their hair, Persephone with a pomegranate, horses and dogs—made a small design. At the bottom was a musician shaking rattles over the grave, and lyre players. At the end, alone and by the sea, was a solitary phorminx player. Glaucos pointed to it. "Yes. That is you. My father's instructions."

The bard looked around him at the graves. "How hard it must have been for your famlly, a son in his prime joining these little ones. The good die young.'" He thought of his own sweet Lydia. "Are you coming back to Athens now, Glaucos?"

He nodded. "I don't want to but probably will have to. Much can go wrong in a state. And a family. When will you go home?" He began to move away.

"Soon," said Teleo. "Soon."

But while he was preparing to go home, his two year invitation spent, Medon asked him to carry a message to Corinth. He wondered whether the archon was contriving for him to sing the Iliad there. It was possible, and he was willing. Corinth was only 50 miles away, and he could ship out of Aegina from there.

Before he left, he said goodbye to the initiates of Samothrace. Each gave the stranger's gift to Teleo. Melissa had woven a soft carrying bag of lamb's wool, sturdy and light. On it she had made an owl, a snake, and a herm, all interlinked with a thin red line.

The smith Makarios held out his hand. "My gift to my friend." It was wrapped in scarlet linen, a broach with double shafts thick enough to pierce the deepest cloak. Its face was worked in a scene in gold, a dog holding a fawn, still struggling. It was a wonderful work. "Thank you, my friend. I will give you a gift equal to it when you come to my city. And in my song." They wept at their parting.

***

The archon lived out his term, leaving office the year that Homer returned in triumph to Smyrna. He became a trusted advisor during the remaining years of his life, as archons would for generations to come. Homer saw him again once at Delos (in 708). They had met suddenly on the harbor path, going separate ways. Medon had been overcome at seeing him unexpectedly, the days of Tes' death flooding through him once more. "Achilles and Tes. Never do I think of one without the other. What could have been done." They clung to each other's company for the whole of the day, while others waited for them, and they parted in uproarious good feeling. "Learn to write, you bastard," Medon called cheerfully. "Join the modern world."

"Only when I forget who I am. Then I will write my name."

Medon did not live to see the ten-year archon term fail, but Homer did.

Three years before he died the Athenians reduced the tenure of all nine archons to one year and expanded the power of the other eight archons. They would keep changing until they got it right, said the independent citizens of Athens.

INTERLOCUTORY

The Voice of Letha Gooding

Why should triumphant beauty lead to pain? How can the best that is in us lead to the loss of those we love? It is one of life's mysteries. How many thousands of men would glorify warfare by calling up the rampant Achilles, forgetting completely the consequences of his wrath?

Tes was not the first warrior, nor would he be the last, on fire from the Iliad. The New Armor had been to him like the immortal armor Hephaistos made for Achilles, there to cover him with a terrible glory. The beauties of technology always entrance the warrior soul. Divine armor, gun powder, satellites, lasers, all are too beautiful not to be used by their worshippers.

What man-created beauty can escape utility? The arts are inevitably at the service of the polis; in fact, the balance between beauty and utility is the aesthetic basis of Greek art.

The poet will find that in Corinth epic flourishes, where no one doubts that art serves society under an oligarchic rule. And so the voyage continues, the journey of Telemachos to see how the world makes use of the bard. And to see how the bard's psyche is polished by the uses of men and how it turns to new subjects.

CHAPTER 15

"Homer"

713 B.C.E. Corinth

So he as well as his Iliad had been politicized, thought Teleo as he came to Corinth with Medon's message for the Bacchalid leaders. Corinth was deeply involved in the Lelantine war on the side of Chalcis, and the Athenian leaders wanted their powerful neighbor to know that Tes' actions were personal ones not reflecting Athenian policy. That the Bacchalids knew already could be considered certain. However, a gesture was important, and a visiting bard with a private message was exactly appropriate. That Medon wanted the Iliad sung in Corinth was also understood. Corinth had a strong epic tradition of its own, one which Teleo was anxious to hear.

The Corinthians were pleased with Medon's message and the courtesy of its delivery, appreciating the skillful rememberer as a political entity, a discreet and trustworthy one. For if a rememberer were false, what city could survive his perjury? Especially in Corinth regard for a man like Teleo was genuine and courtly.

He was housed on the Acrocorinthus in the palace of the Bacchalids and promised passage in the first fleet heading for Phokaia or Kyme. Acrocorinthus was a spectacular acropolis, on a plateau so high that it was an hour and a half's walk from the plain to the summit, so extensive that it has three small peaks, so well watered that it was said to have a well for every day in the year. The pure and lovely Peirene spring of the plain, said to have been formed when Pegasos stamped his hoof, was fed from this very acropolis.

If the gods were to choose an earthly city for their home, one would expect it to be here. The sense of power, of control was overwhelming. Immediately below Acrocorinthus to the north was the flat plain of the isthmus, bordered by the Aegean on the right and Corinthian Gulf on the left, a bridge of land less than ten miles wide between the west and the east coasts. At its highest point this isthmus was only 246 feet above the seas, rocky and covered with low shrubs and dwarf pines; some wheat and barley grew in its sandy grey soil. Towering on the opposite side of the isthmus to the north Teleo could see the jagged peaks of Kithaeron, that fated mountain upon which the infant Oedipus had been abandoned and from which the shepherd had brought him to grow up in Corinth. As son of the King of Corinth, Oedipus must have stood looking at this very scene, thought Teleo. As oblivious of his fate as any man. Mt. Helicon was visible too, far away in Boeotia, the home even at that moment of an unknown shepherd youth named Hesiod. To the northwest was snowy Parnassos itself, sometimes called the loveliest wild country the gods had given to man, the home of the oracular pythoness, the oracle of Delphi, the sanctuary of Apollo. The gulf, he knew, pointed straight toward Ithaca, the home of Odysseus. It was deep, one hundred miles long, with a narrow strait that made it the private lake of the Bacchalids. Southwest, though, on the Peloponnessos, so near that its snowy cap gleamed like a friendly neighbor's light, was the magical mountain of Kyllene, the birthplace of Hermes, sacred to his own souI. And to the east—what could equal the sight of the Aegean and the road homeward, past Aegina and Salamis, jewels in the Saronic gulf below.

Shock struck his heart as he saw that on this clear day he could see the acropolis of Athens—distinctly visible from here, lying below Hymettus, Pentelicon, and Parnes. Did Medon know this? He had not looked for Acrocorinthus from the acropolis of Athens.

What power. What location. What beauty! The center of Greece seemed to be spread out below him. Busy ports, fertile plains, prosperous villages. He wondered at himself—so fond of Athens and now so overwhelmed with the beauty and majesty of Corinth. He found he was not a political man. The world was too beautiful for that sort of aIIegiance. Any man who could climb this incredible acropolis and look at the world around him could be a god. Or should be.

He had to find out why this acropolis had fallen when Athens, much less than this, had survived the Dorian incursion, and his hosts were happy to tell him.

Corinth had fallen one generation after the Dorians had first come to the Peloponnesos. Aletes, the Wanderer, was a great warrior, taking Mt. Solygeius on the Saronic gulf and waging such constant guerilla warfare against the Corinthians that he eventually beat them into submission. But it was this same Aletes who, leading an attack on Athens, consulted an oracle who told him that he could take the city only if the king were not killed. The Athenian king had been Kodros who, as Teleo had heard in Athens, sacrificed himself for the sake of Athenian liberty. Aletes, in the face of such a divine sign, turned away and left Athens free of Dorian domination. Aletes ruled Corinth for 38 years (from 926 until 89I B.C. E.). He was a mild and fair king who treated Dorians and native Aiolians alike. His family, the Aletidai, ruled for four more generations, under Ixion, then Agelas, Prymenis, and then the fateful Bacchis.

This Bacchis held such power and influence that the family changed its name to his. All was orderly for a whiIe. Then, through dramatic internecine murders in 749, Telestes established an oligarchy so strictly in the hands of his immediate family that all marriages had to be within a group of close relatives, about 200 men aIl told. A ruler ruled for one year only as prytanis, and then returned into the family power structure, a pattern that would continue well past his lifetime, until the tyranny of Cypselsus (in 657).

The Bacchalids would have made the latter-day historian think of the Medici family of Florence. They came to power through an elaborate sharing of government in a system of noble families, in an ancient and complex city, at a time when commerce and manufacture was beginning to drive the lives of men. Bacchis and the later tyrants Cypselsus and Periander were not essentially different from Cosimo and Lorenzo the Magnificent. Learned, acquisitive, publicly generous and devoted to literature and the arts, skilIful in commerce and politics, capable of great cruelty, they would bring Corinth and Florence to be foremost among cities for a few brief generations.

Of course Teleo could not have known all this. He stood humble and wondering before the grand prospect of this powerful and prosperous community. It was a city of Poseidon, who ruled the seas around it and the Acrocorinthus itself. Only Aphrodite shared the high places with him, the Aphrodisium already a splendid altar to the love goddess whose hieroduli were to make Corinthian hospitality unique in times to come. The hieroduli were the temple prostitutes, whose fees went into the public coffers to enrich the city and make Corinth a favorite stopover for the traders of the Aegean.

The bard spent many days among the sailors. The city bustled with men of many climes, and the local population was burgeoning here, too, as it was everywhere during these years. There were long sailing delays here for it was worth the effort to move goods across the isthmus instead of around the dangerous capes to the south. A ship-road on the isthmus, the diolkos, ran level and straight from the Bay of Lechaeum to Schrenus. He watched small ships being dragged on a system of rollers from one side to the other. Larger vessels were unloaded and the goods carried across, to be reloaded on other large ships. The illusion grew in him that the world could not do without this central city, this center of its movement. The Corinthians in their high citadel did everything they could to promote that feeling. Tes had been right to consider Corinth a threat to the ascendency of Athens. Their cliffs of greenish chalk made a pottery so lovely—and its craftsmen a shape and design so graceful—that the world had temporarily forgotten the work of other cities. Corinth excelled in its woven fabrics and carpets, its metallurgy, its shipbuilding. Wealth poured into the city, arms merchant for the times.

Ore came in from the north, primarily from Euboea, by sea and land routes, to be made into weapons, the beginning of the hoplite panoply. Settlements in Italy and Corcyra had sent word that the barbarians of the north used heavy plate corselets very like the old Mycenaean ones found everywhere in the old graves of the peninsula. Now Corinth was producing them as fast as she could, unable to keep up with the demand.

The bow was re-emerging in popularity, and that was evident in Corinth too. While it may have been the sign of an old-fashioned hero in the time of Odysseus, now it was a sign of a resourceful one. The Cretans, always excellent bowmen, were a strong influence in Corinth now. But it was the Cimmerians sweeping into Anatolia who were wreaking devastation with their bow-bearing warriors, and word of the terror they brought arrived with every north Aegean fleet.

It was the panoply, though, that men loved. Everywhere in Corinth men debated its best use—not its acceptance, for that was assumed—its most strategic deployment.

⁕⁕⁕

How different the reception of the Iliad was here, in the courts of the Bacchalids. It was the structure that they loved, the way he had made the tale. While the Corinthians understood that their city was a part of Agamemnon's Mycenaean holdings during the Trojan war, they did not relish its secondary status in the epic. Nor did they especially like the absence of the Dorians; Corinthian rulers were Dorians who had not fought in the Trojan war. It was not their history. But they were cultivated men, subtle politicians, wealthy rulers, and they fell under the spell of the great singer. The Bacchalids were patrons of the epic.

In fact, their great epic poet Eumelos was a Bacchalid himself, as Teleo knew. His songs were sung constantly, but Teleo could not meet the great old man, for he had gone to Sicily with Archias (in 735) to found Syracuse, and he might well have died by now. Corinth valued its poets and builders, its artisans and priests, but it was always clear that all of them served the greater glory of the Corinthian oligarchs.

Teleo wondered at all this—that population growth and affluence were such spurs to accomplishment in the arts, that Eumelos the bard was most loved for his history of Corinth. Had he not always been in the same situation himself? To what extent did bards and potters, builders and goldsmiths really celebrate the gods? Did they not celebrate the rulers of the city that gave them patronage even more directly than they did the gods themselves? It was a near thing. Of course, some people thought that their rulers were gods. He marveled at that, and then smiled to himself. How in fact did it differ from believing that their rulers were grandsons of gods? He sang of that every day.

One of the favorite songs of Corinth was that about Sisyphos, the early Aiolian trickster king of the city who escaped from death, the twice-born king. Here he heard a claim that Sisyphos had fathered the great Odysseus, having seduced Anticlea on her way to her marriage with Laertes. He found the version amusing, for to him it only seemed an effort of the Corinthians to claim a Mycenaean hero for their own. It was an interestIng idea, though, for Sisyphos was as clever as Anticlea's father Autolycos, the trickster son of Hermes.

✣✣✣

One shimmering spring day Teleo went with a company of horsemen to hunt near Mycenae, an easy day's ride south of Corinth at the head of the plain of Argolis. He turned aside to go into the ruins of the golden city of Agamemnon. The Dorians had burned it and left the great ruin for all to see. It lay in a fine strategic place at the pass, flanked by two high watchtower hills, approached by a dramatic sweep of road up to the Lion Gate whose massive stones were said to have been lifted in place by the Cyclops. The city backed against a spectacular precipice above a wild, protective chasm. At the very top of the city stood Agamemnon's palace.

He looked long at the wheel grooves worn into the threshhold of the Lion Gate, thinking they were deep when Agamemnon went to Troy, that they were a little deeper when he rolled through them home again to a murderous welcome, that few had disturbed them in the past 500 years.

He thought of the gate at Troy, and picked up another stone to keep.

He walked among the ruins of the great room of the palace where Agamemnon died and looked from there down to the gate where in the next century the Dorians would break in to burn the city. To the delight of his entourage he sang the catalog of Argive forces, the brilliant list of the men Agamemnon commanded at Troy. He looked toward Argos, the capital built a few miles down the plain, closer to the sea. Argos was a powerful city now, some said the strongest in the Peloponnese. But it was at odds with both Sparta and Corinth, and so he returned to Corinth without singing in Argos then.

✣✣✣

At every feasting the talk was of colonies and the war between Chalcis and Eretria. Chalcidians had a rising colony at the tip of the toe of Italy facing Sicily, called Rhegium (founded in 730). Together with Troezen—so near to Corinth—the Chalcidians had begun a new venture at Sybaris ten years ago. There was talk that another of Corinth's allies, Sparta, would be colonizing soon on the north coast of the gulf which formed the instep of Italy's boot.

Ionians from Chalcis had gone early to Sicily and taken the best land. They were joined by other Ionians from the islands, especially Naxos. Sicilian Naxus had begun (in 734 B.C), itself founding Leontini and Catana within five years. One motive in the long-range settlement pattern was control of the strait between Italy and Sicily. Zancle, a small enclave of Cumaean pirates, was made a joint colony (in 730) by Cumae and Chalcis, who imported settlers from a variety of places to build it up—and keep it honest. But the Zancleans had urged Chalcis to settle at Rhegium, and thus the Chalcidians in effect controlled the straits. Corinth was pleased, for they were allies in the Lelantine war.

The jewel in the crown, however, was the lovely Corinthian town of Syracuse, large and flourishing from the beginning. And in Corinth all the talk was of weapons, colonies, and wealth. Hopes ran high and the atmosphere was heady. Corinth meant ultimately to control the coastal traffic between the mines of the Etruscans and the islands and mainland of the Aegean. During the years (to 700) she was to found Molycrium, Maoynia, and Oonidae, all controlling the entrance to the gulf of Corinth.

To colonize one did not throw his clothes in a ship, summon his friends, and leave on a following wind. The colonizer, the oikistes, led a complex preparation before he reached the colony. Every civilized craft had to be represented, as well as representatives of every tribe of the founding city. The cults, the festival calendar, the sacred fire, the constitution or political structure—all went along. If fighting was expected, a softening-up expedition went before.

For most cities, their colonies were autonomous after the initial founding, but not so for Corinth. Corinth demanded first position in all ceremonies that were shared by the cities. Any disputes were settled by the oracle at Delphi, well under the control of Corinth herself. She had sent her surplus population, and even some of the dissident elements, to form attendant cities, but with one important condition: a strong member of the ruling Bacchalids would be the ruler. Archias, the tenth in descent from the first Bacchis, had led the famous expedition which founded Syracuse and Corcyra.

And Corcyra was becoming a problem. It was an island at the mouth of the Adriatic sea opposite the bootheel of Italy and hence in a very important strategic position. Archias had left Chersicrates to rule a settlement there. Many of the settling people had been recruited from Tenea, a village to the south of Corinth said to be made up of inhabitants descended from Trojan prisoners brought back by Agamemnon, proud people who would well serve Corinth's purpose, or so Archias had thought. There were already indications, however, that that may not be the case, for they were demanding more autonomy than Corinth wanted to give. Eretrians were already on Corcyra, too, and the enmity that flared in the Lelantine war between Corinth and Eretria was fueled by knowledge of this rivalry. Syracuse was a much more amenable colony. Dorians from Megara had gone there, too, as had one of a family of prophets from Olympia, the Iamidae, and the people were more traditional. More Dorian.

***

In Corinth Teleo found that the audience for epic was obsessed with Jason. Eumelos, the Bacchilid-turned-epic poet, had composed an Argonautica which now was the rage of the Peloponnesos. That perhaps was a natural subject, because Jason was an explorer, if not a colonizer, and had come to Corinth. Sailing conditions in the Hellespont and the Black Sea lay behind the early adventures of the Argonauts, and Teleo's heart flamed to hear the passage where the Argonauts stopped at Samothrace before setting out on their quest. He wondered whether Eumelos was an initiate. Jason had been an early voyager out of Chalcis, that colonizing ally, and his story struck Corinthians where they lived.

That Jason had brought back from his trip, and brought to Corinth itself, an eastern priestess-goddess, Medea, was a drama of some importance to any colonizing city. Medea was rather like Kybele, and her effort to displace the worship of Hera had tragic results, her children by Jason being kllled by the Corinthians. Corinthian children had then begun to die, so the terrified city set up an altar to Medea. Who tells the tale makes the meaning, and Teleo had no way to know that in Athens only a few centuries later a single poet Euripedes, persuaded by Corinthians, would retell the story of Medea so powerfully that his version—the only one in which Medea murdered her own children—would so overwhelm men that the earlier tradition would be quite forgotten. Such was the power of Euripedes, who used the story to suggest the savagery with which the oppressed can react. Such was the power of any poet. Even that meaning would be lost to many men; their prejudices would grow rather than diminish, for they had never resolved their fear of the Great Mother.

⁂

As he waited for passage to Smyrna, Teleo found himself more and more at the shipyards where he felt at home, where dialect did not matter and the sea lapped at his feet. He loved to hear the sailors' stories and tell a few himself. And it was at the quay at Cenchreai, on the Saronic gulf, that Teleo fell in one evening with a sailor from Cyprus who had known his father Maion.

His heart leaped and the old ache reawakened. No, said Deion, he had not seen Maion since they were young men, but he had always wanted to talk to him. "About the summer he had found the child," he said.

"I was a young man then, building ships for the Greeks and stealing what I could from the Phoenicians," the old Cypriot said. "Helping with the wine trade as well as the oldest and richest one of all, the trade in slaves And I remember hearing at Enkomi that Maion had found the wreckage. I lost a kinsman on that ship and always wanted Maion to tell me what he saw."

"You what?" Teleo asked, surprised. "You knew the ship?"

"Yes. My kinsman and some of my best companions went down with that one. Ha! To Poseidon and Dionysos—who know when a man has had too much to drink! They surely did on that day!" He laughed and drained his cup and stared long into the bottom.

"What do you see there?" He could not ask what he had to know, so he asked something else. Something indirect. Let the old man remember. Don't rush him. "Can you see that time? Were you there?"

"As if it were yesterday," he said. "His bones lie rolling in the salt sea and his sweet flesh has long since been eaten by fishes. He grew up in my village. My cousin."

They both mourned a day long past. The silence hung between them.

"I was on that ship, old man." Teleo's voice croaked. The words fell out of his mouth like jagged rocks, too large, cutting, obstructing, painful. To the other's unsteady look. "I was. I really was. I was a baby. Someone lashed me to the the mastbox and Maion found me."

"You are the boy." He stared at Teleo. "The gods are your friends then."

"Please tell me. Remember all you can." The old man seemed to be rambling and they were talking past each other. Teleo felt panic.

"There are sometimes children on the slavers. But they are usually of a useful age or handsome boys for the courts of kings."

Slowly Teleo tried to draw him out. "We always thought that I must have been with my mother and that she was a slave. Or the child of the captain and his wife. Or a migrating family. Or a famlly

196

fleeing trouble with kinsmen. There are many reasons for rolling around in this old world. But no one remembered such a thing when Maion went to ask at Enkomi. That was weeks later."

"I would have left by then on my voyage to Crete. Well. It would be hard to say." His mind was wandering back. "The slave women, you know, are often pregnant by the time they get to the ports. Women are traded as quickly as possible. They spoil rapidly in the marketplace."

Teleo was about to explode. He brought his heart to heel like a hound.

"A small boy, you say. He would be a child of his homeland, most likely. Wait now, wait. There was something, if I could only just remember."

He drank another draught and sat staring out to sea. Teleo was in agony.

"My cousin was a rough man," he began. Teleo felt like throttling him, but he was afraid to breathe himself, as if a brittle branch might break off and crumble, impossible to recover, against the rocky ground. "He had run away to sea early, and I followed him. He killed many a traveler and threw his body in the sea. He took gifts from desperate women and then sold them as slaves after taking them to his bed. His only desire was gold."

Dear god, thought Teleo, not my rescuer. He could not have been a Samothracian. The old man turned to him with a confidential air.

"He was not the captain of that ship, but he was an ambitious man, and intended to be." His eyes lit up. "I know. That was it. The night we last met he told me he would soon have enough gold to trade for his own ship or even build a new one." His eyes glittered as he talked. "If he had only lived. He would have shared his good fortune with me.

"They were going to take a load of copper to Athens to trade for pottery, but on the way he was planning to stop. Not at Naxos." He paused, searching his mind, looking at his feet. Teleo felt like screaming. "No. Not Naxos. It was Ios. South a little from Naxos." He deliberated. "It was Ios."

He smiled and looked up again. "What about Ios?" The bard tried to steady his voice.

"He was going to ransom a woman and her child there. To her family." He gazed in amazement at Teleo. "Why, that must have been you!"

"Oh god!" Teleo shouted at him. "What else?"

"He thought her family would give him rich gifts. Much more than he could get trading them at Athens." He was becoming agitated now, stammering, overwhelmed finally at what his words meant to the bard. "That doesn't mean you are the same one. There could have been others."

"You've just said a child of that age was unusual," he blurted. "Go on. Go on. What else?"

"Be quiet. I don't know. Let me remember." He drank again, greedily, carelessly, his speech sinking, slurring.

"'This Homer.' 'This Homer child,' he said. He was laughing. 'He will be my fortune.'"

His heart did stop. Completely. "Homer?" The genos name?

"No, no, no. That is not a name," he said impatiently. "It is what we call a hostage. An Assyrian word."

But Teleo would not believe that. Homer. It was his name. At that moment he would have killed to save that name for himself. "Maybe he didn't say exactly that. I don't remember. I wouldn't remember at all except that he died the next week. No one expected such a storm at that time of year." He was beginning to mumble now, and to nod.

Teleo took him home with him and cared for him, but the old pirate never remembered any more than this. His hosts warned him to be skeptical, for many a story was told to those seeking loved ones lost in the world. But he had known Maion and Cyprus. He knew Maion's stem post sign and how he looked.

The old man began to convince himself that it was his cousin who had saved the baby's life, though Teleo doubted it. The scarf of Samothrace was never mentioned, and he knew it would have been had the cousin worn it. He had to consider that, given the cousin's character, he might have acquired the scarf by dishonest means. He might indeed have bound him to the mast to save his investment. Teleo was willing to grant that possibility. He was full of gratitude to Deion and gave him rich gifts. And, seeing the bard's prosperity, the old sailor pressed him subtly for more. Teleo began to fear that he would start to "remember" more. It was so long before he did do this that Teleo was convinced of the truth of their first encounter. Finally the old man left for Crete, promising that he would send word to Smyrna if he remembered more.

It was then that Teleokairos Maionides, at 39, took a bardic name, as he had been urged to do ever since coming to the mainland where the tradition was strong. He felt great good humor at the thought that his chosen name may, in fact, have been his real one. And he determined that on his way back to Smyrna he would stop at Ios.

***

Teleo did see Samothracian scarves in the busy ports of Corinth. He wore his own when he went there and was often approached for hiring on. Captains always needed sailors. It was hard to find a grey-haired sailor, as the saying goes.

A ship captain going west sought him out, wanting crew for a trip to scout land for projected colonies at the mouth of the gulf. "Most Samothracian initiates rise in the world. Why haven't you your own ship?"

"I have, at Smyrna. But I am a bard. My name is—Homer." It sounded strange to him.

"Naturally," said the captain. "Homer means singer, doesn't it? A stitcher-together-of - songs."

"I thought it meant hostage."

"Go with me and I will drop you in Ithaca and reward you for your music. I know you want to see the home of Odysseus."

It was an offer he found hard to refuse. He had delayed his departure for Medon. Now he would delay it for his own sake, for he sorely yearned to see the island of Ithaca. He had seen the cities of Jason and Hector. Why not Ithaca and then down the coast to Nestor's Pylos and home by way of Ios? He would do it. He would leave his goods with the Bacchalids to send to Smyrna for him, along with a message to Zoe. She would want him to go to Ios.

The Bacchalids agreed heartily and, not to be outdone, presented lavish gifts for the family of the great Ionian singer of the Iliad.

But his heart ached at his decision. It had been two and a half years since he had seen Zoe. A Spartan exile, one of the court guard who had become a friend, could not understand his melancholy at not seeing his wife again soon. "You may be sad, my friend, not to see Zoe now," he told Teleo, "but be glad that you have a wife you love. In Sparta marriage is not like that. The family arranges it all and they marry without ever having spoken to each other. Then they meet briefly in a dark room, and after the marriage is over the man then sleeps in the men's hut again. Until he is thirty."

"Incredible!" Homer could not help laughing outright.

"Not only that," said the Spartan. "They never call each other by name, just 'husband' and 'wife' when they speak. And sometimes a man will have children before he lays eyes on his wife."

Homer was gleeful. "No wonder you left such a place! But I don't believe it. Was there ever truly a man who didn't sneak a lamp into the marriage chamber?"

"Well. Who knows. The woman, left alone except for evening visits from her husband, would often take lovers of her own. There is no love between men and women caught in the marriage trap. The man will legitimize all of her children, but those clearly not his own he will disinherit. The important thing in Sparta is not the fabric of marriage. It is the solidarity between the men."

Homer reflected silently. Men who felt the need for such a pattern must still be in thrall to the goddess. Or the fear of her, he thought. The mothers must be strong there. Too strong. "Is that why you left?" He sensed in the guard an intelligence that spoke impersonally, and he was not surprised at the man's answer. "Oh, no. I left before that time."

"You left? Voluntarily? I thought you were an exile, someone who had troubles at home."

"I am, in a way. But I chose exile."

"Some time when you want to tell it, I would like to know your story," he had said. But time kept him from that story, one he wondered about in later times. Perhaps it would not have suited, anyway, because Sparta and Corinth were allies and tales circulated quickly.

He was right about Spartans as allies. They supported Corinth and Chalcis in the Lelantine war, though indirectly. They had just won a long and bitter conflict with the Messenians, struggling (from 735 untll 715), and they were blooming with confidence. The Messenian plain was rich and its people, becoming state-owned helots now, would enrich Sparta immeasurably. Homer observed that Sparta, in this time of expanding populations, was following the policy that Athens was—claiming adjacent territory rather than colonizing. When he mentioned that to his friend, the Spartan laughed loudly.

"Maybe the policies seem alike. But Spartans are like Cretans. They are more unlike Athenians than Corinthians are like either. It makes life interesting, anyway. I prefer the prosperous Corinthians. They're structured enough for me to understand, and they enjoy living. Tell me more about Smyrnan women, though. Maybe I could find one that I could love and trust—as you did." And he winked at Homer.

***

"What will I find in Ithaca?" Homer asked the captain. "Are you colonizing there?"

"No room. The mainland settlements will give Corinth all the control she needs—if she keeps Corcyra, that is."

"What do you think they will think of the Iliad in Ithaca? Do they remember that time?"

"Oh yes. Ithaca survived, you know. Through all the bad times. They say many people from the Peloponnesos fled to Ithaca and to woody Zante. Mycenaean craftsmen that didn't go to Athens or turn pirate went to Ithaca. It was a haven for several generations, shining like a light in the window after everything was gone. Even after the last towns on the gulf went up in smoke, Ithaca remained safe."

Survivors. His own focus was changing. He began to feel kinship to Odysseus. While he had sung in Corinth he had deepened the difference between Achilles and Odysseus. Corinth had been kind to him, but it was Dorian, not Ionian, not even Mycenaean. And it loved Eumelos' epics far more than it loved Homer. He was ready to leave.

In these weeks he had slept often with the heroduli, marvelously sensual women, priestesses of Aphrodite who worshipped their own flesh. His fees went to the state. He knew it was expected of him, and he needed them, but his heart was disappointed in himself. His sacred marriage was far away in Smyrna. His youngest son did not know him. Like Telemachos. He lived a compromise; he was a mortal. Gods or men were keeping him from home; even now he was heading west and then through Ios before he would see the smoke rising from his tall roof and the red mountains of home. As he sailed west along the gulf he looked to Delphi on his right and then to sacred Kyllene, the mountain of Hermes on his left. He poured drops to these great gods of his, and raised a prayer that they would guide him. One more voyage, and then he would go home.

INTERLOCUTORY

The Voice of Letha Gooding

Now he is Homer. He had to earn his way to that name, considering its magic in our minds. And there is still his tomorrow to prepare, his making of the other monumental poem. We are on our journey from here to there.

The extraordinariness of the Iliad would have done for the Greeks what Gilgamesh had done for the Asians. It articulated the condition of being mortal. As time passes I see those two poems as more and more alike. For a long time I had not the courage of intellect to face the Achilles in myself. I had read too literally the raw death of a poem sung for men's feasts, the fate of women as prizes. But Achilles is a universal state of experience, and I recognize his wrath and the beginning of his pity in my own heart. I have blazed like Sirius across the plain, Scamander—my shadow self—behind me. I have given the body of Hector to Priam and have kissed the hand of the murderer of my sons as Priam did, knowing the city would fall. I can say with Leontes in <u>A Winter's Tale</u> that I have drunk and seen the spider. It is human love that makes a mortal of Achilles, that draws Odysseus away from Calypso's invitation to immortality. Because of it I have almost been seduced into accepting death, even while still believing with Goethe's Faust that the struggle never to be content saves my soul from death. Anybody can love a perfect god. Any god can love its own creation. It is human love that is the greatest mystery.

And now to Ithaca. All of the ancient medley of apocryphal lives of Homer include a visit to Ithaca, the reason clearly being Homer's exact description of that place. In the psuedo-Herodotean version blindness first strikes him there, but he is cured. The Delphic oracle is said to have named Telemochos as his sire or grandsire, but the Delphic oracle spoke in mythic riddles, and most frequently to politicians.

Our man is approaching forty. To say that the Iliad is the work of Homer's youth and the Odyssey of his old age does not really help us. Of course we move from youth to age, unless we are Achilles.

How in God's name is it done? That is the burning question. Moreover, don't forget that while the Iliad is now substantially complete, Homer would have been singing it all the rest of his life and feeling quite free to modify any part he wished in the light of his thinking on the Odyssey. Just how he might have done so is an interesting speculation. It is no surprise to find that the shadow Odysseus casts in the Iliad is a long one.

On this voyage Homer will begin the search for Odysseus. Odysseus awaits us, and he is nothing if not patient.

CHAPTER 16

Odysseus Found

713 B.C.E. Ithaca

When that bright star rose which heralds dawn, the ship made landfall at an island. There is a harbor at Ithaca sacred to Phorcys, the Old Man of the Sea. Two headlands form it, with steep sides sloping to the harbor mouth, sheltering it from high waves outside. Once inside, large ships can lie without anchor. At the harbor head is an olive tree covered with long leaves, and a beautiful cave sacred to the Naiads. In the cave are huge bowls and two-handled jars made of stone in which bees store their honey. There are looms of stone where the nymphs weave wondrous webs of sea purple, and perpetual springs of water. It has two entrances: one to the north by which mortals may enter, one to the south, and in the roof, for gods alone. (Odyssey Book 13)

It was dawn when Homer leaped ashore in Ithaca, bidding farewell to the Corinthian ship with a lusty salute from his phorminx. The rising sun flushed them all in one red hue, coloring the sail, the moving men, and his strong image on the sandy beach. Homer cast a long shadow westward, five times his own length, as he moved across the flat sand up to the cave of the nymphs. Resting at the cave until full daylight, he lay there imagining the return of Odysseus to his home. This dusky place was clearly sacred to the goddesses of the sea and had been for a very long time. The steps down to the altars were worn by the feet of the ages. The feet of Odysseus, he thought, with a chill along his spine. The pale light of morning filtered down to him through the opening in the roof, the gods' entrance, and he thought of the cave at Samothrace on Midsummer Day. He prayed to the gods of this numinous place, and to the great gods he knew. A stranger in any land had to be wary, and any gods who remembered him were welcome.

He had come to find Odysseus, but no Athena came to help him. He climbed the low-lying ridge to get his bearings. Ithaca did not seem completely unfamiliar to him; he had sung about it many times. It seemed to lie low in the sea, seen against lofty Same spreading close behind to the southwest. Ithaca was small and rocky, cut almost in two by an isthmus, but it was rich in woods and springs.

More than that, it had probably been a strategic location for many centuries, controlling sea traffic into the gulf and down the coast from the Adriatic to the tip of the Peloponnesos, one of the few tin routes essential to bronze production. So the Corinthian captain had said.

How did a man come to be like Odysseus, anyway? Wasn't he shaped by the needs of his place, if he were like other men and not a god? The island might explain him.

These were Homer's thoughts as he climbed the rocky hill behind the cave and struck out south along the ridge which broadened into a fertile and high plateau. He stopped after two miles at a spectacular overlook. It faced seaward, and a little northeast. The plateau dropped off into a gorge, its edge curving close to him so that all its rugged beauty could be seen from where he stood. Ravens circled out of the mountainside, and a stream plunged off of the crest of the crag, splashing in a distant musical boom along the mountain to slip into the ocean below. He thought of the soaring river of Samothrace, and some of its mystery clung to his mind as he gazed around him here. Perhaps divinity was nearby, he thought. Surely some fortunate creature must be.

Someone did live at Raven's Crag near the waterfall. There was a field stone cottage, all alone and very old, perhaps even dating to Odysseus' time. The top of its rugged outer wall was thick with thorn bushes, a fine defense against any intruder. Dogs barked at his approach, and he knew that someone would come to meet him if he were not among savages. His hand was near his knife.

Someone did. He was very young, perhaps 15, and he seemed disquieted at the sight of the bard, so weary and disheveled from his journey. There was a dog with the boy, large and wolf - like, and the boy controlled him with some difficulty. That they were not master and servant was abundantly clear.

"I have been enjoying your view." Homer smiled to reassure him. "Surely the gods must visit you here, and often."

"If you're right, you are the first I've seen today. And the last, I'd guess. Sit down awhlle. I'll get you water." So the boy had some civility. And humor. And an ache in his voice.

"So it's lonely here?"

"Mostly boring. I went crazy at first. But not so much any more. I expect I'll leave pretty soon," he volunteered.

He was a slave, he said, brought up in the household of Nomius, the king of the island. He was Jason from Siros, an island near Naxos, and he had been kidnapped as a child of five and sold into Ithaca by Taphians going north. He intended to get back to his home, now he was almost a man.

"I was fairly happy here, growing up with the family of Nomius, treated like a son in fact and playing with their daughter, my yearsmate. Then last year they married her away to Same. I will never see her again."

His anguish was plain. "I had been a prince. I am a slave only for the moment. I could not bear to be with them or to see the gardens and the orchards where Nomia and I had been so happy. So I asked to come out here for a while."

"I see." There was a silence.

"How could they have done it? Sending her away against her wishes. My being kidnapped from my home. There is really no difference between them. Now all I want to do is to get to Siros, claim my birthright, and kidnap Nomia myself. My own people, unless they have been destroyed, will be glad at my return and will help me." He stopped. "How did you get here? I have just been praying to the gods for help. And you appear." He looked anxiously at his guest. "Do you have a ship of your own?"

So many emotions came tumbling out of him, as if his words had been dammed within him, that Homer spoke up quickly. "I am not a god. I have no ship. I can do nothing."

"You are a sign, though. Anyway;" he shrugged and changed the subject, turning to pluck berries from the vine over the doorway. "Want some?" He offered a bunch to Homer who accepted them silently. "Who are you? I don't suppose you walked all the way." He grimaced. "Or flew on imperishable wings."

A picture of Odysseus the trickster bloomed in the bard's mind. "I am Homer Melesigenes, of the tribe of Meles, a singer of songs. I was not born of rocks or trees, of course. A cursed Taphian trader put me ashore here, for I had proved unwelcome when my song offended him. My home is across the wide sea, far beyond Siros and Naxos. In—rocky Chios. And here I am."

It was a marvelous feeling, to make up his own life. His heart was glad inside him, risking. Why had he said Chios?

"I can see you are a singer." Jason gestured toward the bag. "Play something for me then. I am hungry for a sad song." Homer invented one for him, and they both had a good cry and sat down to a hearty lunch. The old shepherd who had owned the dogs had died the month before, and Jason and the dogs were glad to have Homer's company for a while, until someone else was sent to join him with the flocks. Homer was glad to linger, roving over the south of the island looking for echoes of Odysseus.

He realized that he had always thought of Odysseus as full-grown, mature, never as a growing boy on a tiny island in the west. But he had lived here, and once he had been an innocent. Not the glorious child Achilles always remained. Not the wounded boy living here now. Not the fated orphan still looking for his father. What kind of child could he have been? And how could he have grown so wise?

Jason was little help, absorbed as he was in his own loss. He admired Odysseus as a man who, against insuperable odds, had got his wife back safely, and he knew the story. Homer's heart went out to Jason. He was not a slave at heart, not even a lost child. He was Jason of Siros, temporarily down on his luck. And very naive. Homer sat with him and began to teach him how to sing. It would ease his heart.

Odysseus had been a child, of course, the child of Laertes and Anticlea. Homer tried to picture Anticlea coming here from Parnassos, on the north shore of the Corinthian gulf, to live on this island with a king who had shipped with that other Jason on the Argo. Laertes had been an Argonaut, although the Corinthian version of the story did not include his name. The child of the trickster and the sailor, that was Odysseus; the famous trickster Autolycos of Parnassos, Anticlea's father, was his grandfather and had named him. Odysseus had traveled to Parnassos as a youth, this Jason told him casually. There he had been initiated into manhood and had received the ritual scar. Homer had not heard that story before. He had of course heard that Sisyphos was Odysseus' father and mentioned that story to Jason, who hooted scornfully at the thought. Perhaps, reflected Homer, that was a story the Corinthians were floating in order to claim Ithaca. He smiled ruefully to himself. He was beginning to think like a politician. He had seen too much of the cities of men.

❊❊❊

The day soon came when help for Jason arrived and when Homer was ready to visit the towns at the north of the island. He said goodbye to his host. Jason knew proper manners, and he gave Homer a parting gift, a stranger's gift, he said mockingly. It was a staff for walking, with four stripes slashed across the upper half. Islanders used the sign to indicate that the bearer had friends here. It had a mystic meaning, Jason said, but no one had explained it to him; still, he thought it useful. So did Homer, who grasped it immediately and set off with high hopes.

Homer returned along the ridge and crossed the isthmus—a mile long and half a mile wide—bypassing a village on Mt. Aeotas, anxious first to reach the seat of Odysseus further north. Three miles' walk found him in sight of the lovely Polis bay, the only good one on the western coast, according to Jason. A small island lay in the channel between Ithaca and Same, about a mile from Polis bay and close to the Samian beach.

He gazed at the northern tip of Ithaca ahead of him. A ridge rose abruptly ahead on the far side of the bay going north in an ascent of three stages, with a col between the first and the second. The first hill, which curved to the west, was small and pyramided; the center formed a hogback ridge which ran into the side of a high, rounded dome, the whole seeming to be a mile or so in length. This was Mt. Neion. At the top of the hogback had been the palace of Odysseus. Homer let the scene sink deeply into his mind, to fix it forever, to see it in his mind's eye when he sang. This rocky island, so wooded, so well watered. He thought of how Telemachos would describe his home to Menelaos, that ineffectual man sitting in his glittering palace bickering with a wife who drugged him into thinking it had all been worth it. He gazed at the beach below and imagined Odysseus here, feigning madness by plowing the sandy waste to keep from fighting at Troy in that sterile folly. The fish-giving sea and fruitful groves whispered all around him. Just as they had that fateful day. No wonder Odysseus had wanted to stay at home.

A man from this tiny island, remote, should not have been difficult to comprehend. Odysseus was sensible, cautious, and steady. While he was an important king, he was an outlander, not one of the Achaean princes, just a man who married into the family, so to speak. Or so the Atreus brothers would have regarded him. It was better to have a smart outlander for an ally than for an enemy, and certainly necessary that such a man not be left at home when all of the princes were going to war.

Odysseus had been given the less glorious and more difficult tasks of the war because he was persuasive and politically skillful. For himself, he knew how to handle the Atreus clan. He did not have their wealth and he did not want their envy. He had seemed satisfied with a lesser woman than Helen or Clytemnestra—Penelope, a cousin from a less illustrious family branch.

And what had happened? Odysseus had survived; Athens had survived; Ithaca had survived. The aristoi fled to Athens when the other cities had burned, and then on to Ionia and the cities of Homer's beloved coast. And now, if Jason had told him rightly, Homer had found the place where the courtiers and craftsmen, the minor nobility, the native population, had come in the great collapse, the makers of the culture that the nobility had fed on. Ithaca and Athens, unimportant in the Trojan war, had kept their continuity and nourished the flame of life—at least for a while. Jason had said that the village on Mt. Aetos had been founded in that time by the refugees.

Ahead of Homer was the home of Odysseus, the sight for which that hero had yearned during all those long years of travail. It was a good place for a palace. The sea lay abruptly below on the west, and watchtowers rose northward on an exposed dome. There was a gentle slope eastward which flattened into a small plateau at its north end; south of it was a slope running eastward with a small river to the sea. A wide bay opened from the river, and the mainland of Greece lay opposite. From his palace Odysseus could have commanded a view in all directions within a few steps of his hearth. It was not grand like the Acrocorinthus, not sweet and warm as Smyrna. But it so suited the man who had been king. Perhaps the place did make the man.

Homer was made welcome by Nomius and the villagers in the town above Polis Bay. He was not the first bard to come seeking stories of Odysseus, nor would he be the last, his host said. "But do come and stay awhile and sing us the songs you know," he insisted. The island had no great city, but it was well populated and growing. There was a defensive acropolis beside the palace site, on the northern plateau. Small groups of houses dotted the bays and the isthmus. A large sanctuary on Mt. Aetos dated from the time of the migrations.

As soon as the singer's presence was known, he was sought out and welcomed in many a home. Ithacans felt their Mycenaean heritage in a more immediate way than had the Athenians—perhaps more as the Samothracians had. For Athens the old songs were spurs to something new. Here among the memories of the past—the living blood of the greatest losers, the technocrats of the Peloponnesos—there was a need for affirmation of the past that rode below the surface for every song he sang. There was Mycenaean armor in the treasure rooms, tablets of clay that no one could read any longer but everyone admired and husbanded because of their existence, such pottery and gold work that Homer was overwhelmed at the loss of such skill—the loss of such a quality of seeing. The islanders loved their antiques and, while they were proud of their forefathers for fashioning them, they were terrified and shamed because they could not reproduce them.

As a result, the joy in the past that he had observed in Athens had disappeared here and had turned to a solemn seriousness. Artifacts were stored and protected, but no one was using them or learning to reproduce them. They were objects of a passive pride Odysseus would not have understood. The true builders of Mycenaean culture had fled here, only to be lost to veneration instead of emulated and surpassed. The price of survival had been high. Too high. He wondered what it would take to put a sparkle back in the Ithacan eye.

***

Homer settled in with Nomius and began teaching songs and making instruments. There were many who sang in this remote place and they flocked to Homer for the latest thing. He was enjoying it immensely. Then one day Nomius spoke to him plainly:

"It is one thing to sing about the suitors eating up the substance of Telemachos' inheritance. It is quite another to have it happening to me while you sing of it. We have modest means here, though the gold in our treasure rooms seems to make us wealthy. Go with me to find a good place for you to school your students that doesn't work a hardship on my family. Feasting is an expensive business. But I will build you a home to show I love you."

Homer was surprised. Not at Nomius' frankness; true hospitality requires it. But at his own blindness. After Athens and Corinth, he had not noticed the drain on the household that his presence had brought. They ate together and set out in the afternoon to find a place for Homer to teach, one easily reached by most of his students, who came after a day's work was done. The north plateau, with its beauty and unobstructed view of the western sea—for they saw past Same from here—was an easy choice. In the next weeks Homer built a small house; many came to help and stayed to listen, the boy Jason among them.

Under the guise of learning the songs, Jason burned to sing of vengeance and power. In Achilles he saw a man who had sacked 23 cities and captured many women. His fair face flushed when he sang of victors taking the captured women to bed, of killing their husbands. Of wreaking vengeance. When Homer went to the hills to visit him once, he found a wooden sword of heavy ash, crudely made and chipped from recent use. His heart chilled at what the Iliad was doing to this young man. He thought of his own bardic name with irony. Jason was a hostage here, and Homer's coming had roused in him a recognition that there were travelers in the world, that his own fate was not done until he died, but that he could not delay too long. The Iliad fed old desires for home, new desires for Nomia.

The plateau was Homer's favorite site. At its eastern end was a sharp cliff which dropped several hundred feet. Cut into the base of the cliff, in the face of the rock, was an ancient shrine predating the time of Odysseus. A temenos surrounded it, still in constant use. Also in regular use was an old defensive wall, probably the labor of Odysseus' own hands, he thought with some excitement; he would have been such a builder and mender of walls. Though the island was low and slight compared to Same on one side and the mainland on the other, Ithaca sat boldly in the critical position for control of the two. Traffic could not even pass outside Same without detection, and, since Odysseus had controlled the mainland north of the gulf as well as the islands, here he must have sat, in this modest place, and ruled. Same, the giant mountain towering over Ithaca, must have reminded him that he was not a god. He was only a minor king married to a relative of the rich and beautiful queens of Sparta and Mycenae. But he and Penelope must have been two of a kind, and he controlled the tin trade to the great citadels. From here. From this plateau. So that is how it was, thought Homer. And he set his school up on the spot.

✻✻✻

Everyone had different versions of what happened to Odysseus when he came home, but they were all substantially the same. He had re-established order in his territory. He had found a center and made it hold. Then he had traveled inland to Elis to build a shrine to Poseidon. He had visited all of his neighboring rulers, the Thesprotians and Taphians, and also the oracle of the dead near Xylokastro in Thesprotia. There was a tradition that he had even gone to Etruria in eastern Italy for a visit among the people called the Etruscans. When he had stabilized matters around him, he had finally come home again. He welcomed all strangers and taught his descendants civilized behavior.

In Telemachos' time, when the world had collapsed, the refugees had fled to this calm sanctuary, where they were received with trust and sympathy. Eventually, of course, the island teemed with people and some set off together to find new homes. It was rare in those times, back in the ages of darkness, ever to know what had become of these emigrants. Still, some came back to tell what lay around them, and gradually knowledge of unfamiliar places began to accumulate in Ithaca, along with the stories of peril in the unknown western seas. All of this lore began to cluster in song around the figure of their greatest king, the wisest sailor as well as the most resourceful man of his time, the survivor king Odysseus.

There was tradition here that Telemachos had married Polycasta, the daughter of Nestor of Pylos. Homer immediately added to his song of the voyage of Telemachos a detail that delighted his listeners, that Polycasta had bathed Telemachos upon his visit to Sparta, just as Helen had bathed Odysseus, her former suitor, when he was an undercover agent in Troy. Homer relived his meeting with Amy and remembered the touch of her fingers each time he sang it.

He began to ache again for the love of a woman, praying that Zoe and the great gods would understand. Even the loyal Odysseus had needed Circe and had accepted Calypso in his long travail away from home. Homer believed in the sacred marriage; he struggled to remember it in a world where marriage was usually something else. He had been too long away. Nomius had offered him a woman in marriage, with a substantial bride price, but Homer had refused, explaining that he had a wife. After that the aristoi would send slaves to him, and that was how Rasenna came into his life. At least, that was what he thought.

Rasenna was a slim girl, young and spritely with lovely feet, high-arched and elegant. She had come, she said, to keep him company and hoped he would not humiliate her with a refusal. She looked straight into his eyes as she spoke, and his body loosened with desire. He took her to his house and closed the rough-hewn door against the brilliant noonday sun, leaving only the filtered light from the eaves to illuminate the chamber. The girl had turned toward him and, gesturing about her, she began to sing

She went to her chamber—her own son Hephaistos had built it for her—with secure doors not even another god could open. She closed them, and first she cleaned any imperfection from her lovely skin. Then she smoothed on oil scented with perfume, a heavenly fragrance potent enough to enchant the bronze palace of Zeus and even of earth itself. (Iliad Book 14)

He grinned in wonder. She was singing his Iliad! To him! A slave woman!

Then she combed her glowing hair, and arranged it expertly in thick, long, shining twists down from her immortal head. She chose a robe woven for her by Athena, a satin brocade, draping it round her shoulders with a golden broach. (Iliad Book 14)

The seduction scene of Hera! She knew it, every sound. As she sang, the girl was loosening her own rough chiton and letting down the plaited length of her shining hair.

She put around her waist a belt with a hundred tassels, and in her ears mulberry drops set in silver. Over her head she arranged shining veils and on her feet tied elegant sandals.

Her chiton slid to the floor.

Give me now love, desire, power over gods and men.

She was moving slowly towards him.

"There is love, there is desire, there is lovers' tender….." Homer interrupted. "Queen Hera smiled with her lips and her limpid eyes.'" He swept her away into his bed, amazed and laughing . "I have just been seduced by my own poem!" The girdle of Aphrodite that she sang of had enthralled the poet, too. Perhaps she was a goddess, this woman who loved his poem, who gave him back the echoes of his own lovely words, full of desire and intelligence. He didn't know what to make of it.

Rasenna explained much later that she served at the feasts and listened to the bards. Sometimes she had been given to other bards who would sing for her if she pleased them. And she remembered. But that didn't explain her.

"Why are you so surprised? There are women who can sing your songs. Don't be such a snob," she said. "Most don't because it never occurs to them. Some don't because they do not care about your subjects."

"What's wrong with my subjects?"

"Women don't like war. They are the biggest losers. You take their sons at seven and teach them contempt for their mothers and the love of warfare and plunder. Then the sons are killed, and the daughters and mothers are sold. Those who survive become old and ignored, little better than slaves themselves. Or their daughters are sold to the highest bidders and sent away never to be seen again and often to die in childbirth. You cannot guess the stories told by the fireside of the women. They would curdle your blood."

Homer looked blank. "I have never cared what the women told each other. I have never tried to imagine the stories women tell." He sat there, puzzled.

Rasenna moved gracefully away from him, to give his body room to change his mind. Later she touched him lightly from behind, enfolding him and rocking gently, and she began to sing him his own song of Thetis and Achilles by the grey sea. She felt his body relax and listen. He turned and watched her carefully, every motion of her throat and mouth. A great happiness surged up in his being and overwhelmed the song. Later they sang the many loves of Zeus and laughed at the improbabilities. They rolled about giggling, taken by all the complexities of eternal sex in a divine setting, concluding that mortals were the only solution for the gods. He had had no idea that there were women like this.

"Where in god's name did you come from? I don't suppose you walked all the way."

She made a face at his old islander joke and would not tell her story at first. "Because you won't believe it. Or, worse, because you will."

She would not tell her name, and so had been called by the name of her people, the Rasennai. She had grown up in Tarquinia, a Rassenian town on the western coast of Tuscany near the Tiber river where there was much contact with the traders who were Phoenician and Greek. Her family had moved south to Pontecagnano only a few years before, to a promising site south of the bay of Naples near the Greek settlements at Pithekousa/ Cumae. Her people had captured an ancient Pelasgian town, an outpost far south of their usual lands, and the danger of the site had been clear to them. Nevertheless they had gone. It was a decision that she lamented.

"My family is dead. Last year. That is all there is to say. All of them. My home stripped and burned. The treasure room emptied and blood slippery on the tiles of my mother's room. Everyone died so quickly that the day was quiet. The cracking wood and crackle of flame at dawn is what I remember—how quiet it was. The fire almost whispered around me. The Taphians had been at it so long that they were business-like, talking briefly in low tones as they went about their bloody work. They stored the wine and treasure methodically, sensibly for convenient trading, laughing occasionally over some grisly joke. It wasn't even fun for them. They didn't even get a scratch, except from the women.

"It was during the following days at sea when the kidnapped women, my sister and aunt and I, were raped and abused. My aunt tried to console us, but when she saw she was helpless and was savagely debased herself, she found a way out of her misery. Under pretense of relieving herself, she was getting ready to sit over the gunwales, her bloody gown pulled up around her waist. Suddenly she grabbed a heavy iron kettle and dropped into the sea. In the gloom they could not find her and finally stopped trying. Then they beat us, furious at having lost such a valuable piece of iron work." She cried softly and was silent for a long time. Homer stroked her face gently and smoothed her rippling hair.. "They did not dare sail north with us toward our own people. Instead they took a route through the straits of Scylla and east around to Greece. They were careful not to scar us and sold us, after a stop at Corcyra, here at Ithaca. My sister died soon after, and I have no people, no village to go back to. I have been saved by the gods for another death."

"Have the Ithacans been good to you?"

"In their own opinion, yes. I expect to be man-handled and I am. That is the fate of Greek-owned slaves and women. I cannot believe what the Greek women endure. Among my people women are respected." She changed tone and spoke directly to him, as a man would, "In the old days the earth gave women their power, and the remnants of that religion still exist among us. The earth was everyone's womb and tomb, and that was what the priestess represented. Somehow—I do not know what happened—the divinity of the receiver of the seed became passive and the giver of the seed became dominant." She paused. "I think one cannot do without the other."

Homer looked searchingly at the face of the thoughtful woman before him. "How did it happen? Why?" He thought of Sardis. "Through force perhaps," she answered. "Certainly by action. Rearranging nature—planting—eventually changes one's attitude toward the earth and its divinity. In the end, though, it is force that imposes belief." Homer disagreed. "No mind or heart can be changed by violation," he countered.

"Oh yes. Oh yes it can. It happens often. The abused become loyal to the abusers and want to please them. The weak begin to ape the strong. If a pathway can be found within the heart, the mind will help the heart toward change. The men from the north knew this."

"The men from the north?"

"Such men always come from the north." She paused and shifted tone." "I must tell you of my people, the Rassenai. They were an immigrant race driven by famine from their birthplace far to the east, a beautiful river valley. But in the famine they held an assembly. Half of them would have to migrate, and they drew lots. The emigrants said goodbye and went to the coast where they built ships and left their sweet homeland forever. Their leader was a man named Tyrsenus."

"Lydians," said Homer. "You are Lydian,"

"Yes. That's right. Do you know the story?"

"You know I am from Smyrna. Where they built their ships. Where I have built ships. My father was Maion the Lydian."

"Yes."

His mind was whirling. "Then it is no accident that you are my bedmate."

"No," she confessed. "I sought you out when I heard you were from that coast."

"And my songs. You learned them for your own reasons." He felt anger and loss, and a bitterness.

"No, no. That is not so. I am Lydian—Tyrehennian, Rassenian, Etruscan-whatever name you call us-and my people love music and words. That is why I love your songs. I am hungry for that. I am hungry for the words that show the world to me—not banquet banter. Not the words of Aphrodite's couch. They mean little to a slave. I am hungry to sing and be sung to, to know the lives of men and women and what they know. This hunger is a terrible thing that even a filled belly and a night of passion cannot help."

She began to pace around the room, showing her mind to him. "Do you know what it is like to be invisible? For people to act as if you were not there? To listen as a servant to men plotting strategies that you know will fail, the weaker plan carrying because of the voice behind it? To live among women who are pleased with their nothingness and are happy just to be smiled on? To abort a pregnancy so as not to mother a slave? To have to remember everything when-" She checked herself.

He finished for her, softly, "-when you can write and read."

She turned away angrily. When she swung back she was calm. "Just a little. I have almost forgotten." She slumped down, pale and exhausted.

He went to her and held her lightly. He would not let her talk then. "Go to sleep now. I will never telI. Sleep." Homer sat, awake, holding the woman in his arms, holding her lightly without sheltering, without passion, as he would a comrade with a mortal wound.

Her father had taught writing to Rasenna. He had learned the Chalcidian alphabet at Pithecousae from the traders. It had been in use there for 50 years and, while still rare among the Etruscans, was useful to the enterprising. "Why do you hide your knowledge?" Homer asked. "'I should think it would make life easier for you."

"I have learned something from Odysseus, after all," she said. "I know to be cautious. I will use my skill eventually, not here, not to keep accounts for a Greek master. It is the same reason I abort a pregnancy, Though the child would be free if the father were, I want no ties. I do not intend to remain a slave."

Homer had seen the same independence in Jason. Was it their youth that rebelled? Did all slaves feel that way, especially those captured in their late youth, those who remembered better things?

Rasenna knew some music, as did many women and slaves, for they had to have something to amuse themselves. She played for Homer on a lyre of Lanthe, wife of Desmentes her master, holding it lightly, letting it rest by her left thigh, the strings upright and between her hands. Her left hand, at shoulder level, damped and plucked delicately, her right hand swinging freely and gracefully, strumming. She would shorten a string by pressing against the upper shell or squeezing strings together, and he watched her technique with interest. It was clear she had much skill for a woman. No, he said to himself. It was clear she had much skill.

Rasenna said she knew the magadis, the old Lydian harp of 20 strings, played with the bare fingers. Homer questioned her closely about it and fashioned one for her as best he could. He made it under the pretext of doing it for himself, and all the villagers looked on with interest. They were highly amused when she taught him how to play it, a mere slave girl teaching an aiodos. All agreed she was very good. Then one day he gave it to her.

"This is yours. You are the best player, and it must be yours to play." When Rasenna's skill with instruments and song became generally known, her master Desmentes was enthralled and set her to playing for his household, excusing her from the most wearying kinds of work, especially hard labor with her hands. She was amused, saying to Homer, "My fingers are more calloused and agile than anyone's in the house and field, but I am to save them for my playing." It delighted her. Homer was pleased with her new notoriety because he knew she was also pleased. And it became easier for them to spend time together.

Rasenna never sang the Iliad for anyone else. That skill was one they kept between them, though she had learned more and more of it. She found she was unable to compose as a formulaic singer did, but she was a fine reciter who repeated verbatim what she chose to remember. She said she was going to write down the Iliad some day, in her own language, before she forgot.

She was indeed surprising. She knew things about the Trojan matter that he had never heard of. "The spirit of Achilles still lives," she maintained one day. "Don't tell me the heroic mode is gone."

"How so?"

"I have learned from the old women. On the mainland north of us opposite the island of Corcyra, there is a place called Epirus. The descendants of Achilles' son Neoptolemos live there, the fifteenth generation of Trojan survivors—they call themselves Molossians. They keep alive the legend of the invincibility of Achilles. And they war against everything—neighbors, land, gods—from all we hear. The Corinthians will have trouble with them, just as the Eretrian colony in Corcyra has had. More bloody slaughter. I heard this too from the Taphians, who fear them."

"Women's talk I am sure. Should I go there to sing my Iliad?" He asked in gentle mockery.

"If you have chosen fame and an early death, yes. By all means." She was irritated with his flippancy. "They are growing in power. Not a peaceable people."

"Rather like the Cyclops?" he teased. "Lawless, godless, uncultivating."

"Seriously. Speaking of your Achilles, though, there is something in your song that bothers me. Neoptolemos-Pyrrhus—whatever his name is—Achilles' son. You sing of an Achilles who is very young. At least he seems so, running to cry with his mother, sulking, reminding Odysseus that he is old. But Achilles has a grown son at home who comes to distinguish himself as a fighter at Troy when his father is killed. If Achilles fathered Neoptolemos at 12, he'd have to be 30 when he died—about the same age as Odysseus. Wouldn't he?"

"Hmmm. Yes, I see your point." Homer had been aware of the problem. "I don't know what can be done about that. The tradition is inconsistent. Maybe I should not mention Neoptolemos in my song. The man Achilles is almost childlike, and I want and need that quality to be clear. When he weeps for his old father, he ought to be weeping for his soon-to-be-fatherless son, shouldn't he? Achilles is less beautiful a mystery if he is imagined as going on 40, His madness less fine, less-"

"Silly. Really. The woman is nothing to him really; it is the principle of the thing. Like children fighting over a honeycake." She snorted in contempt.

"That is the way of war, Rasenna. Women are prizes."

"And it is the way of peace, too. Stealing women and selling them. And, if a woman's husband objects, or his vanity is hurt, then it becomes war again. It is all in the perception. The fate of women is the same." She touched him, trying to soften her words. "It is not a matter of power, as some say. It has something to do with—with what a person can realize and express. Maybe with language."

"I don't know what you mean."

"A man who is cruel to a woman is afraid of the woman in himself. I don't know—of being possessed by the spirit of earth? He is afraid it will overwhelm him, and he seeks strength in being with men and refuses to acknowledge what she is. He is afraid of being swallowed."

He laughed loudly and realized she was angry again. They fumbled into a silence, on the edge of an explanation too partial to be of use to them. Rasenna finally spoke.

"Odysseus, though, is wiser than any of the Greeks, perhaps because he is not really one of them. He is not afraid of women and does not need the boys. The difference between Odysseus and Agamemnon shows in their treatment of their wives. And Agamemnon's daughter Iphegenia."

"Stop," he said. "You may be right. All the same, I weep for Agamemnon who had to sacrifice his daughter." Ardys haunted him again.

***

Homer truly loved to sing the Iliad. It was exciting to every audience. But here in Ithaca he himself was preoccupied with the sailors and survivors. And, as poor Nikos had said so long ago, who tells the tale makes the meaning.

Rasenna told him one day that Odysseus had traveled after the war to the trading towns of the Etruscans. He had heard that before from the islanders. But she went further. "There are families among the Tuscans that claim descent from a son of Odysseus and Circe, named Telegonos. Circe, of course, is the goddess of our western coast. There is a cape south of a village called Roma that is dedicated to her, an island really, that connects to the mainland at low tide. They claim that once Odysseus was there and that his son grew up there and spawned a family."

"I have sung of Circe but not of an island in Tuscany."

"We say that Odysseus left Ithaca and moved to Tuscany and that he died there. Our people will not tell where he is buried for fear his body will be stolen by the Greeks."

"I have never heard a word of that. Where did you hear it?"

"I don't remember. It's one of those things a Tarquinian grows up with."

"Try to remember. You know, he could have done that of course. He very well could have."

Rasenna concentrated. "I remember they called him Nanos. Or maybe that was where he lived. I don't remember. We are like Odysseus in many ways, we Etruscans." She shifted the subject. "There was a version of the Latins at Pithycousae about the vengeance Odysseus took on Palamedes. You know, the man who tricked him into having to go with the Greek forces to Troy. The Latins hate Odysseus because they claim kinship to the Trojans. The Latins say that Odysseus later concealed a letter under the bed of Palamedes and then accused him of treason. When his quarters were searched, the incriminating letter was found and he was executed."

Homer grimaced. "No friend of Odysseus there. Clearly anti-Greek. I couldn't use it where I sing. Besides, my audience doesn't read and they wouldn't believe that he could."

***

To a sailor like Homer the stories surrounding Odysseus as a traveler absorbed him more and more, the marvelous tales, so like the song of Jason and the Argo. Here in Ithaca the tradition that he had travelled after his return had become mingled with fantastic adventures. Every singer had a different set and combination. And there was endless talk about the paths of the western seas. Everyone feared the strait between Sicily and Italy, that wild and perilous passage which even Rasenna paled to describe, whirlpool on one side and rocks on the other. They talked of the cave cults of the great goddess on Malta, where men disappeared, never to be seen again. They talked of the valley of the sun god at Thrinakia on Sicily where the mountain roared like a bull, of giant cannibal tribes to the north, and the ring of Phoenician settlements around the western ocean.

Homer thought back carefully to that long-ago day in Samothrace when the priest instructed the initiates on the sea-gates of the western ocean. It was burned in his memory, and here he was encountering much the same information again. But men did not freely give sailing information to each other. They exaggerated the danger so as to keep their trade routes secret. Many a night he let all these tales tumble together in his mind. He felt a deep excitement, as if fresh water were welling up inside him, spreading, nourishing all he knew.

"Why don't you become shipbuilders and traders here?" Homer would ask Nomius. "You seem to be surrounded by new colonies."

"Exactly. When the world is stopping at your door, there is no need to go to meet it elsewhere. When the old couple who tend our house first came here from Sicily, that was a strange and wonderful place to hear about. Now ships come and go every year. It's about 250 miles west of us across the open sea. However, if you go north to Corcyra, you can see the Italian coast and sail down the coast to Sicily; it's 100 miles longer and should be a lifetime safer. But there are pirates in the bays, as well as savages in the uplands who do not know metal tools. Frankly I am amazed to find a girl like Rasenna to be a native of that country. It is a wild place. The west coast is probably more civilized, with Greek outposts there. Greek influence makes the difference."

He settled in his chair. Homer saw Rasenna's expression when she overheard this remark, and he had great fun teasing her later. Whenever she displayed any special civility, he would taunt her. "Greek influence, of course."

Greek influence must have been early on the mainland north of the Corinthian gulf, he surmised. The oracle of Dodona and the Oracle of the Dead at the junction of the rivers Cocytus, Acheron, and the phosphorescent Pyriphlegeton—all were in Thesprotia, and Greek, before the collapse of the Mycenaean culture. The Thesprotian royal house still claimed descent from Odysseus, by what means he never heard. It was told that Odysseus had led these same people against the Brygi, and that he founded Bouneima. Apparently he had helped the area cities fight off the waves of Dorian invaders, and, perhaps because of his success, Dorians had not taken Ithaca. Here in Ithaca Homer heard tales of Odysseus fighting against the Dorians, and Rasenna told one of Odysseus as king of the Etruscans. He husbanded these new stories, planning to make a new song about Odysseus after his return, one the Ionians would not have heard before.

He would sit late at night before the fire, reflecting. He was not a Mycenaean bard, and the people he sang to were not a palace culture any more. Odysseus had not really been an Achaean at heart—even in blood—and yet he had loved their life—feast and family and wealth—all the benefits the golden kings provided for a few. Homer still saw in all his hearers a yearning for that luxurious past, a pride in the old heroes, an envy of a time when life was more beautiful if even for the few, a helplessness that its material ease was not to be recovered in their brief lives. A sadness.

Here in Ithaca the people saw one overriding truth: Odysseus came home and the Greek world followed him. When all was said and done, Achilles had fought for himself, Agamemnon for his brother, Menelaos for his wife, and Odysseus fought to win so that he could go home to his tall house and his family. Was that heroic?

The tales he was singing about Odysseus began to shift in his mind, like a heavy log settling in the heat, like the early tremors of the ground before Earthshaker moves the mountains. He sat long at the fire before putting it out. When he threw water across it, it uttered a cry like a slain animal.

***

Homer wondered what would happen to Rasenna. "Where would you go if you were free?" he asked her while they ate a midnight feast and listened to the sea pound below the hill.

"My people keep in touch with the will of the gods through divination. And it is important to ask properly. Our gods are not as sharp and distinct as yours of the Iliad. But they are real to us. I will consult them, and I will receive my answers through dreams. There is a place that I have in mind, though."

"Few people in the world can make such choices. Fewer can choose wisely. I think you can. Tell me."

She smiled. "Corcyra. I saw it from the Taphian ship. The women of Ithaca tell tales of it."

"The Corinthian island? North of Ithaca at the strait?" He was puzzled.

"There is a cult to Artemis there—"

"No!" Homer shouted. "That bloody, brutal goddess. Never! Nothing is more alien to your spirit." His heart pounded.

"Just hush and let me tell you. This is the sister of Apollo that I speak of. Not the savage mother of the old country. The women say that at Corcyra Artemis and Apollo bring reason into life. An Artemis that brings reason into the lives of women interests me."

"What makes you think these gods are different?" He was calmer now, remembering Samothrace. "Men seem just as bad and foolish as ever. They don't respect what a god is. They respect his power. And fear his indifference. And they put up with his casual cruelties, as they do a king's, because that is the way he shows his power over them. But don't respect him for doing it."

She took a long look at him and shook her head. "You ask too little." She smiled at him and drew him toward her. "You don't mean that. Your Iliad has made the gods real to man, personal and responsive. And for that to happen, they must have human weaknesses and temporary blindnesses.

"The new Artemis keeps enough rigidness, enough absolute purity, to appeal to my Etruscan needs. Yet she is true to a natural world whose laws man must recognize. Cities are only a small part of the world. The sun of reason alternates with the moons that move the changing weeks, the plants and animals, whether rearranged and tamed by man or not. Artemis is the goddess of the wild things—Feronia in Tuscany—but she is, at her best, a finer concept, an abstraction worthy to be the sister of Apollo. They are a rational duality, sun/moon, those two old eastern gods in their new Greek clothes.

"Artemis of Corcyra looks after the young—children as well as the wild young births of all the creatures great and small. She is the law of the natural world that man must honor, a balance of things that he must not violate."

Homer wrapped her white arms in his cloak against the cold night air. "You are too wise for me, or for your own happiness. How do you know so much about her?"

"I know Feronia from my youth. And women in my culture are not cut off from conversation with men. Wise and priestly people can be female there. Artemis is the protectress of the young against abuses of existing systems. She is chaste to indicate that she is not in thrall to passion, a way of saying her function is rational."

"Would you give up your sexuality?"

"If I must. Of itself it is little to give up, after my experience with sexual slavery. Only with you—with deep love—does it overwhelm me. And I think I know its power, too, after loving you. I can weep for the terrible, life-destroying passions of a Phaedra now." Rasenna looked at him wonderingly. "What I am discovering is that the gods change. Yes, I would go to Corcyra, where there are Pelasgians, Eretrians, Corinthians, people called Illyrians and Apulians, probably even some Etruscans by now."

"You realize 'Corcyra' means 'Gorgon-faced' don't you? You know what kind of goddess that can be, don't you?"

Rasenna was pensive. "Yes. But the gorgon face is on Athena's shield now, too. The old goddesses are dead. The world is changing. But until women are empowered too, humanity will realize only half of its potentiaI."

"I hope for your sake that is true. My own experience with the Great Mother, and my uncle's, was terrible indeed."

She had not seemed to hear him. "There is a sanctuary on the southwest point of the island, at Kanoni. That is where you will find me. If we should have to part." She looked away.

Homer knew from Samothrace that the Great Goddess, who came first, had been superseded by Zeus and that Zeus would be superseded—by whom? What harmonious balance, then, would eventually be possible? He asked Rasenna. "Have you ever heard of Samothrace?"

"No."

"You must go there then. It is an island near Troy where the mysteries are celebrated. Women and children and slaves—and even men"—he smiled slyly—"alI peoples are welcome to initiation there."

"Are you an initiate?"

"Yes. That is where the Iliad first came to me."

Rasenna was thoughtful, "So if that is true, I gather you understand more of what I have said than most men. Can there be a god there who answers to the deep division of the sexes?"

"I cannot say, for the secrets cannot be told. All that can finally be said of any mystery is that the initiates live by what they learn. The world says that initiation at Samothrace makes people better. More moraI."

"Did it have that effect on you?"

"I think so."

Rasenna sighed, "Then there are two places in the world where I might go. If I can ever get away from here. Right now," she looked at him "Ithaca is fine. I am content to be with you."

"This beautiful world," Homer gazed. "I wonder what will become of us all. Are you the way you are because you can read and write?"

Rasenna laughed. "Or can I read and write because of the kind of person I am? Or because I don't fit into any one society. I am no longer an Etruscan of my country, having moved south. I was of a family that destroyed a Pelasgian town and then was destroyed by Taphians. I learned an alien language because my father traded with foreigners. I am unwed but sexually experienced, a literate who pretends not to be, a free spirit who is enslaved. I cannot imagine innocence. As a woman I have no hope that Greek men will respect me except as a priestess. And then there will be their old fear again. I wonder how it feels to be just what you are, having always been that, safely, with no hidden nature, no tricks, no ambitions."

"What kinship I feel for you now, Rasenna. I am an alien and a seeker, too. I can't be otherwise. But there is beauty in what we lack. My Zoe has it. She is what you describe." He had spoken thoughtlessly and had seen her stiffen as he spoke. "I think that is why I need her so, you see. And why I feel so like you."

"Yes." She smiled up at him with infinite sadness. "If what you say is true, you need her. You are fortunate. But do not be so sure you understand her. If she is true to her name, her simplicity and innocence is very complicated indeed."

Homer nodded. "How terrible that you understand." And they stood together, small figures against the profligate sweep of island and sea and sky.

***

Homer began to search out objects that could be dated from the time of Odysseus. He thought he would add some local detail to his songs to delight his hearers, bring Ithaca to Smyrna when the time came. Nomius was doubtful that everything could be precisely named after all this time, but he agreed to help in the search. They visited all the altars in the natural groves and by streams, as well as the sacred altars surrounded by temenos walls. Since sacred objects were never thrown away but could be transformed into new shapes, the process was both rewarding and confusing. Fountains, glades, altars abounded, and then one day they came to the cave on Polis bay that was sacred to the nymphs, especially revered by the islanders.

Great wooden beams, polished and grooved and inlaid with ivory and nacre, gleamed in the lamplight. They appeared to brace the cave walls, though that seemed quite unnecessary. The altar at the far end was lower than the entrance, and Homer took two steps down the wide floor before coming level with the sanctuary proper. The altar was a dressed piece of bedrock five feet long and almost as broad. A pipe channel ran across it to control the flow of sacrificial blood, the stains of which shown darkly at the ridges. The rest was polished clean. Before and around the rock altar stood an array of bronze cauldrons on tripods, thirteen in all and identical, lighting up the cave as if it were day inside. The intricate chased design along the tripods' thin legs was uniform in all of them, and Homer's heart rose. A set of matched gifts! Truly expensive, from a great king indeed! The legs were on wheels, and the handles elegant and circular, graced with figures of horses, men, and hounds. "Surely this is Odysseus' treasure!" he exclaimed, in awe before them. "Brought here by the man himself while the sun still rose over Mycenae."

"No, no," said Nomius. "They are said to be molded after the old things but date from a later time, gifts from the islanders to the gods in time of great danger. Perhaps the originals were from the palace of Odysseus."

"What became of Odysseus' treasure?"

"That is still a mystery."

"And what became of Odysseus, Nomius? Why is there no great tomb here? And most of his palace is rubble."

"The bones of that man may indeed be here. Look carefully at Ithaca, my friend. It is eroding. The old tombs, once well below ground, often sit above the surface now. I believe the tale that Odysseus died at home among his people. But the tomb has not survived, either because the barrow site is forgotten or the cave site lost. Or the whole site eroded or plundered many ages ago."

"The island is riddled with caves. Do you think he lies in one of them ?"

"That is more likely than not. Remember the prophecy of Teiresias: 'death will come from the sea in peaceful old age.' That could mean anything. Monster. Fish hook. Pirate or Poseidon himself. Or it could simply mean he was buried on a headland that has since dropped into the sea."

"Strange that no story exists."

"But it does—they do. Every place within a week's sail claims him, since we have no certain tomb."

And surely the man had died, for he was not a god and chose not to be. He had come home not to peace but to chaos and difficult times. All the heroes who had sons continued in the songs for that generation of men. And then there was silence. There were no songs after that.

✳✳✳

No bard could ever tell of the death of Odysseus, though many tried. He was a mortal man, a teller of tales himself, and every poet understands that silence, the death of another voice. In the underworld, if one had had the trust of Odysseus, and had asked him how he came to die, he would have said that Teiresias had been right, that death had come from the sea. So Homer imagined——

Old. Still vigorous of mind, but old. In his late seventies. His people flourished about him and every day was still consumed with duties. He had led expeditions to the mainland in the years after Troy, and to Tuscany, and slowly he had reestablished his domain, although the world was now awash with newly displaced people from burning cities. Telemachos was now formally in charge and he would have sore problems in the coming years.

For now, for today his territories-Telemachos' territories-were serene. It had taken a lifetime—his lifetime. Such an eventful one. Now he rested on the terrace over the courtyard wall, a flagon of his finest wine in hand, alone, looking peacefully out to sea. Eastern and western waters were visible, and to the north past the towers water stretched all the way to Levkas. He imagined he could feel the old undulations of the black ship beneath him, his island like a ship floating in the wine-dark sea. But no. Ithaca was firmly anchored. It was home.

He had loved it so. It had always been his greatest love. He sank into a reverie, gazing to the western sea past the edge of woody Same. The sun was beginning to slide behind her pine trees, playing tricks with the forested hills, casting shadows across the island behind him.

He thought of his childhood, of summer evenings and of his first flush of youth on Parnassos at the home of Autolycos his grandfather. Odysseus glanced eastward at that peak barely visible on the horizon, in his mind's eye more than his own now. The home of the Muses, the beautiful Graces, the most beautiful women of all.

No. There had been one far more beautiful. Even now his heart ached to remember her beauty. As if it were yesterday he could see her at her father's palace. That was the first time he had seen her, Helen, the daughter of Tyndareus of Sparta.

Odysseus had been young then, strong and dark and kingly. He had come at 20 with all the other princes of Greece, to sue for the hand of Helen. Her beauty so astonished men that they claimed she was the daughter of Zeus by Leda, for Tyndareus could hardly have conceived her. As word of her legendary beauty spread she had been kidnapped by Theseus of Athens and had caused a small war. Her beauty had become a political issue, and now Tyndareus had to get a husband for her to settle it all. The people of Ithaca and the west, so proud of their clever young king so darkly powerful, had insisted Odysseus join in the suit for her hand.

And so he had come to Sparta. The life of Odysseus had been easy until then. Though he was shorter than the blond Achaeans, the Mycenaean aristoi, he was rugged and brave, a clever strategist, and with ease he had kept the Achaeans out of his lands, even becoming an accepted ally. His Greek was flawless; his eloquence became legendary.

Helen was quite taken with this handsome young suitor who so knew how to speak to her. Odysseus smiled at the memory of his courtship. Helen was intelligent and they had become friends. Her touch had sent sparks flying between them. She was as blond and voluptuous as a goddess. Only her palace guard had kept him from her bed; he had tried and she had seemed willing. He was sure that; given her free choice Helen would become his.

It had been his own idea, the plan that Tyndareus finally announced to keep peace among all the vying suitors. Each would pledge to abide by Helen's decision; and furthermore each would pledge his army to defend the right of her chosen husband should she be kidnapped again. Even now, Odysseus smiled ruefully to himself and shook his head slowly at what he had planned. He was so sure she would choose him. So sure.

Who could explain it? She had not. He had stood shocked, feeling the blood drain from his cheeks, as he heard the announcement. Menelaos. She had chosen Menelaos. Why?

In a deep reverie he turned to look west where the light glittered in the waters of the channel, still bright enough to dazzle his eye. He was gazing toward the offshore islet by Same when something caught his eye. Someone seemed to be there. In the light breeze he thought he heard a sighing. Was it a voice? Or only the sea sloughing out of the grotto below the hill? He stood very still to listen.

It came again, this time closer and more like singing. Odysseus began to move toward the sound, walking slowly, curiously, down toward the shallow beach. Maybe someone was calling from there. Familiar. He had heard this singing before. Somewhere long ago. He moved to the edge of the strand and stood looking out to sea.

There it was again. The soft singing. He could surely hear it now, and it was moving closer. He could see the shapes in the setting sun, their dark silhouettes against the sky and waves, drifting closer; beckoning. Now at last he knew. It was the Sirens' song.

"Come this way, Odysseus, glory of the Greeks. No man has ever passed us by but you on your voyage home, and then you heard our song! Come this way. We will sing again to you all that ever was on this fruitful earth and all that ever will be. Listen to us now. We will answer any question. Anything you cannot understand! Come to us and ask..."
(Odyssey Book 12)

They sang and Odysseus listened. No bonds to hold him now, his eyes on their dusky figures so indistinct against the radiant sun, he began to go slowly toward them into the murmuring surf. The sea curled around his ankles and then his knees as he moved. Unaware of anything around him the heart of Odysseus drew him to the Sirens, his last question moving from his mind to his whispering lips.

That was the tale that Homer never sang, though it did occur to him, more than once. Men didn't sing such songs as that, even in his time.

***

The year wore on at Homer's school on the plateau, and Homer found himself sitting gazing out to sea, wishing to be home again. As dear to him as she was, Rasenna was not Zoe. She was student and teacher, lover and friend. She was not Zoe. She found him on the bluff one day watching the sea bird's flight. He reached for her and smiled. "Come back with me to Smyrna. I will buy you from Desmentes and give you your freedom."

"Buy me?" she said quietly, shocked.

The sea looked grey and choppy under a sudden wind from the north. The mainland seemed far away under a low sky, and the sea birds wheeled out unexpectedly from the rocks below, scattering. "I cannot live in Smyrna with your wife. Your children would resent me. When you leave, I will go to Corcyra."

"No temple priestess. No!" Sardis burst open inside him.

Startled, she pulled back in anger. "What have you to say about my future? There will be safety and kindness there. They will be proud that I can write. I will be a woman of the world who does not have to beg a man to speak for her."

Homer wasn't listening. "You don't understand. Artemis is a savage. The barbaric Epirians live within sight of the island."

"The Epiriot women are skilled in herbs and healing. Wonderfully knowledgeable, according to the old women."

"With poisons, you mean."

"You are the one who doesn't understand." They stood miserably silent, then walked aimlessly, not together, around the plateau's edge. Homer spoke softly, standing near the edge.

"Once a woman of my family was sacrificed to Artemis on Mt. Tmolos. Perhaps she was flung from such a crag as this." He stopped moving. "I expect she leaped by herself. Gracefully, like a panther stretching out." His voice trailed away.

Rasenna's voice was level and clear. "I have been a sacrifice already. I will never again be a victim. I love you, Homer. I do not apologize for what I ask of you now. You must help me to escape."

"You will not go home with me."

"No. If I cannot have you for a husband, then husbands do not matter to me. I will have men as they have had me, as a convenience. They must not inconvenience my life."

"Then I will buy you from Desmentes and give you your freedom to say goodbye. I would not want to hurt my hosts."

"That is a problem for you. Not for me." But Desmentes would not sell her. He had paid a great deal for the two girls not two years before. One had died and the other had not had a child to make up for his loss.

Then the gods intervened. It was festival year at Olympia, and a youth of Ithaca, Stavros, a beautiful boy, had been there for a month training for the competition. Quite a few of the island's men were going to see him run, and Nomius wanted Homer to go, too, to sing, although there was no musical competition. Olympia was not far from Ithaca, just over the strait and ten miles up the river Alpheus, about fifty miles in all.

Most of the Peloponnesos would be there, so it would be easy for Homer to catch a ride after the Olympics down the coast and even further. It was the 17th Olympiad, and nobody wanted to miss it.

When Desmentes heard that Homer was leaving, his heart filled with anger; his slave would bear no valuable bard for him now. That night, sullen with wine, he sent for Rasenna and forced her, telling her grimly that if the great bard could not give her children, he would give her to others until someone could.

Rasenna, determined to escape immediately, demanded Homer's help. He sought out Jason and the three began to plot. Jason was naive, but Rasenna could not go alone, and they could not go with Homer. Naive though he was, Jason hit upon a sensible plan.

Jason and Rasenna would go to Nomia on Same when Homer and the men left for Olympia. He would find a pretext to take a small boat there, just across the channel west and south, with Rasenna a stowaway. Jason swore that Nomia would help them, and even dreamed that somehow she would want to run away with them. His face shown with the thought of seeing her again, and Homer's more knowing heart ached for him. Still, it was safer than going east where traffic and the wild north coast would surely defeat them.

They needed a good excuse for the trip, and Homer was quick to invent one. Next day he told Nomius of a dream he had. He saw a ship sailing for Same, laden with sheep for Nomius' daughter. The gods had smiled and sent a following wind.

Nomius looked at him askance. "You can't fool me, singer. You are even dreaming of leaving. You are like Odysseus on Calypso's isle: we offer you the eternal love of our people, and you mourn alone for another place." There was disappointment in his voice. "The gift to Same is a good idea, though. I will send Jason before we leave. He was always devoted to Nomia."

It took some doing for Jason to delay his errand until the festival ships were going, but he contrived it. The night before departure when Homer went to the women's quarters, Rasenna was playing in the courtyard and he stopped to hear her song. It was the lament of Ariadne for Theseus, a wonderful, wistful song. She sang of the loss of her lover, sweetly and intensely, and the keen of her sorrow cut through the night to the edge of the forest of Neriton where it echoed and died away. Their leave taking was tender and wordless.

Homer was full of fear for them. He watched from the palace ruins as Jason pulled away in the grey dawn, Rasenna concealed under the backs of the milling sheep. He left for Olympia a few hours later, in high sunshine at noon, going the other way.

✳✳✳

Nomia did help the fugitives get to Corcyra, but Jason abandoned hope of ever having her as his own. She was to be a mother now and could not leave with him. She did not want to, she said, even if he came back again with an army of hoplites. Rasenna took Jason with her, consoling the broken-hearted boy who was almost as old as she in years but as innocent as she was not. Nomia put them on a trader whose captain she trusted, sending gifts with her old playmate to soften his pain.

Jason was to get home eventually, to Siros, to find his famlly had all forgotten him and were uneasy with his inheritance. He took his due and returned to Ithaca, buying his freedom and living as a bard and friend to Nomius, often going to Raven's Crag and singing the songs of Homer himself. When Nomia's children came to visit their grandparents, they played on the slopes and in the gardens and sat on Jason's lap while he told them stories about when their mother was a little girl.

Rasenna became a priestess at Corcyra. She sent rich gifts to Desmentes which he grudgingly accepted, ten times the price of her freedom. She led the cult of Artemis into a brilliant generation of temple building. To this day the temples of that island are adorned with marble scenes from the Iliad on their pediments. The hero cult of Odysseus spread and flourished there until that world withered. Corcyrans to this day believe their island to have been Phaeacia, the home of Nausicaa and Alcinoos, and Arete, the wise queen who remembered matriarchal times.

The Ithacans were sorry to lose Homer, but they were survivors.

INTERLOCUTORY

The Voice of Letha Gooding

How do you like my "death of Odysseus"? That is my contribution to the myth and I state it for all to know, to save you a computer search.

It does no disservice to Odysseus' character. As the alleged Homeric epigram to Thestorides said, there is no mystery like the human mind and no human mind that can comprehend the heart.

But it wouldn't have worked anyway, Odysseus. The treaty that bound you to go to Troy would have meant nothing to the Achaean war lords if you had won what they wanted. No one could have saved you then. The flames from your forests and villages would have been visible from the Acrocorinthus. Is that what the Sirens told you? It is still no answer, is it?

To continue the voyage. Our Olympics have been running for almost a century now. Not a bad beginning, but only an infancy. The ancient games ran for 1,168 years in the four-year format, which didn't include at least five hundred years of earlier ritual games. Every now and then some one like Jimmy Carter or the Spartans during the Peloponnesian War will disrupt its continuity, but the world averts its eyes in embarrassment and goes on with the games. Most people have more grace than to punish their countrymen.

The Greek Olympics drew the best soldiers, so a truce had to be declared during the months of training. Would that we could be so civilized, even for so poor a reason. But we have matched the ancients in allowing for safe transit through hostile territory. In classical times the reward system for Olympic winners was just like ours. Though the immediate award was the sacred olive wreath and palm leaf, cities honored winners with triumphal procession, naming of streets and erecting of statues, even food and shelter for a lifetime. Some tombs became revered as divine heroes' tombs, but we save that for rock stars and Elvis.

You have only to read the funeral games of the Iliad and the sports in Phaeacia in the Odyssey to see how dear athletic contest was to Homeric life. In fact, Greek time began when Zeus' Olympian games began. The cultivated classes marked historical time from the first Olympiad of Zeus (in 776) just as Christians mark historical time from the birth of Christ. They would have said that Homer was born in the year of the seventh Olympiad and the Iliad was composed in the third year of the thirteenth.

Did Homer compete in song here? No. But from the very start of Panhellenism, artists and poets, historians and philosophers came to read and sing here, for no broader or quicker forum for dissemination of their works existed.

The place had been holy long before the first Greeks came (in 2000 B.C.E.), an oracular earth mother Ge speaking from a cleft in the rock called the Stomium, still honored in classical times. The invading Greeks absorbed this worship but made their earth-mother-with-saviour-child the dominant figures, agricultural deities like Demeter (wheat), Dionysos (vine), and Heracles (olive tree). When the Epei and Pisatans- -Achaean Greeks- -came in Mycenaean times, their dominant god Pelops married the old earth mother, calling her Hippodamia now, and took over the sanctuary. Then—you guessed it—the next invasion by Dorians ended that age and Zeus, their god, dominated the sanctuary, reducing Pelops and Hippodamia to mortals and calling the mother Hera. Rituals stayed but meanings changed. No people simply obliterated the old ways, which probably means some of the natives survived.

The last big change came in 776 when an EIian king needed to reassert his power. He changed the festival from eight to four years, to weaken the old worship, but he revived the ancient Heraclean foot races, in the name of Zeus, of course. Notice how clever he was: festival would be more frequent, more fun, and tradition would be preserved but transferred to the realm of the newest god. Tell me that myths aren't made by politics. Who tells the tale makes the meaning.

Heracles, both a Dorian and a Cretan/Mycenaean hero, had long been credited with originating the foot race and setting its length at the distance he could run in one breath—a stade, giving us the term stadium and setting the distance at 200 meters. At the finish line stood his sacred wild olive from which wreaths were fashioned for the winners, an unusually large tree for its species and one with leaves of unusual color.

Now let us attend the ancient festival in the year when it became truly panhellenic.

CHAPTER 17

The Long Way Home

712 B.C.E Olympia

In early September the broad valley of the Alpheus lay brown under the heat of the late summer sun. Crowds had been camped by the river for two weeks in colorful tents and lean-tos spotted across the flat valley, clustering close to the Hill of Kronos where additional wells had been dug for the throngs of visitors. Everywhere hawkers were trading votive gifts and food. In the cool evenings under a bright moon music and dance swirled around the campfires. The athletes were quartered away from the crowds, and each competing city had sent officials, anticipating victory for its contestants and honor for its people.

Homer was in great demand as soon as he arrived. When word spread of his new Iliad, Spartans and Pisatans and Epei flocked to his camp to hear him sing of the great war of their peoples, of battles, of embassies and funeral games. The holiday atmosphere livened his Muse and she made him think of new things. He surprised the Ithacans with a new version of Odysseus' homecoming, of the reunion of father and son at Raven's Crag, with precise details of their island which gave all of them immense delight.

The highlight of the festival was to be the afternoon of foot races, the day after the full moon. However, this year delegations from the Peloponnesus had come early to parley, for the festival was entangled in political struggle. The trouble was that the Sparta-Messina war, (from 735 to 715) had disrupted the games and no one was satisfied. Messenians had won many competitions before the war began but none since. Elians won almost exclusively during the war; then, (in 716) the first Spartan had won a race. Whether political bias or heavier participation had caused the results was a moot point. The victorious Spartan king Theopompos was here to argue, magnanimously but to his own state's advantage, that the games needed to be protected from such wars between the cities. And cities seemed to agree but for varying reasons. It seemed clear that the Spartans planned to wage more wars, and to win more games. However, a Panhellenic faction interested in extending the influence of the sanctuary and at the same time diluting the influence of Sparta, was supporting Sparta's position.

This faction, which included sanctuary officials, maintained that, in 776, when Iphitos of Elis had restructured the games, he and Lycurgus of Sparta and Cleosthenes of Pisa had made the Truce of God, the Ekecheiria, on the advice of the Delphic oracle. It was the old agreement to give safe passage through their territories for festival. Now this faction maintained that the oracle had also decreed that the sponsoring Elians should maintain strict neutrality in wars of all Greek cities who, in turn, would respect their position. The Elians argued that the record indicated exactly that policy. Whatever the truth of it, the truce now must be agreed to by every city sending delegates and apply to the whole month of training, giving safe passage both ways; no wars would be fought, no executions carried out, and Elis would be neutral territory.

Such a policy had captured the imagination of Panhellenists and the support of war-weary delegations. More practical minds would say, as the subject dominated camp conversation, that such a pact was absolutely necessary if the best warriors of every city were to have a chance to compete, and that even the Spartans didn't enjoy fighting in the August heat. Homer thought that Odysseus himself could not have conceived a better way to centralize Peloponnesian power and at the same time neutralize politically the people controlling a powerful religious center.

He noted that Athens was represented in the games and congratulated Medon's perspicacity. Change was not new to the Olympics, of course; rule changes, new events, controversy was always present. When the eight-year festival schedule was changed to four years and the games revived in 776, only one foot-race had been run, the dromos, one length of the stadium track. In 724 a two-length race was added, the diaulos, so successfully that in the next Olympics, in 720, a long-distance event had begun, the dolichos, 24 lengths of the stadium. Only free born Greek men who could prove legitimate paternity were eligible to compete; that rule, they said, would never change.

An important procedural innovation made in 720 still provoked discussion. All trainers and athletes had to participate naked. Some said this was to keep women from competing in disguise. Others said that sweat-stained clothes ruined the beauty of the event. The priests simply said that the race was a pure offering to Zeus, a sacred ritual of men before gods. Whatever the reason, the races that lovely afternoon in 712 were magnificent, bodies honoring the gods with every ounce of strength commanded by disciplined minds.

Beautiful, thought Homer, as the winners were handed palm branches and cheered by thousands of voices. Stavros was second in the dolichos, so Ithacans celebrated with a great feast at which Homer sang of how Ithacan Odysseus had excelled at games.

On the day following the race Homer watched the solemn procession to the altars of the gods, which ended at the ash altar of Zeus. There wreaths of olive, cut from the sacred wild olive of Hercules which marked the finishing line, were placed on the heads of the winners. A huge feast would follow the sacrifice. While it was being prepared the priests of the sanctuary presented to the assembled delegates and athletes a broader agenda for the next competition (in 708). Wrestling and the pentathlon would be added.

Athletes demonstrated what would be the basis of judging; the games were designed to reward military skills. Lengthy debate followed as to the appropriate order of events in the pentathlon and their timing. Finally it was decided that emphasis on arms and legs would alternate in the first four events-discus, long-jump, javelin, foot-race; then wrestling would come last, demanding coordination and strength in the whole body. The crowd agreed enthusiastically and broke up to feast and plan for the next festival. Officials talked quietly about getting ready for twice the crowd next time.

Homer was thoughtful as he sat at the campfire watching the dancers; he saw the agility of dance, the swing of field labor, the harmony of the men at ship's oars, as at least as beautiful as the Olympic races. Years later, in his Odyssey after Odysseus took part in the sports of Phaeacia, the King Alcinoos would praise such graces and Homer would describe a marvelous dance, two men tossing a fine purple ball into the clouds and to each other, all the while dancing in the midst of a circle of men clapping in time to the music. The bard's exhilaration at the sight of the Olympics was as genuine as anyone's; still, it was ironic that the very suspension of wars indicated that the games were for warriors. He began to look for a ride home.

✳✳✳

A vessel from Naxos was short-handed and gladly hired Homer as crew. Thus began a trip homeward that was to stretch across the next two summers. He sang his way along the western coast as the ship rested on legs of the voyage, and around the cape of Malea, until storms rose and almost drove them out into the western sea. The Pleiades had set by the time they reached Melos In the Cyclades.

Under threatening clouds they set out again, determined to reach home. Homer thought with heavy heart of Nikos heading for Lemnos those many years before under such a sky. When one of the sailors told the worried crew that Homer wore the magical scarf of Samothrace which would save them at sea, Homer laughed and assured them that it was true. At once came a thunderclap, a good omen. Then a wild storm broke and they were driven perilously toward Siphnos and the islets off Paros. But the crew now was confident, skillful. They cheered lustily when in the darkness the blue flames of the Dioscuri played around the mast. Homer stood amazed. Ever after they would tell of the potent scarf that saved them. Nor would a subdued Homer ever forget; the gods had rescued him from Poseidon once again.

Winter passed comfortably at Naxos where every household welcomed him and the aristoi showered him with costly gifts. He bought a slave boy he called Aidon, because he was talented in song, to help him manage the belongings he carried with him.

At the first hint of spring Homer said goodbye to his hosts and set out for Ios, so close to the southwest that he had watched its outline all through the winter dreaming of what it held for him. He approached it as he had Samothrace, with a sense of destiny. Its peaks were half as high, its perimeter about the same, its position among the close and friendly islands of the Cyclades quite different.

King Kreophylos welcomed him with high courtesy; indeed, Homer's Iliad had preceded him. Medon's heralds had been busy, and every city that had sent delegations to the Olympics had gone home to spread the news of the new song of the wrath of Achilles.

When Homer first broached the subject of his parentage, reaction was quick and intense. Few families had not been touched in these generations by piracy and emigration, and they took a personal interest in his plight. They looked intensely into each other's faces, Homer and the islanders, hoping to see echoes of their own. Rememberers listed for him the families who had migrated eastward in the past two generations, to Kolophon, and Chios, and Kyme. The fates of daughters who had married into distant lands were often obscure.

There had been one couple who they knew had died young somewhere in Anatolia and had left a daughter named Critheis, but no one knew what had become of her. Her family had once been prosperous but the direct line had since died out. None had been bards. Homer's heart quickened when he heard that there had been blindness in the family. The oracle of Klaros burned suddenly in his mind—the blind bard of Chios?? Maybe. Maybe there was a connection.

He listened to stories of piracy and loss. Many families were happy to claim such a sweet singer. They took him to their hearts. Surrounded by possible kin at every feast, he saw no certain flesh, no certain hand on his shoulder, or voice saying, "I have longed for you. Come home." He

229

wanted to claim Ios as his mother's home, and so he did. He enjoyed these warm people and enter-tained them all. Yet he felt like Asian Ionians when they returned to Athens. Perhaps Ios was his family home once, but now he smiled to himself because home was somewhere else and he knew where to find it.

Then Cretans came offering rich rewards if Homer would winter on their island. He needed to go home; yet he remembered Maion's visits to Crete, and rich traditions of Mycenaean Crete in epic tales. He knew he would never have the chance again. So at 41 Homer went to Crete, where he was received with adulation. During the season he sang a great deal, and, when weather allowed, travelled over this huge island. Echoes of the old time were everywhere. He saw at Knossos some of the bright frescoes Maion had seen, in the half-buried ruins of the old palaces.

After the burgeoning optimism and forward vision of the mainland, here he was plunged into the past again. Having lived so immediately as sailor and performer and guest, he was again drawn inward, and sought solitude. Fresh thoughts, like underground springs, watered his mind, and seeds stored there began to germinate. Like tree roots in winter when branches seem passive and simple, the mind of the singer was spreading and growing, absorbing the oldest myths and memories of the Crete of Idomeneus. His Odyssey would resound with Cretan echoes.

Homer travelled through the islands and finally reached Delos from which he would cross to Asia again. He gave Aidon his freedom and told him to go home, but he would not. At sacred Delos Homer sang the song of the slaughter of the suitors on Apollo's feast day, when the bow of Apollo restored order in Ithaca. Some sober Delians had been prepared not to like the singer of the Iliad who had treated Apollo so lightly. Now they were pleased with the singer whose tact equalled his talent. He was, after that, the god's special gift, the child of the Muses indeed. The Pleiades were setting, and it was in the last fleet returning (in 710) one golden afternoon Homer saw the warm red hills of home.

Lionized, heavy with feasting, laden with memories of the Ionian islands and Crete, Homer arrived in Smyrna. He had become a name. Since he had left Athens and Olympia, his poem had spread across Greece like a fire before the wind. At Mycenae a cult to Agamemnon had begun, and near Sparta a cult to Menelaos and Helen. Though these were Dorian lands, they were part of a wave of patriotic fervor for a heroic past. Everywhere on the mainland the old tombs of the heroic age became revered again, the old burial practices and games temporarily resurrected, and potters began to paint scenes from epic and myth rather than rituals, animals, and gods. In Attica an artis-tic convention began of depicting scenes from the age of heroes by the use of a special double-axe-shaped shield. There never had been one like that, but the shape stood for the age. What part the Iliad had played in all this enthusiasm no one could be sure, but Homer was already legend.

***

Zoe was waiting and reunion was sweet for them both. This time they needed words to help them back, reassurances, narratives of what had happened, of what they were together, of things to come, of the present moment.

The twins had not survived to see him again, and Homer had to have time to grieve for them and to comfort Zoe. His Dioscuri, his comfort in the loss of Lydia, were themselves lost, gone quickly in the fevers of the last spring. He imagined himself being delayed, feted at the courts of kings while his sons died, and he was bitter with self-hatred. He had come home to a family diminished in number and unrecognizably older. Kristos, seven when he had left, was turning a sober twelve. Iannos at five did not know him and did not think about him. His brother Iannos put Aidon to work with the ships.

Only Zoe had not seemed to change. "But you have, Teleo," she said quietly, smoothing his hair and holding him close. "It has been a long five years for you, I think. For me," she shrugged, "there is growth but there is no time. There are seasons, but each will be the same. Festivals and crops and funeral games are, finally, alike. There is always pain. And joy again."

His family was wealthy now by Smyrnan standards, and Zoe took frank pleasure in the gifts from far-away places, gifts given out of joy. "So different from booty," she would say to her family, "taken from burning homes where men lie dead with clutching hands. Freely given, out of delight. How beautiful they are." She would polish the tripods and dishes, hang gleaming weapons and cups on the walls, store all the richly woven fabrics in the coffers. The children proudly wore cape and sandals, gifts from Athens. And a story went with every object.

The genos had nourished and cared for his family loyally, and Homer felt a great surge of love toward them. Their demands on him to perform and remember he met with a willingness and sense of loyalty that was new to him. He took the children with him wherever he went, except to his cave.

Homer had to search for the cave at the head of the Meles. Its entrance was overgrown, the sheltering saplings now sturdy trees. But inside it was the same, his old footprints barely disturbed around the slabs of limestone where he had sung so often. He stared at the evidence of who he had been. It seemed a long time ago.

Zoe became pregnant again almost immediately, to their delight, and life seemed to return to normal. She didn't like his bardic name because in Aiolic it meant "blind one," but his trip to Ios made the long homecoming worth delay. Now her husband knew his mother's homeland. That was important.

Homer's great reputation in the world, as well as the visible wealth it had brought, made many fathers' sons want to become singers. His own sons were hungry for stories, too, and it was with pleasure that he taught them, thinking of Theophilos. When he sang of Achilles he thought of Tes and looked warily at Kristos, so inflamed with the nobility of warfare. It made his heart ache. He considered for the first time the importance of these songs to the minds of the young boys. He relived his life in Kolophon with Theophilos, when he was not much older than Kristos. But most of all he spent time at the business of restoring order at home.

***

Homer caught up with the regional news. Erythrai had a new colony, founded jointly with the island of Paros in the summer of Homer's return. It was Parium, situated at the junction of the Hellespont and Propontis. Paros had also begun a settlement on Thasos in the same summer. They were moving boldly at a time when colonization had become cautious because of the Lelantine War and the threat from the Cimmerians. Caution turned to consternation in 709 when the Cimmerians destroyed Sinope, Miletos' colony since mid-century. It lay on the Black Sea at the Halys river. The Cimmerians could move south rapidly now, into Phrygia, as Ardys had predicted. They had not moved west to Troy or Samothrace. At least not yet.

Writing had come to Smyrna while Homer was gone. The youngest rememberers learned it and undertook to keep the rolls for the city. Potters signed their pots, especially the ceremonial funeral urns and sanctuary gifts. Trading families kept written records, and now almost every life was touched by some knowledge of the strange new markings. It would take a while before a word became an image rather than a sound, but the process had begun.

Aikathara was born in 709, a lovely daughter Homer welcomed with all his being. His heart ached for Lydia, so much like this baby, who would have been old enough by now to care for her new sister. He thought too of Ardys, now so long in his grave, and the pain he must have felt looking into the face of the daughter of his return. He thought of Amy and their son, somewhere among the Phrygians if he lived and saw the light of the sun. All lost so long ago. But now was a time to be joyful. If sorrow had taught him anything, it was that. Home was sweet as honey.

A few weeks later Sargon of Assyria took Cyprus. Homer could not endure the thought of that magical island in enemy hands nor could he believe how easily it had fallen; some cities had survived the destruction by paying tribute. He wondered what the men of the heroic age would have thought of that, and who was wiser. Sargon II had been king of Assyria since 721, when he took power from his brother Shalmaneser and built a new palace complex at Khorsa. A poet as well as an engineer, Sargon knew how to write. In fact, he contrived a new writing method, beeswax plates in walnut boards instead of clay, very quick and graceful and easily done.

That monarch was busy everywhere. After putting down rebellions at home he had attacked the Phrygians in Cilicia and campaigned with his son in Iran where his heroic deeds made him revered by his people. Rumor said his son Sennacherib was as dauntless as he. They were moving westward.

✳✳✳

Homer would hear snatches of the Iliad on the lips of travelers on the road, resting at noon in the fields, and especially at festival times when hearts were expansive. Every bard in Ionia, and there were many, sang his song but also had his own way of telling the events of the war and the returns. A few had knit together long poems, none so long as his, with the difference that the songs remained chronologies of actions rather than becoming dramatic narrative like the Iliad. The Trojan matter still was uppermost, as were songs about the gods and their misadventures. Lively episodes on Olympos were welcomed at the feasts, and a new attention to the gods of the cities spread like a smile over the face of Ionia.

In the spring of 707 Laura was born, and now there were four children thriving in the house. Kristos was a young man of 15, quiet and mature for his age, much like his uncle Iannos. He sang the songs of the bards well, but his heart was with the land and the people of Smyrna. No akrasia, no longing to roam the world, to test the edge of things, ate at his soul; in its stead was the image of civil order, of the wise and responsible citizen. He had grown up in Smyrna as man of his house while Homer was in Athens, happily destined to be head of the genos. Everyone loved Kristos and began to wonder who he would marry.

At mid-summer word came that Gordia, the capital city of Phrygian King Midas, had fallen to the Cimmerians. That great golden king Midas, the friend of the Aiolian Greeks, drank bull's blood as his city burned, and died most horribly rather than be taken.

The life of Midas had been a marvel of Homer's time and he had hoped to sing before the legendary king, but now it was too late. Midas had ruled for the past 15 years, the pride of the Aiolian Greeks, for he had married Hermodike, the daughter of King Agamemnon of Kyme. He had been the first barbarian—Phrygian—king to worship Apollo at Delphi. In fact, he had presented the sanctuary with great treasure including a golden throne. His admiration for things Greek was welcomed by the coastal cities who had basked in assurances of a generation of peace. Trade had exploded inland and the promise of such wealthy allies had drawn mainland eyes to the east.

Midas was in fact so rich that many tales grew up around his name, some edged with envy. He was a worshipper of Kybele, of course, and had once come to Mt. Tmolus to worship there and bathe in the sacred spring of the Pactolas. People maintained that the goddess blessed him and had washed gold dust into his very bones. One version went that he had done a kindness for Silenus, a priest of Dionysos, and had been granted one wish to be fulfilled by the god. He had wished that everything he touched would turn to gold. When this proved disastrous he had to bathe in the river Pactolus to rid himself of the curse.

Now magnificent, magnanimous, golden Midas was dead. The Greek letters, which he had ordered adopted and used, stared out from broken pillars and temple stones, their uses turned aside.

Homer accepted when the sons of Midas, Xanthus and Gorgus, asked him to compose the epitaph for their father's tomb. They had heard the Iliad and loved it, as their father had loved the Greek language. Below the bronze figure of a mourning maiden Homer's lines would say:

A maiden of bronze, I sit on Midas' tomb. /As long as water, like my tears, can flow,/ As long as leaves unfold to make great forests/As long as rivers tumble to the sea/And that sea tumbles back upon the shore,/ As long as sunlight burnishes my shoulders /And the calm moon comforts my sad breast/ I will abide here on this tombstone mourning/ To tell the traveller where great Midas rests. (Homeric Hymns and Homerica)

The two sons of Midas gave Homer a silver bowl in payment, which he dedicated to Delphi because Midas had loved that shrine most of all. He smiled to think his words were written in the alphabet of Phanes the Poet.

***

With fame came students, fresh young voices to carry on the songs of the Ionians; even Thaddeus' son spent a summer with Homer. They all loved the songs of war, the battle scenes of the Iliad, just as Kristos had. Homer began to think about generations, about fathers and sons, especially about the sons of the heroic age.

Each son seemed to live a fate decreed by his father's character. Both daughter and son of Agamemnon suffered extreme fates because of their parents' rashness. Achilles' son Neoptolemus went fatherless, eventually becoming embroiled in the jealousies between his wife, daughter of Helen, and his mistress-slave, the widow of Hector. Menelaos' sons were bastards, and the divine Helen had no son at all, a telling fate in a patriarchy. Nestor's favorite son died at Troy, but he had many more, and his distinguished line continued. Odysseus alone had a son who sought his father and who actively helped him regain his throne. Homer looked around him at the sons of Smyrna, where sons would live more prosperous lives than their fathers. Would they be better men? The Mycenaean heroes' sons had been doomed by the fates of their fathers, by the fates of their doomed cities. Were they better men?

He and his brother Iannos talked about this, sitting together in the courtyard after eating, their families busy around them. It was a question the age of heroes raised, the same one that chimed repeatedly in the Iliad and would be imbedded deeply in the Odyssey: Could you tell about a time by asking whether its sons were better than their fathers?

"Who the hell can tell?" Iannos exploded. "Who is the question important to—except the sons?"

"Every father is also a son, Ianni. I dream just like Telemachos. Maion is still Odysseus—if he were to walk in the door right now, I wouldn't really be surprised, would you? Really?"

"No. But you can't think about that. It's not the way to survive."

"I know. I am in my forties now, and the subjects of my life are not those of a boy. I am somehow tired of Achilles. I know well that I am mortal. I yearn to make my listeners happy. Sing something to comfort the survivors next time."

"Next time?"

"Look around us, Ianni. Cimmerians to the north, Assyrians east and south, Lydians at our doorstep. Even Aiolians who remember the day their fathers lost Smyrna. They sing the songs of Thebes, thinking the sons are better than their fathers. Athens lusts for us, Corinth courts Sardis Lydians, while Athens and Corinth eye each other like stags on a mountainside. Spartans are children of Ares plain and simple."

"My generation at Smyrna hasn't fought any wars," Iannos said, with some geniality. "Maybe because of the Panionian. I guess I thought the fighting was over."

Homer let out a laugh. "The gods love you, Ianni. And they should. You are a good man." He prayed silently that his brother would never see the face of Ares.

"I hope to God my sons are better than their father!" Homer raised his cup.

"I'll drink to that," laughed Ianni.

***

One season followed another as the children grew. Kristos married a woman of Chios (in 706) and built a fine new home as close to Homer's as he could, close enough for singing and teaching and absences. It was built in the rectangular style, much to the disapproval of the old men.

In 705 a beautiful red-haired son was born to Homer and Zoe, and they named him Pyrrhus accordingly. Iannos now was 10, Aikathara 4, and Laura 2. When Kristos' new baby arrived next door, children sounded through the house, warming hearts and trying patience. When he needed to concentrate Homer still went alone to his cave.

Suddenly, (in 705) Sargon II was ambushed and killed while fighting in northwest Iran. His son Sennacherib left him unburied on the battlefield and removed all mention of his name from public inscriptions. Homer wondered what their tragedy had been. Sennacherib abandoned the great new city of Sargon and made Nineveh his capital as old factions rose against him in Babylon. The Panionian league, watching the swirl of wars around them, was clearly worried. The Greek element in Sardis was very weak, and there were signs that the Lydians were arming, ostensibly against the threat from the northern war. Arms production began to dominate their forges. Phrygian refugees were fleeing into Lydian territory. The masses of people were moving again and trade was more hazardous than it had been in Homer's lifetime. Perhaps Homer's own sons were to live in a warlike generation after all.

"Smyrna is as safe a place to live as any;" son Iannos observed. "But men do not shirk the responsibilities of their times. Who knows what will come in mine." He practiced vigorously with sword and spear.

Hearing the distant rumble of armies, Homer sang less of Achilles and more of Odysseus. The survivor king of Ithaca became his central interest; the man who had to go home and straighten things out in his city. What should a man be, after all? What values made a settled city possible? It was easy to rally men to fight, but even Odysseus could not save his men. As he thought of Troy he knew that hot ashes smoked that very morning in places where men had thrived the day before. On the day after disaster what did a man do?

Now word came that King Leodamas of Miletos had been murdered, brutally slain on his way to a festival of Apollo. A rival kinsman, Aphitres, had seized power as Laodamas' family and allies fled to Assessus pursued by their enemy. Now the city of Assessus was beseiged. Shock reverberated through the Panionian as the defenders sent to their oracle for advice. Ionia hoped the dispute could be settled in Miletos. However, the oracle had surprised them by advising that the city send to Phrygia for help. Homer wondered if this were the first crack in the Panionian alliance. If it disintegrated, they were all in danger.

Yet Smyrna smiled back at Homer every day. Trade flourished, children grew, the seasons rolled by in festival. Zoe was there. Life was as it should be.

People still talk about the singing contest between Homer and Thaddeus at the funeral games for the king of Teos. Friends from boyhood, frequent competitors in festival singings, they knew each other's techniques well. Now almost fifty, with schools of their own, they met in a famous game. They drew lots to see which would compose the first half of the line, setting the trap, and which would complete it and escape. The first fell to Thaddeus:

Thaddeus: They ate the flesh of oxen and their horses' necks—Homer:—they unbridled, dripping sweat when the battle was done
Thaddeus: This man is the child of a brave father and weak—Homer:—mother; war is too cruel for a woman.
Thaddeus: Agamemnon prayed earnestly that they would die—Homer:—at no time on their voyage. And then he said
Thaddeus: Eat and drink, my guests, and may none of you return to your loved homeland—Homer:—in misery but may everyone return again in joy. (Hesiod, Homeric Hymns and Homerica)

They sang for two hours, riddling and gaming until everyone was exhausted from suspense and laughter. In later days men said it was Hesiod who was Homer's opponent, but the truth was that those two never met, though Hesiod flourished in Homer's old age. Homer would have mourned to know that his old friend Thaddeus had been forgotten.

Word came that the siege of Assessus had been lifted and Amphitres slain, at the hands of the sons of Laodamas. Two Phrygians had come to the city gates carrying in a chest the mysteries of the Cabiri. After the city had celebrated these new rites, the two priests had led the inhabitants into a ferocious battle and to victory. Peace had come to Miletos, but kingship was replaced by a benevolent tyranny.

Late in the sailing season (of 701) a battered trader limped into Smyrna and anchored at the seagate. It was Phoenician. The young captain had come to see Homer.

"I'm David's son, from Tartessus," he said, and all was joy in Homer's house. Moved by the sight of him, full of a thousand questions, Homer could only gaze at him at the feast.

"I am Hiram." He paused. "Named for my uncle who died many years ago."

"How?" Homer grieved.

"Pirates. Off Sicily. On the way out to Tartessus." Homer mourned. "Hiram then. Ah, my boy, how I loved your uncle. Now then. What has brought you back here?"

Hiram laughed. "I'm Phoenician! A sailor. This is my first trip east."

"To see the cities of men and know their minds."

"Ha!" Hiram grinned. "I've heard that line before."

"Tell me of David."

"Happy. Rich. He's taken up horse breeding and given up the sea."

"Your ship looks weary. Stay while we do some repairs."

"Yes. I'll do that. I was hoping you'd ask." And Hiram began to tell a tale of woe. He had been to the Levant to find Cyprus in Assyrian hands and every Phoenician settlement in jeopardy. Trade was almost non-existent in that area. Egypt, Palestine, and the Phoenicians had organized to oppose Sennacherib and been soundly defeated, the Assyrian taking all rebel cities except Jerusalem. The Assyrians had laid seige to Jerusalem but had fallen prey to the plague and abandoned the attempt. Judah paid tribute even though the city had not fallen. Sennacherib had put his son Ashur-Nadin-Shum on the throne of Babylon. The world waited to see whether this son would be better than his father.

David's son was much like his father, but the Phoenician world was changing too. Times were bad in the south, but Phoenicians were flourishing on Thasos now and in the west.

"Tell me about Samothrace, " Hiram said. "I plan to go there after Thasos before I go west again. My father wishes he had gone when he could." They talked long about the island, its public ceremonies, its effect on Homer's life. "I would be a different person if I had not been initiated," Homer said gravely. "In fact, had there been no scarf of Samothrace I would never have lived at all. I want to give you some messages for my friends there."

Then Hiram talked about Tartessus, drawing pictures, describing proudly everything he could remember. "Typically Phoenician. Gadir is the name of our town. It began four hundred years ago on a small island, which we joined to a large one very near the shore. We may even annex the mainland some day." Tyre had founded it near a fertile river valley, and, contrary to the usual pattern, a number of Phoenician villages clustered together there, raising cattle and mining tin. Olives and figs, fish, horses, and purple dye from shellfish provided a sound base for trade. Now Greeks and Italians were coming to settle near them.

"It's the place to be. The old world is dying. I can see that around me here. We are right outside the Gates of Herakles with a vast ocean before us. Who knows what can happen. I long to go home again."

"Has David ever come back east?"

"No. He had too much to do at Tartessus to leave. It was a critical time. How he talks about you, though. He said for me to bring him some of your songs."

Homer made a special song and sent it to his old friend. By the time Hiram reached Tartessus the Iliad was there, too, and David's heart rose when he heard that the great bard Homer was none other than his old friend Teleokairos.

Maybe Hiram was right, Homer reflected. The old world did seem to be dying all around him. Still, Smyrna smiled with his singing, his children were growing up safely, nearby cities were bursting with activity. Yet amid festival and work and lovemaking, ominous news came with every ship's landing. What about Medon's hopes for a panhellenic world?

Were the old destructions coming back again? He had made his Iliad to show that no one wins in war, no matter how glorious the fame of men. He prayed that the center would hold. At least Samothrace was safe. And so was Smyrna.

CHAPTER 18

Earthquake

700 B.C.E. Smyrna

It was during a decade of such events that Homer's children were growing up. To find himself fortunate finally was something Homer enjoyed quietly. He thought often of the lines in his poem of Odysseus' return: "Of all creatures that live and breathe upon the earth, nothing is bred that is weaker than man…let him enjoy in silence the gifts that the gods may bring." Now was his own time, with his sons next to him and now his grandchild whom he had named, just as Autolycos had named Odysseus. He sat the blue-eyed boy on his lap and declared, "Because I have become a famous guest in the world, he will have the name Xenocles."

And now as the century turned, Homer was over 50. He had grown heavier with the years, but he was still agile and powerful. His mild look deepened and sharpened around the eyes, his high cheekbones and heavy brow becoming vast caves of blue-green light, places from which a sibyl could sit watching the world. His mouth was the mouth of a singer, mobile and generous. His great round head began to grey, but he still moved with a measured grace and quiet tension. Though he listened carefully, as if by himself, he could instantly be a companion, sharing his own pleasure, and delighted with what others were willing to give. The bounties of the earth seemed marvelous to him, as were the works of men.

And in this fall (of 700), Zoe was with child again. She was a beautiful woman at 39, and he watched her with great love. Kristos was due home from singing in Phokaia with a gift he had ordered to surprise her. Fine Egyptian linen which the Phoenicians traded up the coast, scarce now, it was byssus, made somehow by a secret process, a mixture of flax and silk with the silky fibers from mollusks of the warm southern ocean.

Homer was strangely anxious to see Kristos safely home. They had had a very dry summer that lasted later than usual, and heavy rains had pounded them since the middle of October. Now it was December and there was water everywhere. The four streams of the plain south of the Hermos had run full all fall and the Hermos was flooding its banks.

When Kristos came home Homer was relieved and Zoe delighted with her byssus. Kristos was full of news about trade and wars and the way of the world. The songs of the Argonauts had become the latest fashion, and he sang one he had heard at Phokaia. Sennacherib was resting for the winter. The wells were down all along the way home and the Hermos had returned to its banks in spite of the continuing rain. They were at first relieved, since they had feared floods. But when they checked their own wells, they too had dropped remarkably, becoming clouded and faintly unpleasant to the taste. They didn't understand it yet.

Deep beneath Sipylos Poseidon was stirring. He pressed the rocks together, and fine cracks shivered through them, in infinite numbers. The waters of the autumn seeped between, washing radon into the ground-water and increasing electrical conductivity. The earth warmed slightly as gases began to move into the air.

Strange things began to happen in January. The cabbages in the fields began to sprout again, and the vines bloomed. Everyone was astonished and uneasy. The gods were sending a message, but no one could say what it was. All privately expected disaster because the earth was forgetting her pattern. Fish no one had seen so close to shore were huddling along the entrance to the Hermos, some drifting close below the surface. Strange fish were passing along the coast, high in the water and easily caught. The Lydians who ate fish a great deal were delighted to find the fish literally jumping out of the water into their nets. Small fowl and animals seemed unafraid of people. In Smyrna anxiety grew.

Deep under the village's base, where rocks held a high proportion of quartz microcrystals aligned when the mass had cooled aeons before, the bedrock began to burst apart, releasing an electric field into the air high above it, blanketing the earth with charged aerosol particles, unseen but felt in many ways. By mid-January the wells of the city had become so heavy with the smell of sulphur and chlorine they were almost unusable. And now the smoke of many sacrifices could be seen rising daily over the city. But as January ended nothing new had happened in two weeks, and Smyrna began to relax again. The gods had heard them. It had been a late autumn, after all, and the warmth had simply stayed in the ground. The unusually heavy rains had caused a second spring, and it was natural that the wells were muddy. January had been the middle of the singing season and the baby was due soon. Homer and Kristos were busy every night. They were singing the new Jason, joining in the current fashion. No one ever asked a question about the Argonauts' initiation at Samothrace, which seemed odd to Homer.

Zoe had become strangely depressed, very unlike herself. She felt heavy and ill, and the baby moved constantly. She had found a snake in the house, something that had never happened before, and had killed it, an act that had brought her to the edge of hysteria. She was sure of impending disaster.

"There are snakes everywhere today, mother," Iannos had said, trying to calm her. "Something has driven them out of their holes. I killed two at the baker's this morning. The worms are up, too, as they are after the rains."

In the early afternoon walking up to the cave on the Meles, Homer looked up to find that the deer had come down from the mountains. They stood huddled in herds on the open slopes of the lowlands, unafraid of man. He stood, suddenly very still. The hair prickled along the back of his neck and he shivered. He turned back to the city and began to run.

When he reached the village he could feel alarm in the air. Dogs were barking continuously and people were tending to the animals. Geese and chickens would not go in their coops. The rats had left the granary and fled the city. No birds sang and all the cats had run away. Mullets were splashing in the shallows of the bay, and crabs were crawling ashore below the city walls. The pigs, restless for days, now in great anxiety were chewing at their tails.

With his family around him, Homer tried to be calm. He told them, "There are signs of real trouble, I fear. I have never seen all this before." He was struggling not to show his own fear. "When the animals are like this, trouble will not be long in coming. Stay near the city and acropolis because the mountain is not safe, and the rivers of the plains could flood as the earth shakes. I expect the ships to be ruined. Don't let it worry you. Now, Iannos and I will help with guard duty. Kristos will be in charge here. Take everything off the walls and shelter yourselves under the sturdy tables and chairs. They will protect your heads."

In spite of the tension—or perhaps because of it—they ate a fine evening meal full of love and laughter. Homer even thought he would go out to sing, but he knew few wanted to listen. The afternoon had brought a haze on the horizons. It was like a reddish mist hugging the ground, and it stayed there as the night drew on, the stars overhead unusually bright and near. Flashes of lightning, like heat lightning of the summer, spread across the sky. Then long jagged cuts of light would split the sky and noise like thunder would rise from the ground.

In the early watch of the night Homer had stayed at home with Zoe. The air was oppressive, sparking their dry hair, and the dogs barked without stopping. Zoe was unable to get comfortable and sat propped against the pillows, breathing great breaths, her eyes shut, holding his hand.

Near midnight Homer went to his station on the acropolis. Two others were with him. He stood there, looking out upon the sweetest prospect earth could offer, a beloved scene transformed in the eerie light. The sense of Poseidon's power had taken hold of him and now ruled his body. Earthshaker was preparing a terrible fate for his children the Ionians, this god of the children of Neleus. Homer wore his Samothracian scarf and ring, for he knew he would confront the god soon. He thought of the story he had sung of the Phaeacians, the lovely civil people who had brought Odysseus home safely whose kindness had been punished by Poseidon. As their boat had entered the harbor on the return voyage, Earthshaker had turned it to stone and rooted it to the spot. And then he had raised a ring of mountains around the city, cutting it off forever from the sea. Homer looked at the midnight sky, thinking of the terror of that ancient metamorphosis. Who had lived through the earthquake? Could such mountains be raised around Smyrna? He remembered the god's wrath against Odysseus, that patient man. Was Poseidon his own enemy? Why would he threaten Smyrna? Then Homer remembered Samothrace and carefully calmed himself. The old gods would always retain their power. That would not change, he thought. Mortals can only do what they will to survive the wrath, and the Olympians would help. He concentrated his heart on Hermes.

Over Mimas large glowing apparitions shimmered on the horizon, burning for two or three minutes at a time. It looked as if the sun were coming up in the west. Late in the hours after midnight when Homer's watch was almost up, Poseidon struck.

At the moment the first tremor hit he felt electrified, magnetized, and his ring lost its power, the decorative filings falling away to the ground. Fire rose out of the earth before the sentinels, wild and crackling, moving across the ground, but it did not consume the dry grass. A smell like sulphur filled the air. The mountain heaved and rolled beneath them, throwing them to the ground. Explosions erupted behind them, and strange voices seemed to sound in the wind. A row of round balls of blue flame burned low across the gulf in the flickering sky. A river of lightning split the now cloudless sky over Smyrna and the stars watched like desperate eyes. There were flames in the form of snakes, red-violet, hovering above the quaking earth as the red fog was being swallowed into the mountain.

Homer and the men of the watch fled the acropolis, racing in the howling, rumbling hillside toward the city. Trees and boulders crashed around them. Their only thought was to reach their families. Now as the shock subsided, Homer strained to see the city; he was disoriented, not certain where it was or where he was. But the city was there. Even as he looked, with relief that it had not been swallowed as Tantalis had been, he saw a bright tongue of fire lick to the roof of the granary. In seconds it was blazing.

He sprang forward, shouting, racing down the hillside, falling, crying out to warn the village. "Fire!" "Fire!" tore from his throat as he saw, in the eerie earthquake light, people coming out of their homes again. The scene was obscure to him, dusty and distant. As he moved he realized he had seen the walls. They were still there, but something was wrong with the roofs and the houses. At wall-top level he stopped, stunned at the sight of a wave of fire washing across the thatched roofs of the city whipped by the wind. Figures of people, his people, were scattering everywhere. He scrambled on, shouting at the top of his power, sobbing for breath. He could see the city gate before him, torn off the wall and lying in pieces, as people staggered around it. Out of the flames as he drew abreast of the gate came the shape of a monstrous horse, his eyes raging unforgettably, pounding directly toward him. The great chest hit him squarely and spun him around in the air like a leaf in a summer storm. As he was flung upward, Homer saw in the sky to the northwest a tremendous burst of electric-blue fire that shot from the horizon to the zenith. And darkness came upon him.———-

The blue flame. It was all around him. All he could see. He was being pitched and tossed, rolling abruptly and sliding away, clinging to something, straining to reach the incandescent blueness. He was calling, calling for someone. Maion. Zoe. Someone he needed to reach. The children and Zoe. They were in the ship and it was gone. Terrible pain in his head and his leg. He could not breathe and had to rest. As he did, as he lay seeking with his heart alone, in his mind's eye, the blue flame focused and flickered and glowed, coming closer, seeming to approach him in the air.

He was intent, breathless, praying and willing it to come to him. He could feel the earth moving beneath him, groaning and heaving, and his hair was wet with salt water. The blue glow bobbed nearer and seemed to hover around a center, slowly coming closer. It was aeons before he realized it was playing around the mast of a ship. Its prow was clearly visible now as the boat hovered alongside and rough hands pulled him aboard.

Pain shot through him in great shivers as he lay in the boat. A single sailor sat near him; there was no other crew. He wore a Phrygian hat and played upon a phorminx as the ship traveled of its own will. Homer could not see his face, but he knew it was Odysseus come to take him to Samothrace. He wore the scarf and ring and sang, but he did not speak.

And as Homer watched, the figure changed his shape. Subtly the cloak and cap, the swarthy beard and broad shoulders shifted into a finer form, a nobler head, a longer reach. The face was turned away and, try as he might, Homer could not make it out. Then inside the cloak he seemed to be able to see as if it were a cave, the clever babe of Maia laughing in the darkness. Waves of dimness pulsed at the edges of his vision while he watched the figure change again, turning slightly toward him, moving his whole being slowly, as if it floated in water. Homer saw the glint at the ankle, the imperishable shoes that took him over moist and dry to the ends of the earth. The caduceus, the herald staff, was in his hand, and the god turned his full gaze on the poet for the first time. It was Hermes Argeiphontes, the boundary-crosser, sitting alone in the ship with him, the world around them lit by crackling blue fire. And by this fire of Samothrace, Hermes wore the face of Odysseus.

For a long moment the bard of Smyrna looked deep into his eyes as the darkness gathered round them. The coast of Ithaca lay on the horizon and the sea was calm as they sped toward it soundlessly, on a broad reach before the wind so that they seemed to be skimming above the water, motionless, wordless, soundless. It was with a shock that he found himself alone in the ship just before a brilliance like a thousand suns burst open in his head. In that timeless instant the glory of existence shuddered through his being. The god's infinite love surrounded him like all the dawns since the world began, moving west to the second bloom, when the sun went down and all the ways became dark.

——Homer woke to unspeakable pain. Noise swirled around him, crying and the crackling of fire. He must be in a room, he thought, but it was too dark to see. He had to call Zoe and be sure everyone was safe. His voice, loud, was a shock to him and hands touched him instantly, holding him down. Fire burned in his head and lights stabbed like needles across his eyes.

"Lie still. Lie still. Don't move." He heard Kristos' voice, but he couldn't see him. Why were they all in the dark?

"You've hit your head badly. How do you feel, father?" Kristos was speaking again.

"I'm alive. Light the fires. Let's get some light and see how everyone is. Your mother. How is she?" He struggled to rise and gasped with the pain of it.

"You're by the fire now. Mother is all right. Now rest." The voice turned away and he could feel the fire's heat. And it was only then that Homer knew he could not see.

"Help me up. I must find Zoe. I can't see now. My head is killing me." He was panicking. He could hear anguish in Kristos' voice and demanded the truth.

"Oh father, please. You are badly hurt. Mother is hurt, but she is alive. Iannos and the girls are just fine. Now rest."

"Pyrrhus. You didn't say Pyrrhus."

"No, father. He must have run out. He is probably with the others. We have not found him yet. Don't worry. I am going now to look."

They found Pyrrhus crushed under the courtyard wall, and Zoe, grieving, went into labor that evening. Sightless, his leg broken, Homer was moved into the shelter beside her, and they clenched each other's hands through the agonizing night. The baby, a girl, was born at daybreak, amid the still smoking ruins of Smyrna. Homer could feel Zoe slipping away, weary with another child's death, with so many deaths, too weary at last to stay. "Name her Zoe, for me, my love," she said. "I love you." And she was gone. If he could have moved, he would have gone with her.

***

In the months after the earthquake that leveled Smyrna, the survivors sorted themselves out and tried to begin again. Only the city walls had stood, along with five houses. Everything else had been damaged beyond hope. Surrounding cities sent clothing and food if they could, and families took shelter, some never to return. A wave of looters, pirates who had heard the news, came to pick over the ruins and were repelled. The survivors of Smyrna took time to grieve, and then ate their supper and lay down on the earth at the coming of spring to rest for tomorrow's labor.

Kristos headed the family now while his father lay injured. He decided, after the funerals, that his father and sisters should be taken to Chios to live with his wife's people while he and Iannos began the rebuilding. It was March and they had to hurry, for planting and sailing season was upon them. He acted at once, carrying his helpless father, who was alternately placid and distraught with grief. Aftershocks were still frequent, and with every tremor Homer seemed to relive a vision that made him tremble with its power. He could not and would not explain his terror.

In the darkness he could still see the eye of the horse that had trampled him, full of high anger, majestic, awful in its divinity. His bones still felt the earth rolling beneath him. The gates of the city were breached. His life lay in ruins. Poseidon was his enemy. Forever. There was no mistaking now. His body shuddered involuntarily before the knowledge of that eye.

But a deeper eye had looked at him, blessedly, slowly, humanly. The timeless eye of the redeemer, his rescuer, the eye of Hermes in the face of Odysseus. His agitated spirit could calm itself. The eye of Hermes was a giving one. Instead of drawing him out and taking away, it filled him with being and will. It gave him himself again, himself in his best and truest form. It filled him with joy that dissolved horror and despair. He hung suspended, taking it into himself, healing his brokenness.

Then he would sleep, to wake in unspeakable pain again. Dawn would have come for others, giving them confidence and beauty. He could feel the spring sunshine on his face. To live and see the light of the sun. They were equivalents.

PART FOUR

Kadmilos, Herald of the Coming God,/ Hermes, consciousness, enabling Air:/ Give song to substance, sight to eyes held hostage/ Give breath to message from the gods to earth/ And sing the song of the survivor there.

Interlocutory

The Voice of Letha Gooding

"O dark, dark, dark amid the blaze of noon,/ Irrecoverably dark, total eclipse/ Without all hope of day!" So Milton's Samson spoke, in the drama by that other epic poet blinded at the height of his powers, twenty years before <u>Paradise Lost</u>.

I need. like others, to honor the tradition of Homer's blindness, even though it is debatable. Some say it came from his moving words about the bard Demodocus in the Odyssey, some say from the lines about the "blind singer of rocky Chios" in the Homeric Hymn to Apollo. Whatever the reason, it has crept into the early "lives," though coins copied from a fifth-century statue in Smyrna showed Homer seated, holding a scroll. That he was sighted part of his life seems clear from his poems.

Milton's Invocation to Light in <u>Paradise Lost,</u> in which he likened his infirmity to that of "blind Maeonides," touches our feelings now.

Thus with the year/ Seasons return; but not to me returns/ Day, or the sweet approach of even or morn,/ Or sight of vernal bloom, or summer's rose, / Or flocks, or herds, or human face divine! (Book 3, ll.40-44)

Thus blind Milton sang, his greatest work still in the making.

Chapter 19

"The Blind Singer of Rocky Chios"

700-695 B.C.E. Chios

The blind singer came to rocky Chios at 52 with the death of Smyrna still fresh in his nostrils, to Emporio, a village on the southeastern coast, where there was a sanctuary to Athena Brighteyes, the goddess of sight.

In Homer's time Emporio was a complex of villages on the beach and two terraced hills, one north of the bay. The houses were built of stone, the rough conglomerate of Chios, and had clay chimneys. Roofs, supported by posts, were networks of wooden beams covered with slabs of rock and mud which had been waterproofed with clay.

They brought the famous singer in his recovery to a house on the north hill near the shrine of Athena, the house of Kristos' wife's uncle. The family welcomed him with love, and all of the village strove to help the divine bard from Smyrna who was widowed and blinded by Poseidon. He slept a great deal at first because in his dreams he could still see. There were all the dear faces again, the green valley and cave of the Meles, the frozen ridges of Samothrace, Athens from the Acrocorinthus. The sight of faces rapt in heroic song. He could not endure the darkness of waking. How had he offended Poseidon? He struggled with the certainty that he had, although he could not place it. Yet it was a knowledge he had always had. As he had sailed through the islands, had walked above the endless tremors of earth, he had known the god was stalking him. Even now Poseidon waited.

Homer grieved for Zoe. He received with a silent nod the condolences of others, formalities Zoe would have considered important. There had been so much death that day that this unique death had not seemed unique. The young, too, could accept the loss of a woman at 40 as almost inevitable. After all, she had lived a full life and she did not suffer long. How could he tell them it was never all right to die! It would not have helped his grief had she been 90. He could not think of a world in which she did not breathe and see the light of the sun. Indeed.

He imagined Herophile the Sibyl across the straits behind Erythrai, with her knowledge of events, and did not envy her. All the burned cities he knew. Life itself may be permanent, yes; Zoe had taught him that and he had to remember it. But any man, any woman, any golden city was as ephemeral as the wind he felt blowing at his beard. The great burial caves of Chios held the bodies of others like him who once could feel the wind.

His last sight had been the gates of the burning city. He remembered suddenly Melissa of Athens, so long ago now, and her vision. This was what she saw, not Troy. What else was it that she had seen? A long gash in the clay of the mountain? Well, there were certainly many gashes now. He thought of the last decade—the years since his return—with a soaring ache, and tears streamed from his sightless eyes. Smyrna had seemed so sweet amid the ravages of conquest nearby. So far away from grief and war. While soldiers torched the cities to the north and east and south, Smyrna had decked herself with flowers and drunk the Pramneaian wine. The black ships had covered the beach below the city wall like so many hummingbirds clustering at the nectar of a lovely myrtle. Zoe had always been there. Zoe and her fertile body. Now gone with the flames across the rooftops, whipped by the wind. Ashes.

What of the cities of men then? Melissa had seen Smyrna and they had thought Troy. Troy had been wrecked by earthquake not long before it was burned by the Greeks. Now Kristos and Iannos were rebuilding Smyrna. For what destruction? He knew it would come. Herophile had said so. He thought again of the ruins of his childhood forays in the Hermos valley, and the lost city of Tantalis. Men built for themselves and their children, and it was only an illusion that the city would not die. His conviction—and Tes's and Medon's—that the dark ages were over and a new spirit was alive in the world—was just an illusion, too. Sons and fathers were all alike, doomed to death, and, alas, so were the cities of men.

In blessed sleep, where vision still lived, one dream began to emerge. It had lain all along at the bottom of his mind, deep under all the turmoil, and when anguish had blown all the rest away, there it was always, more real than his life. He had looked into the eyes of Hermes. And he had known the god as Odysseus, not certain how, but certain nevertheless. He strained to dream it again, to relive that instant, to recover that precious vision and hold it, the instant before the blinding light had enveloped him. The light had brought him unspeakable joy, an ecstacy that transcended any mortal feeling. Any mortal scene. What had followed it, his waking to darkness and death, had been inevitable, unbearable. He had looked on the eyes of the god and was blinded. He had seen Hermes.

Acceptance would finally come to him, but not through the agency of Athena. It would happen when he ceased to consider his blinding as Poseidon's wrath and began to see it as Hermes' gift. He had looked into the eyes of the god. The white light of revelation had burst upon him, burned away his eyes, and now he was ready to see. He knew that, if he waited, the way would be shown to him. And it was in the waiting that he was drawn back into the world of the living.

It had been the move to Chios, Kristos said, that was helping his father recover. Or the sound of his new daughter's presence, for the women insisted that he keep his small Zoe nearby. Laura sang to him, and Aikathara learned about herbs from the women of the southern coast. She brought him potions to heal him, which he dutifully complained over. "I should have named you Herophile," he would grumble, and she insisted her medicines had saved his very life. The family haunted the sanctuary of Athena, convinced that their gifts and prayers would be heard by the goddess whose praises he sang.

Homer first learned to know the footfalls and the smells of the people around him, seldom startled by the touch of a hand on his body. He realized that vision kept people at a distance from each other. Now, when he wept, the children huddled together with him and their tears mingled. But the day finally came when, in spite of it all, the needs of daily life became important again. Knives needed sharpening, handles smoothed, seeds sorted, and ships repaired. He was glad his hands had had such a busy life, and in many things they did not need his eyes. His walk was stiff, but he needed to make himself strong again. There was desperate need among the rebuilders, and Homer set about to do what he could where he was. His costly gifts which remained, the presents of many, he gave to those who had nothing, and they were traded away for mules and grain and iron tools. The craftsmen of Smyrna and Chios made phorminxes for the blind bard who had lost his with his home.

The young men of Smyrna, Kristos and Iannos among them, upon whose shoulders the labor had fallen, prevailed upon the elders to rebuild Smyrna in the new fashion, with a grid of streets oriented north-south, with houses terraced and close together, rectangular and efficient, with more spacious rooms. The work became easier for them, close to an adventure, since the city would rise all at once, rational and modern in every way. They questioned Homer endlessly about what he had seen in Athens and Corinth, and about the towns of Aiolia. With every new idea they would fall into a welter of debate and decision.

The kings of Chios town, twins Amphicus and Polytekna, presented the divine singer with a trained pup, a beautiful hound he named Argus of the Hundred Eyes, thinking Hermes would enjoy the joke. Together, Homer and Argus learned the way around Emporio. When he fell off a terrace or stumbled into the wrong houses, everyone laughed good-naturedly and helped him on his way. "It's not that I'm spying out Troy like crafty Odysseus," he would say, "though it would be worth it to bathe with Helen. Just point me toward home," and he would set off again. He learned to ride a mule down to the port and finally came to spend part of his days in the sun on the waterfront. He did not need to compose alone in the cave now, because he carried his privacy around with him. Where it was quiet he would sometimes sing, and if mortals or gods cared to listen, they were welcome. The ships would hail him as they arrived, and he came to keep up with the world again.

The turmoil of the earthquake had touched the whole area. The king of Erythrai, across the strait, was a man named Knopus, a descendant of Athenian Kodros. He had been having political difficulties for some time, before the tremors had damaged the port village of the city. He felt a need to consult the Delphic oracle to settle part of the local dispute, and so he set out with his retinue of trusted nobles. Among them was Ortyges who, with two co-conspirators Iros and Echaros, took over the ship soon after it got well into the channel. They killed resisting crew members and, binding King Knopus, threw him into the sea. Then they put into Chios Town to announce their coup and enlist the aid of Amphicus and Polyteknos. These kings recognized them and agreed to supply soldiers to help them at Erythrai, making a treaty with the rebels. The revolutionaries sailed back under cover of night to take Erythrai. Homer wondered why Knopus had not consulted Herophile, instead of undertaking his fateful voyage to Delphi.

Ortyges, the leader of the insurgent band, had sounded the trumpet at dawn, and Erythrai had fallen with little resistance. Homer wondered if the new king had been among the men who had attacked Phoinikous with him so many years ago at another dawn. But Ortyges did not refrain from bloodshed, as they had tried to do. He drove the citizens outside the city walls, executing indiscriminately any that he felt he could not trust—and there were many. Knopus' queen escaped to Kolophon, but she had little power and was promptly forgotten. The revolution was a great success, to hear the twin kings of Chios talk, but everyone was wary, afraid a new era of petty warfare could be upon them, Ionian against Ionian, as in the days before the Panionian league. Citizens of nearby towns, who had come to help Smyrna clear ground, went home to let the region settle down a little.

But the oligarchy at Erythrai was oppressive and arbitrary, every trader bringing horror stories from the miserable city. The Chian people were uneasy in their official friendship with such a regime, and, though they had always been close to the Erythrians, began to be restive toward their own twin rulers. Homer listened and nodded, wondering how many ways there were to destroy a city.

✸

Homer did not move back to Smyrna. It had become a completely new place, with little for his memory to touch. Fertile and welcoming Chios, his refuge in his great travail, became his permanent home. He knew Emporia well. This ancient site had quite a history itself, dating back to Mycenaean times when it was a strong and fortified city. (In 1100 B.C.E.) the southern acropolis had been destroyed and abandoned, but its terraces were still in use, though most of the villagers lived on the north, farming the fertile land between the hills.

The people of the world all seemed to have washed ashore on Chios at some time, leaving Pelasgians, Carians, Minoans, Lydians, Euboeans, and now Smyrnans. The island was larger than Mimas peninsula and famous for its vintages and pottery. The hills in the south were low and rounded, and fertile country lay between them. The sacred ground of Athena Brighteyes and the hospitality of kin kept him at Emporio for two years.

Homer began to sing again, often at the oddest times of the day and to strange assemblies of people. The shipmen loved his Odyssey, which he was changing radically now. Students from all over the island accumulated around him. The Chians said Homer meant the Blind Man, and others said it meant the Singer. Homer would say, with a great laugh, "Why, I am the blind bard of rocky Chios. Apollo knows my name!" The god of mousike—music and poetry—was very much a healing god.

Homer would not argue with Apollo, who claimed both healing and the Muses, but Hermes had come first. It had been Hermes, after all, who had supplied the healing balm and incantation on Parnassos that had healed the boar wound of Odysseus. Now Parnassos belonged to Apollo, but, if Autolycos had lived there in the time of Odysseus, then he knew it had once been Hermes' mountain, for Autolycos was his son.

Language healed him, too. It was the total effect—the euphony—the exquisite combination of senses and intelligence—that triumphed in his songs, that triumphed over his tragedy, that brought harmony back into his life. Into the life of every man, he told himself. The total harmony of form was as important as the echoing vowels in a phrase. Whatever it was, it healed him.

In what Homer would say to his students he could hear Theophilos again:

"Large open vowels and consonants force the mouth open. Words of size should require muscular opening, stretching, reaching out. Practice words that, in saying, touch the lips lightly, that grind the teeth, that scour the throat. Words that suffocate and spit, that clash, and force great distortions of your face, horrible words that drive the breath from your body. Words with short vowels sitting in the top of your head above the passions. A feeling, a thought? Find the sound and the word for it. It lives while it is spoken. A word is indeed a concrete thing, my boys. It is said with mind and muscle at the expense of breath, of life itself."

✸

With some foreboding Chians heard that the brother of Knopus, one Hippotes, rightful heir to the kingship of Erythrai, was in the Ionian islands raising a force to retake his city. There would be many at Erythrai who would help him, and great resentment of the whole island of Chios. Emporio began to stand watch.

Some of Homer's new students were rememberers who could read and write when they came to him. He was to find that they excelled in memory, in verbatim memory. But they were never very good in spontaneous composition. There seemed to have developed in them a sense of line, they said, or of words themselves as symbols, something that kept them from it. It would take a new kind of mind to see beauty in the letters as they live in the mind. Socrates never did, many centuries later, and neither did Homer. But these boys were the finest singers of <u>his</u> songs, with the truest memories of all. And, when they had time to compose and memorize, they could sing exactly, verbatim, the same song time and time again, something never really considered desirable before. Homer remarked upon it, willing to suspend judgment as to whether all this was good or bad. It was different. And he knew the epic would never be the same. He was not sure it should be. He found the change exciting, and he had sung a new kind of song himself, hadn't he?

He wearied of the same old destructions. Was every generation doomed to begin again? He had a love of the story of Odysseus now, the survivor, the restorer of order. But what should the order be? Only the past month Ortyges had been defeated and Hippotes enthroned at Erythrai. Homer smiled and wished for the best. Wickedness had been overcome.

But he knew that was not the end. Would the survivors be wiser? Who should decide the pattern of civil order? What values would carry people in peace? What practices and laws gave citizens hope and a full life? That was what Smyrna needed now. And Erythrai. And Chios Town. And Miletos and the rest. And he quietly came to understand what it was that he must do.

It was not by insight on a mountaintop, sudden and dramatic, changing his life; it was by reason, by constant reaction to his time, by remembering Hermes, by living near the shrine of Athena, dependent upon others.

If he could not save a city, or a wife, or a child, or his own sight, he could design the song of Odysseus into a vehicle through which the maturing of one mortal, step by step, would demonstrate how civil order can rise from the ashes for survivors. He could show all the skills a man must have to survive. Further, he could show a man struggling, when all civilizations were in the balance, to find a pattern that was good. The great gods of the city—Hermes, Athena, and the rest—would be his guides. And, true to his vision, Homer would represent Hermes in the character of Odysseus. He made the great decision: he would compose another very different monumental poem.

***

Now there was constant trouble in the channel. The Erythrians blamed the Chians for the success of the despicable Ortyges, and provocations against shipping were constant. Trade fell off at Chios Town, and came to Emporio instead. Then the gods must have taken a hand, for something unexpected occurred.

Amphicus, one of the Chian kings, was killed in a drunken riot at a wedding at Chios Town. The slayer and a number of his supporters fled to the mainland and attempted to set up a settlement there. The outraged Erythrians tried to drive them out. But finally, when Erythrai understood that the new founder had killed one of the hated allies of Ortyges, albeit accidentally, the Erythrians took it as a sign that the gods had a hand in this just punishment. And so the settlers were allowed to stay. The Chian king Polyteknes was prevailed upon to leave the coast alone for the sake of cities trading through the channel, and all became serene again. Homer smiled to himself. The bitterest enemies in the long stretch of time became friends. It is the gods who don't forget.

There would be deep purposes in his new song of Hermes, his new Odyssey. He would show forth the nature of Hermes in the behavior of Odysseus, a sweet trickery in itself. And, most daring of all—dare he do it?—he would layer into the Odysseus tale a confessional narrative under which the matter of Samothrace would be preserved for the initiated. Dare he do it? Sing the mystery? The enormity of his thought quite overwhelmed him and he took to his bed shivering, quite consumed by the risk. He was convinced, however, that this was the purpose of his vision. Samothrace would fall, like all the other cities he knew, and he could not let the wisdom of that sacred place die to the minds of men. He would be Proteus, the transformer, the shape shifter who held the truth through many subtle and dangerous changes, for the man who sought the truth of things. He was burdened by the enormous task before him. Even as he was, he thought of the Trickster's eye. He told himself not to be afraid.

He imagined a scene in Olympos where Hermes and Poseidon had argued his case before Zeus. Some god had snatched him from death twice before and put him on borrowed time. Had he done it again in the earthquake? Giving him time to compose an epic for men that would see them through all the destructions to come? Taking his sight to make him see the god's purpose for him? What arrogance! To believe the gods had chosen him. After such a thought, he laughed uproariously. It was the kind of pride, of hubris, that led men to disaster.

His family saw a change come over Homer. He would sit within the sound of the sea, holding his phorminx, seeming to listen and to concentrate with a ferocity that chiseled lines into his face, that burned his brow, that drew his lids down over eyes so luminous that it was hard to believe they did not see the light of the sun. He was so busy inside himself that all he needed around him was the sound of the sea. When he wanted human company, the wonderful eyes opened again, the color of seas around a magic island.

The solution came to him quite clearly one morning, effortlessly, following long days of anguished confusion. The confession. The test of Samothrace. Keep the pattern true. The personal tale of how a man became whole would be sung in first person and in the language of the psyche, of myth. It would naturally be fantastic. And, under the fantastic voice he would layer the practical, precious sailing knowledge of the western ocean. Only the initiated would know. It would be saved when Samothrace was sacked as the Cimmerian swept over Asia. All the rest of the epic would be in third person narration, but that was the core of it—the confession. The placement of it, however, was a problem. He could not represent Odysseus as a naive person before this confession, this spiritual rebirth, for the tradition made everyone see him as the wise counselor of kings and the warrior awarded the armor of Achilles. He would have to solve that problem. But even as he thought, he knew the answer would come.

***

When Homer was 54, (in 698), a stranger, a singer, came to Emporio with Kristos and Iannos from Smyrna. Ianni told Homer of this man's arrival.

"Father, there is someone in the courtyard I wish that you could see. He is refreshed and wants to meet you. First, I need to tell you that he looks remarkably like you. Remarkably."

"Well, there may be such people in the world, Ianni. Is he from Ios? How old is he?"

"Not from Ios. He looks over thirty."

Homer grinned, "Well. I am over thirty, too, Tell him to come in." There was a going away and moments later a shuffling of sandals in the portico. Then a voice said to him, "Greetings to Ionia's great poet. I have come to sing for you, songs you may not know yet. And I long to hear your Iliad from your lips."

"Welcome. Your voice is not that of a boy. What songs do you mean?"

"One is a song the singer of the Iliad would love, from far away in Phrygia. It is 'The Lament of Enkidu'."

"Ah," said Homer, rising, "Let's go out under the trees. Sing it for me now. I long to hear it."

The song was sweeter and sadder than he had remembered. Ianni and Kristos and the others gathered around to listen. When the words had died away no one stirred for a long moment. A fly buzzed and far away a mother was calling to her child.

"You are Phrygian then. But farther east. Of Assyria? Babylon?" Homer could not place him. "I have heard the song before, many years ago in Lydia."

The man seemed tense. "It is a very old one. I learned it in Phrygia where it has long been written down. Gilgamesh has been popular since before the Hittites."

"Phrygia." Homer said it flatly. "Are you one of the defeated and dispossessed that fell with Midas? You honor me with your visit. From what I have heard you sing, I doubt you have come here for lessons. But we will make you welcome and listen to your sweet songs."

The man came nearer, near enough to touch him. Pleasure shone in his voice. "I am happy that my song pleases you. But it is hard for me to speak. It is not as I imagined it would be."

Homer felt his tension. "You want to tell me something now. Sit by me, then, and tell me." He braced himself against his chair.

But the stranger stood. His words came haltingly. "'I am Dionysos, a singer of Gordia in Phrygia. I have lived there since I was stolen as a child in a raid on Sardis. I was presented to the king and trained as a singer, for I showed the gift by the time I was seven. Then he apprenticed me to a carpenter to learn to make fine instruments for the court.

"Of course you know what has happened in Phrygia. The day the Cimmerians came to Gordia was terrible, full of blood and death. At the height of the sacking, I killed a horseman, threw him to the ground and bounded aboard so fast that the steed hardly broke his stride! Out of the city gates I tore and rode like the wind, going south.

"I won't bother you with all my trials. Just know I came at last to Sardis, to the temple of Artemis from which I had been taken. One of the ancients there, an old crone in the household, remembered me and wept. The tale she told me made me weep too. My mother had died, a sacrifice on the mountain. Though the temple officially said my father was the river god Pactolas, my true father had been a singer of Smyrna. In Smyrna—" he was talking with difficulty, watching the shock in the blind man's features, trying to ease it, features so like his own that he could hardly speak—"I was told to come to see you. I was told you would—know my father." This last very softly.

Homer could feel the hot tears begin to course down his cheeks into his beard, splashing on his cloak. He struggled to speak, even as he was reaching forward. "There are many charlatans in the world who think a blind old man is fair game," he said huskily,

The voice said, "I am sure there are. I cannot prove a thing, All I remember is walking out into the courtyard and being snatched, being hit and thrown, bleeding, over the back of a huge grey horse."

"I heard of that. My sons who have brought you to me, they would seem to think this is so. Good men who love me. You believe this? Kris? Ianni?"

They murmured their assent.

"They say you look like me." Homer hesitated for only a moment. "I saw you once, when you were born. You were red and ugly." He cleared his throat again, "You have probably changed, as I have. Come here, Dio," he said, "I have something for you."

He took Ardy's ring from his finger and gave it to his son. "Your Lydian grandfather's ring." He stood up, opening his arms. The man he embraced was just another person, a body, to everyone else. Never to him. His son! Amy's son! They clung together in the dusk weeping, his heart almost smothered in happiness. In the distance a child was calling his mother, knowing she was listening.

Dio seemed to confirm for anyone who thought about it that a bardic gift was inherited. There had been no family tradition in his early days, as there had been none for Homer in Smyrna. They had the gift. Kristos and Iannos did, too, but they had also expected to be bards from the day they were born. Homer began to be sure that, whoever his family had been, his father might well have been a remarkable singer. He thought again of Phanes. The thought introduced a new possibility, that his father had been gone when some disaster had struck his home. That his mother—wife or mistress—had not necessarily been with his father at all. With the miracle of Dio's homecoming Homer allowed himself to hope he might know the truth about himself before he died. It was a cruel hope, but hope nevertheless. The oracle had said the blind bard of Chios would, some day, see the sun again. He would have given his life to be able to gladden his own father's heart as Dio had gladdened his.

CHAPTER 20

Making the Odyssey

700-695 B.C.E. Chios

In the time of recovery he would go in the hours after midnight to the temenos of Athena across the court. Steeped in dreams of visions, in memories of dreams, there he would wait for the day's awakening in the precinct of the goddess who brought sight. Only the owls who nested there and Argus of the Hundred Eyes, his Laconian hound, would keep him company until the small birds sang. There he might meet the boundary-crosser as night turned into day. There he would wait for the Muse. Often he would lie on the chiseled terrace stones, face up to the stars, knowing exactly where each constellation was in the harmonious whole.

Finally one cool autumn night Argus would not enter the precinct, whimpering and circling away, whining with fear.

"Who's there?" Homer's voice was crisp and small in the quiet. No breath stirred in the olive trees. Even the owls were silent.

Then a soft shuffle sounded on the terrace and an indistinct voice spoke. "A traveler. Come to restore my vision."

"Ah," said Homer. He could feel a presence near him.

"Why are you here?" the voice asked.

Homer hesitated. "I am blind, as you would know if you were a trickster, or a thief. My dog is afraid of you."

"I heard him. You need have no fear of me. I come to honor the goddess." He repeated his question. "You are here because you are blind?"

Homer was alert now. He smiled within himself. "I am here because I seek to see."

"Ah," said the voice.

"You are Theban," Homer said. The voice held surprise and pleasure. "Yes. I go to Klaros to the tomb of Teiresias, the Theban prophet."

"The famous seer. The priest of Apollo."

"Famous, yes. Never the priest of Apollo." There was a pause. Homer waited. "That visionary lost his sight when he looked upon the secrets of Hermes and Athena. People forget so easily and the truth is lost. That is why the gods must meddle in the lives of men."

The sound of steps moving away muffled Homer's response and then melted into the distance.

Homer stayed a long time, meditating. To know the secrets of Hermes and Athena moved life within oneself, transforming vision. Transforming the level of being.

That was the morning when he began to remake the stories of Odysseus into a sacred song of Hermes, disguising it as epic. Had not his nocturnal visitor said the truth is lost unless a means of preserving it is found? Had not his whole life been moving inexorably to the point where he would be such an agent of the god? The god had given him purpose. Now he must trust his Muse to give him inspiration.

***

Hello. Letha Gooding here. This is not an interlocutory because it is not marginal commentary. We come to the center of the mystery, the message in the bottle. In dark and fertile communion with the Muse, Homer composed the song of the survivor—vigorous, exciting, and structured to carry his wisest conception of how mortal life can be lived. Odysseus is flawed, a paradigm of twentieth-century man, and the Odyssey is still the greatest literary work in western culture.

That is not to denigrate the Iliad, the child of his youth. Achilles is the hero of force, Odysseus the hero of guile, of indirection, of patient intelligence. While Achilles is the tragic mortal sacrifice, Odysseus is that more difficult hero, the wise survivor.

He is also that ambiguous trickster with words, the politician, the strategist, the man who would rather reach an accommodation than fight because he knows in war everyone is the loser.

If you are not interested in the meaning and structure of the Odyssey, you can skip the next few pages.

You remember it, the Odyssey—Homer's version of the return of Odysseus, the man who thought of the device of the Trojan horse which brought victory to the Greeks after ten years of war at Troy. Homer begins forty days before the end of his hero's eventful ten-year homeward voyage, with Telemachos setting out to find his father and Odysseus escaping from Calypso's island only to lose his raft in a storm and wash ashore on the isle of the god-like Phaeacians. At a great feast he recounts his famous Fantastic Voyages before his hosts send him magically home to Ithaca where, united with his son and disguised as a beggar, he successfully plots to avenge the insult to his family from the hundred suitors who have been terrorizing his home, and reestablishes his relations with his family and his subjects.

It is a really masterful and suspenseful plot, full of perils, politics, humor, and a great variety of memorable characters. The Fantastic Voyages—tales about Polyphemus the Cyclops, the beautiful witch Circe, the Kingdom of the Dead, the Sirens, the Lotus-Eaters—are as much a part of our childhood as the idea of an odyssey is synonymous with seeking beyond the common experience, and Odysseus/Ulysses the archetype of the wise and successful questor. We enjoy his resourcefulness, tenacity, intelligence, duplicity as well as the love he feels and inspires. Homer's Odysseus is very—well, very mortal.

No one has ever told a tale any more successfully, or originally, or as full of trickery as Homer has told the Odyssey. Let me lay it out simply, my friends; it will amaze you. More than that, you will see that what you think of Odysseus is inextricably bound to the way the story is made.

Basic, of course, is the familiar cosmic principle of prosody Homer used for the Iliad: the hexameter line, fundamental to Homer's aesthetics. The Odyssey's twenty-four parts are the twenty-four beat lengths of the line; the caesura falls at an incredibly appropriate and precise point in the adventure in the Kingdom of the Dead where a shift occurs in the tales; the bucolic diaeresis falls at the point where Odysseus arrives at his own threshhold after twenty years, still in disguise but back home again. The spondee is the last two books in which Homer outshines himself, the famous reunion with Penelope in which the trickster is tricked, and the miraculous restoration of Laertes.

A masterful use of plot. I am dumbfounded by people who consider Homer to be a primitive singer of traditional tales.

As to the remarkably intricate order of the Odyssey, the whole epic is a sacred song of Hermes designed around his number Four: four books of Telemachos' voyage, four of Odysseus' escape and reception in Phaeacia, four of the confessional Fantastic Voyages; then four with Odysseus in disguise at Eumaos' hut, four in disguise in his own home, and four of discovery, slaughter, and restoration. Of the fantastic episodes Homer uses four wandering adventures before the pivotal Circe-Underworld tales, and four foretold adventures following it. In Ithaca there are four recognitions of the hero which carry much of the epic's meaning. Well, you get the idea. And you remember from Samothrace the meaning of Four.

Hermes is a Trickster, so Homer is true to his god. One of his best tricks is beginning action in medias res, in the middle of things: Telemachos opens the epic forty days before the end of a twenty-year plot; Laertes, the father, closes it. But, if you consider Homer's purpose, to show the development of mortal man, he begins at the beginning—youth—and moves to old age. Not in the middle at all! It's a wonderful device of language that has a great unconscious appeal for us. One of four organizational designs for this monumental epic.

But we have just begun. Homer's holy book of Hermes appears to be about Athena, with Hermes only running errands for Zeus. But Hermes is central; he is Odysseus. They even wear the same kind of mystic pointed cap in vase paintings of the following century. In the Iliad Helen describes Odysseus as looking like a ram, the holy animal of Hermes, which the hero clings to in escaping from the cave of the cyclops. I am coming back to this; first let's go on with the tricks, games, deceptions of structure that the blind bard contrived for the Fantastic Voyages.

***

Within the four books of the Fantastic Voyages Homer uses four overlapping but distinct systems of meaning, the first of which Ernle Bradford discovered and explained in <u>Ulysses Found</u>. Homer conceals a mariner's guide to the sea gates of the western Mediterranean under the narrative. The key to sailing those seas safely—with foreknowledge—distances, wind directions, descriptions of landfalls, even local human reception of the voyager—all are there. What Bradford doesn't explain is the reason for concealment, though it was common to keep sea routes from other traders. But why in an epic tale? What better way to preserve precious information for the Samothracian initiate than to conceal factual data under the cloak of fantasy? I love the mind that thought of that! Hermes would have been absolutely delighted.

Another system of meaning in the fantastic tales is also Samothracian—a first-person confession by Odysseus as if it were just the conventional song at a feast. When the Phaeacians/Samothracians finally ask him who he is, Odysseus tells them, profoundly, who he is and how he got to where he is now, in first person and the language of myth, the language of dream and the psyche. He recounts the great Second Voyage of Man, his inner transformation in the process of centroversion. It is the second voyage because Odysseus has already experienced the first, the voyage to manhood of Telemachos: the boar wound on Parnassos is its mythic equivalent.

Yet another vital layer of meaning in the fantastic adventures is about the nature of the social fabric. As Odysseus wanders from place to place he encounters all kinds of societies and stages of civilization. Before Homer's time, when the Mycenaean bards told these stories, civilization was literally up for grabs. It could take any direction. The cities of the heroes were gone and everyone had become a wanderer or an exile, just as Odysseus had. The population was decimated, literacy lost, commerce ended. Homer's own cities of the eighth century B.C.E. were bursting with new problems that the old order couldn't solve by old methods. At the same time cities were turning to ashes again as the Assyrians and Cimmerians moved into Asia. It is no wonder that men would want to hear as the episodes pass through a progression of social systems from the passive lotus-eaters to the barbarian cyclops all the way to the god-like Phaeacians, giving Homer's audiences retrospectives of each of those societies. That content, coupled with the politics of Ithaca in the latter part of the epic, was painfully important to Homer's aristos.

The fourth system is subtler: the relationship between gods and men and, to some degree, between gods themselves. Harder for us to grasp, perhaps. These are not the playful gods of the Iliad, though they are lively enough when they appear. Great Poseidon is of course the natural enemy of the voyager, just as the unconscious always tries to reclaim the conscious hero. In fact, for Odysseus death will come from the sea; it could not be otherwise. Zeus complains that mortals blame the gods for the ills they bring upon themselves, a position quite advanced from Agamemnon's in the Iliad. Calypso complains rightly that the Olympians neglect the earth goddesses. Athena aids the mortal Hermes.

Retribution comes for the terrorist suitors on Apollo's feast day by means of Apollo's bow. But the greatest religious act is that of Odysseus when, drowning in Poseidon's storm off Phaeacia, he accepts the veil of Leucothea—the porphyris of Samothrace—thus acknowledging his proper place in a harmonious cosmos. After that he faces only human enemies. Understanding himself, he can lead the polis back to order.———What a stupendous work.

One old puzzle of the Odyssey I can answer now: why, if Odysseus was so anxious to get home from Troy, did he sail in the wrong direction when he headed out, going north to raid the Cicones? There were plenty of places in the Troad and south to raid on the way home.

We told ourselves it was because the Thracians were allies of Troy, but so were cities in the south. We said he wanted booty. Come on! He had just sacked the richest city on the coast and was loaded to the gunwales with booty. Homer's real reason is apparent now: he had to get his hero to Samothrace, but without naming the island and giving away his meaning. Storms there always blew to the southeast; so he took his ships to the only place from which a storm would blow them onto Samothrace. They stayed for two days and two nights, the length of the mid-summer festival.

At the end of the fantastic tales Odysseus is rescued from storm with the scarf of Samothrace, and is tossed about for two days and two nights again. Then the Phaeacians fete him and send him home safely in a magical ship. They are the Samothracian initiates who hear his tale and who guarantee safety at sea. They do not guarantee safety in the perilous world of mortal men, but the initiate is ready to confront what will happen—with the aid of Athena, of course. Homer does some very clever designing so that the first person voice doesn't begin and end too neatly, and Calypso, in a sense the last adventure, is the first mentioned.

***

The best place to get to know Hermes is in Norman O. Brown's <u>Hermes the Thief</u>. Hermes emerged from the mists of time as a god of the stone heap, at the boundaries between people, a protector of wayfarers. Since that was where trade took place in fairs of exchange, Hermes became a complex of trader-god, boundary-crosser, craftsman—a power presiding over contact with strangers and new things. Hermes' binding power became verbal, sexual, athletic, and mercenary, as well as trans-substantial.

Through his making of music and language, he was the god of the bard and of the herald who presided over all rituals and assemblies—his rod was held by speakers in assemblies, denoting who held the floor, not really unrelated to the healing cadeuceus representing his physical healing power. Hermes was a pastoral ram god, too, from the days of the boundary festival. Most of all, he moved between life and death as the messenger of the gods to men and the conveyer of souls to the underworld.

We are well aware that such a power is inevitably allied to trickery, for who knows how transformation takes place? The god of the boundary fair is full of deception by his very nature because fair value is always relative. The god of language is a profound trickster. The god of crossing boundaries is also inevitably a thief, for loss is present in every gain. But what joy, what delight, what promise comes with change, acquisition, understanding! To tell a tale is itself enthralling. To tell a tale of boundary crossing is doubly so. To tell many tales in one is to play the games of the gods. And to tell a tale of the Trickster tricked is to be Hermes himself.

***

Hermes is said to be the great-grandfather of Odysseus—through Autolycus and Anticlea—an indication of similar natures. But in Homer's epic Hermes is Odysseus. Their personalities are identical except in the healing power which the god retains and uses. If you have wondered where Odysseus' very complicated character comes from, here is your answer: from a complex divinity with a whole cluster of subtly inter-related powers.

Look for yourself: Odysseus goes to the Kingdom of the Dead and returns, he crosses boundaries of all kinds in his adventures and even plays the stranger-in-danger in his own home. He loves games and prizes and feasting, as he tells the Phaeacians, and demonstrates there, sublimely. As a craftsman he builds the escape raft and is the inventor of that engine of doom, the Trojan Horse; he blinds Polyphemus with a well-tooled olive stake and plants an orchard as a child, along with his father. In the Iliad he is a horse-thief, wearing the very same cap of his great trickster grandfather Autolycus as he rides the horses of Rhesus into camp laughing aloud from sheer pleasure in his stealthy expedition. He is swimmer and wrestler and champion who wins the armor of Achilles from Ajax. Versatile. This man is versatile. And smart.

He is a killer, too, when he has to be, as was Hermes. That god's epithet "Argeiphontes" means killer of Argus of the hundred eyes. After the dog Argus dies Odysseus confronts the hundred suitors he will slay. A twisted similarity, perhaps, but there.

The god himself intervenes as healer, bringing moly to save Odysseus from Circe and the balm to heal his boar wound on Parnassos in his youth.

I think the clearest and most daring identification of Odysseus as Hermes happens in Phaeacia. Odysseus approaches the palace of Alcinoos in a concealing mist of Athena's making, which miraculously dissipates at the very instant when the feasting Phaeacians are pouring a libation to Hermes. As they think of that god, Odysseus appears out of thin air at the hearth by Arete! How plain does it have to be??

The most important attribute of Hermes, already basic to the character of the Ithacan king,

is his skill with language. As ambassador to Troy and speaker in the councils of war, Odysseus was an important figure in the Iliad. In the last song of that epic Homer told of Hermes disguised as a young Greek who intercepts Priam's embassy to Achilles and invents precisely the same kind of tale to conceal his identity that Odysseus does in the Odyssey and who then acts as boundary-crosser for Priam and conductor of the body of the dead Hector.

In Homer's new epic Odysseus is the wily punster in the cave of Polyphemus, the great spell-binding storyteller of Phaeacia, and the indefatigable liar, composer of identities when survival requires it. It is here where Homer's heart lies, for Hermes is his own divine guide! Homer makes a wonderful simile when Odysseus strings his bow to execute his vengeance:

> Then as easily as a master musician stretches a new string on his lyre, making the sheep gut fast at each end, so with great ease Odysseus strung his great bow. Then he twanged the string with his right hand, and it sang a note clear as a swallow. (Odyssey Book 21)

When Homer sang this passage, at the height of the suspense, he must have stopped his phorminx, and, imitating the motions of the simile, used the instrument like a bow, directing everyone's attention to his hands. At the end of the line he would stop singing and twang the string, just as he had described it—high drama. He would have loved it. I <u>know</u> he did that.

He must also have enjoyed hugely passages in which bards would be honored, singing them with a bold humor or high seriousness, as when Demodocus is given the finest cut of boar's chine by Odysseus, who says

> For in every country on earth bards are honored and admired, for the Muse taught them their craft and she loves them every one. (Odyssey Book 8)

That would have spread smiles and cheers among his listeners. But Demodocus' blindness is a corollary to skill: the Muse "had given him good mixed with evil; she took away his sight but gave him the power of song." Homer's audiences would have been moved at that.

A clearer feeling as to Homer's own delight in mousike comes when Eumaios tells Penelope of the ragged stranger at his hut:

> His stories! He will enchant you. He's like one of those bards who learn the Muse's songs—everyone is enthralled and won't let him stop. That's how I felt when he sang for me at my fireside. (Odyssey Book 17)

Homer saves both the herald and the bard from the general slaughter in the hall and makes them the major voices of reason in council the next day who try to restrain the families of the slain suitors from blood-feud retaliation. They are dear to Homer's heart, the children of his god.

Now, Homer had a real headache over Odysseus' father Laertes. Because his poem celebrates the metamorphoses of human life, Homer needs a live Laertes to stand, together with his son and grandson at the end of the epic, beside Athena, the new patriarchal triumvirate. Trouble was, this old hero who sailed with Jason in the Argo was already dead in the old stories. Those ended with the slaughter of the suitors and an assembly at which Athena declared the strife over.

So Homer had to prepare his audience for a live Laertes well before the character made his appearance. He did it by changing the story of Penelope's weaving strategm and repeating it as a stock passage at several points in the epic. In the old songs the clever Penelope had delayed a decision about who to marry by insisting she had first to weave her wedding finery and dowry, then at night unravelling her day's work. Homer changed her task to weaving a shroud for Laertes before she leaves his family for another. Not half so strong a reason, but one that works, because she actually is weaving a shroud—a symbolic shroud for the suitors.

The metamorphosis of Laertes back to manhood again is essential to Homer's meaning. We forget that for a Greek a very old man fell into a category outside of manhood and that, with exceptions like the heroic Nestor and divine seers, ordinary men passed out of manhood into sad old age, the state of Laertes until he sees his son again.

Laertes' resurrection is obscured because it is one of the four famous 'recognitions' of Odysseus, each significantly different from the others and definitive of the ways a man is recognized in the world: his dog, his nurse, his wife, and his father. First is his dog who knows Odysseus even in disguise, instinctively, and is content just to see him again, wag his tail, and die. He is a Laconian hound, a long-lived breed, indeed, according to Aristotle. Readers are always deeply moved by this first great dog story. Odysseus cannot respond to him without giving away his identity, and so he walks on with tears in his eyes.

The second recognition is of course by his old nurse Euryclaia, when she bathes his feet and sees his scar from the boar wound of his youth. This is where we learn of that wounding, the equivalent of Telemachos' voyage into manhood. A man is known by the nature of the scars he has, from the battles he has fought. It is the same sign Odysseus uses later to identify himself to Eumaios and the drover Philoitios. The third recognition is the most famous, when Penelope tricks her husband into revealing the secret of their bed, the post of which is a living olive tree. The trickster is happily tricked; a husband and wife know each other by the private secrets that they share. The scene of reunion had been a favorite all through the years in the tales about Odysseus. Homer does probably add certain things to deepen the profundity of their relationship. The youthful Telemachos is impatient with his cautious parents. And Homer interjects, in the first meeting of Penelope with her beggar husband, lines that suggest to the careful listener that Penelope does indeed recognize her husband and trust his methods. Such an idea has to be merely hinted at so as not to destroy the focus of the suspense and so as to suggest the subtlety of the wife herself. Homer must have taken great delight in working over that recognition.

I marvel at the last of the four recognitions, entirely Homer's own invention, elaborate and difficult and important to his meaning. Odysseus goes to the hills, to find his old father lying on the ground, widowed, useless to his family, weeping for his lost son. Odysseus gives his father <u>two</u> recognition signs—he shows him the scar on his leg and then points out the trees and vines they planted together, things that had grown and flourished through the years. At this double recognition, this old shell of a man sinks against his son, overwhelmed. Odysseus physically pulls him up from the ground and holds him upright again, at which time the spirit and intelligence of Laertes becomes <u>instantly</u> active. The metamorphosis occurs at the recognition and physical contact with Odysseus, as if Laertes were touched by a god.

After that Laertes goes to a ritual bath where he is made tall and strong by Athena. In the battle with the avenging fathers of the suitors, he is the only man Athena allows to slay an adversary, a clear sign of his return to full and heroic stature as a man. He cries, "What a day is this for me, generous gods!" and Athena claims him as dearest friend.

Doesn't it seem that the former state of Laertes is that of a man without the knowledge of the meanings implicit in the signs? Is Homer saying that old age will come, but empty old age need not? That knowledge of the Second Voyage, in the person of Odysseus, will bring Athena to one's side at any age? Without this second life voyage, the life of an aged man has lacked all meaning, sinking toward uselessness, toward resignation and unconsciousness. With this second life voyage, man can restore and transform himself. And, while Telemachos still thinks his is the only real voyage and that his father's suffering has been only a dangerous interruption in his life, both Odysseus and Laertes know better.

So the poem ends with father, son, and the man transformed by spirit, flanked by the goddess of intuitive wisdom, Athena. They seem to embody the mystic statement of the Osiris cults of Egypt whose rites involved use of a pillar cut from a sacred living tree and the raising of a man from the dead. In that tradition the divine reborn son sires his own rebirth and that of his father, so the priest says, "I and the Father are one." And, as the generations of mortal men pass but are ritually the same, the patriarchal system of relationships is seen as spiritual more than physical.

More than one people have sought words and representations for such a concept.

***

And so the great story ends, with the last book full of balances and resonances from the opening ones: The opening of the epic describes a disguised Athena standing in the road in front of Odysseus' palace watching the rioting suitors and his helpless son. The last lines of the epic describe Athena standing in front of Laertes' house beside the reunited father, man, and son, binding Ithaca to civil law.

At the beginning Hermes frees Odysseus and at the end he leads the suitors into Hades, the one act the direct result of the other.

Agamemnon's speech at the end about his wife's treachery is the same topic Zeus discusses at the start; Penelope undoes the treachery of Clytemnestra, as Telemachos cancels the fate of Orestes.

The opening and closing assemblies are even more elaborately interwoven, with all that intricate footwork about the fates of slain fathers and slain sons.

The "stock passage" on Penelope's weaving is repeated verbatim—a beautiful ritual repetition, for Athena is the goddess of weaving, of making useful in the polis the four-dimensional reality of Hermes which the act of weaving signifies.

No one forgets the loves and lovers of Odysseus. After all, it is human love that brings him home, that he chooses over immortality at Calypso's island. The intense loyalty he provokes in both men and women is part of his fascination. Eurycleia and Argus know the loyalty born of nurturing; affectionate memories lie in the minds of Nestor and Menelaos for the comrade who brought victory. Helen knows him well, from his courtship and his spy mission at Troy; well enough to recognize his son on sight. His mother? She longs for his quick and gentle ways, and so she dies. Nausicaa loves and admires him when marriage is on her mind; he tells her he owes his life to her,

262

a lovely but inexact fiction. Then there is the love of Penelope, the trickster wife, a counterpart of himself, mother of a son who seeks him, keeper of his place in the world.

The night of the reunion of Odysseus and Penelope, when time stands still, marks a cycle of time just short of twenty years, at the conjunction of the orbits of sun and new moon. That must have been an ancient theme. The Greeks revered what Odysseus said to Nausicaa about marriage, which they carved on their walls as an ideal to remember:

> The gods grant you your deepest desire—husband, home, and one mind between you, a sight to gladden your friends and sadden your enemies, but you know it best yourselves. (Odyssey Book 6)

I've said enough. We must get back to the blind singer. Perhaps Hermes can be author, text, and reader, but each of us in the metamorphosis of reading is, at the same instant, both Orpheus and Eurydice, and only mortal.

CHAPTER 21

Homer Speaks

698-685 B.C.E. Chios Town and Volissos

Two years after the earthquake Iannos married and came to live at Chios Town to sail his father's ship out of that flourishing port. He had helped Kristos and Uncle Iannos build fine new houses at Smyrna and restore their fields and orchards. Now Kristos farmed and sang, sailing sometimes with his uncle and cousins. When Dio, a master carpenter, joined the family, he helped Iannos build a new house in Chios Town, with spacious rooms for Homer and his daughters. Such carpentry was in demand, and Dio soon married and settled nearby. In 696 Homer's daughter Aikathara married Phesinos and moved to Volissos, a quiet village on the northwestern coast of the island.

Homer enjoyed Chios Town immensely. His singing was always sought, and he was deluged with students. Sons and daughters around him, Homer thought often of how Zoe would have enjoyed life now. Even so, that other level of his life still ruled his days and nights. He needed to work on his poem. He needed his cave on the Meles again, or some serene place to compose. He found himself going more and more often to quiet Volissos.

The intense life of composition during these years brought a change in Homer that nothing else could explain. He was in a space so peopled with life that to see him sitting alone by the sea, letting his words loose on the sea wind, was to feel all audiences, all wars and heroes, all god-like visitations—all possibilities—in the space around him. Men swore they would see the Muse there with him. Some even said he would walk the hills with strangers. They said sometimes he moved as if he were sighted, as if Athena had given him his eyes again.

He began to lose weight, the result of his preoccupation, he said. He would just forget about eating, this lover of feasts. Still, when he did come to the feasts and sing, his songs of Odysseus were funnier and cleverer than ever, fresh and exciting in their new arrangement, and Homer was more beloved than before. The house of Phesinos and Aikathara was near the sea, on a cove about a mile southeast of Volissos. It was part of an ancient settlement dating back before Mycenaean times, more than a thousand years old, the villagers said. On the northwest promontory of the bay stood a temenos to Leucothea, much to Homer's delight. The gods had understood and brought him here to finish the core of his poem, the confession of Odysseus, with her blessing. He had already refined the fantastic voyages a thousand times over, but he vowed to continue until he had spun them into pure gold.

Homer sang the mystery of the human struggle, in lucid narrative, long before the philosophers reduced that precious matter to prose; long before the psychiatrists dismembered it, swallowed it, disgorged it, and stitched it back into myth again; long before everyone became his own priest and analyst. It is all still there in the song of the bard, composed almost 2700 years ago and fresh as the sun this morning.

❖❖❖

Homer speaks:

Of all of my songs, this one is my best. The voyage of Odysseus is my own night sea journey composed in the voice of the psyche, its images speaking to the deep listener within. Silently, out of a fruitful darkness looms the single ship and the voyager, the sea around the hull phosphorescent, a film of blue flame playing over the spars, and, amid the rich chaos, pattern and infinite dimension. Even my Muse trembles in the presence of such mystery; yet when that mariner turns his gaze to us, the song begins.

The Fantastic Voyage is my truest song, too, though it may not seem to be—my critics all praise me for my skill in picturing the "real world!" I want to tell you about it myself, in the literal language of your time because that is what you trust—though I see little that is engaging about explanation. Its plainness is like bones bleaching in the sun, devoid of narrative life. Give me a knotty, vital myth any day. You seem to need to draw the bones out of the living creature and pull its sinews apart before you can see what it is. Still, I honor you for what you are, and I'm glad you enjoy my stories.

Thank the gods Letha Gooding seems to know I cannot be made real except through narrative. This curious woman has told you something of what my Odyssey is about, its design. In fact, she has told you a few things I didn't know myself! In the main, though, she got it right. Odysseus is Hermes, and the voyages are part of the Samothracian initiation told in my own way. I thank her profoundly for loving my songs.

When it comes to my life she often misses the mark. That is no surprise, since no one has done my biography since classical times. I must tell you immediately that she is quite wrong about Laocoon. I never thought he was my father. By now I am sure you have guessed who that father really was!

She leaves out so many things that were important to me. For instance, she doesn't show how close Maion and I were. And she really idealizes life in Smyrna in my boyhood; we worked very hard. In spite of that, her chapter on Smyrna is my favorite. The world was once like that on a sunny day!

But gods! How she distorted the initiations! They were poetry, woman! Stories, magical stories, and objects, and deeds. Not explanation. How lost a world is when it needs explanation! Sorry. Just give me the stories, the images, and a song in my Muse's head.

Ah, Zoe and I. That iron-bound closeness to Zoe. It doesn't surprise me that I went blind when she died.

Letha makes me more high-minded than I really was, and a too-serious entertainer. I was a dead-serious thinker, of course, but in performance I was very amusing and charming, witty and dramatic by turns. Unpredictable, too. She doesn't write about the glorious women I had in my youth, or how desperately I suffered from being different, or the petty jealousies between bards. She doesn't know that I was a rough man among men and a very skillful hunter. I don't see how she could have missed that, with all those animal similes in my songs. Zeus, how I missed hunting after I lost my eyes. I loved the bow and arrow—you can see that in my Odysseus tale. And I did learn to write my name.

Thank the Great Gods she didn't make me into some latter-day Prometheus. I guess I was more like—well—Chaucer, probably, or Dante, if you need examples. Or, rather, they were like me.

The poets all acknowledge me as the master. I made daring new kinds of poems, yes, but was very much a creature of my century. No wild rebel. Rather well-behaved and canny. I saw the cities of men and knew their minds. Akrasia? Of course. But doesn't everyone who is truly alive feel that?

I wish her manuscript had seen the light of the sun before her evil fate engulfed her. Then I would not have to speak to keep Samothrace from being lost again. Let me tell you now about the core of my mystery poem of the voyage. I will try to speak appropriately and in your idiom, as I said.

Imagine me as your guest speaker, or better still, in a television interview, or on a tape for radio. We are together on the beach at Volissos, and I am sitting on my favorite rock. I am wearing a long Ionian chiton, freshly washed, and my daughter Zoe has trimmed my beard for the occasion. The wine skins are beside us, good Chiote wine (Letha Gooding says Chian!), and my favorite Praemnian which Kristos sends me from Smyrna.

Now. Close your eyes, and keep them shut. No. Put this dark scarf over them. Feel the heat of the sun. Hear the sea, and the cries of the birds. Let me talk to you, though now and again I will have to sing. If you'll hand me my phorminx now I will set it here between us. Ha! You're not used to the darkness yet. I suppose we need no opening hymn, as I used to give before a singing! So I will simply begin.

The fantastic voyages were the challenge of my life. So many tales to choose from, so many problems to work out. To tell the tale so that it makes the meaning is the hardest work I know. The Muse provided my mousike, but I had to think the tale out for myself.

First I had to plot the mariner's chart to the sea gates of the western ocean. I left out the Aegean leg to obscure the starting point at Samothrace; everyone knows the Aegean, anyway. Rounding Cape Malea, where the storms are legendary, I drove the ships down to Jerba off the Libyan coast for the first adventure. From there Odysseus sails north again to the west coast of Sicily, thence to the Aeolian islands. The next sea gate is between Corsica and Sardinia, from which he drops down the Italian coast from Cape Circeo past the Galli islands, through the strait of Messina past Etna to Malta, then west to the mouth of the Adriatic at Corcyra, and then home to Ithaca. I mention the sign of Stromboli's volcano, too. In each adventure I include details of the landfall and rivers. What a help these descriptions proved to be to initiates roaming out into the wide world!

How incredible foreknowledge is, after all.

I needed to hide my purpose, so I included incidents with no sailing directions, like the trip to the Kingdom of the Dead. Mortals find that place soon enough, with no directions! You cannot know how agonizing, how soul-wrenching this part of my epic became. In an agony of concentration I would bring myself here to the beach at Volissos and compose with my feet in the sea. Sometimes I would swim. The very rhythm of this world crept into my voice, the ebb and flow of water never quite concealing earth tremor, never quite overwhelming bird cries. "You know what I miss most about seeing right now?" I asked my daughter Zoe once, for she looked after me. "The fish. I have utterly lost the fish. They are so silent and so beautifuI. So elusive. Why didn't I look more at the fish? I do know red mullets, of course. I remember them well.

Zoe shrugged my mood away. "You can smell them, father. You can always smell them when they come ashore!" We laughed together a lot.

✳✳✳

I begin the myth of human transformation at the beginning, with nothing, in the land of the lotus-eaters in a tale I got from the Phoenicians on Mimas peninsula. Anyone who is borne along on the lotus flower in the world sea exists only passively; there is only pleasant aimlessness, and timelessness, and meaningless acceptance. No one has a name or a relation to anyone else. To be thus is to refuse even to refuse to act. And, as with drugs, no one can rescue himself from such inertia. So I have Odysseus literally carry the victims back to the ships, as if they were infants. That episode is plain enough and I sing it quickly. Not so the next. It is critical.

The next step—from lotus-eaters to cyclops—takes Odysseus from nothingness to barbarism and beyond; of course, as destructor of Troy, he is still a barbarian himself. He carries the Ciconian wine taken as a bribe during the sacking of a city and enters the cyclops' cave to help himself. He is hardly better than the giant cyclops who lives in a country ideal for civilized man, yet who exists in a cave as a lawless and godless cannibal. Note my long, admiring description of a lush place and its promise for civilized people. This is an old trickster story, you know, a child's favorite.

I had to laugh about it, the irony I mean. Here I was, pacing the sand of Chios as blind as Polyphemus myself! I kept thinking of Orion, a son of Poseidon who was drugged on wine and blinded by a trickster son of Dionysos, King Oenopion of this very island. Orion got his sight back, as you know, by gazing east where Helios rises from the ocean, but that did not happen until after many adventures. I even composed a short song about him. I confess I have tried the same thing, but no oracle instructed me and so it failed. I really was obsessed with Orion for awhile and put him in my underworld. Letha should have thought of that; he was a hunter, too.

Everybody always enjoyed the episode about Polyphemus and the terrible destruction of his eye. It ends a way of seeing that he represents, a way of seeing for Odysseus as much as for himself. The uprooted tree stake that blinds him is sacred—for me it is the staff of Hermes, the club of Herakles dedicated to Hermes, the olive of Athena, the phallus of Dionysos—and the wine of Maron that Polyphemus drinks is Dionysian. I suggest in this single act the fundamentals of the move toward human culture, but first the point of the olive stake has to be hardened by the fire of Hephaistos. I pile up the symbols of technology and fire in double similes to show this meaning. Remember? Let me sing it for you—

> You know how to bore ship's timber with an augur—you hold it in place while others keep turning it round and round with a strap. That's how we turned the heat-sharpened pole in his eye and the blood bubbled about the charred point, eyelids and eyelashes curling as the roots crackled. Just as a smithy plunges a red hot axe in cold water to make strong steel and it hisses loudly, so did the giant's eye sizzle around the olive wood. (Odyssey Book 9)

Sheer horror? Audiences loved it! A profound action, on any level of meaning. Then after the blinding, having been tricked by the vine, the olive, and fire—the great civilizers—Polyphemus is tricked by words! Since Odysseus has said his name is NoMan, Polyphemus tells the cyclops who run to his rescue that no man has harmed him, and so they leave.

But, you see, for one of my meanings, Polyphemus is right! Odysseus has not misspoken; he is no man—he is Hermes—and so he spoke the truth and everyone has been deceived by language!

Don't you revel in that?—Oh, so do I. Zeus, how I enjoyed singing that! It is no meaningless action, either, when I have the Greeks escape under the bellies of rams because the ram is sacred to Hermes.

I always got a huge kick out of singing the Polyphemus adventure. Somehow people sense its importance. Something deep inside them delights in it. In the blinding I tell of the coming of the civilized arts and the movement into—what you call a dualistic mode of being. I am showing you the price you pay for consciousness when Odysseus announces his name, rejecting the namelessness of the lotus-eaters, defeating the grotesque deity of the one-eyed giant, but taking on an opposite, an enemy, the mighty eternal unconscious in the form of Poseidon. The curse of Polyphemus is the curse of accepting evil with good in a world of opposites, of saying who you are and accepting the certain opposition of what you are not. You understand, then, why Polyphemus has one eye, one which must be penetrated and disabled in order to escape from the cave.

***

Few of the tales I tell are as important as that one. So I put in the next two episodes to show what happens in this new world: the welcome and rejection by Aiolus, and the awful loss of Odysseus' men in the land of the Laestrygonians.

Aiolus, as King of the Winds, is ancestor to more noble women and heroes than most men can name: Salmoneus, Tyro, Nestor, Jason, Bellerephon, Melikertes; as seed-carrying wind, he was indeed fertilizer of the earth! As our myths say, the wind is procreator after the sea. But his island floats and is encased in a wall of bronze, that metal of the age before iron. The people welcome Odysseus, entertain him, and give him the precious gift of a favorable wind. Their inbred but hospitable society is Mycenaean in flavor, even pre-Mycenaean, and they cannot respond except in traditional ways when my poor hapless Odysseus, betrayed and asleep when his men loose the winds, is blown back again. So they cast out the emerging individual. Sleep, we all know, is a sign of mortality. In this world even Odysseus cannot control others whose acts stand in the way of fulfillment, of getting home.

I love to sing all the cannibal stories, you know, like Polyphemus and the Laestrygonians. They seem so savage, and we all have a fear of being devoured and a buried shame at devouring other life. When we would kill and prepare our own meat, we never forgot to honor that dead body as a sacrificed life. I feel sorry for people who have lost that proximity and would guess that they have lost their religion, too. For many of us the sanctity of plant life was destroyed when we rearranged nature with planting. That's the <u>real</u> reason the power of the old earth goddess is dead. Eating is a ritual act that you will pay back in kind. You don't like that thought, eh? Yet it makes the beauty of the feast.

I still remember from my youth the orgies in the field furrows at harvest and planting time. They were always numinous, fraught with fundamental truth. An impotent man or a prudish woman scared Hades out of us. The children born of those unions were truly conceived in, invested with, divinity. Especially the women. And I will tell you something I never tell anyone else, ever. My wife Zoe was such a child of the furrow. She used to tell me when we were in bed together and in deep union that she knew my mother conceived me at such a time. She was wrong, of course, but that was a need of hers, then.

On to the Laestrygonians, who have houses and councils rather than isolated caves, but are hunters without agriculture, cannibals who attack without mercy, like gluttons, destroying all but one ship. Did you recognize the setting? I got it from Rasenna, who knew of the savage tribes in south Corsica. A spectacular place. I understand another slaughter took place there 2000 years later! Does that make me a prophet?

Anyway, in these two episodes I show the stagnation of the planter culture of Aiolus and the violence of the hunter Laestrygonians, rather like the coming together of the ancient Mediterranean peoples and the tribes of northern Greeks. Rather like the lotus-eaters and cyclops multiplied—I could not say socialized! Our man seeking a new order of civilization rejects and is rejected by them both. My emerging individual is a threat to such orders. But make no mistake. There was a time and a level of being for which those orders were adequate enough. I sang before history was invented, of course, and did quite well, really. My audience understood.

These are my first four adventures—lotus, cyclops, winds, and cannibal attack. I take my hero through social time as well as through an emerging notion of how he can see the world around him. Almost as if he were growing from infancy in the same way that the social unit is evolving. Nowadays you call it ontogeny and phylogeny, pretentious terms, I think, for a simple idea.

No, let me pour the wine. You will likely spill it, so freshly blind are you.

❊❊❊

Now Odysseus, directionless, comes upon Circe's island. This is the center of my whole poem, you know, because it embraces the trip to the Kingdom of the Dead, where he confronts his own dark side and, hence, acquires self-direction—you call it centroversion. The heart of the mystery. In a highly dramatic and personal confrontation, my now careful hero meets the power of the Great Goddess in her most enticing aspect—as Circe.

Many a man has succumbed to her worship, accepting his earthly and animal nature, and never left her pens again. She is the Goddess of the Wild Beasts, and I know her well. For me, both she and Calypso must speak the language of men, not of the Olympians. Only the direct intervention of Hermes with the sacred herb of Samothrace saves Odysseus from her. He accepts his sensual nature after he has set limitations to it, yet he stays a year. It is Circe, not Zeus, who requires the perilous journey to the Kingdom of the Dead, for death is of the earth and not the spirit.

You see, what Odysseus gets from the Kingdom of the Dead is foreknowledge. Blind Teiresias prophesies his return and eventual death, warning him not to eat Helios' cattle. The rest of his adventures, except Calypso, will occur only after they have been anticipated either through Teiresias or Circe. So not only Odysseus but also my audience is ready for the event when it happens.

The song of the Kingdom of the Dead must be done carefully, but dramatically, and must be told by a survivor, in retrospect; otherwise it would be too numinous. I could always feel the dread in my listeners, without seeing their faces. I begin with the ghost of the dead sailor Elpenor, Odysseus' seaman who falls off the roof at Circe's, sleepy from wine, and lies still unburied, a comic death but a terrible fate. I have Odysseus say, as his tears fall in pity, "Elpenor, how did you get here? You have beaten us to this dismal place, and on foot!" That always gets a laugh, for relief, as we move into the gloom.

After Odysseus' talk with Teiresias comes the touching conversation with Anticlea, his own mother, whose death is new to him. She tells him the situation in Ithaca—foreknowledge again—

and when he asks what killed her, she says that life was no longer sweet for her. There are always sentimental tears here, and I linger over it as she talks about the dead. Then comes my catalog of famous noblewomen, mothers of great heroes of the past.

In the last part, after a pause, my dear Odysseus meets and commiserates with those Greek heroes who failed to return: first comes Agamemnon and his slaughtered retinue—where I hint at the fate of the suitors. Agamemnon and Achilles both ask about their sons. Ajax won't even speak to him now, a sulking suicide because Odysseus defeated him in a contest for Achilles' armor. You notice how I changed Achilles—-some of my audience—warriors—objected to this, by the way, but I always sang it boldly

"But you, Achilles, are most blessed of all humankind. We honored you alive, as if you were a god; now you rule among the dead. So do not regret your death."
He answered at once, "Don't praise death to me, Odysseus. I would rather work as a plow-man for a poor farmer on a small patch of land than be Supreme Lord of the Kingdom of the Dead....But tell me please about my son. (Odyssey Book II)

Ah, my sweet, proud, mortal Achilles. My heart aches for him. And I close with Odysseus seeing Minos judging the dead, the great sufferers who defied Zeus—Tityos, my Tantalos of sunny Smyrna, the trickster Sisyphos. I put in my beloved Orion, and end with an elaborate and terrible picture of Herakles, who tells Odysseus that he succeeded in his labors with the help of Hermes and Athena. I was very plain-spoken there.

❋❋❋

Now, let me stop here a while. I want you to see the best trick of all, how I center the song as if it were skewered on a spit! The caesura I set in here separates the poem into before and after.

This is how I do it: After Odysseus has seen his mother and the mothers of the heroes, I have Odysseus stop his story, saying it is late. I return my audience to the audience in Phaeacia's palace. Everyone pauses, everywhere, for a moment. Including me!

What a caesura! Monumental! I have to smile when I think of it—so obvious—but few ever said they saw it. Right at the corresponding point in the epic where the caesura goes in the hexam-eter line. Forgive my agitation. I have never explained this before, and I find it most invigorating.

After this pregnant pause, I have Queen Arete speak up and refer to Odysseus as <u>her</u> guest, so pleased is she by his praise of the mothers. Then, notice now, the elder statesman Echeneos, while flattering her, says that the decision whether to continue rests with the king, Arete's husband, who is also her uncle. In this man's speech I remind the listeners—both mine and Odysseus'—that, while Arete is the child of the former king, it is Alcinoos who wields the power. Matriarchal tradition.

When Odysseus does resume his tale, it is at the meeting in the Kingdom of the Dead with Agamemnon where the murdered king speaks scathingly of women and of his son's heavy burden of vengeance. Do you see? Do you see the sea-change at the break? Everything heretofore in my poem, in both the fantastic voyages and in the epic as a whole, differs fundamentally from what follows it. The old caesura break in the line upon which the whole epic pivots!

After it, consciousness reigns. The king rules. Odysseus is <u>direction</u>-oriented in his confessional tale. I put in an interesting little conversational touch right there at the center, too, something of a mystery too. See if you can find it. I love it when a plan comes together like that.

We need a break here, too. Let's stretch and walk on the beach. I have to tell you what I said right at the caesura, right where Odysseus puts all my audiences together and pauses...

There is a long silence in the shadowy hall. The pleased queen offers to share her guest with the men, inviting them to give gifts. She is ready for the story to end, though she asks her guest to stay longer. At that central silence comes the shift to consciousness that maleness represents, the shift from mother right to patriarchy. And then I place, in the sacred core of my poem, a magnificent, outrageous statement about myself and my poem!

Authority in his hands, King Alcinoos urges the tale-teller—both me and Odysseus!—to go on, saying—I'll have to sing this without my phorminx—we left it by the rock—

"Dear Odysseus, plainly you are no imposter, like so many others. There are many such men in this dark time spinning their lies which no man can counter. But there is the spirit of honesty and sense in your story as well as poetic art; you have told it like a skillful bard who understands his craft." (Odyssey Book II)

Ha! Do I give myself away? My true intent! The poet's craft indeed! Sometimes when I sang this I could hear a low chuckle and feel a delightful lightness among my listeners. And my heart would laugh. Working with words and narrative. Singing. What is it anyway? Who tells the tale makes the meaning. And narrative is not like life. If one expects a narrative to be life, then the singer is simply a liar. Who can, after all, tell the tale of how he came to be what he is? Can confession tell anything other than another narrative, another lie?

And what about all the lies I have Odysseus invent? That my audience took such delight in? They are true stories I heard, tales far more believable than the fantasy I spin. Are they lies then, after all, if they happened to the men of my—or Trojan—times? My listeners believe them, however gruesome or tragic they are. That is the saddest trick of all, for life is hard and death is certain. And there is no real test of the truth of the stranger's tale, is there? Even of this one.

But the voyage continues. The four remaining adventures will have marked resemblances to the earlier four; however, they are of a higher order and Odysseus has foreknowledge of them until he fails again. The ones I finally select are the Sirens, the double choice of the Clashing Rocks and Scylla and Charybdis, and the Cattle of the Sun God, which leads to the unexpected sojourn with Calypso.

Now do you see my whole design? I put within the fantastic voyages the exact same structure as that of the total epic: the first four adventures I mean to represent the fall into time, the world of Telemachos; the episode with Circe and the underworld is the second stage, of inner metamorphosis, with the descent at the center—at the central point of which I insert a reminder of the longer epic pattern which has arrived at the same pivotal point itself. Then will come four further tests, rather like the four recognitions in Ithaca—call them precognitions since he expects them—upon which Odysseus acts before he is able to accept and return Leucothea's veil. That veil, the scarf of

Samothrace indicating completed initiation, is the same sign of cosmic harmony as the closing image of the generations of Laertes with Athena.

You see how the epic and voyage overlay each other? I wove this web of words as substantially and densely as anything Penelope ever did. Or Athena. The core of the whole pattern lies at the caesura. The essence! I am immensely pleased with it.

***

Back on my rock again. I think I've worn it smooth through the years. You can, I suppose, anticipate the final four adventures, all of them thought-provoking, I hope. The first is the Sirens, whose song is too strong for human flesh to resist. A touchy subject for a bard to sing about.

Our sirens were death goddesses, shaped like bees or fantastic birds, with women's heads. It is their promise of knowledge that men have always succumbed to. No one had ever escaped them before, but Odysseus has foreknowledge and so he endures, by means of wax plugs in the ears of his crew and ropes binding him as he listens to their song.

You must realize that this episode touches me where I live. Odysseus is tied, his mortal body bound while his mind and heart strive to break away. It is one of the agonies of the seeker, of the initiated. I cannot ignore that the Sirens are singers, like myself—though I am both singer and listener—that the content of their song is simply that they sing, their song so enticing that men listen until they die. Can their captured listeners live their own lives, or are they bound up in the past and the future while their bodies turn to skeletons? The beauty of the Sirens' language and the depth of their music can tempt men away from living, in the same sense that the lotus-eaters, in the first set of four tales, tempted men. However, I make this last temptation of a higher kind, appealing to the self-aware and to the noblest parts of spirit. .A self-aware Odysseus, having heard the song and, bound within his own mortal body, having gone on with his life, can live in a world made more beautiful by their tempting song.

As a bard, I can imagine the horror of the death of the Sirens, when no one will listen. I could not put it in my song. I know well the dangers implicit in epic and the complex passiveness of its victims. It is an episode I trembled to consider, and I would tear myself away to pace the sand, full of anxiety. I could hear the warships pass, the piping of the auletos carrying with it a clarity that brought back the days of my youth. I remembered standing, back to the mast, while I piped the song to the oarsmen, watching the wake from the narrow black hull fold apart behind the ship as she went. I could imagine Odysseus tied, back to the mast, listening to the Sirens' song as the long wake flowed behind him in the stillness of a sultry afternoon. And my own heart would flutter like a caged bird beating its wings at the memory of a bright sky.

Ah, well. Shall we go on? Next I have Odysseus confront the matter of choices: he must either try to slip between the Clashing Rocks, at that terrible volcano of Stromboli, or he can go through the straits of Messina where he must maneuver between the rock of Scylla and the whirlpool of Charybdis. You recognize the Clashing Rocks from the story of Jason, which I use as a symbol parallel with the eye of Polyphemus. In fact, at that point I remind my audience of that blinding. But Circe has forewarned Odysseus, advising him to avoid repeating that test, and so I take him past, to the strait, to the very nature of choices. He must keep his head and accept that there is always some loss in choice—that is what I mean by the whirlpool Charybdis and the monster Scylla—oblivion and certain sacrifice. Circe had advised a quiet and cautious approach to Scylla, telling Odysseus not to rouse the old earth forces she is part of. Still Scylla snatches six of his men, who call to Odysseus for help he cannot give. Here I have Odysseus stop his tale and express his emotion to the Phaeacians over this loss, calling these deaths the most pitiful thing he has seen in all his troubles on the sea. Odysseus realizes that he could have prevented at least some of the tragedy—he stopped to arm himself, against the advice of Circe. Nor did he forewarn his men, for fear they would not take the passage.

After Odysseus' failure to be frank with his men, they mistrust him and insist on landing at Thrinakia against all that he can tell them. This is the dread island Teiresias had warned them about, and Odysseus forewarns his men this time—to no avail. I don't complicate the ancient meaning much here: the cattle and sheep number the days and nights of the old lunar year and so represent the life of man. The crew forget the gods in their mortal hunger, eating up their days, so to speak, and bring on their doom. Odysseus is asleep, as he was when his men opened the bag of winds; he too is mortal and can save only himself. Then, as the Laestrygonians had destroyed his fleet, Zeus destroys his last ship and his men. Odysseus alone survives. You can imagine with what passion I sang of the castaway hero clinging to a sail-tangled mast.

Now, because Odysseus has failed to heed Teiresias' warning, his foreknowledge deserts him. Out of control, he is swept back to Charybdis the dread whirlpool, where he is saved by hanging to the overarching branches of the wild fig tree. The gods of the tree show it to stand for procreation. You would say that the generative principle saves dualistic man from death in time. I would say that his sons live on. Forgive me if I say that I like my way of expressing this better than yours. In fact, my image of the fig tree and the maelstrom is better than both.

Well, now Odysseus floats, at the mercy of the ocean's currents, to the island of a goddess, this time Calypso. Just as Circe's island lacks a clear locale, Calypso's is hidden in the navel of the sea, remote from Olympos. She is an earth goddess, not an Olympian, part of the same oblivion as the sea, and she offers immortality to the weary mortal. He must give up his search for home if he is to live outside of time, as she does. After the disastrous realities of the straits and Thrinakia, I think I make Calypso a genuine temptation, the final sweet appeal. In fact, she and Poseidon are my final symbols, one benevolent and one hostile, of the old preconscious world.

I struggled mightily to find a way of showing the agony of Odysseus' choice of mortal consciousness. Finally I made it simple: as it happens—in time, in silence, and in tears. I guess such a choice cannot finally be explained, as I have Odysseus gently tell the sad Calypso. His mortal loves—home and family—do most to bring him back to the "real" world our consciousness imposes. I am suggesting here that he learns he is mortal at heart.

It is of course Hermes who comes to free Odysseus, through Athena's intercession with Zeus. And Poseidon, more powerful than ever, assaults him one last time. Even now a humbler but ever-resourceful Odysseus does not depend on the divine aid of Leucothea until the very last minute, when he is drowning in the great waves. When he finally does accept and use the scarf of Samothrace, he sits astride the mast, binds the scarf about him, and throws himself upon the turbulent sea.

Of course we all know that the battle with the sea will continue, but he does escape the angry water by reaching a place where a river flows into the sea and by praying to the river god: "Mercy, Lord, I am at your mercy!" He places himself in harmony with the gods and man, with full knowledge that he needs the gods and must obey them, knowing the nature of mortals in the order of the cosmos. He takes shelter among the roots of the twin olive trees, one wild and one cultivated, his sheltering spirits of Hermes and Athena.

***

I have kept you too long. An Odyssey is a long voyage, no matter who is the voyager. I brought the epic form a long way, too, from the songs of the old tradition. You know how I wanted my fantasy to work, and it is all for Hermes' sake.

This is not the tale of <u>how</u> I did it—now that would be a different tale of suffering! Exquisite suffering. I would not put you through it. But it is done now.

The certainty that, if my sacred song were to survive with the meaning intact, it would have to be written down, grew on me slowly as I made the poem. The accompaniment on the phorminx would of course be lost, for we had no system to record it. There was no help for it. Some mainland singers even then did not use the phorminx as they recited. So I tried to forget that some of my lovely effects would be lost. At any rate, I had to do something to save the poem. So I called my sons and my students together. That was a day to remember.

I told my sweet singers—I loved them one and all—that the Odyssey was a song to Hermes containing a mystery which would be lost unless they kept precisely to its structure. In the end I asked those who knew writing to make a copy and keep it for the school. Each one gave me his solemn promise. From that day they called themselves the Homeridae. To this day I believe they were all true to their word, substantially. They did make some improvements, I must admit, and add some junk, too. But they kept their word to the god. Bless them.

My heart has always warmed as I work with meanings. I love the lover of words, the givers of themselves to mortals, the agents of the Muse, the tricksters and the sufferers. I know that man without mousike is trapped in the present moment. Trapped at the surface. Like the beast of the mountain. In a deeper darkness than mine.

***

Homer had been drained by the work of these years and by his blindness, for every day his blindness was a new thing. His task now was to sing his sacred song and make it known. Athens would help him, as would Corinth and Ithaca. And so, the role of the great singer became that of boundary-crosser once again. Accompanied by student or son, invited everywhere, Homer spent the 680's singing the Iliad still, but singing his new Odyssey, the delightful and suspenseful song of the trickster, and loving every minute. He went once more to Delos and even to Argos, but never as far afield again as Athens or Ithaca. Or Samothrace.

One day when he was at Volissos he had a visitor. It was Prax's son, Andrus, come to hear him sing the Odyssey.

"What does your father say about it?" Homer inquired.

"He heard about it, your newest version of the old tales, from a bard seeking initiation, the young bard Monakribos from Klyzomenai. He listened closely through the whole song, enjoying it hugely, looking at the ground, or staring into the distance, or covering his head with his cloak and weeping.

"But when the bard had finished and we all asked Prax how he liked the song of his old friend, a slow smile began in the back of his eyes and spread, as if it were a fire inside him, and he began to chuckle. He laughed, and then he roared, overcome, as if some delightful private joke lived inside him. He was like Laertes himself at the end of the epic, with a new spring in his carriage and laughter at the back of his voice. All that he said was that it was great, magnificent, that he wished that he could hear Teleo sing it. After that he always smiled when we would mention your name. And he told me that I must make the journey to see you. And to hear you sing. He said that you are the wisest man who ever lived."

Homer let loose a great laugh of his own, and his heart smiled at the thought of his old friend .

❖

Smyrna was flourishing again by 688 when the city sent a delegation to the 23rd Olympiad. Kristos went along, and came back with songs to celebrate Smyrna's great new hero, Onomastos, who had won the first boxing matches ever to be part of the Olympics. On the day of competition twelve boxers were entered, and the excitement over the new event was high. Each winner of a bout had to fight another winner immediately; it was a punishing competition. Onomastos had electrified the multitudes with his combination of endurance and graceful, dancing movement. The herald of the games had proclaimed his victory with the overwhelming approval of the crowd, handing him the palm and later crowning him with the wild olive wreath made from the tree Homer could still picture in his mind. The judges had pronounced his skill so just, so sensible, so natural that the rules of all Olympic boxing events for a thousand years were to be modeled upon his performance. There was wild jubilation in Smyrna upon their return, and Homer went to his old city to hear Kristos sing a tale of his friend's great triumph. Every young boy in the gulf cities began to train for boxing.

Kristos brought news to his father about Ithaca. Kristos had met Jason at the games. He was free and living in Ithaca. "Tell him I am 40 now," Jason had told Kristos, "the same age he was when he came to my hut at Raven's Crag. The age of Odysseus when he came home. Tell him my life is good. I was never a slave, but slavery changed my life nevertheless. Give him my love."

Kristos paused. "Jason told me how you helped them to escape. The woman sent her slave price back to Desmentes. She is now a priestess in Corcyra. She was your woman, I gather. Did you have children by her?"

"No. She was a forceful woman, of the Etruscan race. A delight. And she sang my songs! You cannot imagine how she could sing them! So. She has what she wanted and I am truly happy for her. Poor Jason. It is hardest of all to return. To reclaim the past. His hopes were so high." He sighed.

"He is only a passable singer, I'm afraid." Kristos was eating figs as they sat quietly in the autumn sunshine. "He sings as if he has banked his fires. Without power. I wonder sometimes how I sound. I wonder if a singer whose life has been easy, as mine has, can truly sing well. Jason's pain has not made him better. But look at you and Dio! Anguishing things lie in your hearts. But not in mine. It was hard when you were away, but I knew my home, and love was all around me."

Homer smiled warmly and reached for his son's shoulder. "You have it, Kristo. You have felt the anguish of others and so lived their griefs. Why Jason is lacking I cannot say. It is usually the self-important, those who sing for the attention to themselves, who cannot sing truly."

"That may be. But what is it that has made you able to do what you have done? To keep the tradition and change it, too? What was it that made you <u>want</u> to change it? That is the important question. I twist my heart over it."

"Oh, dear Kristo. My boy. Who knows quite how he comes to himself? I will tell you what I never tell anyone else. I was a good bard—an excellent bard—but just that. Until I went to Samothrace. I made the Iliad there."

"Then I will have to go for myself."

"Samothrace speaks only to those who seek it out. I am happy that you are going."

And so began the pilgrimages of Homer's children and his students to the sacred island. Unobtrusively each would be initiated. His family then was united by more than a blood bond, one that taught them a purer harmony. They understood the Odyssey and sang it just as he did, without so much as a glance between them betraying the great secret of its structure. Even before Homer's death, then, the Homeridae became rhapsodes, literal reciters, of necessity, because they knew that the meaning of the Odyssey lay in its forrn, in its very bones.

✶✶✶

Jason went back to Ithaca afire with Homer's new epic, much of which he had learned from Kristos at Olympia. Whether it was the love that shone in that song's Eumaios, or the transformation of his own life into art—who is to say, when vital forces coalesce?—Jason bloomed with his singing of the Odyssey. And when travellers thronged to Ithaca again to honor Odysseus the wise man, the modern man, Ithacans bloomed too, their substance reinvigorated, their artifacts only evidence now rather than frightening icons. And so through the years to follow, Ithacans grew equal to the gift of the great singer, the bard who gave them back themselves, blest among men and beloved of the immortals.

INTERLOCUTORY

The Voice of Letha Gooding

"Where is Homer, who possessed the throne?/ The immortal work remains, the mortal author's gone," as Lucretius observed.

All mortals enter the house of death, however magnificent their spirits. All of them hope to find loved ones there. Many of them pray they may meet the souls of the great, as Odysseus did in the Odyssey. Plato's Socrates, speaking to the Athenians who had just condemned him to death: "What would not a man give if he might converse with Orpheus and Musaeus and Hesiod and Homer? Nay, if this be true, let me die again and again." (Apology, trans. Benjamin Jowett) I am not the first person, nor will I be the last, who has hoped that, in this life or another, I might know the truth of Homer. Dante, in The Divine Comedy, meets him in Limbo, where Homer leads the school of great pre-Christian poets—Horace, Ovid, Lucan, Vergil—striding ahead, "lord of the lofty song, who soars/above the others as an eagle" (Inferno, Canto iv, 89-90). They hold high converse there.

It may be that the bard will sing some day for me, perhaps a beautiful passage or two about this lovely world I too will leave behind.

CHAPTER 22

Death of Homer

686—680 B.C.E. Chios

The news spread like wildfire through the Greek cities. Sardis had fallen to the Lydians! Confusion abounded, for there had been no approaching armies, no siege, no knowledge of civil strife. The Candaules, or ruler, for many years had been Myrsilus. He was weak but backed by the tradition of 500 years of consecutive rule by sons of the line of Heracles and Omphale.

The story of Myrsilus' death brought by refugees was highly dramatic, one of love and betrayal. And, Homer reflected privately, highly suspect. Myrsilus had been so in love with his wife Toudo that he wanted other men to be impressed by her beauty. He talked incessantly about her to his closest counselor and friend, a Lydian named Gyges, son of Dascylus. Finally he insisted that Gyges hide in the royal bedroom and watch the queen disrobe to see her magnificent body, escaping as she came into the king's bed. Gyges was horrified at the order, but the king insisted, and it was done.

The queen saw him. She did not let the king know that she had seen Gyges, but she knew he had contrived it and she privately swore vengeance. The next morning, having her trusted retinue with her, she summoned Gyges to come before her. She gave him a choice of murdering the king and marrying her to make his knowledge of her legitimate, or of dying on the spot. Her courtiers stood with swords drawn. Gyges chose to live. He murdered his old friend the king that night as he lay asleep in his bed.

Though Gyges and the Queen had the support of a strong palace faction, the city rose in tumult at the assassination and usurpation. Terror reigned for a week before it was decided that, if the Delphic oracle proclaimed Gyges king of Sardis, resistance would cease. And so a delegation had been sent and all of Ionia waited for the answer. It was all that men talked about.

"Why do you want to know the news," Homer's maidservant would ask, shaking her ancient head. "It is always bad. Men are bent on destruction and women on mischief. You are better off sitting here on your rock making tunes."

Homer would laugh. "I expect you're right. The world is madder than ever. But that's what my songs are about."

Now another story of the assassination was circulating, "the official one, no doubt," commented Iannos, "definitely Lydian in flavor." It said that Gyges was a Lydian shepherd, a simple and honest man serving the great house of the corrupt and weak Heraclidai. One day after a tremendous storm on Mt. Tmolos, Gyges had come across a broad chasm newly bared by a mudslide. At the foot of the ravine was an entrance to a cavern that held marvelous things. He saw a horse made entirely of brass and the corpse of a huge giant who lay sprawled the full length of his palace floor. On his hand was a magic ring which Gyges took, along with all the wealth that he could carry. He discovered when he turned the crown of the ring toward himself that he became invisible. So, by various machinations he gained influence and access to the king and queen, access to their confidence, and through assassination access to the throne.

The Chians hooted with delight. "Who wants to bet that the Delphic sanctuary is much richer now?" Homer smiled to find the bones of both stories to be identical. The invisible ring of the god of Mt. Tmolus, the invisible power of power.

And indeed the Delphic oracle approved Gyges on the throne, qualifying his triumph only by saying that the Heraclidai would be avenged in the fifth generation. And who cared about that?

"Smyrna will be lucky to still be Greek in five generations," Kristo said glumly. "I think the chaos is close to home now."

✳✳✳

Even in the years since his blindness Homer was a commanding figure. He had a presence like a god, straight, and graceful, and alert. One would not know at first that he was blind. He delighted in puns and word games, in dancing, delivering opinions at civic councils, composing curses and love songs, playing at Nestor, perhaps, with a wry self-mockery. He had never really learned patience; it was a willed kindness instead. The world still came to him and begged him to sing in their cities.

At Delos Homer was honored in an assembly of all the Ionians, each city bestowing citizenship on him, the greatest honor they could give. The Delians at the same time dedicated a marble tablet to him in the temple of Artemis by the port. Such celebration almost overwhelmed the old singer. But he was wise now, and he took it for a sign to be joyful.

Here in the sunshine on the sacred island of Apollo he knew that for the Greeks the center was shifting from Poseidon's Mycale to Apollo's Delos. He knew that, intentionally or not, his poems had played a part in it. As Athens and Medon had. He did not forget, though, that every day he felt the earth tremble and heard the surge of the sea. Nor could he forget that the light of the sun had been taken from him. Poseidon was watching him, yet he knew to seize the joy of the day.

Homer went as far as Argos then, persuaded at Delos by the archon of Argos to go home with him after festival, drawn by the memory of that city in the distance when he had stood among the ruins of Agamemnon's palace. In verses from the Iliad, he sang of Diomedes the Argive so powerfully that all of Argos swelled with love. They heaped gifts on the famous singer and voted to raise a bronze statue to him, honoring him as a man from the Heroic Age himself. The archon decreed that sacrifice be made to him there and that every five years a sacrifice be sent to honor him in Chios. Below the bronze figure these words would be inscribed:

> Here divine Homer stands, whose glorious stories honor all of Greece, but most of all the Argives for their part in throwing down the mighty walls of Troy for bright-haired Helen's sake. Our great city sets his image here, giving him honor as we do the gods. (Homeric Hymns and Homerica)

And Homer enjoyed it hugely. He was a bard, after all, and he loved his vulnerable and foolish mortality, and everyone else's. This was a time to snatch happiness and share it. He sat at the center of Greek love and respect, often shaken by tears, often smiling. The Iliad was a classic by now. And his Odyssey said it all—eloquence was in. Resourcefulness and political savvy, patience and family loyalty, education in the ways of the world—Hermes in the flesh of the Ithacan with the blessing of the city goddess Athena. That was the modern man who could survive and even bring order into the lives around him. It was a message so important to men of his time that it took his breath away to feel how they fed on it.

He did not sing as well as he used to, and he always had one or two of his students with him to spell him while he rested. It was not that his voice was failing; it was too many years without seeing his audience react. He could sense a great deal, of course, and he had learned to respond to the hearers. But there was another thing: his new Odyssey, so carefully thought out, did not respond to circumstances as singing always had before. His own thinking had changed so much that bards who did not grasp what he had done with his epics privately criticized him very sharply. They began to blame him for the decline in the quality of the literate bards' work, blaming it on the length of his monumental poems. The old man, they said, clung too closely himself to his poems. He was not adaptable any more. Poor man. It was sad to see genius decline, they said, and tried to continue the old traditions.

There were always women, at home and abroad, who enjoyed the beds of the famous, and he knew how to woo them, moving close and saying miraculous things. They said that he was lusty. For Homer, what could have been profoundly sensual, profoundly mortal, seldom was anything more than sex. Still, it would do fine until better came along. It was a gift of life to be enjoyed. He still worshipped Aphrodite, if not as often as in his youth.

There was a wave of Homer-worship in Cyprus when Stasinos married Homer's daughter Laura and came back to Salamis with her. Stasinos had gone to study in Chios, hearing from Athenian traders of the celebrated blind bard. When he had arrived Homer was in Delos, and he had waited. He had loved Laura at first sight and, when he had studied with the Homeridai—Homer's students—for two seasons, had married her and taken her back to Cyprus. Bringing the Iliad and Odyssey with him, Stasinos composed a great epic of his own, the Cypria.

Homer's epic stories took the island by storm. Kings had their beds crafted like that of Odysseus, and interest in the Mycenaean traditions of Cyprus was at fever pitch. The Assyrian conquerors may have held the cities in tribute to them, but the hearts of the people were Greek, and the poems gave them opportunity to show it. There was no way to separate art from politics. Homer smiled to himself when he heard. Odysseus would have loved it.

Homer spent most of his time at Volissos. There he would go riding or stroll the island hills easily with Argus of the Hundred Eyes. Homer had always had a fine palate for wine, and now it was a delight to go among the vineyards. He could tell almost to the hour when a certain hillside would be ready, just from the days of rainfall, the feel of the soil in his hands, the slant of the morning sunrise. He would gather the grapes and stomp them with fine exuberance, singing the songs of Dionysos as he swung about.

It had been Zoe, his fresh young daughter born of the earthquake, who had enlivened his life in the early 80's; she had been on the edge of womanhood but still loving the world of the child. She would take him with her or accompany him on visits, holding his hand and gossiping, questioning, suffering girlhood, fussing over Argus, wondering what her mother was like. She had been too much a bard's daughter to be the kind of woman Zoe was, for her youth had been very different. There was less of Demeter, more of Athena, he thought in his heart. They told him she looked more like him than like her mother, especially around her eyes, that luminous blue-green that was the envy of all who saw her. She was Homer's daughter.

Zoe became a remarkable singer. Inventive. An intuitive poet. She had the gift of her father in greater proportion than the boys did—clarity, wit, even power, enough to make them envious. The family was amazed and troubled. Why had such gifts been wasted on a woman? Homer would only smile. "Ah, my boys. You know the nature of Hermes. It is his joke again. Maybe you need to consider women a little differently, as he taught me to.

"As for Zoe, we must be careful to marry her well, for she will be a fine mother for bards. Always listen to her, in matters of mousike." He said this to them all, grieving in his heart that she would never have an audience for her great gift. Such a world. He sighed and shook his head. And he had helped to shape it.

**

One morning Dio, now a man of 54, came to Homer's bedside. Small birds made the sounds of early morning. "Father," he said, "I need you now."

"What's the matter, Dio? You are full of despair."

"My son. He has left us." He began to weep quietly.

"Georgi? Why? He is only—"

"Fourteen. He has gone to Sardis. It's my fault, I know. I have filled him with tales of Ardys and Amy, of Maion and the Lydians."

The old man sighed heavily. "But surely he will not kill his grandmother's people because of what happened to her so long ago."

"No, no. You don't understand at all. He is filled with Lydian fervor." Dio said bitterly. "He has gone to fight against the Greeks! I will not see him again. His mother, my sweet Olivia, mourns him as the dead, tears her face and casts ashes over her hair and bosom. I cannot make her speak."

"He may be back. But many children die and parents are alone. I will send to Sardis to see what can be done. I know Ardys' sons will answer me." Dio sat with him all morning. "I married too late and he was too important to me. It is not good to care too much about a child. He will not love you for it." That was all he said. The old man kept his silence, aware that he would not live to know the fate of these dear spirits.

Gyges did not love the Ionians. He began to look for provocation to move against them, and it was not hard to find. There was in his court a young poet and musician from Smyrna, one Magnes, a lover of Gyges, a handsome and clever man who was enormously promiscuous. While he was singing in Magnesia-near-Sipylos he seduced so many wives that the citizens physically attacked him, shaving his head, ripping up his costume, and maiming him so as to prevent any recurrence of his behavior. Gyges pounced upon this as an insult to his court and mounted raids against the village, finally conquering it outright. He boasted that Smyrna would be next.

This Gyges, Homer told Dio, was apparently very good at manipulation, if this and the assassination were any indication. It was no surprise, then, that the reply to Homer's plea about his grandson was discouraging. Gyges sent greetings to the foster son of Maion the Lydian and congratulated Georgios on having two such illustrious bloodlines as Ardys and the orphan Greek, the great singer of rocky Chios. But even such a fortunate man as Georgios had to make choices, and the Lydians welcomed and honored the bright young descendant of a priestess of Artemis whose father was a born Sardian. He said he wept for the parents who would not see so fine a son again, but they should be comforted that there was a glorious future ahead of him in the Lydian army.

Homer wondered what Georgios would do when the time came to attack Smyrna. The old pattern again. The incessant mixed loyalties. His had never been so harsh as Georgios's, though. Perhaps the safest way to live, with the purest thoughts, would be to choose your parents more carefully and never leave the side of the mountain you are born on. Then you can know your loyalties, your place. If you are buried there. Soon enough.

⁂

During those busy years there had been no reminders from Poseidon. Some of the children died, his grandchildren; gone to be with Lydia and the Dioscuri and Pyrrhus. The normal quarrels and jealousies erupted, but there was no one in the family who wished any other member ill or worked away at destroying memories of the past. There was some ambition and greed; but that was never dangerous unless it was coupled with sloth. Olivia, Dio's young wife, went mad from grief at Georgi's desertion. The physician kept her sedated and pleasant. Dio sought solace in his craft.

Something went out of the great blind singer when word came in the spring of 689 that the Lydians were laying seige to Smyrna. All that beautiful country between the fated cities was as real to him as the spring sun on his bare arm. During the previous winter Smyrna had been preparing for the inevitable, and Kristos had sent his family to Chios for safety. He had stayed to fight, as had his oldest son Xenocles, whom Homer had named for himself as the most famous guest of Ionia. Georgi would be with the Lydians.

As the Lydians had approached, Smyrna had launched a cavalry attack on the plain east of Warrior Pass. A Smyrnan warrior, a new Achilles, had astonished both armies, blazing like Sirius for an hour and sending the surprised Lydians streaming away in great disorder. But he was soon slain, and in the long days to follow the Smyrnans were driven inch by inch along the ten miles of plain back to the city.

On one fateful afternoon Georgios and Xenocles found themselves face to face on the banks of the Meles near Homer's old cave. "Turn away from me," Georgios had said. "I will not fight my own blood. I remember the blind man's song. Glaucos and Diomedes were only friends, not brothers." He held out his hand in friendship.

Xenocles took it and they embraced for a moment. "We must prove ourselves in other ways than breaking the heart of an old man." They looked at each other for a long moment and then parted, never to meet again.

The fighting was prolonged and bitter. Cities as far away as Sparta sent relief to the beleagured city in Ionia. Once Smyrna actually fell, but a courageous counter-attack drove the Lydians out again. One story went around that the Lydians, finding their soldiers restless, had sent envoys into the city announcing that they would not withdraw unless the women of the city were sent out to them. A Smyrnan slave girl, the property of a citizen named Philarkos, suggested that the slave women dress as free women and pretend to accede to the Lydian demand. The debauchery which followed allowed the Smyrnan army to attack and give the city a temporary respite from Lydian pressures. No one remembered the valiant slave-girl's name.

Many stories came out of the siege, a seige which Homer did not live to see lifted. In those last months whenever he sang the Iliad it was with an irony and anger that only the immediacy of Smyrna's pain could explain.

✳✳✳

As he had aged Homer had enjoyed visiting the potters and the workers at the famous clay pits of Chios. Their vessels were popular all over the Aegean and the operation well organized but never hasty. The workers would dig a trench six or eight feet deep in a carefully selected area. Then with picks and shovels they would remove huge chunks of clay from the hard-packed earth. These would be loaded into reed baskets and raised by a line of workers to the surface. It was hot work, and there would always be a sack of wine and a bag of fruit or nuts hung to cool in the breeze over the shady side of the trench. Other workers shifted the soil, washing it out and refining it for use at the potters' wheels. Then they would divide it into units to go to the craftsmen. Most pots, shaped and dried, went into immediate use on the local market, but the finest ones were reserved, to be skillfully decorated and carefully fired, and sold abroad.

Homer had taken to singing for the potters every now and then, making charms and curses, singing hymns and snatches of epic. They had taught him to hand mold and even to throw a pot on the wheel. His hands were good, sure and strong, but the years of calluses on his fingertips put delicate work out of his reach. Still, he enjoyed the atmosphere, and the potters were glad in their hearts to see his familiar figure outlined on the ridge above them, coming for a morning of banter and song. Argus the Hundred Eyed, now ancient and slow, would be with him, sometimes a grandchild and often a student. They would bring delicacies to the men, wine and meat and sweet fruit to share.

It was after the rains had begun in October and near the end of the year's production that Homer planned to visit one fateful morning.

As the great bard walked the sea-path, he heard two boys laughing as they talked on rocks by the promontory, and he stopped to greet them.

"Hey;" he called the usual question. "How is the fishing today?"

They laughed again. Their poles held fast by rocks, at that moment they were picking the lice from their ragged chitons, shaking them out in the clear air of day after sleeping meanly in an infested hovel. They glanced at the blind old man, so familiar and so clever.

"It's Stavros, Homer," one boy called in high spirits. "Yes. Fishing." And then he added, full of mischief as he deloused himself. "What we catch we leave behind. What we don't we carry with us."

The old man seemed suddenly stricken. "Ah," he said slowly. "Ah. You have been talking to Herophile. She said that to me once."

The smile faded from Stavros' lips. Puzzled, he stood looking at the blind singer. "No. Does Herophile have lice?"

They all laughed hugely. "You are a clever riddler, Stavros. Wiser than you know," Homer said softly. He seemed slighter than before, as if he were already moving away.

Lice. He smiled to himself. In fact, he had to laugh. Quite a reminder. Such music in his head. And soon the worms would have him. He sighed.

It was the riddle Herophile had warned him about. It had come and now he suddenly understood it. With a peace he could not explain he knew its meaning now. What he had done, in the

284

great itch of his creation, he would leave behind him. To the Homeridae. And, alas, all the rest would go with him to the underworld.

All that he had not sung. The Third Voyage. The song that had been forming in his heart. It would have been the greatest song, Odysseus' third voyage inland, bearing an oar on his shoulder. He would talk tonight with Dio and Ianni, try to tell them about it.

When he hallooed from the top of the ridge the potters saw him start down the old path with Argus, in a leisurely way, carrying his bag with his phorminx and lunch. A student, one Cleon who was interested in clay tablets to write on, was trailing behind.

At the same instant all of the potters watching his approach realized that the path had washed out at a turn near the top. In one voice they shouted a warning and raced toward the hill. But Homer had slipped, and he and Argus came sliding toward them. Loosened soil from the diggings gathered stones and tufts of grasses, and as he tumbled part of the mountain came with him, rushing into the pits at the bottom of the slopes. Cleon stood aghast at the top of the hill as men scrambled through the mud to reach the crumpled figure, lying on his side near the washing sheds. Cleon saw him move and then raced back to town for help.

Homer was gravely injured. He was like a man badly beaten and struggling to breathe. With help came a pain-killing potion and a stretcher, and the potters carried him back to his home. A broad gash was cut in the side of the mountain where the earthslide had occurred. People gathered solemnly to see the spot where the great bard had fallen. Cleon blamed himself for not going before him. The potters said it would have happened even if Homer had been sighted. Earthshaker had been loosening the hill for a long time.

The family hurried to his bedside knowing his chances for recovery were poor. His body was crushed inside and only the strong herbs of Herophile kept him lucid. She had sent them from her cave across the strait before the accident had happened, a gift for his old age, the messenger had said.

He called the Homeridai together for one last talk, repeating the familiar pledge they had made. "Sing however you wish, and continue the school as long as you like. But remember your pledge to me never to change my long poems, either by omission or addition. I have shaped them for a purpose, to honor the god. Let Hermes be your guide." He would not tell them all even now his gift to the Trickster God, the secret of Samothrace imbedded for the initiated to discover. Some of them understood. As long as Greek continued as a language, as long as bards would sing, as long as Athens and Olympia promoted Panhellenism, so long would his gift to men endure. If they would try to understand, the message was there for them. That was all that one man could do for mortals. If the gods were going to punish him for this—well. He would know soon.

On the third day Homer said his farewells to his family. They were tearful and private, outside of time. Oh, the time. It had gone so quickly. And yet he had had the span of two men's lives, at least. He tried to think when the best moments had come. Was it waking on the mountain at Samothrace? Or the fall of dark hair across the sun in the glades of Sardis? Zoe and their generations, before and after them, living the pattern? He wondered what would become of them all, all of the people he loved. Only too soon they would join him.

He wondered if he would meet Achilles and Odysseus, and his heart raced at the thought of what he had made of them. What if, when he met them, they were just brutish killers, coarse and arrogant, unable to feel the shades of being he had given them in his mind. It was the kind of joke Hermes would pull, to have that happen. There were so many, so many things to discover the truth of. In the underworld. Ah, but this sweet earth. It was so incredibly lovely. He would take a nap and see it again, once more. He was so weary.

When Homer woke they had left him alone and gone in to supper, with only old, wounded Argus to keep him company. But he knew someone was there although he had heard no one come on to the terrace to his door. Old Argus was not breathing, though he could feel his weight beside his feet. Tears came, but he could not reach down to touch him. Hundred Eyes indeed, he thought.

Homer sighed and shifted, with pain, bumping his battered knee along the wall as he turned toward it on the bed. He let the pain settle, as he did, into the pillows. And then a strange thing began to happen. He thought at first it was the color of the pain that shot before his mind, but this was different. A sheen of color swam up at him, a soft rose, for only a moment, so faint he was sure he had imagined it, a residue of dreaming. It came again slowly out of the dark, not from directly ahead, but as if it rose from the eye sockets, emanating from out of his brain, from behind him.

It was the color of sunrise now, but flowing and full of pearl, like a seashell washed at dawn. His heart overflowed at its beauty. He rested, watching, holding still, afraid he would lose it if he moved. And very slowly, very gradually, like the rising of the mind after sleep, a texture came into focus before his eyes. It was rough and grainy. It was the wall before him; and it was bathed in color. A dark shadow, like the mountains of his life, lay below its rosy expanse and it moved as he shifted his shoulder. In the silence he knew that he could see.

With infinite pain he moved, rolling his bones around to look toward the direction of the light. White stabs of lightning cut through his flesh, and the breath struggled through the crumbling rooms. He fell against the wall then, his whole being drinking in the full glory of the western sun. He wondered if he were just remembering his childhood home in Smyrna, but he knew he was not. He was not surprised that he could see, just immensely joyful. The tricks of Hermes were infinite. A wonderful laugh was born in his mind as he saw Argus move again.

Someone was there in the doorway, the presence that had awakened him. It did not block the light which shone toward him over the gleaming ocean, past the high-streaming radiant clouds. He knew that with his eyes he would see what was waiting in the underworld. With great joy he smiled at his visitor. Hermes had come for him.

✻✻✻

There is a hero's tomb to Homer in Ios, near the temple to the Samothracian gods, which faces northwest towards the sea. The divine bard of Ionia was honored there like a god during the long centuries to follow. And no one can gainsay that he lies in that storied tomb. But a whisper passed through the world once that said otherwise.

One cold December, when rosy-fingered dawn reflected palely on the snows of Moon Mountain, two Samothracian priests came to the quayside, where a trim black ship pulled in out of the misty morning sea. They had been waiting patiently, knowing the way was hard. As if in a dream they now moved slowly up the pathway, the earth lying muffled and silent, echoing only their steps. The leafless trees were burrowing with their roots toward a new spring, ice glittering in their jeweled branches. As for animals, the survivors were curled away waiting for the sun. They placed him in his rock-cut tomb, with the symbols of the gods beside him. The cleverest craftsman of all rolled the stones in place and built a barrow over the entrance, placing on top a stele in the Samothracian language which few could read, even then. After a suitable interval the priests gave the travelers the stranger's gift. Kristos, Iannos, and Dio finally left for home, and a grieving Athena sent them a following wind.

INTERLOCUTORY

The Voice of Letha Gooding

We still have the spondee to put on our hexameter line- -two final accented syllables, each quite different from the other but parallel, both the logical result of the action at the caesura. The caesura—Homer's initiation at Samothrace—still echoes through the world, like ripples from a center, like a sound uttered once but reaching the ear even now. Homer was the first great Greek epic poet and Nonnos of Panopolis the last, more than 1100 years later. Samothrace lived through all of that time, shut down only twenty years before Nonnos was born, when the Christian Emperor Theodosius closed every pagan sanctuary and forbade sacrifice. Nonnos presents us with his own absorbing detective story, as I heve contrived for you to see. Also, you deserve to know something of what happened on Samothrace in the past 2700 years. Our two chapters, then, tell the story, first, to Nonnos' time, A.D. 400-450, and second, to the present—to the last syllable of recorded time, so to speak.

The death manuscript you are about to read is from a fictional librarian to a very real Nonnos of Panopolis. Our aged and gentle Paulus is one of the great number of displaced persons of a violent time who is a survivor with his own peculiar voyage to relate. He lived in a time as anguished as any in history, especially for Egypt. Let me set the stage for our learned librarian and his talented former student and friend, Nonnos, author of <u>The Dionysiaca</u>.

When our Paulus first came to Alexandria near the turn of the century, he walked into a turbulent city. Christianity, the official state religion, had recently banned observance of all others, even as it was at war within itself. Profound conflict still existed between the Christians and the outlawed followers of every pagan sect, public or private. Egyptians still twisted under the hand of foreign rule, once Greek then Roman and now Byzantine. The learned Greek-speaking Christian patriarchs of Alexandria were locked in an ideological struggle with the desert monks. Terrible economic upheaval was loosing a great horde of dispossessed within the country itself. And language, as a tool of reason, was turned against itself.

Since the time of Alexander the Great, Greek had been the language of the nobility and the state in Egypt. When Rome conquered Egypt, Latin became the language of administration but Greek remained the language of the noble educated class. Now, when Christian enthusiasm swept like a wave over Egypt, not only were temples sacked but manuscripts with any reference to paganism were burnt without a second thought. The secondary library at Alexandria went up in flames immediately. Educated Christians, who believed that God wanted man to seek His highest knowledge, stole and concealed what they could against a more rational time.

The Alexandrian Christians were tragically at odds with the Byzantine Christian hierarchy, too, and at mid-century would be formally deemed heretical. The educated churchmen had no allies. To add to the turmoil, a legislative reform of the previous century had torn the civic fabric asunder. The Romans had abolished the ancient nomes, or provinces, in 310 and reorganized the local governmental unit as a "metropolis." For the first time in Egyptian history the city became responsible for the land around it, much of it then in small private and large public holdings. But they made the mistake of turning the taxation system over to city officials, thinking it would promote prosperity.

We know better, don't we? It led to feudalism. Taxes were administered by those with a vested interest: small landowners become tenants on their own land; great estates gobbled up the public holdings, their owners living in town as city officials legislating wealth into their own pockets. By Paulus' and Nonnos' time masses of people were reduced to penury, all the public land was gone, estates had their own churches and armies, education was dangerous and forgotten.

The monasteries, having slipped from the hands of the secular leaders, became largely Coptic sanctuaries filled with the dispossessed, the ascetic, and the dissatisfied. The poor gave their children to the monks to raise, and many did not rise above servitude. We know that monasticism and the accompanying feudal structure were to dominate the West for another thousand years. Ironically enough, Christianity ruled only another two hundred years in Egypt. So deeply at odds were the "heretical" Egyptians with the Byzantine church that they were happy to be freed from their domination by the conquering Arabs of 641, who had a tolerant policy toward Christians in Egypt for another three hundred years.

Thus, when to be an educated Greek pagan in Egypt was equivalent to a death penalty, Nonnos wrote a monumental epic to Dionysos!—in Greek! He lived in Panopolis, a city whose very name was changed to cast out the Greek god Pan. We know nothing of Nonnos the man, except that he must have become Christian since he also began a paraphrase of John. I burn to know his story. Nonnos was born in 410, too late to be a Samothracian initiate—that is why we need an influence, a Paulus. But The Dionysiaca is full of references to Samothrace and Homer. So this is how it may have been. Perhaps we have another man who, watching the world around him burn, decided to try to save something for the survivors. It is not his fault that Nonnos is not Homer.

CHAPTER 23

The Paulus Letter

A.D. 430 Alexandria, Egypt

These words of Paulus librarian of Alexandria to Nonnos of Panopolis, most gifted scholar and my dear young friend:

In a few days the sun and the new moon will be wed again at the winter solstice, for the fourth time since my birth almost eighty years ago. At that propitious time please God I will die in this life and be reborn in Heaven, leaving the cares of this tortured world behind me. I leave a legacy to you which my loyal Hileus will deliver when the time comes. Welcome him and give him shelter if you can, for he has devoted his life to my service and I can leave him only his freedom. He brings you my treasured papyrus of the Odyssey, and this letter. Both are confessions of sorts, to be sure, but of the kind a good man may find useful.

During your schooling here with me in Alexandria—a few short years ago—how long it has seemed since you left. Well. We never spoke of my youth, being so much concerned with yours. I was a stern mentor and you the finest student of Greek poetry Egypt had ever seen. No question. A fine copyist, too, though I still claim mastery there. Alas, in these times, who is there to rival us? Well. That is not my matter here. Time is short and I have much to tell.

You know me as a Christian, a follower of Alexandrian patriarchs, and I die a believer in my faith, as true as one may be. I was not always so: in fact, I came to it through much travail. But that, too, is not the story I must tell. Be patient, hear me through. Then I will make a request of you, knowing you will not deny the wishes of a dying friend. Let me go back to the beginning.

My name was not always Paulus. I was born Talthybius of Samothrace, and my life has been stormy, true to the name. Samothrace had been sacred to the Great Gods for two thousand years, and I was born into a priestly family in the year of our Lord 350. The world was changing swiftly even then. Although Constantine and Licinius had struggled to agree in AD. 313 on a policy of religious freedom which ended persecution of the Christians, it was only a few short years until, in 330, Constantine declared Christianity the official state religion. By the time I had become an initiate of the Great Gods, mid our ancient marbles in the lavish festival of Mid-Summer, there had been a falling-away from our worship. Samothrace is very close to the Hellespont and Constantinople, the new eastern center of official Christian power.

I was 40 and had been a priest of the Great Gods for fourteen years when in 391 the emperor Theodosius decreed that all pagan sanctuaries be closed forever and public sacrifice forbidden. My life seemed to end. The entire island was a sacred place, you see—like Delos—and so life literally came to a standstill. The fame of Samothrace was so great that the Emperor's fleet stood by to ensure no worshippers could come to the festival.

The destructors landed, they said, to oversee the evacuation of inhabitants desiring to leave with their goods. They swarmed over the island, and the sacred treasure houses were sacked. I can still remember standing in the Hall of Votive Gifts, looking around after the looting. Shards of broken dishes lay scattered on the echoing tiles, a jewel winking here and there out of the dust, the winds whipping debris over floors never neglected since they had been lain centuries before. I am still astounded at how quietly it died. That special sacredness, pure and isolated, simply cut off. Now quite forgotten.

Well. When nothing was left, and settlers had already begun to dismantle the sanctuary buildings to make their cottages of marble, when my wife died of grief and poverty and barrenness, I became a wanderer in the world. I wore my scarf of Samothrace and more than once suffered for it. Drifting down the coast of Asia Minor, through the towns and islands which had sent delegations to our festivals for a thousand years, I found many who knew me and would help me. But they suffered persecution too, while their children embraced the shining new state religion with an eagerness that twisted many a heart.

Of course I had no trouble accepting a state religion. I could also accept that the newest Great God was Christ. But I could not understand why our worship, so practical and inclusive, so great-hearted and rational, had been silenced.

At last I came to Alexandria in the most terrible of times, when Christian fought Christian as savagely as pagan. Monks from the desert had burned the secondary library in 391, but there were many Christians in the city still devoted to the continuity of learning, as was the patriarch Theophilus and his successor Cyril. I was able to join their ranks and, in the fullness of time, became a devout convert. Well. You know something of those times yourself, having been born into an ancient family a generation after the dissolution of their priestly functions. You have told me how they suffered at Panopolis, and the price they still pay as Alexandrian Christians in a region dominated by the stern plain men of the desert monasteries. You know I must still call it Panopolis, though the Coptic name has changed to Akhmim. The power of naming is something we both understand.

Your family sent you here to Alexandria for your Greek and Latin, the languages of education and power. Now you are thriving again in the state beaurocracy. I too have lived well among the librarians and keepers of annals. In all of the tragic controversies of our time, I am true to the patriarchs of this city who are hated for believing that seeking the fullest wisdom is a true path to God.

That is why I must tell you now of my home island. At 80 I am surely the last living priest of a great mystery religion that stretched back into the third millenium before Christ. I believe with all my heart that its existence, its slow work through the centuries, has helped mortals toward a consciousness that has made comprehension of a Christ and acceptance of Him possible in this world. When I reveal to you this history—and I must since the sanctuary lies abandoned—you will become the keeper of the mysteries, perhaps you alone. May God forgive me if I do wrong. I will face Him soon enough.

I stop to weep. I cannot help it. A place in this hard world that would have welcomed and listened to the Gallilean, that did give shelter to His disciple. Did you know there is a church on the shore below the ancient sanctuary, built where Paul rested on his way to Neapolis? Yes, it is Paul's name I took at my conversion when my stormy life was saved.

I pray I may impart to you, a devout Christian and a deeply learned modern man, what Samothrace has meant during the past one thousand years. You know better than most, having Greek blood in your veins and a lineage that goes back 750 years to the founding of Alexandria itself, this first city in all the Greek world to be named for a man. The ties between Alexander the Great and Samothrace are as strong as those between Alexander and Egypt, perhaps stronger.

The island of Samothrace had always been sacred to the Great Gods, its holy language so old that no one knows its source, its rituals so rooted in the natural world that its myths, even for the initiated, obscure historic time. The public myth tells of the birth of Dardanus on Samothrace and his later founding of Troy. Well. Since Troy existed in the third milennium before Christ, what vast span of time, what generations of people, how many lives do we speak of? My God cannot ask me to believe that all this humanity, all of those seekers, are among the lost.

Aiolian Greeks were in Samothrace by the eighth century B.C. and, even though the mysteries were ancient then, Hellenes influenced the growth and form of the sanctuary from their first settlement, altering and refining belief but not changing the fundamental Pattern, or even the ritual language. It was in the eighth and early seventh centuries, when populations were swelling everywhere, that buildings began to rise on holy ground. As they did all through Greek lands. As colonization and commerce became important to the Greeks of the Aegean, so did the island of the Great Gods who protected sailors and who made men better through knowledge of its mysteries. In the sixth century before Christ the island city became larger than it has ever been since that time. Everyone knew the tale that Orpheus the Thracian singer brought Jason and his Argonauts to the island for initiation. Odysseus and Aeneas, those epic voyagers, and Heracles also knew the secrets. Men understood that what the heroes learned had an impact on their nature, and they were led to emulate them. So through the centuries the sacred island welcomed the sea traveler to its holy mountain.

By the fifth century Samothrace controlled land on the mainland opposite its northern shore, and the Samothracian navy became a force to be considered in the northern sea. And in the south? The great awakening of the Greek spirit in Ionia came in cities that now knew the Great Gods. Herodotus was an initiate, as he reveals in his history. Thales came to the island, too. Although the political and religious influence of Samothrace was always greatest in the Aegean islands, in Asia Minor and among the Black Sea settlements, even mainland Greece sent many a pilgrim to us. Aeschylus—that tragedian who was a monotheist and an initiate at Eleusis—wrote a Samothracian play, the Kabeiroi, and Aristophanes seems to have been an initiate, considering his references to the mysteries. Plato mentions us with admiration. And that is only the beginning.

Let me tell you now the most absorbing tale—the tale of Alexander the Great and his family. What exactly his great teacher Aristotle knew of our island remains hidden. Aristotle was born, of course, not far away, and he wrote a history of the government of Samothrace—part of a series on many cities, to be sure. One wonders at that great teacher during those fateful years, the man who gave his corrected copy of the Iliad to his royal pupil, the one Alexander placed under his pillow every night of the rest of his life.

Would Aristotle have considered Samothrace important to his student? Undoubtedly. For the parents of Alexander, Philip of Macedon and Olympias of Epirus, met and fell in love on Samothrace at the Mid-Summer festival. Oh, yes. That was a fateful encounter indeed. At their wedding they had the Samothracian public ritual re-enacted, the marriage of the earth and sky. From that time their family poured treasures into the sanctuary coffers and inaugurated a building program that created during the next one hundred years one of the most spectacular sanctuaries the world has ever seen. The island also became a strategic center, as it had been to the Second Athenian League and as it was to be to the Ptolemies, the Selucids and later Macedonians. Alexander considered himself to be a descendant through his mother of Achilles and always carried the Iliad. But part of his vision of himself must have been rooted in his belief that he was a blessed offspring of the Great Gods of Samothrace. A belief in the evolution of new gods, of transcendent mortals, is part of that mystery. And Alexander made Samothrace the religious center of Macedon. In fact, at the farthest extent of his march into India, a little past the river Hyphasis, are two altars. One reads: "Here Alexander stayed his march." The other invokes all of the major gods of his army and his people: "To Father Ammon, to brother Heracles, to Athena Providence, to Zeus Olympos, to the Cabiri of Samothrace, to the Indian Sun, and to Delphian Apollo."

He was so like Achilles, Alexander was. But he was far more. He was a founder of cities. He re-founded the city of Homer; did you know that? Oh, yes. On his passage through Lydia he left his army and went to the ruins of Smyrna. That city of the fair prospect had been destroyed in 600 B.C.E. and in Alexander's time had sat a burnt-out shell for almost 300 years. The story goes that the great Alexander stopped to rest under a plane tree on Mt. Pagos. There he dreamed a vision of the new Smyrna, being told to re-found it on the spot. Being Alexander, he did. Yes, the magnificent city we know today, the city of Polycarp and Paul's visit and a thousand Christian saints, is the city not of Homer but of Alexander's dream when he was paying homage to the bard. Just as our lovely suffering Alexandria is his child.

And what a child it is, our beloved city. He connected it to the island of Pharos—the one Homer mentions in the Odyssey?—Well. Alexander connected city and island by the mole, the Heptastadion, in the old Phoenician pattern, making two harbors. Under Soter I and Ptolemy Philadelphus the great lighthouse was made which still stands, dedicated to the Great Gods who save the lives of mariners. Its several stories are of significant geometric shapes, the bottom being the square of Hermes/Thoth. The Ptolemies, of course, were Macedonians and continued in Alexander's reverence for Samothrace.

I honor most of all Demetrius of Phaleron, that able man once ruler of Athens, who came to Alexandria and, as counselor to the first Ptolemy, began our famous libraries and museum, the greatest the world would ever see. A man of action and a scholar, a translator of Homer. Had I had a son, I would have named him Demetrius.

But I get ahead of myself. With the untimely death of Alexander, every faction, though at odds with the other, seemed to court the Great Gods. Wealth poured into the sanctuary, and Arhiddhos, Alexander's half-brother and later Phillip III, together with Alexander's young son continued the construction program on the sacred island. So did Arsinoe when she was wife to Lysimachos from 288 to 281 B.C.E.; she commissioned and built the Arsinoen, the largest round building in Greek history, a wonder still to behold. I have heard that she planned at its center a huge iron statue of the Great Goddess, to be suspended in thin air between two giant lodestones! Imagine! But that was not to be. Lysimachos died in battle and the power struggle shifted. It was to Samothrace that this tragic woman fled when, at the murder of her sons, weeping, disheveled, in the company of a single slave-woman, Arsinoe found sanctuary there from capture by her brother Ptolemy. That she was persuaded to wed this same brother and rule as queen of Egypt is part of the bitter story too, as Alexander's empire was torn asunder. And Samothrace? It grew in power as Ptolemy and his wife/sister brought Samothracian ideas to Egypt. Some would say back to Egypt, but I do not know. It can be no surprise to find the great lighthouse is dedicated to the Savior gods of navigation.

I am so weak now. See how my hand falters. God grant that I may finish. Alexandria, the Greek gem on the brow of Egypt. The seat of learning. The great library. Is it no wonder that the great librarian of Alexandria at its height was Aristarchus of Samothrace? The man who collated Homer's works and began the art of literary criticism with his careful purification of the texts of the great bard? It thrills my breast even now to think what that man did. And to suspect why. Aristarchus grew to manhood on that small and sacred mountain and came to Alexander's city as an initiate of the mysteries revered by the Macedonian house ruling Egypt. Determined to purge and reestablish the text of Homer. I am suggesting to you, Nonnos, that the two actions are connected. Be patient and you will see.

There are other initiates, too, whose connections with Samothrace had an impact on the history of the world. The Spartan king Lysander, who installed the tyranny of the Thirty at Athens, was famous for his luck at sea. He was an initiate. That decisive battle of the Hellespont, which ended the Peloponesian War, took place at Aegos Potami two miles from Sestos within sight of the peaks of Samothrace, and he was said to have been guided by the Great Gods. Remember how Plutarch writes of it in his <u>Lives</u>? A great stone fell from the sky, blazing for 75 days before it hit. Many said it was a sign of divine intervention, and that Castor and Pollux were seen on each side of Lysander's ship.

One of the saddest and most notorious incidents in Samothrace's history tells the defeat of the Macedonians, the fall of all Greece before the Roman armies. You must recall it from Livy. Remember how the power passed to Rome? Perseus, last king of Macedon, fled after the battle of Pydna in 168 B.C.E.to sanctuary at Samothrace. With all of the treasure he could carry, said to be 2,000 talents. The Romans under Aemillius Paulus were hot on his heels. They surrounded the island but respected its sanctity. Finally the admiral, Gnaeus Octavius, landed on Samothrace and before the assembly of citizens accused one of Perseus' lieutenants, Evander of Crete, of polluting the sanctuary. It was known throughout Greece that he had tried to kill King Eumenes at Delphi.

Ah, what treachery came then! When the Samothracians called Evander to be tried, Perseus advised his friend to choose death instead, for he feared that Evander would reveal that Perseus himself had ordered the murder. While Evander secretly planned his escape, Perseus ordered him killed. Thus the desperate king defiled "the two most hallowed sanctuaries in the world," in Livy's words. With the murder of his closest friend, Perseus lost all support. His retinue went over to the Romans and Perseus decided to flee to the court of a Thracian ally.

Secretly he engaged the vessel of a Cretan, Oroandes, to take him away under cover of night. At sundown the treasure was smuggled aboard and at midnight Perseus, with great danger and difficulty, reached the beach. But Oroandes was gone, far out to sea with the treasure. Perseus and his eldest son hid for a time among the temples, while all of his people and his young children accepted a Roman amnesty. Finally, he surrendered too, and was taken to Rome where he was displayed in triumphal procession. Such is the fate of those who pollute holy ground.

Well. That story you must remember. The Romans had suspected that some delegates to the

Samothracian summer festival—theoroi who were sent from many cities—had used their time on the island for political meetings. I expect that happened more than once, as it must have at Delphi and Delos.

I have just been carried back from vespers and write by the light of my candle. It is a short one now and I am weary. Well. When the world became Roman you might have thought that the glory of Samothrace would diminish, for the Macedonian house was gone and Rome ruled Egypt, too. But quite the reverse happened! Romans revered Samothrace more than mainland Greeks ever did. Had not Aeneas the Dardanian founded Rome, and had not Dardanus been born at Samothrace? They believed that the holy relics of Rome had been brought by Aeneas from our island. Many a Roman came to the festivals of the Great Gods. The sacred center bloomed through the Republic and the Empire. When it became fashionable among the wealthy to carve initiates' names on the walls of the stoas, famous names appeared. I remember seeing that of Caesar's father-in-law Piso Caesonini. And especially that of my revered Varro, whom Caesar had appointed to head his great library at Rome and who was considered to be the most learned Roman of his age. Yes, you have seen his discussion of Samothrace in his writings. Some said that Varro's good friend Cicero was initiated on his way to Asia Minor, but I never saw his name. However, he speaks in de Natura deorum of Samothrace, Lemnos, and Eleusis, saying "these when explained and rationally analyzed are recognized as involving the nature of the material world rather than the gods." To know this he must have been an initiate. Sulla was; that is certain. And the great Hadrian. Poor Germanicus sailed to Samothrace to become an initiate, but storms kept him from landing, indicative of that good man's evil fate.

Oh Nonnos, how good it was to be a part of such a holy place, one that taught harmony and strength to everyone who sought it, that spurned the wicked and taught knowledge of how the world was made. Where enemies worshipped together, however briefly, at the shrines. How much good was done. Only once was it desecrated by pirates, in the rampages of 84 B.C.E. when countless cities and holy grounds suffered from the terrorism.

Through the centuries Romans came to festival. Until the very end official Rome was always dutiful in honoring Aeneas. Even so, most of the initiates continued to be Greek-speaking commoners of the Aegean basin. Mainland Greece, because of Athenian influence, centered on the mysteries at Eleusis which began like ours but meant very differently.

While every initiate had to come to the island to be introduced to the worship, many of them held parades and festivals to the Great Gods in their native towns. Some even built a local Samothrakion. The sacred island of Apollo, Delos, built a Samothrakion as early as the fourth century B.C.E., and worship of the Great Gods flourished in the Greek settlements of the Black Sea and Propontis. Who could have imagined that today Samothrace would be just a poor island, famous only for its onions and black stone? I can still see the winged Victory standing on the headland, lifting her hand in farewell to the ship that carries me away.

How my spirit yearns for rest. My eyes grow dim. Dear Nonnos, my letter reaches its end. I would not write those secrets in this letter, where they might fall into alien hands on the way to yours. You must find them with your memory. Dear Nonnos, there is a manuscript that I have written and hidden where only you can find it. Pay attention now.

Scribes have hidden many scrolls in secret places in the desert, that same desert which harbors the sackers of libraries. I know of many of these places. Think now, Nonnos, of the time when you and I went out to such a place. I showed you a certain cavern and a hidden corridor, and you memorized the way. Please God that you remember now. I showed you how to recover the precious hoard of papyrus from its hiding place. Go there as soon as you can. Find among the scrolls a bundle bound together by a length of purple wool. I entrust it to your keeping as I die. Soon you will understand my other gift to you, that comes with this farewell. The Christ I worship would have our souls seek the highest truth. May God grant my dying wish and visit you with many blessings. The Galilean be with you in these troubled times. Farewell until we meet again in Heaven. Paulus

CHAPTER 24

Nonnos

A.D. 1990 Nicosia, Cyprus

Letha Gooding looked for a long time at the final lines on the monitor: "The Galilean be with [you in these] troubled times. Farewell until we meet again in Heaven.   Paulus."

It was over at last. Weary to the very bones, she ejected the disk from the computer, filed it carefully, cut off the juice, and stared into vacancy. How long had she been working on this? Three years? Four? It had been seven since the bundles of manuscript had been found, one year's delay for the contents to be listed, and then two years of red tape and byzantine negotiations to get to come to Nicosia to work on the "Paulus" letter. Sabbatical and grant money had run out two years ago and they were living on their savings, having decided that this was what savings were for. Now, finally, the translation and commentary was done. And, along with it, the other manuscript. The life of Homer. The "Paulus" letter was a minor piece in a bundle of far more significant discoveries that had excited the whole world of classical studies. Badly damaged, its only significance had seemed to be that it was apparently addressed to the Greek epic poet Nonnos, author of <u>The Dionysiaca</u> from an early teacher of his, a hitherto unknown librarian of Alexandria. No one had looked at it carefully, and no major scholar had vied for the privilege of examining it. She had been lucky.

Rousing herself, Letha stretched in a long outward movement and called into the bedroom. "I'm through!" She waited a moment and then called again. "Hey! Guy. It's done!"

"Wonderful!" She heard a shuffle of papers and his feet hitting the floor. They met in the middle of the room, smiling and reaching for each other. Circling in a half-dance, they gradually began to laugh, to throw their heads back, to hug each other, immensely happy. And to sigh a great sigh and collapse together on the sofa. Guy bestirred himself long enough to fix their drinks, and with a solemn toast to Paulus, they lapsed into reverie.

There was no way to determine now where the letter had lain for 1500 years. The bundle of scraps of which it was a part had probably originated in Antioch or Alexandria, but it had changed hands so many times on various markets that when the Bureau of Antiquities at Cyprus had bought it, it was part of a cache of mixed papers ranging in date from the second century A.D. to 1840. She had heard that the letter was to Nonnos and had set her sabbatical aside to look at it. That leave had stretched into four years, most of it here in Nicosia at the museum, much of the time, too, working out the novel.

The life of Paulus, she reflected, had been concurrent almost to the year with that of Augustine of Hippo. She wondered whether Paulus had endured the same terrible spiritual suffering. Somehow she doubted it; he did not burn with the same intensity, either of love or hate. His was perhaps a greater torment, she thought, too dispassionate, seeing good in the enemy and evil in the acts of the righteous. Knowing that the patriarchs of Alexandria, those Christians he followed and revered so much, were considered to be heretics by influential elements in the official church. For Augustine there was late but vigorous certainty.

"How do you feel?" Guy was looking at her thoughtfully.

"As if Paulus had died only a moment ago. I want to close his eyelids and take his letter to Nonnos. Tonight. I want to read it—all of it-on the way." Letha laughed and shook her head softly. Then she brightened. "No. I want him still to be alive. I want to shake his old bones until he tells me where to find the other scrolls in the cavern. God. What that place must have been." She was staring again.

He roused her. "How do you know they aren't all still there? How do you know Nonnos got them?"

"Oh, he did. He did all right. And that's my next project. To study The Dionysiaca from a purely Samothracian perspective." She saw his look of horror. "Not soon. Not tonight. But nothing is ever really done, you know."

"I'm beginning to understand that. Still, today is yesterday now. Let's go to bed and get up late this morning." He helped her back into the twentieth century with some long, sweet lovemaking and they both slept like babies.

Guy Gooding had sold his investment firm at the end of '86, though he still did a little consulting work occasionally for old clients. His time was his own now and he unashamedly said so. His wife was still absorbed in her career, sharing with him her enthusiasms. He carried his interests wherever they went—books and chess, golf and finance, and he was a fair closet poet. The children, so wonderful and dear to them, theirs for such a short time, were grown and gone, but life was still good.

It wasn't so much that Letha was enthralled by The Dionysiaca. What had interested her was the human problem of a Nonnos: Why did an Egyptian Greek living down the Nile at Panopolis write an elaborate pagan epic poem when that worship had been violently forbidden in the passions of the times? Even before the decree of Theodosius in 391, which closed pagan places of' worship and forbade sacrifice, Panopolis had not been a center of learning. With Greek being rooted out in the river cities and villages, Panopolis was hardly the place to find a Greek epic composer, especially one as original in his poetics as Nonnos, using Latin stresses in the epic line. The battles between Pan and Perseus in The Dionysiaca had probably reflected a rivalry between cults in Panopolis, but that must have been in the previous century. It was puzzling.

"Paulus' letter doesn't solve the problem," Letha had concluded, "but it does suggest a reason, an impulse. Perhaps Nonnos was stimulated by Paulus to revive the pagan epic, even in the face of Christian prohibition. Or did he write it in response to his teacher's last request? The Dionysiaca is saturated with talk of Samothrace, you know, and he was born too late to be an initiate. Nonnos was—or became—a Christian, you know. He began a paraphrase of John before he died."

"Or," asked Guy, "did he take a poem popular in Panopolis for many hundred years and re-write it? Or record it so it wouldn't be lost? People have done such things. Or did he want to make something new and just literary, not religious? Will we ever know?"

***

They had talked about the problems of Nonnos over supper one evening shortly after coming to Cyprus, with three new friends, Telly Panayides was a local official, a colonel in the Greek

Cypriot army, sensible, proud of the island's history. Ian Cowan, a Scotsman from the University of London and Cory Danton, a young American from Arizona State, were also doing research at the museum.

"Your Nonnos," Ian observed, "couldn't have picked a worse time to be alive. Fifth century Egypt must have been pure hell."

"How so?" Guy asked as they settled comfortably for their after-dinner brandy and conversation.

"Combination of economic and religious factors, actually." Ian settled in, lighting his briar self-consciously, for he was trying to quit smoking but was addicted to the rituals of the pipe. He decided to enjoy it. "Well. That was the time of the rise of monasticism, wasn't it? Much bitter opposition to Greek paganism and learning,"

"But the monastic movement started long before Theodosius' decree," Cory objected.

"Quite so. As early as 270 Antony moved out into the desert. By 295 his followers had caught up with him—he was living in a deserted fort, you see. He helped them establish a community and then left again, to live in a remote cave somewhere. That was in 305, I believe. A good century before Nonnos." Ian paused to accept his brandy.

"Those settlements were called coenobia, A lot of them by Nonnos's time. Secular monasteries, I suppose." He pulled thoughtfully on his forbidden tobacco. "Solitaries grouped together under a teacher. For example. Pakhom made a settlement at Tabennisi about 300- 305, too, a deserted village near Akhmim. It grew, and he founded another north of Akhmim at Pabau, and so on, until finally he had a group of communities that spread all the way to the Mediterranean. Under one control."

"That sounds like a contradiction to me," Letha said, "How can anyone be alone in the desert surrounded by people?"

Cory intruded. "You don't know the desert then. So big. So empty." He grinned. "So dry." He took the proffered brandy snifter from Guy's hand. "Thanks."

Ian went on, "The community would divide into 'houses' each responsible for a certain trade. Otherwise their time was their own. The monks could eat together or alone, but they all had to meet for vespers. Variations on such a pattern. Many of the coenobia of Pakhom shared their lives with the peasants as the hard times deepened under the Roman reform. Even the great Athanasias himself once visited Tabennisi and gave it his blessing—he was an early patriarch of Alexandria."

Cory laughed. "Old Athanasias took a bunch of desert monks to Rome one time and shocked the church fathers out of their skulls. They called them Asian fanatics."

"All the same," Ian added, smiling at the irony, "by Paulus' death, at 430, a monastic group was in charge of the Catacomb cemetery at Rome. The church knew a good thing when it saw it."

"Nonnos lived in a Nile river city, but the country round about was full of monastics," Letha said. "I wonder where they all came from. Who they all were."

Ian grimaced. "Just about anyone who needed sanctuary, really. And they lived where they could. With temples abandoned and villages burned, there were many places to commandeer. Besides, there were the old tombs and caves that had had such use since ancient times. They were filled with the homeless. The persecuted. The poor. The murderer and the saint. The religious ascetic and the social reformer. Everybody flocked to the desert."

"Not everybody," Letha countered. "Fine Greek scholars must have lingered for a while. In the large cities and along the Nile. A whole class of educated Christian converts."

Telly spoke up now. Ordinarily a quiet man, he accepted that in his times, in Cyprus, it was necessary to be military. He had helped in the terrorist crisis of '88 and supported the peace efforts of that year between Greek and Turk. Cyprus had known many masters since Greek had come to its shores in Mycenaean times, but most of it still spoke Greek.

"Some of the monasteries founded in that time flourish, uninterrupted since that time. Not near the Nile, though. In the western desert of lower Egypt. The Berbers almost drove them out, but they survived, and became the showcase for medieval Europe. What was the trouble with Egyptian Christianity, anyway? Why did Byzantium condemn it?"

Ian put on his lecture voice and talked a while about Monophysitism. "The conception that Christ has one nature, that he was never of the Fallen. The international church condemned that position officially in the Great Schism of 451."

They fell silent for a moment. Letha commented, "Then Egyptians were really not Christians at all."

Guy said soberly. "I'm sure they thought they were. But I leave that to heaven. I guess they all know by now."

Thoughtful laughter.

Cory said, "I'll tell you someone who must have really bugged Nonnos. Someone he probably knew in his childhood."

"Bugged?" Telly asked, eyebrows raised.

Cory laughed. "Irritated. A celebrity monk named Shenoute. He grew up near Akhmim—Panopolis, sorry—and was the nephew of an abbot, so he must have had some advantages and known people in the area. In fact, he became an abbot himself, important enough to attend the Council of Ephesos the year after Paulus' death—431." He paused to savor his brandy. "But he broke away and founded a reform movement, probably about the time Nonnos was writing his epic. A stark reform movement, complete with beatings and spare diet. He would accept only the simple Coptic peasants-the fellahin-for membership. His discipline was very harsh. While he kept his people unlettered, he wrote tons of tracts, in Coptic, not Greek. A pretty poor Coptic, by all accounts, which unfortunately set the standard for the church. He died in the year of the Great Schism, '51. I can't help wondering what a fine poet like Nonnos, working on the lush music of his epic, thought of the famous Coptic zealot Shenoute and his hard-working, world-rejecting disciples."

"But none of you have mentioned the thing I wonder most about. Whether there were two Nonnoses," Letha glanced around for a response, "or were they one and the same?"

"Here we go," Cory said. "I say they were one and the same man."

Ian bridled, clearly at odds with that point of view. Letha turned to Telly to explain, "Two Nonnoses lived at the same time, one in Panopolis and the other at Tabennisi, right outside of town. One was a Greek epic poet and one was a Christian saint! Isn't that beautiful?"

Telly shook his head, "No Christian saint back then would write a poem to Dionysos." He laughed, amused at the incongruity. "Now, today, maybe so! I've known some good fathers who worship him surely and devoutly."

Cory interrupted, "OK. Case for one Nonnos: poet was born 410 and death date unknown,

Saint died 458 and birth date unknown. A man could write <u>The Dionysiaca</u> in his youth—he was 20 when he got Paulus' letter—and then convert to live another—give him five years for the poem—twenty-three years as a Christian! Well educated in his youth, he'd rise rapidly in the church to bishop by 448. Plenty of time to repent and achieve sainthood. In fact, the greatest sinners make the best saints! I say he was one man."

"Five years for composing that epic? He could hardly have copied it down in that time!" This from Letha.

Ian countered, too, "I say he wasn't. First of all, the saint is supposed to have traveled to Heliopolis and have been a bishop at Edessa—that's Antioch."

Letha said, "Of course the poet is said to have converted. He began a paraphrase of John. Maybe the press of affairs kept him from writing,"

Ian scoffed, "Not a man as prolific, as voluble—as florid—as the author of that huge poem! Bishop Nonnos converted Saint Pelagia in Alexandria in that famous tale."

"His eloquence was legendary," Cory said. "That sounds like a poet to me."

"What famous tale?" asked Telly.

"I don't like that story. But I can see Ian is going to tell it."

Ian raised his brows at Cory's remark and began dramatically, "While Bishop Nonnos was preaching, a famous actress Pelagia passed in the street and was captured by his eloquence. She sent for him and he converted her. She gave all her goods to the poor, disguised herself as a man, and took to the caves of the desert. Years later—note the long time, opponents—when Nonnos heard of the good works of a desert monk, he sought him out, to find he was Pelagia, alas, by now on her deathbed. Church made them both saints."

"I ask you," Cory looked around the group, "seriously, which life served man best—God, too—the ragged hermit helping a few poor folks, or the consummate actress who gave pleasure to thousands of weary people?"

Letha laughed. "Why is it you can tell the answer from the way the question is phrased? Students learn that first of all."

Telly turned to Guy. "Well, what do you think?"

"It was a case of Dr. Jekyll and Mr. Hyde" he said soberly. "Remarkable opposition of ideals, but with the same eloquence and passion. When the pure desert dried him out, Dionysos filled him up again with the world. Clear case of split personality. Plus lots of energy. And money. It'd make a great novel." And all agreed about that.

Letha had a last word. "Still. What an intriguing juxtaposition. What lives—or life—is lost to us! I'd like to believe it was one, but such a famous conversion would be in the record. There must have been two—maybe father and son. Who could give up all that extravagance of Greek music in his head?"

Cory growled good-naturedly. "I think we're all wrong. What happened was that the stuffy bishop saw what he had done to Pelagia and he went back to Dionysos and was last seen dancing on the mountain among the maenads!"

"Sounds like one of the desert holy, in a frenzy. Maybe they weren't that far apart," said Guy. "Anyway, let's toast: to the memory of Nonnos, wherever they may be."

✿✿✿

Guy and Letha loved Cyprus. "But even here, today," Letha protested, "are the same savage conflicts. Greek Christian and Muslim Turk. This city itself, this beautiful and ancient place, is divided by a wall separating Greek and Turk, with armed guards on the wall and bright flags flying in the wind. The distrust grows. You've heard what Telly says. Every Greek fears that time is on the side of the Turks who, he says, are importing settlers to reproduce as fast as they can. In another generation many, many Turks can claim passionately that Cyprus is their birthplace. He had asked, "What will happen to this beautiful city? to the ancient ruins which they say Turks neglect, just because they are Greek? What anger do the Greeks here feel, seeing themselves as having come with the Mycenaeans 3200 years ago. Knowing that religious warfare is setting the whole Middle East aflame? In other words, what in the name of humanity have we learned since Nonnos' time?"

"Since Nonnos' time? Why not since Homer's? Since Hector's?" Guy asked.

Letha grimaced. "Whatever time. Still there, stupid little blindnesses to kill each other over. To blow up the treasures in the ground below. To make life miserable during the short time on this planet, to alienate other generations so they must hate the enemies of men long dead. Why do people let themselves be used so?"

"If you're saying most religious conflict is about many other things besides the state of the soul, I agree. Let's leave it there, OK?" Guy closed the subject.

"OK. But these destructors do not sit there and decay, like those parchments did. They feed in darkness. In the battle between the destructors and preservers, it is clear who is winning."

He looked at her sharply, seeing her deep anger. "All the more reason to be a preserver."

Letha had glossed her translation of Paulus's letter with copious notes, many on Samothrace, an area of interest new to her. She had relied primarily on the publications of the Bollingen series Samothrace, the work of general editors Karl and Phyllis Lehmann and their colleagues in the excavation of the island, both excavation and publication still in progress. Letha would shake her head in disbelief as text after text in her reading did not index the island or in some cases even identify it on maps. That finally seemed to be changing, probably as a result of the archaeological excavation.

Since 391 the history was a melancholy one, the tale of a holy place abandoned. After the closing of the temples and the sacking, the sanctuary was rifled for building stones and allowed to decay. In the very century of Nonnos, lime burners had even built a kiln right next to the Rotunda of Arsinoe, that unique building. Natural destruction of the sanctuary buildings came when, about 550 A.D. a tremendous earthquake shook down all the remaining ruins. Thus did man and nature conspire against it. The island itself was apparently not depopulated right away. She had used the Lehmanns' description:

Soon its further history became shrouded in almost complete obscurity. It remained part of the Eastern Empire. Ravaged by pirates and eventually becoming their hideout, shaken by earthquakes and deprived of resources by progressive deforestation and erosion, it began to sink into oblivion. The process was slow and extended over many centuries. The ruins of numerous Christian churches, mostly small in design, are found all over the island as are traces of a still dense population in the early Byzantine Era. (Guide 20)

When the northern harbor silted up in the eighth century, the ancient Aiolian town shrank in size. The tenth century must have been a time of turmoil, with fortifications built on the north coast and all the civilian population moving inland to Chora. She was reminded of the old Mycenaean time, when palaces could not risk being built by the sea, and her heart ached for the human race.

Except for two visits recorded from the fifteenth century, the island was forgotten. From 1500 to 1800 no historical records exist of the island. Three hundred years of utter silence. However, one of those two visits was memorable: that of Cyriacus of Ancona in 1444.

The Lehmanns had told it so well, and Letha struggled to get the same delicious sense of events when she told Guy about it. They were spending a long afternoon picnicking near ancient Enkomi on the beach. They had eaten and napped and now rose to stroll at the edge of the water, kicking the foamy border, letting it slip around their ankles, feeling the sand give way with the rhythm of their walking.

"Cyriacus says he approached Samothrace by sea from the south, in a boat from Imbros. He was thinking about the Iliad, Homer's 'divine song', and Alexander. The highest peak, he says, is called 'holy wisdom.' The governor of the island, John Laskaris, himself took Cyriacus to the ancient city on Sunday, the Lord's Day, which Cyriacus considered to be 'auspicious': He writes that he thought of Plutarch's story that Phillip and Olympias met here, and he marvels at the walls and 'towers and gates' with their 'varied architectural style...partly still extant.' The Hieron he calls the Temple of Neptune, probably because Homer says Poseidon sat atop Samothrace and looked at Troy. It was still beautiful though in ruin."

Letha pulled at the notepad in her pocket and read: "fragments of huge columns, architraves and bases, doorposts beautifully decorated with garlanded heads of oxen and with other sculptured figures." Most of the sanctuary, she added, was overgrown, with only the ruins of the Hieron, the Rotunda of Arsinoe, and the Propylon of Ptolemy Philadelphus visible still. He observed that many blocks from the sanctuary were used in the castle of the tenth century perched above the harbor. He even made sketches of some of those blocks.

Then Cyriacus made a sketch of a bust of a bearded man. Letha read Phyllis Lehmann's description:

Clad in a barely visible garment and seemingly wearing a skull cap, his somber features attracted Cyriacus in spite of their severe weathering. Here on this island where Philip had met Olympias, he saw in this venerable image a portrait of their son Alexander's celebrated tutor Aristotle. Plutarch's Life of Alexander had been uppermost in his mind as he approached the ruined site and thought of its ancient glory..... What could be more natural, it must have seemed to Cyriacus, than to find a bust of the great philosopher here in this place where Philip had met Olympias? Nor is it surprising that this learned man of the Quattrocento, accustomed to medieval representations of philosophers as bearded men clad in caps and flowing garments, his thoughts revolving about these very historical personalities, should have interpreted the unidentified statue before him as a portrait of Aristotle.. ... a bearded man about whose torso a vaguely classical garment falls in diagonal folds. Over his skull, he wears a slightly peaked cap from which his hair escapes to fall on his shoulders in long, undulating locks. His eyes are curiously downcast, his nose

aquiline, his lips tightly pursed, and his wide, flowing mustache merges with the mass of his long beard.
(Lehmanns, Samothracian Reflections 15-17)

Letha closed the pad and looked up thoughtfully at Guy. "The Lehmanns believe the bust Cyriacus drew and labeled ARISTOTELES was in fact one of the prophet Teiresias. They found the bust."

He objected. "Wait a minute. That is a strange confusion." "Not really," Letha countered, "The drawing shows the eyes to be deep and ambiguous. Pictures in this book and extant copies of Cyriacus' sketch of the bust indicate a striking likeness. Only two things seem different to me—the beard has been shortened and stylized and the eyes have been reworked. People resculpt old pieces. It happens. It happened to this one. There is a fillet around the head that could be interpreted as a cap. I don't know."

"But what would either of them—Aristotle or Teiresias—be doing in the sanctuary of the Great Gods?" Guy was puzzled.

"Well, of course, no one knows exactly the sacred story that was told there. Teiresias is in the underworld in the Odyssey, and an underworld story is likely as a part of the initiation. The Lehmanns make the case that the figure seems to be stooping forward, as if he were emerging from the underworld." They found a cool spot and sank to the sand, feeling it as they talked, letting it slip through their fingers.

Guy sat back, thinking of the ironies of time. "Well. That's an interesting problem. You know, there is plenty of reason to connect Aristotle with Samothrace. Why shouldn't there have been a carving now lost but there in 1444? Of Alexander's tutor, clearly marked ARISTOTELES, that stood somewhere in the city? He wrote a history of the city's constitution, after all."

"It's possible. The bust, the Lehmanns assume, was definitely part of the sanctuary. And they think the eyes were originally blind and certainly strange and downcast. The mysteries surely involved a trip to the underworld; at least, in Homer Teiresias is involved in such an adventure. He was Theban, like Cadmus, whose marriage the Samothracians celebrate."

He agreed. "Right. So the extant bust is probably Teiresias. It makes sense." He smiled across at her. "Besides, the only other ancient I know of who was blind was Homer."

Letha stared hard at him and looked away, lost in thought. "Homer. Yes." A sudden wind from the sea lifted her hair, a sand devil curled along the earth and threw itself into her lap, making a fan of fine dust. Infinitely beautiful, she thought. Infinitely real. It was as if someone had touched her.

"Something about the old eyes of the statue just crossed my mind. The ancient representation of blindness was a groove almost across the eye socket—horizontally, of course. That is the same symbol, if you lift it off of the face, as the theta letter—you know—the letter for the gods. I wonder if there is a connection? Could blindness be a sign of the touch of the gods? Or could it mean that godhead lay within? That the person had an inner sight, not necessarily that he was literally blind at all."

✸✸✸

With Letha's work complete and the school year soon to begin, Guy arranged for their departure. He was good at such things, clear-eyed and relaxed. Letha collected all her materials for the publishers, ready to send to them.. She had borne them, like children, but so differently. How hard it was to explain one's own meaning, even to Guy, she reflected. Reading, concentration, all the turmoil of thought happens so chaotically, so discontinuously, so intuitively, even as one struggles to impose reason on the process. Even when she could look back and recover how one thing led to another, that was never the order used when she tried to articulate her thought. So no one else could ever really know the landscape of a mental journey. The scenery of ideas. When she talked about them Guy would have to begin with the latest structure in the process, the logical conclusion of the journey she had experienced, the ideas altered into as rational a form as her conscious mind could shape.

It was such a struggle to share the mind, even with someone so close as to be almost like herself. No, not like herself. Like the other part of herself. Their bodies and the long years together made them one, their roots and hearts almost indistinguishable and inseparable, but in their minds, in their heads they moved freely. No, that was not exactly it either. Letha turned back to her packing.

She wanted to go to Samothrace. It was presumptuous of her to have written of it without knowing it firsthand. It was the common ground for her translation and her novel-biography. Even with the careful work of the Lehmanns' volumes, she knew the gap between knowledge and deed. Still, they had shown her around the sanctuary with the eyes of those who understand what they see, who see carefully, honestly, trying not to apply meaning generated out of preconceptions. As she had? Yes. Guy is right, she thought. How remarkable people are, after all. The work of the excavations was by people who honored the nature of the sanctuary, who strove to understand it with as much passion as any initiate who had shared in its festival. The forms of worship in the human soul, how various they were. How delicate the messages between the brain and the heart. The soul. She wanted to climb to the top of Moon Mountain before she died. Cyriacus had called it Holy Wisdom.

Letha thought back to the Appendix of Lehmann's first volume, to Nicostratus, and to the time she told Guy about it. A little gem saved out of the centuries of unrecorded Samothracian existence.

"Who the hell is Nicostratus?" He had shouted cheerfully in reply whlle they were sailing. "I know you are going to tell me." They had rented a boat and spent the morning in a brisk breeze, soaked by the spray, on a bright September day off Mykonos. They had agreed the first time they had seen the Aegean, leaving Piraeus, it was indeed wine-dark. Now it had reminded Letha of Nicostratus.

"He saw Samothrace from the sea and described it. It crossed my mind just now. Nobody knows who he was, really. Piacenza quotes him a lot." "Who the—"

"hell is Piacenza?" Letha had pulled hard on the line as the boat leaped into a wave and sent spume over the bow. "Hey. Slow down. Really." They eased headway and relaxed. "Let's share the same ocean." She hugged him and brought out the wine. "Shall we pour libations to the gods, and especially to Athena—"

"who taught us the paths of the sea? Why not?"

Letha said then, looking across at the island passing on their port side, "Nicostratus told how, on high ground to the west of the sanctuary, there stood a magnificent statue of Kybele, mother of the gods. It faced toward the sea." She was looking at the promontory passing beside them and he looked too, trying to think how it felt to come upon such a sight on such a mountain. "Nicostratus said its effect was powerful, commanding, expressing the power to defend the sanctuary and at the same time inviting the traveler to worship." Guy stared, forgetting the sheets, then having to trim.

"The Nike. The Winged Victory of Samothrace? The headless lady of the Louvre!"

Letha was delighted with his delight. "Yes. He saw it. As it was then."

"When was then?"

"Nobody knows." She saw his disgust. "The Lehmanns cite Hemberg and Rubensohn as placing him between A.D. 800-1150, closer to the end than the beginning. Piacenza's book was published in 1688, and he refers to Nicostratus' works often, but the time is not clear. Sometime between sixth-century Stephanos Byzantius and twelfth-century Tzetzes. Nicostratus—now that's a text I would love to see come to light."

"What else?"

"Wait a minute. Piacenza adds that there was a Zeus statue to the east of the sanctuary, the two apparently framing the holy valley from the sea, like two beacons. He doesn't say Nicostratus told him that."

Guy was ahead of her. "Then the Nike statue couldn't have been destroyed in the great earthquake of 550. Not if they say 800-1150. The disaster that brought every single building down? Come on. That delicate statue? So beaten by the wind? Balanced on the prow of a ship in a fountain? I don't believe it. Sorry." She didn't dispute him. After a silence he added, "Nope. Either Nicostratus didn't see it himself because he's quoting an older author, or Piacenza has him dated wrong and he belongs before 550. But somebody recorded seeing that—sight." He glanced again at the island and whistled softly to himself.

"I'd have to agree to that," Letha said, "and the Lehmanns seem to, too, in their <u>Reflections</u>. The pieces of the statue and the fountain base were found exactly where he says the statue of Kybele stood. For all those centuries. It isn't mentioned anywhere else—and I think that's odd. The goddess of mariners, of Parian marble, standing there for 700 years, facing the tempests, balanced against the wild strong winds from Thrace, at the prow of a stone ship surrounded by the fountain's sea. Signs that fish sported beside the hull—perhaps dolphins or the sacred pompilius fish—have been found on the site. A reflecting-pool basin was below, which would catch the statue's image bracing against the windy sky. What a sight that must have been for the sailor on the stormy Aegean. I wish the Louvre could put it in context."

"No. No phony scenery. It would need this sun," Guy said, "and this glorious wind, and that is impossible."

"They've found the right hand of the statue. It was held high and forward, palm open to the winds and worshippers. By the way, a similar right hand has been found. Could that be the hand of Zeus? Frankly, I don't believe the statue is Kybele. With wings? Probably Athena Nike. Ship monuments like this existed at Epidauros and Lindos—at Lindos near the sanctuary of Athena. Remember? The Lehmanns locate eleven such ship monuments, with metal or stone figures atop them. All dwarfed by the artistry and size of the Samothracian."

***

She sighed and checked the apartment carefully. It already had the feeling of a place one is leaving. So much had happened here. So much had grown from a simple marginal note and from the Paulus letter. She had mailed the disks and manuscripts and they were safely home. Her epic about epics. She remembered a talk with Ian and Cory in the sunny plaza over coffee. What good friends they had been.

"There is a strange tradition about the writing down of Homer that I have never understood," Letha threw out. "Tzetzes identifies the 'four wise men' that Pisistratus is supposed to have charged with collecting and writing down Homer. That would have to be the third quarter of the sixth century B.C.E., since he was tyrant from 560 and died in 527."

"Well?" Ian said, "Tzetzes is late and unreliable, but it's an imperfect world and we take what we can." His Scots face bloomed into a smile. "What's the problem?"

"The 'four wise men'—'four very famous and learned men.' Well, it's who they are. One is totally unknown now, one Coneylus, or Epiconcylus, with no city named—presumably Athens. The next is the Athenian Onomacritus. His reputation indicates learning, but it is sullied. He was hired to collect and make an edition of the oracles of Musaeus—an important charge indeed. But he was said to have been discovered falsifying them, adding one in which Lemnos is supposed to disappear into the sea."

"That's an old image," Ian said. "Sign of a sacred island. The island of the soul. Should be no surprise, should it, given Lemnos' mysterious associations?"

"Well, he was supposedly disgraced over it."

Cory interjected, "Wasn't he suspected of having invented the Orphic poems himself? Have we here a man who can be looked at from two perspectives—one learned in mysteries but suspect because of it?"

Letha nodded at her young curlyheaded colleague. "Yes. And if he had a reputation for such learning, why would he be charged with collecting and editing such an important text as Homer?"

"Homer and Musaeus are both early singers," Ian countered. "He must have been regarded as expert in that area."

Letha objected, "But Musaeus is mythical. And Homer is so clear-eyed, so of-this-world."

"Clear-eyed, I love that," Cory laughed and they all did. "Go on. Who were the other two 'wise men'?"

"Orpheus of Croton—"

Cory interrupted, "Orpheus? Croton is the city of Pythagoras, for Chrissake! What are you suggesting? That Pisistratus appointed a bunch of mystics to collate Homer? That's crazy!"

Letha threw her hands up in a gesture of amazement. "I know! I know! That's what I mean."

Ian went on quickly, suddenly caught by the problem. "Who was the other one?"

"Zopyrus of Heraclea." "The Heraclea on the Gulf of Tarentum? Near Croton?"

"I guess. I don't have any idea. Just the name and city. From Tzetzes."

Cory jumped in. "This is wild. Where would such a list of names come from? How about the dates. Was Orpheus in Croton and then called to Athens by Pisistratus? Or was he an exile?"

"Who knows." Letha sat listening to their speculation. Cautious, Cory said, "Just because he was from Croton doesn't mean he was a Pythagorean mystic. Pythagoras took power there in 531, but went there earlier. And nobody knows when—or even if—Pisistratus gave the charge. Just that it would have had to have been between 560 and 527."

Ian shifted direction. "Croton was founded by Achaeans. About 700, perhaps in Homer's lifetime. There could have been a tradition connecting them with Homer that has nothing to do with Pythagoras."

"Right." They all soberly agreed.

"Still," Letha added, "some time somebody saw Homer as relevant to the mystery tradition. Else Tzetzes couldn't have reported such a curious list of Homeric editors."

Cory mused, "I find it interesting that there would be four of them, given the Pythagorean significance of numbers. I wonder what that indicates. If anything. The Hermetic number."

Letha added, "Some say that Pisistratus himself was a writer and mystic. And I have heard the old saying, 'who tells the tale makes the meaning.'" And they had fallen into a fertile silence.

She had begun her inquiry and had gradually come to see a completely new Odyssey, one not at odds with accepted views, just deeper. She had written her new life of Homer now, as full as she could make it, hypothesizing Samothracian initiation in the Odyssey. She had written an argument on it as an Afterword to her manuscript on Paulus and Nonnos, and the publishers had not seen any of this yet. The Paulus text was what they had agreed to publish. She tried to imagine their reaction.

She came back to the present, to her editors and their expert readers. She knew her Afterword might not see the light of day. Nor her novel-life. So many wise minds—wonderful minds whose thoughts she had fed on for so long and that she loved so, who were so clear-eyed and articulate—they would advise caution, and they would be right, of course. The direction of commentary in recent years was towards examining the non-conscious elements repeated formulaically in Homer. Her thoughts would point to Homer as an elaborately conscious artist. Still, both could be true, she thought. The bones of the epic were evidence. Maybe someone qualified would rally behind her hypothesis and make it a legitimate area of study. She could hope.

Letha looked at her watch again. What was keeping Guy? The battered luggage stood forlornly in the middle of the room. She would travel light to Samothrace next summer. Somehow. She wanted to see it all for herself. Especially the curious finding along the wall under the hill. Built against the retaining wall was the entrance to a Mycenaean bee-hive tomb. It led nowhere; it was only an entrance. But why? Whose tomb? What ritual was performed before it? It seemed to prove the legends or the rituals reached into the times before the Trojan War, well before Homer. To what Mycenaean king did the festival do honor? Be patient, she told herself. The work there continues. And they are digging again at Troy, she heard. Wonderful.

She saw in her mind's eye the pictures from the island excavation and tried to imagine Samothrace at its height. Two elaborate marble initiation halls, the Temenos and Altar Court, the Hall of Votive Gifts, the Rotunda and theater, the fountain and dining halls—so magnificent.

Letha closed her eyes, sad at leaving this sunny Mediterranean. Image after image rose in her mind. Wildflowers had shivered in the crisp wind as they had stood in the sanctuary of Athena at Lindos. The sun was warm and bright. After prayer and meditation—Guy had suggested it—they had begun to walk up the broad, long steps to the acropolis. They could see only the high step advancing into the sky ahead of them, the brightest and bluest sky she had ever seen. They would go right into it. Then the temple came into view, and the terrace. The power of place. Place and belief together. The power of it. She found herself tense with memory. That was fifteen years ago.

How much more powerful then would a visit to Samothrace be? She believed it likely that

Homer knew that place. Alexander had been there, and Herodotus, and Hadrian. How would it feel to walk the sacred routes, knowing what Schelling thought the rituals had taught? What magic lay in a place where so much learning—and power—had been? She was suddenly not sure that she could risk it. If the priest loomed out of the night into the torchlight at the swearing-stone, and demanded that she confess her darkest actions, what would she say?

There was so much. No murders. Much worse. She had raised a family. The deepest wrongs she had done were with the certainty that she was doing right, and to those she had loved so. Like every mortal mother. Like Niobe, she had made mortals. The gift of life was also the gift of death. Guy would tell her, "Death is only a part of it. It is God's gift of life that matters. That is the experience that smacks of the divine. Life under the sun." Letha sighed. She was learning. Life was good. Continuing good, however brief. She thought she knew what to say to the priest, after all. But Niobe's tears would flow as long as it was God who gave life and mortals who gave death to their children.

Guy found her there, tear-stained, and pulled her close.

"Sorry we're going? A lot has happened in these rooms." He wiped her tears and kissed her. "Good things. Wonderful things. We have so many happy memories. But today it's London and then home."

They smiled and shook off their sorrow at leaving. With considerable commotion the luggage was loaded and they left without a look back.

The plane was late leaving, the cabin was hot, security was tight. Security had always been tight, especially since the hijacking in 1988. But this was unusual. Luggage and carry-ons had to be completely dismantled and reassembled. The delay was occasioned by much attention to several parties of dignitaries on their way to the big peace conference in London. A number of delegations had been traveling for some time. They had deplaned and were casually gathering again. Deputies bustled about them, and bodyguards prohibited anyone from entering the front area of the aircraft, from the 26th row forward. Guy and Letha entered from the side, well back of the official parties.

"There's plenty of security on this plane," Guy confided, smiling. "I think you are safe from muggers and pickpockets. These people have more immediate concerns. Iraqi, Irani, Arab, Israeli, Greek, Turk, Afghan, Russian, Christian, Muslim, Lebanese, Libyan. My God, Letha. And we can still hope? I'm glad I don't have to solve all that."

Letha nodded. "And those are just these people's concerns." They settled down for the flight to Athens, where there would be a comfortable stopover. "We'll fly over Mt. Tmolus." Letha was looking at her pocket guide. "<u>The Dionysiaca</u> must mention it a thousand times."

"Then let's break out the Dionysian wine and wear garlands on our heads. We have every reason to honor the god of exuberant life, whatever you want to call—Him." Guy's sense of deity was profound as his sense of humor.

"We'll see Smyrna—Izmir, that is. And maybe even the Old City. What I'd give for a walk in the Old City." Alexander's Smyrna, she thought, was not like Izmir now. Through all the centuries—the wars and earthquakes and persecutions—the city had been there, absorbing each shock and each new infusion of peoples. A glorious city. It had harbored the archetypal exiles, the Hebrews. She thought of Cadoux's book on ancient Smyrna, written with such loving detail, and of its emotional Preface. Cadoux had lived in Smyrna the first years of his life and been exiled in one of the most tragic and ironic of times. In the early 1920's after the first World War, the Greeks had attacked and taken Turkish Smyrna. When the Turks recaptured it, they destroyed everything Greek they could find in the city—buildings, libraries, manuscripts, statuary. Everything Greek. And changed the name to Izmir. Cadoux had wept over it, for the sake of Greek and Turk; for the sake of mortals.

Now it was beautiful again, thriving and Turkish. She cast her eye over the coastline of Asia Minor visible ahead of her. Turkish now. Or Phrygian? Or Greek or Persian or Carian or Lycian or Cilician or Assyrian or Lydian or Hittite. For how long? Did it matter? A thousand years more? Two thousand? Then what? Conquest. Holy war. For a woman? Money. Boredom. Power. Survival. She thought of the delegations in the front of the plane. Men as bold as Agamemnon or Sennacherib or Hiram or David. Wily as Dolon or Gyges or Odysseus. Rich as Midas or Croesus. Polished as Darius or Pericles or Solomon. Passionate as all of them, as convinced of the right as all of them. Women too. Meir and Aquino, Cleopatra and Amazonian Myrine.

All good people intending good. Just as she had intended it. Well. She was breathless at the beauty of the world she saw turning below them, a beauty borne more truly in the intellect than the senses, stronger than any hate or failure. She could only be full of love.

She turned to Guy and lifted her glass, looking into his eyes. "To the ecstatic beauty of living," she said.

"To the Giver and the Gift," he replied.

***

The first report came over Athens radio:

"Olympia Airlines Flight 124 to Athens, carrying dignitaries to the Conference for Peace in London, exploded in mid-flight over Turkey this afternoon and all 260 passengers and crew are presumed lost. Airline officials can say only that apparently a bomb was smuggled aboard. Seven terrorist groups of sharply opposing factions already have claimed responsibility for the act. The plane blew up as it was approaching Izmir, scattering wreckage over a wide area. Sections of the rear of the plane reportedly plunged into a chasm on Mt. Tmolus. Identity of the delegates aboard awaits confirmation by their governments."

Achilles went back into his tent and sat on a bench facing Priam.

"Hector's body is ready. We placed him with due courtesy in your wagon, and you can see him when you leave at dawn. But now, old king, come eat with me. I think of Niobe in her terrible grief when Apollo and Artemis killed all twelve of her children. After ten days, when they were buried and she was haggard and exhausted with sorrow, even Niobe remembered food. It is time for us, too, old man. Weep for Hector when you get back to Troy, as I will for Patroclus."

Then Greek and Trojan, knowing their own deaths were near, sat down together, reaching toward the savory meal before them. (Iliad Book 24)

AFTERWORD

To build a life around a predetermined point of view is not scholarship. It is thoughtful entertainment, however valid it may prove to be. The inevitable errors and monumental hubris—enough to invoke the unquenchable laughter of the gods—are my own.

Most of this manuscript was written in the 1980's while I was teaching English literature at the University of Tennessee at Martin. Let me acknowledge here my debt to colleagues and administrators for their interest and support, especially to Marie Chester, Phil Miller, A.L.Addington and Milton Simmons. Special thanks go to interlibrary loan directors Margaret Weaver and Sandra Downing and Betty Hornsby of Murray State University. I owe an immense debt also to family members Anne Hoffman for publishing information and to Maggie and Todd Morris for their technical support in manuscript preparation—I couldn't have done it without them, nor without the help of Roy Francia and Pamela Prince of BookSurge. Now, nearing 80, I want to share this story because it seems too interesting to throw away.

The material on Hermes and the structure of the Odyssey has appeared in the 70's and 80's in my articles in <u>Southern Humanities Review</u> and <u>The Comparatist</u> and in papers read at professional meetings. Rather than use one translator's words for Iliad and Odyssey citations, I have paraphrased based on the tone and content of quite a few, primarily to avoid causing discomfort to anyone by associating their work with this imagined account of Homer's life.

My debt to many fine authors and translators is beyond acknowledgement and thanks. They have given so much pleasure through the years. Below are listed some of the major sources used to build plot. Then, for further reading, find the names of only some of the many authors and translators who have contributed major work in Homeric subjects.

Ernle Bradford, <u>Ulysses Found</u> (Harcourt Brace, 1963). Norman O. Brown, <u>Hermes the Thief: The Evolution of a Myth</u> (Univ. of Wisconsin Press, 1947). Cecil John Cadoux, <u>Ancient Smyrna: A History of the City from the Earliest Times to 324 A.D.</u> (Basil Blackwell and Mott, 1938). Rhys Carpenter, <u>The Discontinuity in Greek Civilization</u> (Univ. of California Press, 1966). J.N.Coldstream, <u>Geometric Greece</u> (Ernest and Benn, 1977). Ludwig Drees, <u>Olympia: Gods, Artists, and Athletes</u> (Frederick Praeger, 1967). Lewis Richard Farnell, <u>Cults of the Greek City States</u> 5 vols. (Clarendon Press, 1896-1909). Robert Graves, <u>The Greek Myths</u> 2 vols. (Penguin Books, 1955). Hesiod. <u>Homeric Hymns and Homerica</u> tr. Hugh G. Evelyn-White (Harvard Univ. Press, 1936). Herodotus. Homer, <u>The Iliad</u> and <u>Odyssey</u>, with many fine English translations. G.L.Huxley, <u>The Early Ionians</u> (Irish Univ. Press, 1972). Karoly Kerenyi, <u>The Gods of the Greeks</u> tr. H.J.Rose (Thames & Hudson, 1959). Karl and Phyllis Lehmann, general editors, <u>Samothrace: a Guide to the Excavations and the Museum</u> (Institute of New York U. Press, 1955) and <u>Samothracian Reflections</u> (Bollingen Series Princeton UP, 1973). John S. Morrison and R.T. Williams, <u>Greek Oared Ships: 900-322 B.C.</u> (Cambridge U.Press, 1968). H.W.Parke, <u>Festivals of the Athenians</u> (Cornell Univ. Press, 1977). Richard Stillwell, William MacDonald, Marian McAllister, <u>The Princeton Encyclopedia of Classical Sites</u> (Princeton Univ. Press, 1976). Curt Sachs, <u>The History of Musical</u>

Instruments (W.W.Norton, 1940). Freidrich Von Schelling, Schelling's Treatise on "The Deities of Samothrace": A Translation and Interpretation by Robert F. Brown, No.12 American Academy of Religion Studies in Religion (Scholars Press, Univ. of Montana, 1977). Anthony Snodgrass, Archaic Greece (Univ. of California Press, 1980) and Early Greek Armor and Weapons (Edinburgh UP, 1964). W.B. Stanford, The Untypical Hero (London, 1958), The Ulysses Theme (Univ. Michigan Press, 1968), with J.V.Luce, The Quest for Ulysses (Praeger, 1974).

From a wealth of fine materials on Homer, here are a few further names of authors you will enjoy, an alphabetical—and incomplete—list: T.W. Allen, Norman Austin, Rachel Bespaloff, Carl Blegen, Charles Beye, Cecil Bowra, Walter Burkert, Joseph Campbell, Ernst Cassirer, H.M. Chadwick, Howard W. Clarke, J.M.Cook, Vincent d'ADesborough, E.R.Dodds, M.I.Finley, Cyrus Gordon, Barbara Graziosi, Jasper Griffin, W.K.C.Guthrie, N.G.L.Hammond, W.A.Jaynes, R.C.Jebb, G.S.Kirk, W.F.J.Knight, Joachim Latacz, Walter Leaf, Albert Lord, H.L.Lorimer, W.T.MacCary, Paul MacKendrick, Gilbert Murray, George Mylonas, J.L.Myers, Gregory Nagy, Erich Neumann, Martin Nilsson, Walter Ong, Walter Otto, Denys Page, Leonard Palmer, J.W.Perry, Andrew Ramage, J.M. Redfield, H.J.Rose, John A. Scott, Bruno Snell, Denton Snider, George Steiner and Robert Fagles, J.A.K.Thomson, Emile Vermeuli, Paoli Vivanti, H.T.Wade-Gery, T.B.L.Webster, Cedric Whitman, William Woodhouse.